I0654506

Rebel of the Forsaken: First Spark
Book One of the *Rebel of the Forsaken* Series

Written by Sarah Penberthy
Story, World, and Characters by Johnathan Penberthy
Copy Editing & Proofreading by Jo Cipriano
Cover Design by Sarah Penberthy
Series Development & Lore Architecture by Penberthy Family Entertainment LLC

Published by
Penberthy Family Entertainment LLC
Eagle Mountain, Utah

ISBN (Paperback): 979-8-9943587-1-9
ISBN (Hardback): 979-8-9943587-2-6
ISBN (eBook): 979-8-9943587-0-2

For more information, visit:
www.RebelOfTheForsaken.com

Rebel

of the

Forsaken

First Spark

Johnathan Penberthy

Sarah Penberthy

Chapter 1

Flicker in the Dark

The warehouse looms at the edge of town like a skeleton, its rusted panels catching the moonlight in jagged streaks, its shattered windows staring into an unknown darkness. A chain-link fence sags around it, more a suggestion of protection than an actual barrier. The place exhales rot and abandonment, signaling the kind of forgotten ground the earth is eager to drag back into itself.

I've been near spots like this before. They always carry the same weight: half-forgotten, half-rotting, like the bones of some animal better left buried. But tonight, the cold claw curling in my stomach isn't about the warehouse. It's about JP.

Wait for me, Evelyn. Don't move until I get there. His voice had been sharp, hard as iron. The way it always is when he means business.

And I want to listen. Damn, I want to.

But sitting out here in the dark while this building watches me back is its own brand of torture.

The warehouse doesn't just *sit* in the night—it broods. Every jagged window feels like an eye trained on me, waiting for me to slip, waiting for me to breathe. The wind moves through the broken metal siding with a low, hollow moan, and every time it scrapes across shattered glass, it sounds eerily like a footstep.

Every shadow stretches far across the ground, like it wants to crawl toward me and hook itself around my ankles. My pulse throbs so loud in my ears that I glance over my shoulder, convinced something else can hear it too. Like I'm giving myself away with every beat.

And the longer I sit here, the more the dread pools in my stomach like oil.

What if I do wait? What if by the time JP arrives, whatever is inside has already vanished into the dark? What if this hesitation—my hesitation—costs someone their life?

The thought scalds.

I'm not some rookie hiding behind JP's shadow. I'm not helpless. I've survived things that should've ended me. I've trained for this. I've earned my way into nights like these.

But a part of me—the quiet, stubborn part that remembers fire and smoke and the way JP had torn through the flames to pull me out— still whispers caution. Still whispers, *wait*.

My fingers twitch toward the knife strapped to my boot. Its weight is familiar, grounding. The promise of steel feels steadier than my own breath.

My body leans forward before my mind even fully decides: a slow tilt toward danger, like gravity itself has chosen a side. My nerves buzz hot under my skin, strung so tight they feel ready to snap. My breath quickens, my thoughts sharpening into something reckless and bright.

I tell myself the same lie I always use when I'm about to do something stupid, something brave, something that feels, in all the wrong ways, like becoming who I'm meant to be:

You've got this. You're not a kid anymore.

I slip through the fence, the metal links rattling behind me like a warning. The tear in the chain-link scrapes against my jacket, snagging at the fabric as if even the rusted wires want to pull me back.

My boots crush broken glass, each step cracking so abruptly in the stillness, it feels like I'm shattering the night itself. The sound ricochets across the empty lot, too loud, accusing. Every echo announces me, rippling out into the dark, like a beacon I can't take back.

The warehouse looms larger with every step, its gravity swallowing me whole.

And still, I move.

Inside, the air is thick—with mildew, rot, something metallic underneath it that clings to the back of my throat. I wrinkle my nose, but the stench only sharpens, burning all the way down to my stomach.

Every instinct screams at me to turn around; instead, I force my breaths slow, steady, counting them in my head like JP has drilled into me. *Control your breath, control your fear.* My chest is still tight, like my ribs are straining to hold something wild inside.

You've got this. You're not helpless. You're not a kid anymore, I repeat to myself, over and over.

The words don't silence the nerves—they just give them a leash.

I edge around a stack of crates, their wood swollen with damp, their corners softened and black with mold. I squint through the dim, searching for anything—movement, sound, the kind of shift in the air that tells you you're not alone.

Nothing.

The silence is worse than noise. Thick. Oppressive. Like the whole warehouse is holding its breath, waiting for me to make the wrong move.

A drop of water falls from the rafters and hits concrete with a sharp *plink*. I flinch, knife-hand twitching. My laugh comes out thin and shaky. "Jumping at water. Nice, Evelyn."

But then, the shadows shift.

Not with the lazy roll of moonlight through broken glass. Not with the sway of wind through cracks in the walls. This is different. Intentional. Like the dark is peeling away from where it belongs.

My breath hitches hard in my throat.

I'm not alone.

Suddenly, something slams into the back of my skull: an iron-hard blow that detonates white-hot pain behind my eyes. The world lurches. My knees give out, legs folding uselessly beneath me. The concrete rushes up in a blur, tilting sideways as my vision smears into streaks of light and shadow.

Then, everything goes black.

Consciousness returns in jagged pieces, each one sharper than the last.

First comes the pain: deep, pounding, nauseating. A hot pulse radiates through my skull, each heartbeat a hammer-strike behind my eyes. Then, cold awareness slides in: my arms wrenched behind me, shoulders screaming, wrists bound so tightly the ropes feel fused to my skin. Every tiny movement makes the fibers saw deeper, biting down to bone. My fingers are numb, tingling at the edges like they don't fully belong to me.

I'm slumped in a chair—hunched and off-balance, held in place only by the ropes cutting into my arms, pulling me at an angle that feels all wrong. One leg of the chair wobbles with every breath I take, threatening to pitch me sideways but never quite following through, keeping me trapped in a constant, nauseating imbalance.

The room wavers in and out of focus as my vision struggles to catch up. Shapes bleed together, then snap apart. Cracked concrete prowls out around me—pitted, stained, mottled with patches of dark that look horrifyingly like old blood left to dry in lazy circles. A moldy dampness clings to the air, sour and wet. Underneath it all is the sharp copper tang of something fresher.

My stomach twists.

And then, the haze clears just enough for me to see them: four figures.

At first glance, they might pass for human—men in worn jackets and grimy boots, the kind of drifters you avoid on the street. But their movements are wrong, too fluid where joints should catch, their smiles stretched too wide, splitting their faces into grotesque parodies of humanness. And their eyes—bottomless pits of wet onyx, swallowing the light around them—pin me where I sit.

Demons.

A tremor slices down my spine, cold and electric, leaving my breath trapped somewhere high in my chest. They don't need blades or teeth to be dangerous; their danger is the air itself—warped, soured, vibrating with a wrongness that makes my skin crawl.

Predators disguised in human shape, like in their creation, someone had been asked to sketch people from memory, but had forgotten all the details that makes a human real.

One crouches low, dragging chalk across the floor to make symbols that shimmer faintly and twist in ways that hurt to look at. Another paces in slow circles, boots clicking softly, claws twitching at its sides like it's impatient for me to move. The other two mutter in guttural tones, voices scraping the air raw, their words not meant for human throats.

The sound doesn't just echo—it *crawls,* buzzing through my bones with a slick, unnatural resonance, like whispers slithering straight into my marrow. My pulse hammers so violently it feels like the whole room can hear it.

They know I'm awake. And they've been waiting.

The nearest one notices me stir. Its grin stretches slow, deliberate, until it shows teeth too sharp to ever make sense in a human mouth. It crouches low, close enough that I can see the way its black eyes reflect the faint shimmer of the chalk circle like an oil slick. Its breath hits me in a wave: smoke and ash, thick enough to choke.

"Awake already?" it rasps, voice dragging like claws on metal. Its grin wideness, a sickly performance of kindness. "Good. Wouldn't want you to miss the show."

I pull against the ropes instinctively, wrists twisting hard, testing for any weakness. The fibers bite deeper, skin scraping raw. No give. No escape. The chair wobbles under me, its legs creaking against the cracked concrete. My pulse spikes, wild and unsteady, panic clawing for control.

Don't lose it. Don't give them that. Panic doesn't help. Thinking does.

I swallow, forcing my voice to steady, but my throat felt tight as wire. "What are you doing here?"

The demon chuckles—low, rumbling—and the sound vibrates through the concrete, straight into my bones. It rises with a fluid, lazy grace and begins circling me, slow and predatory, as if tasting the air around me with every step. Its boots scrape across the floor, a deliberate drag, like it wants me to hear it coming even if I can't see.

With each pass, the demon's shadow stretches long and thin across the cracked ground, brushing over my legs, my arms, my throat—a silent promise of what it intends to do.

It stops behind me first, close enough that its breath ghosts against the back of my neck. A shiver rips through me. The demon moves to my side, crouching low so our brows are level, its eyes, nothing but pits of black that swallow the dim light whole.

"Brave little thing," it murmurs, voice curling around the words like smoke. "Trying so hard not to tremble."

The demon reaches out with a mock tenderness that freezes my blood—two fingers brushing along my cheek before tucking a strand of hair behind my ear. The touch is slow, deliberate, intimate in the worst possible way.

Revulsion hits me like a fist. I jerk my head away, bile burning the back of my throat. Its grin widens, pleased by the disgust twisting my face.

"You'll make a fine offering when the circle is ready," it croons, tilting its head as if admiring a piece of art. The void of its eyes gleam, hungry. "Your blood will sing beautifully in the chalk."

My stomach spirals, fluid clawing up my throat, but beneath the fear something else flares hotter: defiance.

They think I'm prey—something small to toy with, to unravel, to carve open until I scream for mercy. They think my fear makes me weak. They're wrong. So very wrong.

Suddenly, the door *detonates,* slamming against the wall with a bone-rattling crash. The sound cracks through the hollow warehouse like a thunderbolt, scattering shadows and demons alike.

Gunfire splits the silence—each shot deafening, each flash briefly painting the walls in stark white light. JP's figure, broad and unflinching, fills the doorway, then moves with the efficiency of a man who's done this too many times to count. His pistol barks fire, rounds burning blue as they strike, and two demons shriek before collapsing into smoke, their bodies unraveling faster than they can react.

But the other two are faster.

One whirls toward me, lips peeling back in a snarl, teeth catching the glow of the chalk circle. The other slams into JP with the force of a wrecking ball, sending his pistol skidding across the concrete. The impact drives him down hard. A flash of claws tear across his chest in a spray of blood that gleams dark in the half-light.

"JP!" His name rips out of me before I can stop it.

I twist against the ropes, fibers sawing deeper into skin already slick with sweat. The chair creaks and groans under the strain, threatening to topple with me bound to it. The demon's shadow stalks closer, grin widening with every step, black eyes devouring me whole.

Something in me snaps. Heat surges through my arms, sudden and violent, racing under my skin like wildfire. Suddenly the rope shreds apart in my hands. I stumble free, and my breath hitches in shock.

No time to think.

The demon lunges, claws arcing toward my throat. I throw an arm upwards by instinct. Pain explodes across my forearm, hot and blinding, and my nerves scream as blood sprays wide and splatters across the half-finished chalk circle at my feet.

The reaction is immediate: my spilled blood hisses as it hits, glowing bright and unnatural, the runes beneath it rippling like water disturbed by the throwing of a stone. The circle pulses once—alive, hungry—and the demon freezes mid-step, its black eyes widening as if it has just recognized something terrible.

I don't let it finish whatever thought has stolen its grin.

My boot knife. Thank every star in the sky. My fingers wrap around the hilt like they've been waiting their whole life for this single moment. I wrench the knife free—steel singing as it clears the sheath—and ram the blade up through the demon's jaw.

The impact jolts up my arm. The demon's body seizes, every muscle snapping tight. A rattling hiss sighs as black smoke geysers from its mouth and eyes, thick enough to burn my lungs. The body shudders once, twice, then collapses into a mound of ash.

For a breath, silence presses down—broken only by the sound of JP grappling with the other demon, his breath ragged as claws scrape bone.

The knife drips in my hand. My blood burns in the circle. But JP is still pinned, the demon's claws hovering inches from his heart, the weight of it crushing him into the floor. His face twists in pain, blood dark across his chest.

Something primal tears loose inside me.

I don't think; I move. My boot slams into the demon's chest with a crack that echoes through the warehouse. The force of it shocks me as much as it does the creature. Its body rockets backward like I'd been hiding a sledgehammer in my bones, smashing through a stack of crates. Wood explodes into splinters and dust rains down in clouds.

I am on the demon before it can rise, knife flashing in my hand. My blade plunges deep into its chest, sinking through skin that splits too easily, through bone that crumbles like rot. The demon convulses, black smoke convulsing out of its mouth in desperate gulps. Its body jerks once, twice, and then collapses into ash that scatters across the floor like burnt paper.

Silence falls, sudden and absolute. My uneven breathing fills the hollow space.

The only thing that moves is the chalk circle, its lines glowing faintly, pulsing once like a heartbeat buried in stone, before fading back into the cracked concrete as if nothing had happened.

I stand amid the wreckage, breath tearing in and out of me, the knife in my hand dripping a tar-black residue that steams against the cold ground. My pulse thrashes wildly, rattling my ribs as if trying to escape my body entirely. The trembling in my limbs isn't fear—not exactly. It's sharper than that, hotter.

Adrenaline surges through me, flooding every nerve with fire. And tangled beneath the fear—coiled around it—is something reckless and raw. A dangerous, intoxicating thrill. A rush that makes my hands tremble even as the knife stays steady.

I hate it. Hate this part of me that wants more. But—heaven help me—some part of me *likes* it.

"Evelyn." JP's voice cuts through the haze like a whip crack.

I turn, breath still ragged, to find him standing in the doorway. His pistol hangs low at his side, smoke curling faintly from the barrel. His eyes find me, relief flashing bright for half a heartbeat before it hardens into stone.

"What the hell were you thinking?" he snaps, voice rougher than the gunfire.

I wipe the blade on my jeans, forcing my hands steady. "I was thinking we didn't have time to wait."

His jaw flexes, tight as a bowstring. "You were supposed to stay outside." He moves closer, boots heavy on the cracked floor, every step a punctuation mark. "One of them knocked you out before I even got here. If I'd been five minutes later—*five*—you'd be bleeding out on this floor."

My chin lifts, heat flaring sharp. "But I'm not. I handled it."

"Handled it?" His voice spikes, raw with anger. "You got lucky, Evelyn. And luck doesn't keep you alive out here."

The words slice deep because I know he's right. My head is still throbbing from the hit that dropped me. Rope burns have scorched angry lines across my wrists, hidden only by the way my skin is already beginning to knit itself back together. *If I* didn't heal the way I do... If *he had been any later*...

I shove the thought down, bristling instead. "I can't just sit on the sidelines. I'm not a kid anymore."

JP's tone drops low, heavy, like a weight pressing the air flat between us. "No. You're nineteen. And that makes you reckless. Until you learn the difference between bravery and stupidity, you're going to get someone killed." His eyes lock on mine, sharp and unyielding. "Or worse—you'll get *yourself* killed."

The words land harder than any claw, sharper than any blade. My throat tightens, but I refuse to look away. Because underneath his anger isn't just rage—it's fear. Fear for me. Fear of what losing me would do to him.

And it terrifies me too.

I look away, jaw tight. He isn't wrong. I know he isn't wrong. But the fire in my chest—the desperate need to prove I belong out here— burns hotter than the shame his words carve into me.

JP drags a hand down his face. "Come on," he mutters, voice rough with exhaustion. "We're going back to the office. We need to talk."

He holsters his pistol without a second look and strides out, each step a heavy, controlled strike against the concrete—war drums marching away from the battlefield. Moments later, his truck roars awake, and the sound rumbles through the empty space, rattling the broken windows before it disappears into the dark.

When the echo dies, all that's left is me.

I stand alone in the wreckage, lungs heaving, the air thick with the metallic bite of blood and the scorched stink of demon smoke. Ash clings to my arms in gray streaks, gritty and cold when I brush my fingers against it, its dust smearing dark under my fingertips.

And beneath all of it—the trembling, the exhaustion—my chest is still throbbing with adrenaline, feral and electric, refusing to quiet.

The silence presses close again, broken only by the faint creak of the building settling. For the first time since the fight, I realize how badly I'd been shaking. Forcing my legs to move, I step outside, and the night air rushes cool against my overheated skin, a relief so sharp it stings.

My motorcycle waits by the fence, chrome catching what little moonlight is still bleeding through the clouds. A steady thing. Familiar. Mine.

I pull my helmet from the handlebar, but hesitate and tilt my head back instead. The stars glitter bright against endless blackness, uncaring and untouchable. I used to love them. When I was little, I'd lie in the grass with my mom, tracing constellations with clumsy fingers, pretending they held secrets meant only for us.

Now, they just remind me how small I am. How little I understand about what I've just faced. How close I've come to being nothing more than another body in the dark.

And yet, a stubborn warmth stirs in my chest. I'm still here. Bruised, battered, aching—but alive. Stronger than I should be. Faster to heal than anyone else. Different. Even if I don't know what it all means, staring at the stars, I feel my future's inevitable weight pressing down on me.

With a sigh, I slip the helmet over my head and twist the key. The engine's low growl vibrates through me, grounding, steady, and the bike roars to life with a defiant snarl in the empty night.

I gun the throttle and tear away from the warehouse, wind lashing against me like it could strip everything away—the fear, the anger, the questions tugging at the corners of my mind.

By the time I pull up to the office, JP's truck is parked out front, gravel and dust long settled around it. Figures. He never wastes time when he's pissed.

Inside, the lights blaze warm, golden against old wooden beams and leather chairs, cozy in a way that almost mocks me. After the warehouse, the air here—paper, coffee, dust—smells too safe, too peaceful. But the look waiting behind the desk tells me peace is the last thing I'll get tonight.

JP stands in front of me, his arms crossed, a wall of muscle and thunder. His blue eyes are sharp enough to pin me where I stand.

I shut the door behind me with a soft click, drop my helmet like a gauntlet on the couch, and brace myself. The storm breaks instantly.

"What the hell were you thinking, Evelyn? I told you to wait for me! I told you not to go in alone." He leans forward, his weight hitting the desk like an exclamation. "You could've been killed. You almost *were* killed. Do you even understand what would've happened if I hadn't shown up when I did?"

The words grab hold of me, reminding me of the demon's claws.

I stand with my arms crossed tight, nails biting into my sleeves, letting the storm wash over me. My jaw aches. My throat burns with words I want to throw back at him but swallow instead. There's no point arguing when JP is in full lecture mode.

After several minutes of pacing and scolding, JP's voice finally drops into something steadier, though its edge never leaves. "So. Tell me everything. What did you see?"

I hesitate, sifting through the fight in my mind: the shadows writhing at the edge of vision, the guttural snarls that I can still feel in my bones, the chalk circle glowing faintly with my blood. But one detail claws to the surface, clearer than all the rest.

"One of them had a tattoo," I say slowly. "On his arm. Some kind of symbol. He was the one calling the shots, doing most of the talking."

JP's eyes narrow, quick enough to slice through the air. "What kind of symbol?"

I move closer to the desk, my fingers twitching with restless energy. Grabbing a notepad and pen, I let muscle memory guide me. The lines spill out easily, burned into my mind like they've been seared there on purpose: looping arcs, blunt angles, a pattern that seems to shift if I stare at it too long, like the paper itself doesn't want to hold it.

My chest tightens and I slide the sketch across the desk.

JP studies it in silence—too much silence. His jaw clenches, a muscle ticking at its edge, his eyes darkening with something I can't read—recognition, maybe. Or dread.

The quiet stretches until it becomes unbearable. "Well?" I demand, though my voice comes out thinner than I want it to.

He doesn't answer—doesn't even look at me. Instead, he reaches for his phone, his fingers moving fast, like they already know who to call.

"Stay here," he mutters low, as he presses the phone to his ear. His tone isn't a suggestion; it's an order—the kind he doesn't expect me to question.

But the knot twisting in my gut tells me whatever he sees in that symbol—it's worse than he wants to admit.

I sit on the couch for a while, arms wrapped tight around myself, listening to the low rumble of JP's voice carrying from behind the desk. He sounds calm, measured, but I know him well enough to hear the strain threaded underneath. Whoever he's calling isn't just some contact; they're one of his ghosts, one of the names etched into the scars he never talks about.

After a minute, the air in the office feels too heavy. I push myself up and wander down the hall. The bathroom light buzzes when I flip it on, flooding the room with a sickly yellow glow that would make even the healthiest person look half-dead.

The mirror doesn't do me any favors either. A girl stares back— dried blood smeared across her cheekbones, shadows pooled under hazel-gold eyes that look like they belong to someone far older than nineteen. Dark hair clings to my skin, framing a face that looks young and tired at the same time. A girl who should be in bed, safe, normal. Not being tied to chairs in warehouses while demons whisper about carving her open.

I twist the faucet. Water sputters, then runs hot, and steam curls up from the basin in ghostly ribbons. I cup my hands and splash it onto my face. The sting against my wounds lights up my nerves, but the burn is grounding—real, at least.

When I look up, the rivulets slide down my reflection's skin, catching in the hollow curve of her jaw. For a moment, with the water dripping and the yellow light painting her pale, she almost looks ordinary. Almost.

But she's not—I'm not.

"I should be scared," I mutter, watching my lips move in the mirror. "Normal people would be scared."

The girl doesn't answer. She just stares back at me, stubborn, unblinking, daring me to admit what I already knew. And the truth is, I'm not scared—not exactly. My heart is still racing, my hands are still trembling, but fear isn't what has me shaking. I feel unsettled. Confused. Haunted by the same gnawing question that's followed me for years:

Why me? Why do I walk away from things that should've killed me—twice, three times over—when other people don't?

The silence presses in. My own eyes stare back, hard, accusing.

"Because you're a freak," I tell the mirror. The words crack with a bitter laugh, though my half-smile falls flat before it can take real shape.

I snatch a towel, dragging it across my skin until my face feels raw, like maybe I could scrub the wrongness off if I just pressed hard enough.

Then, I turn back into the hallway. The bathroom light buzzes once more before flickering out, leaving the mirror in shadow.

JP is pacing when I step back into the office, phone pressed hard to his ear. His movements are sharp, almost mechanical—boots striking the floor in clipped beats, shoulders squared like he's on a parade ground instead of in an office surrounded by leather chairs and file cabinets. His jaw is worked tight, a muscle twitching with every word he doesn't say out loud. His eyes are dark, distant, locked somewhere far away in a memory I can't reach.

When he sees me, something flickers across his face, then disappears before I can name it. He ends the call mid-sentence, slides the phone into his pocket, and turns toward me like he's already decided how this conversation is going to go.

"We might have a lead," he says without preamble. His voice is flat, controlled, but there is an undercurrent of dread he can't quite hide. "Someone thinks they can connect the symbol to a group in the area. They'll meet us tomorrow night."

"Tomorrow?" I echo, frowning. The adrenaline still humming through me snaps sharp. "Why not tonight? You just love dragging this out, don't you?"

He shoots me a look—the kind that used to stop me dead when I was younger, the kind that says *don't push me*. But it doesn't land the same anymore. I'm not a kid he can shut down with a glare. I've grown into my own stubbornness, assured and unmovable.

"Because you need rest," he says, his tone crisp and commanding. "And because I need time to prep."

I flop onto the couch with exaggerated drama, rolling my eyes so hard it almost hurts. "You and your prep. What are you going to do, color-code the demons? File them alphabetically?"

For half a second, the mask cracks. His mouth twitches, fighting a smile. "You joke, but my system keeps us alive."

"Sure," I say, stretching out across the cushions like I own the place. "Meanwhile, I'll just be over here, recovering at superhuman speed and twiddling my thumbs." The smirk slips out before I can stop it, even though I know he hates when I lean into the whole *not normal* thing.

His eyes soften just a fraction, the storm easing at its edges.

"Fine," I add after a beat, my voice dropping quieter. "I'll wait. But don't think I'll sit this one out."

He gives me a half-smile then—small and reluctant, but real. "Wouldn't dream of it."

For a moment, if fragile, the tension between us thins into a truce we don't have to speak out loud, the kind that says: *we're still in this together, even if we want to strangle each other while we do it.*

When we finally head out, the office lights flicker off behind us, plunging the space into darkness. The warm glow inside vanishes and is replaced by the raw bite of night air. It's sharp, bracing, the kind that cuts straight through skin and bone. My breath fogs faintly before it's carried away by a knowing wind.

My hair whips across my face, strands stinging my cheek until I shove them back behind my ear. My eyes scan the shadows automatically, the way JP has trained me—edges first, then distance, then dark corners.

That's when I see it: movement at the tree line. Just a flicker, gone in an instant. But still enough to send my pulse skittering into overdrive.

"Did you see that?"

JP freezes mid-step. His hand hovers near his holster, body angled toward the threat before I even finish speaking. His eyes narrow, sharp as a blade. "See what?"

"There—" My finger points before I can stop it, trembling slightly despite my effort to keep steady. "Something moved."

His entire body shifts, the soldier in him snapping into place like a switch inside him was thrown. "Stay close."

The air changes. Heavy. Dense. Like the atmosphere before a storm, thick enough to taste. The wind carries with it something that sounds almost like whispers—too faint to be real, too scattered to form words. But my instincts scream otherwise.

Without thinking, my knife is in my hand, cold metal biting my palm. My back presses to the wall, every muscle taut, waiting for something to come tearing out of the dark.

"I swear I saw—"

"Shh." JP's firm hand cuts the air. His eyes stay locked on the tree line, his whole body frozen with the terrifying patience of a man who's survived too many ambushes. Listening. Waiting.

The silence that follows is more haunting than any scream. My heartbeat thunders in my ears. The shadows stare back, unblinking. Still.

Nothing steps forward; the unease crawls across my skin like static, alive and insistent. Every nerve stretches tight and every instinct screams the same thing: that flicker of movement wasn't my imagination.

The night isn't done with me yet.

Chapter 2

Ghosts of the Fire

JP and I share a tense glance, the kind heavy enough to speak without words. My lungs tighten against the night air biting through my jacket and into my skin. We stand frozen in the gravel lot, eyes locked on the tree line where shadows pool thicker than they should be. Every branch, every sway of wind looks like it's hiding something ready to peel itself out of the dark and strike.

The silence is the kind that makes your own heartbeat sound like betrayal, beating so loud you swear the whole night can hear it.

"Nothing," JP mutters at last, though the word lands flat and unconvincing. His brow stays creased, jaw sturdy and defiant. He sweeps the tree line again, his gaze moving like a rifle barrel. Watching. Calculating. Waiting.

Only when he's certain the stillness will hold does he shift his stance, the tension in his shoulders loosening by degrees, but not disappearing fully. With JP, it never does. He doesn't release tension—he buries it. Tucks it just beneath the surface where it can smolder until the next fight pulls it free.

And standing there beside him, knife still in my hand, I realize I'm starting to do the same.

I try to mimic his calm, but my own eyes burn from staring too hard, too long. The flicker I is gone now, swallowed whole by the dark like it was never there. My chest tightens, every inhale shallow, like my lungs are refusing to fill all the way. Still, I force out the words, thin and brittle: "Maybe it was just a trick of the light."

Even as the lie leaves my mouth, I feel the weight of it sink. I don't even believe myself.

"Could be," JP allows, his voice low. "Doesn't matter. Stay sharp. Don't let your guard down."

We move together across the lot, side by side, our footsteps crunching on gravel that sounds fragile, like the earth is warning us not to break the silence. My veins buzz under the surface of my skin like static electricity, and prickle through my arms and inside the back of my neck. Every breath carries a faint metallic tang, sharp on my tongue, like the taste of fear.

Behind us, the office towers in the dark, no longer warm and safe but cold, haggard—like an abandoned corpse hollowed out and waiting to collapse. Ahead, the night presses in, every shadow stretching, smothering.

When I swing a leg over my bike, the leather seat is icy beneath me, seeping through my jeans. I hesitate before pulling on my helmet, glancing back toward the trees one last time.

Shadows ripple at the edge of my vision, and for half a second, I swear I see it again: a figure peeling loose from the darkness, its eyes gleaming faintly.

But when I blink, there's nothing. Just the heavy, waiting silence pressing down, waiting for me to choke. And somehow, that feels worse.

The unease doesn't leave. It just burrows deeper, curling low in my gut like a snake waiting to strike. "Head home safely," JP says. His voice is even, but his expression is stone, every line of his face etched with a worry he'll never admit out loud. Serious enough to make my stomach twist tighter.

"You too." I try to shape my lips into a smile, but it feels brittle, stretched thin over bruises that haven't healed yet.

He studies me for a long moment, eyes narrowing just slightly—that look of his, the one that weighs every risk, every threat, every way this night could've ended differently. It's the kind of gaze that feels like armor and a cage at the same time—a protection I don't want, and a restraint I can't escape.

Then, without another word, JP turns and climbs into his old boxy pickup. The paint faded, the body dented, but the truck still as stubborn and unyielding as he is. The engine grumbles awake, a low growl, like an old warhound refusing to die.

I watch the truck bounce once as JP's weight settles in, then watch it rumble forward, taillights bleeding red into the dark until they vanish completely. A small, silent promise lingers in the empty lot behind him: no matter what else comes, JP has my back.

Even when he isn't here to prove it.

I sit here longer than I should, the weight of the night like hands on my shoulders. The stars overhead gleam faintly, cold and indifferent, their light too far away to matter. The silence stretches deep and wide, but it doesn't feel empty.

Because somewhere beyond the tree line, beyond the restless shadows that twitch at the corners of my vision, something else is waiting. Watching. Breathing the same night air we are.

We haven't been alone tonight. Not even close.

The road home is quiet, my bike's engine purring steady beneath me, the vibration seeping deep into my bones. The wind whips against me, cool and sharp, tugging at my jacket until I think it might peel me away. I breathe deep, letting the wind carry the leftover heat of battle off my skin, the acrid taste of smoke still lingering in the back of my throat. For a fleeting second, I almost let myself believe this is normal—that I'm just another nineteen-year-old out too late, hair tangled by the wind, the night mine to enjoy.

But the shadows at the edge of my vision don't let me believe the lie for long. Every tree lining the road feels too still, every dark corner, too deep. The empty streets whisper like they're hiding something with teeth.

My mind replays the fight, every detail sharper now that I'm alone. The way the demons had moved—not like mindless hunters, but with deeper purpose. Coordination. And that tattoo... etched into memory, carved across my thoughts like the rope that had cut through my skin.

Three attacks in one month. That's not coincidence: that's pattern. That's intent. The town isn't the center of this anymore—I am.

They—whoever they are—are drawing tighter and tighter, their orbit shrinking until all that remains is me at the center. Are they hunting... *me*?

By the time I pull into my driveway, the spell of the open road has worn off. Our house crouches in the dark like it's trying to disappear, its silhouette leaning against the night. Ashford, Oregon isn't a big town—some people even call it cozy. I call it suffocating. But even here, this house manages to stand out for all the wrong reasons.

The porch light burned out years ago, allowed to die without a second thought. The siding peels from the house in long strips, curling away from the wood beneath like skin shedding after a sunburn. Every line of the building droops, weary, as if the place has given up on holding itself together. It's a place where comfort and shame tangle into one roof, and I've been living beneath it my whole life.

I kill the engine, the sudden silence roaring in my ears that had grown accustomed to the steady purr of the bike. For a moment, I sit here, staring at the house as if it might finally collapse in on itself. Then, I swing a leg over the seat, boots displacing the gravel at my feet, and make my way inside.

The door creaks open, loud, like the house is announcing my return.

The air hits me instantly: thick and musty, heavy with stale beer and cigarettes that seeped into the drywall years ago and never left. It clings to me like grease, sinking into my skin; I know I'll carry it with me no matter how much I scrub.

The living room greets me with its usual chaos: empty bottles lined up across the coffee table like soldiers on parade, ashtrays overflowing with half-smoked butts, the stench of them lingering bitter in the air. The carpet is worn down to threads in the places my father stumbles most, pathways marked by weight and routine. Shadows stretch long and jagged along the walls in the dim light, twisting the wreck of the place into something uglier. Like in this light, the house is allowing me to see it for what it is.

From the back bedroom, my father's snores rise and fall, uneven, slightly muffled by the thin walls. Relief and bitterness tangle tight in my chest. At least he is alive. At least he's out of my way. But even when he is here, he isn't. Not really

It hasn't always been like this.

I think about before the fire, how we lived in a little white house with green shutters on the east side of town. It wasn't perfect—drafty in the winters, too hot in the summers—but it was hers: my mom's house. Her laughter filled the kitchen, bright and effortless. Every windowsill overflowed with plants she insisted were "resilient," and the whole place smelled faintly of lemon and soap, the scent of someone who cared enough to keep things clean. It was small, but it was warm. It was alive.

After the fire, after she died, everything good in my dad burned, too.

This house was supposed to be a fresh start. A rental. Nothing special—just four walls and a roof to keep the rain out. But ghosts don't respect leases. They followed us here, whispering through empty rooms, filling the cracks my father refused to mend. And he welcomed them with a bottle in his hand, drowning in the same grief I couldn't escape.

Now, it isn't a home at all. It's a shell. Hollow. And I'm the ghost rattling around inside it.

I step deeper into the living room, boots sticking slightly to the floor in places where spilled beer or ash have long sullied the carpet. I should clean. I should care. But the weight in my chest tells me what I already know: no amount of scrubbing could ever wash the rot out of these walls. The stench has sunk too deep. It's part of the house now, just like him.

Upstairs, my room waits like an island in a sea of ruin. The only space that still feels like mine. I head for the stairs, each step slow, careful not to wake him.

The stairs complain beneath me as I climb, each groan of old wood familiar as a scar. My hand trails the rail out of habit, fingertips grazing notches carved there from years of wear. It feels like the bones of a dying animal beneath my palm.

I slip into my room and shut the door softly behind me, exhaling like I've crossed into another world. My sanctuary.

The walls are plain, bare drywall that should look empty, but that instead remind me of everything I've refused to lose. Stacks of books line the corners, their spines bent from being reread. Notebooks litter the desk and floor, pages filled with sketches, half-finished thoughts, fragments of the chaos I could never say out loud. Drawings I've never shown anyone—shadows, faces, fire. Scraps of who I am, tucked away where no one can judge them.

The air up here is cooler. Cleaner. It doesn't carry the sour bite of cigarettes or the stale heaviness of beer. It's free. Untouched. The only space in the house that still feels alive.

I collapse onto my bed, the mattress dipping beneath me in recognition, like it remembers every weight of me after every long night. My muscles ache, but not nearly as much as they should. The bruises that should've left me limping are already fading to faint shadows, yellowing out of existence. The rope burns around my wrists still sting, but even they are beginning to smooth away, my skin smoothing over itself like nothing happened.

My body feels like a lie—healed on the surface, shredded inside.

I stare at the ceiling, my eyes tracing the cracks spidering across the plaster. I count them like constellations, lines crisscrossing into shapes that mean nothing. My thoughts refuse to quiet. They never do after nights like this. The silence only makes them louder—echoes of gunfire, snarls, smoke.

And beneath it all, that circle. Glowing. Waiting.

The shadows outside. The way the demons had moved with purpose. That strange tattoo burned into memory. Questions spin too powerful to ignore. Who are they? What do they want? And why does it always feel like the answer is *me*?

27

I roll onto my side, curling deeper into the blankets, as if their weight might soothe the restless knot in my chest. But it won't loosen. Sleep edges closer, exhaustion tugging heavy at my limbs, but my mind thrashes against it, unwilling to surrender.

And then, memory drags me under anyway. Suddenly, I'm twelve again:

The living room glows gold with late-afternoon light, curtains softening the brightness into lazy patterns across the carpet. The radio hums a half-forgotten tune, the kind my mom never quite knew the words to, but sang anyway. Her laughter bubbles through each line, filling every corner of the room, turning the off-key notes into something beautiful.

She twirls barefoot across the floor, a dish towel in one hand like a ribbon, her hair catching the sun in flashes of burnished copper. Her smile is a sun of its own, warm enough to burn away anything that tried to touch me.

She is my anchor. My shield. My whole world.

I can feel the warmth of her hand tugging mine, pulling me into her orbit. From somewhere above me, I can hear her words in a whisper, the same words she always said when I was afraid— *everything will be okay*.

For a moment, the memory feels alive, close enough to touch. Like if I reach far enough, I can bring it back with me.

But then, it twists. The gold fades to red.

The light turns harsh, broken by smoke. The air thickens and fills my lungs with ash. The radio dies in a sputter of static, swallowed by the shriek of sirens outside. Curtains blacken, curling in on themselves, and the room that was once ours becomes a cage of fire.

Her laughter is gone. Her hand slips from mine. And no matter how hard I search the smoke, she isn't there. There's only fire.

Sirens continue wailing outside, alarms blaring like the world itself is screaming. Smoke floods the house and rolls over me in waves that sting my eyes and claw down my throat.

My father stumbles out from the back room, wild and broken. His eyes are red, panic carved deep into every line of his face. "Evelyn! Get out!" His voice cracks apart on my name, raw with desperation.

But I can't move.

My body locks, frozen by terror. Fear slams into me like a wall, rooting my feet to the floor. My chest seizes, my heart pounding against my ribs so hard, it feels like it's trying to escape. I spin in the smoke, searching—begging—for her. For my mother. But she's gone. Lost. Swallowed whole by the fire.

The roar grows louder, the flames blistering hot as they surge closer, devouring everything I know, everything that is safe. The walls groan and crack, paint blistering into bubbles before peeling away. The house screams as it burns.

And then, through the haze, a figure emerges.

Tall. Steady. His outline framed by fire, impossible and immovable against the chaos. Shadows twist around him like wraiths, clinging and writhing, but his eyes—damn, his eyes—burn with a determination that cuts through the smoke like steel.

"Come with me!" he shouts, his voice carrying above the roar. His hand reaches out, firm, unyielding, waiting for me to take it.

Terror claws at me, my instincts telling me to hide, to curl in on myself, to run from this unknown savior. He isn't supposed to be here. He doesn't belong in this nightmare. But the fire surges closer, devouring floorboards, devouring air, devouring *me*.

My hand moves before my mind can argue, clutching his like it's the only solid thing left in the world.

His grip is iron, pulling me forward, dragging me through the storm of heat and smoke. He is sure-footed where I stumble, steady where I hesitate. Walls collapse behind us, sparks rain down like burning stars, but he never falters. Step by step, he carves a path through the choking black, through a world that's ending.

And somehow, impossibly, we burst into the freezing night.

The cold slams into me like another shockwave, so sharp it makes me sob. I collapse onto the icy ground, my body convulsing as it wheezes for air. Each gasp scorches my throat, each breath a painful victory against the fire's grip. The smoke still burns in my lungs, rattling out of me in violent coughs as the night spins overhead.

Alive. But everything else—everything I loved—is gone.

My mother isn't there.

The realization guts me more than any other loss ever could.

The rest comes in pieces, jagged and out of order. Sirens wailing, harsh and relentless. Firefighters shouting commands over the roar of the blaze, their voices distant, muffled, like I'm underwater. My father staggering across the yard, hair singed, eyes wide and empty, moving like a man already broken. The house collapsing in on itself, flames eating through every beam, every wall, until all that's left of my life is smoke and ash swirling into the night sky.

And me—clutching JP's hand like a lifeline, knuckles white, skin raw, unable to let go. Caught between grief and survival. Confusion and terror.

The fire had taken everything I was. All that remained was the hollow shell of someone I didn't recognize.

I roll back onto my bed, the present bleeding back in around me, heavy and raw. Tears prick my eyes but don't fall—they never do. That night carved me open and left me empty. My mother was gone. My father drowned himself in bottles to forget her, and in the process forgot me, too.

And JP—this stranger who'd dragged me out of the flames—slowly became the only steady thing I had left.

I used to fear him. His silence, the intensity of his eyes, the soldier's stillness that clung to him like a shadow. He seemed more weapon than man. But fear gave way to something else: Dependence, Trust, a bond forged in fire and loss.

He became my anchor in the chaos, the immovable weight that kept me tethered when everything else wanted to sweep me away. He taught me to fight, to keep breathing when every instinct begged me to stop. To survive when survival felt impossible.

Every lesson came with the same reminder: I wasn't normal.

Stronger. Faster to heal. Different. He called it a gift, said it made me special. He said it gave me a chance most people didn't have.

Some nights, though, it feels less like a gift and more like a curse. Because the fire may not have killed me, but it never stopped burning inside me.

My hand finds the necklace at my throat. The chain is cool against my skin, familiar, a weight I've carried for as long as I can remember. My mother gave it to me, her fingers warm as she fastened it, her voice promising I'd always have a piece of her close.

It's the only part of her I still carry—the last tether to the warmth I lost in those flames.

I clutch it tight, knuckles whitening around the pendant, clinging to her memory—her laughter in the kitchen, her soft voice singing

31

along to half-known songs, the sunlight in her hair. Her love. Her light.

The only thing strong enough to remind me why I fight at all. And why I can never stop.

It wasn't until puberty that I started realizing just how different I was. As a kid, my differences never stood out. Scrapes and bruises faded faster for me than for anyone else I knew, but I figured I was just lucky. Resilient. My mom once healed from a nasty cut almost overnight, and I thought, *That's just what bodies do if you let them.* I didn't see it as strange. I didn't see *her* as strange.

But after she was gone, my own signs only sharpened.

Once, I crashed my bike on the gravel road behind our house. The handlebars twisted out of my grip and I went flying, skin tearing open across my palm. Blood slicked down my arm, hot and sticky, and the pain was sharp enough to make my vision blur.

My father barely looked up from his bottle. His eyes glazed past me like I wasn't even there. I wrapped the wound myself, pressing an old rag into it until the bleeding slowed, expecting agony in the morning.

Instead, when I woke, the skin had nearly sealed. Two days later, it was gone—smooth, unbroken, like the crash had never happened.

At first, I told myself it was a fluke. A miracle.

But it kept happening. Every cut, every bruise, every twisted ankle—gone in days instead of weeks. It should have felt like a blessing. But all it did was remind me I wasn't like anyone else.

And then, by fourteen, the strength came.

I didn't notice it all at once. It slipped in quietly, showing itself in the smallest moments. Like the night I reached for my dad's arm to steady him when he stumbled too close, only for him to jerk back as though I'd crushed him with my grip.

Or the afternoon at school when a group of bullies cornered me in the hallway, shoving me against the lockers like they always did. This time, when I shoved back, one of them hit the ground so hard his head rang against the tile.

The look on their faces wasn't pity anymore. It was fear.

And for a moment, staring down at their wide eyes and pale skin, I almost believed them when they called me a monster. Because taking down someone twice my size hadn't just been possible—it had been *easy*. Too easy.

I hated it.

Some nights, lying awake in my room, I wondered if maybe it was punishment. A cruel joke written into my bones. My mom died. My dad drowned himself in bottles. And me? I was cursed to carry a body that healed too fast, hit too hard, felt too wrong. Maybe this was my penance for not being able to save either of them.

That's when JP stepped in. He never flinched at what I could do. Never called me a freak. Where others recoiled, he leaned in. He showed me what to *do* with it.

"Strength without control is chaos," he'd tell me in that gravel-deep voice, his hands steady on the boxing pads while I hammered at them until my arms shook. "Strength with purpose? That's survival."

So he drilled me. On stances, balance, breath, footwork. Pushed me to run until my lungs burned, to fight until my legs gave out. Every time I thought I'd hit my limit, he proved me wrong. The harder I pushed, the more I discovered I could.

And when the nights came—the ones when shadows were more than shadows, when something slipped through, hungry for blood—he didn't shield me from them. He threw me straight into the fire. Sometimes barking orders, sometimes dragging me back by the collar before claws tore me apart.

"Demons don't care that you're young," he told me once, after I'd nearly gotten gutted. His eyes were sharp, but his tone softened in a way that stuck. "They only care that you bleed. If you're going to fight them, you fight to win. No hesitation."

I hated him for how relentless he was. For every bruise, every exhaustion-soaked night when I collapsed into bed thinking I couldn't take another step.

But eventually, I understood. He wasn't hard on me to break me; he was hard on me so I'd live.

And I did.

Still, the feeling of wrongness never left. Every time a wound sealed too fast, every time my fists landed with bone-breaking force, the unease crept back in. The gnawing sense that I wasn't just different—I was something else.

One memory sticks clearer than the rest.

I was fifteen, sweating through my shirt in the dim basement JP had turned into a training room. The air was thick with the musk of effort, hot and stale, layered with the scent of dust and rubber. Bare bulbs hummed overhead, their light harsh, stripping every shadow bare. My knuckles throbbed, raw from pounding the pads, and my arms trembled like overstrung wires about to snap.

"Again," JP barked, bracing himself behind the pads.

I glared at him through sweat-stung eyes. "I've hit you a hundred times already."

"Then, hit me a hundred more." His tone was calm. Maddeningly steady.

Anger boiled in my chest. "What's the point? You don't even move. All I'm learning is how to bruise my own hands."

"You think demons stand still for you?" His reply was quick, clipped, a verbal strike. He lifted the pads again. "Stop whining. Focus. Control your stance. Control your breath. Power comes from control."

I wanted to scream at him. To throw the gloves across the room and shout that I wasn't him, that I never would be. But the words stuck in my throat, swallowed by the stubborn fire that refused to let me quit. So instead, I planted my feet, tightened my fists, and swung again.

The crack of impact rang through the basement, sharp as a gunshot. The force reverberated up my arm, bone-deep. And for the first time, JP staggered. Just half a step, boots scuffing against the mat. His eyes widened, a flicker of surprise breaking through his stone face.

I froze, breath caught in my throat. "Did you... feel that?"

His lips twitched into something almost like a smirk. "Yeah. Finally. Thought I was training a pillow this whole time."

I groaned, rolling my eyes, but the corner of my mouth betrayed me with the ghost of a smile. "You're impossible."

"But you're getting there," he said, voice dropping lower, serious now. He lowered the pads, his gaze sharp but softened by something I didn't often see from him: pride. "That punch? That's you when you stop doubting yourself."

I flexed my fingers, staring at them like they didn't belong to me. Stronger. Faster. Tougher. And instead of feeling powerful, the weight of it pressed down heavier. *What am I?*

JP must've read it in my face. He set the pads aside and leaned against the wall, crossing his arms. "You're not broken, Evelyn. You're not a freak. You're different. And different doesn't mean bad."

The words sank deep, warming something raw inside me, but they didn't erase the unease. Different was still dangerous. Different meant I would never be like anyone else.

But at least, for the first time, I wasn't alone.

That night, when I collapsed into bed, my muscles screaming, I stared at my hands until sleep dragged me under. They didn't look like the hands of a scared kid anymore. They looked like the hands of someone who could fight back.

The memory unravels into darkness, fading into the soft, shifting blur of dreams. I blink, and my room comes back into focus, the ceiling's thin spiderweb cracks greeting me like old scars.

The mattress pulls me down, heavy and warm, exhaustion tugging at me with the steady drag of an undertow. Pain echoes through me in slow waves: bruises blooming along my ribs, knuckles scraped and throbbing, muscles tight and trembling from the fight I barely survived.

I know they'll fade by morning. My body always lies for me. But for now, the pain is sharp enough to remind me of the truth.

I am still here.

Downstairs, my father's snores rumble through the floorboards—uneven, ragged, broken by the occasional cough. When I was younger, the sound terrified me: proof that monsters existed inside these walls just as much as they did outside. Now, it doesn't scare me. Not exactly. It just makes the house feel emptier, my father's presence only a shadow of what a father should be, submerged in liquor and silence.

I reach for the necklace at my throat—my anchor. The only piece of my mother I still have. Evidence that not everything was lost in the fire, even if most of me was.

The ache in my body spreads into my chest, heavy and insistent, like the day itself has settled inside me. I squeeze my eyes shut and will sleep to take me before the thoughts spiral again.

Tomorrow will come fast. The demons won't stop. And I'll have to be ready—whether I understand what I am or not.

The house descends deeper into silence, my father's snores droning on like a broken engine. For once, I don't fight the pull of exhaustion. I let it take me.

Because for tonight, sleep is the only escape I have left.

Chapter 3

The Shell of Home

It's my day off. No early shift pulling lattes at the Bean & Gone, Ashford's only coffee shop worth stepping into. The kind of place where the espresso machine hisses louder than the gossip, and regulars argue over crossword clues, like the fate of the universe hinges on a six-letter word for ocean bird.

The job doesn't pay much, but it covers gas for my bike, and throws a few dollars toward the bills, which is more than my dad manages most weeks. Between shifts and training, it's a rhythm I can keep. A routine. Just normal enough to convince people I'm another small-town kid with a part-time job and predictable dreams. Just enough to make it look like I belong.

I snag my phone from the nightstand while tugging a shirt over my head. The cracked screen flickers to life, lighting the dim room with its glow. One notification waits: another text from Maya, one of the girls from the shop who, against all odds, has become my only real friend.

Maya: *You alive? Thought you fell off the planet.*

Maya: *Party at Jackson's tonight. Come on, you need it.*

Maya: *And before you say no—yes, there will be pizza.*

A laugh slips out before I can stop it. That's Maya for you: persistent, dramatic, absolutely relentless. She doesn't just tug me out of my shell—she pries it open with glittered fingernails and sheer willpower. She insists on dragging light into places I've long learned to keep dark.

And somehow, it works.

The normalness of it hits harder than it should: pizza, parties, stupid inside jokes. Arguments over song playlists. Cheap beer spilled on cheap carpets. The kind of things kids my age are supposed to worry about. Not demons. Not chalk circles that pulse when blood hits them. Not secrets that burn holes in my chest every time I try to breathe.

For a heartbeat, I let myself imagine it: a night of greasy pizza slices drooping off paper plates, music turned up too loud on a speaker someone found at a garage sale, laughter bouncing off walls decorated with Christmas lights that never got taken down. A night where shadows don't slither. Where every sound isn't a warning. Where I can just... be. Just Evelyn—not whatever else I'm becoming. But even as I smile, the lie is already unraveling.

The idea of standing in someone's living room, pretending to care about who hooked up with who, or which teacher assigned too much homework, feels almost laughably foreign. Their problems are soft around the edges. Safe. They revolve around grades, crushes, weekend plans.

Mine revolve around creatures with black eyes and human skin stretched too tight. Around knives etched with symbols older than this town—older than this world, maybe. Around the knowledge that something in the dark has learned my name.

Their world is small, gentle. Mine has teeth.

Still, I type back.

Me: *Can't. Rain check?*

Three dots blink like she's already loading her counterargument. Then, they vanish. A moment later:

Maya: *You're impossible. But fine. Next time.*

I set the phone down with a sigh, guilt pricking persistently behind my ribs. I want to say yes. Damn, I want to say yes. I want greasy pizza that leaves oil stains on napkins. I want to laugh until my cheeks hurt, feel the warm, buzzing blur of a room full of people who aren't running from anything. I want to lose myself in the harmless chaos of a party where the biggest crisis is someone spilling a soda on the couch, or fighting over the aux cord.

I want to feel normal. Just for one night. But normal doesn't fit anymore. It hasn't for years. It's a sweater I outgrew long before I realized I was changing.

The silence settles in around me, thick and expectant. I pause, listening for any sign of life down the hall. Nothing. No shuffling steps. No muttered curses. No familiar clink of glass bottles knocking together.

Either my dad isn't up yet, or he passed out harder than usual. Both possibilities sit heavy in my stomach. And honestly, both feel the same.

This house has a way of holding its breath, of making me strain to hear something that isn't there. It's like living inside a ghost story with no ghosts left, just the empty echoes of what used to be.

Pushing off the mattress, I step into the hallway, floorboards creaking under my weight like they want me to be discovered. The house is too quiet; the kind of silence that amplifies every sound until even my breath feels intrusive.

The bathroom mirror catches me on the way in, and I almost flinch at the sight. My hair hangs in a tangled mess, damp with sweat I never shed, and my hazel-gold eyes are shadowed with fatigue, rimmed faintly red from another night without real rest. For a second, I just stare. Then, I stick my tongue out at my reflection, mocking the girl staring back, as if a stupid face could disguise how wrecked she looks.

40

The pipes rattle angrily when I twist the shower knob, coughing and groaning before surrendering a stream of water that gradually warms. The first rush of heat strikes my skin, and a sigh escapes me before I can stop it. Steam fills the small room, curling its tendrils around me, wrapping me in its fleeting cocoon. It carries away the grime and sweat I should've washed off last night, peeling off the layers of smoke and ash that still cling in memory.

My bruises sting under the spray, a tingling reminder of teeth and claws, but already the ache is dulling. The soreness slides away too quickly, muscles loosening as though they've forgotten how close they came to tearing. My body insists on healing, but the pit in my chest refuses to ease.

My mind doesn't let me rest.

It keeps circling back to last night: the demons moving with intention not hunger, their attacks too coordinated to be instinct. The cold fury in JP's eyes when he dragged me out of that warehouse alive, a fury that wasn't aimed at me, but that burned all the same. And that tattoo—etched so deep into my memory that every time I blink, I still see the lines glowing behind my eyelids, pulsing like a heartbeat that isn't mine.

We might have a lead. JP's voice slices through my thoughts, sharp and heavy, echoing in the spaces sleep refuses to fill. As if those five words carry miles of history I'm not allowed to know.

Who are we meeting tonight? What kind of person knows about symbols carved into demon flesh—and knows them well enough to identify them from a messy sketch I drew while my hands were still shaking? And what will they tell us?

Answers? Or something worse: new questions, ones I'm not ready to face, but won't be allowed to ignore?

The uncertainty buzzes in my stomach, like a wire yanked too taut. Information like this never comes clean; it comes dripping in blood, in warnings, in choices no one can undo.

41

And tonight, I'll have to face whoever—or whatever—knows more about that mark than I do.

I crank the water hotter, scalding against my skin, as if I can burn the unease away. But it clings stubbornly to my ribs, a pressure I can't shake. If anything, the heat only drives it deeper. Last night wasn't random. None of it is. Things aren't slowing down; they're escalating. And every step pulls me closer to a truth I'm not sure I want.

When the water cools, goosebumps prickle across my skin, and I twist the knob tight. Steam trails after me in soft white ribbons, dissipating into the hallway like ghosts slipping back into the walls.

The mirror is fogged over, a shield of clouds softening me. For a second, I consider leaving myself that way—safe behind the blur, hidden in the distortion, just a vague outline instead of the truth I never seem ready to face.

But habit—or maybe self-punishment—wins out. I drag my palm across the glass, cutting through the mist. Warm droplets smear under my hand, and my reflection emerges in streaked fragments before finally settling into clarity.

There she is.

Light brown skin, damp and gleaming under the bathroom's unforgiving fluorescent glare. My mother's skin—warm, rich, alive in a way that tugs something in my chest. The faint dusting of freckles across my nose—hers too, a constellation she used to kiss one at a time just to make me laugh.

My dark hair hangs heavy with water, clinging in uneven strands to my shoulders. It drips slowly, rhythmically, tracing chilled paths down my spine. The motion frames my eyes—those damn eyes I wish I could hide.

Hazel-gold. Too bright. Too aware. Eyes that shimmer when my emotions surge, betraying me even when my voice doesn't crack, when my hands don't shake. The glow is faint right now, but still there—like embers that are never fully extinguished.

I hate that shimmer. Hate how it gives me away, how it makes me look like something other than human. Like something I don't have a name for yet.

My gaze drops to the rest of me. Lean, wiry muscle sits under my skin, etched into me by years of training in basements that smelled of rubber and sweat, by fights in back alleys where fear and instinct were better teachers than JP's lectures. Every inch of me looks purposeful. Efficient. Built for movement, for momentum, for damage.

Not bulky. Not soft. Not the body of a girl who gets to worry about parties and crushes. Every line gives away the same truth I keep trying not to face:

I'm not normal; I'm built to fight. Whether I want to or not.

My throat tightens. For a heartbeat, I swear I see her face layered over mine in the glass—my mother's warmth in my freckles, her light flickering in my eyes. Her hand brushing hair from my cheek. Her laugh.

And it hurts. It hurts so badly I have to look away before it swallows me.

I break the gaze first, reaching for the towel and dragging it through my hair until it's only half-dry. The motion is rough, mechanical, like if I work hard enough, I can rub away the reflection I don't want to see.

Jeans. A plain black T-shirt. Simple. Practical. The kind of outfit that lets me blend in anywhere—hallways, sidewalks, coffee shops. Just another face in the blur of people who don't know monsters exist. Clothes that act like armor, like camouflage, that make me small and unremarkable.

Clothes for someone normal.

I catch my reflection in the mirror as I tug the shirt over my head. The fabric settles against my skin, neat and unassuming, trying its best to play the part. For half a second, I imagine that this version of me could walk down the street unseen, unnoticed, untouched by the things clawing at the perimeter of my life.

I almost believe the disguise. Almost.

But the girl staring back from the fog-framed mirror has something in her eyes normal people don't—something bright and sharp and impossible to hide. And the illusion cracks before it even forms.

Downstairs, empty bottles litter the living room floor, some tipped over, others standing tall like little trophies of my father's surrender. I gather them up one by one, glass clinking against glass as I drop them into the recycling bin. The sound is loud in the silence, rattling through the house like an accusation.

The kitchen isn't much better: crumbs scattered across the counter, dishes stacked precariously in the sink, the faint smell of old grease clinging to the walls. I push the clutter aside, set a pan on the stove, and crack a couple of eggs into the heat. The sizzle fills the air, sharp and comforting all at once. For a moment, it almost feels normal. Almost like mornings from years ago, when my mother would hum at the stove and my father would stumble in half-awake but smiling, his arms around her waist.

Almost.

The floorboards creak.

My father shuffles in, rubbing at his eyes, hair sticking up in uneven tufts like he'd fought sleep and lost. His shirt hangs wrinkled and stained near the collar, the sour trace of last night's whiskey clinging to him. He squints at me as though he can't quite believe I'm standing there.

"You're up late," he mutters, voice rough and raw, like pebbles worn to dust.

"I needed sleep," I answer flatly, flipping the eggs. The spatula scrapes the pan in a rhythm that feels more disruptive than it should.

His gaze drifts from the pan to the bottles I cleaned up. His jaw tightens, lips pressing into a thin, brittle line. "Didn't need you cleaning up my mess."

"Someone had to." The words come out sharper than I mean them to, but I don't take them back.

Silence stretches between us, filled only by the angry hiss of the eggs as they spit against the pan. He lowers himself into a chair at the table, the wood groaning under his weight. His shoulders slump forward, rounding him in on himself, making him look smaller than I remember—shrunk by years of exhaustion and something heavier, something he never names.

It's only when he settles that I really look at him.

Michael Cross used to be a big presence—broad-shouldered, steady-handed, the kind of man who filled a room with quiet confidence instead of noise. But the man sitting at the table now is a collapsed version of that memory. He's pushing fifty, but his face looks a decade older. Deep lines crease his forehead and frame his mouth, etched by grief and alcohol more than time. His eyes, once warm and open, are bloodshot and cloudy: dull marbles swimming in red.

His hair is unkempt, graying unevenly at the temples, and the stubble on his jaw is days beyond intentional. He wears a flannel shirt wrinkled enough to hold its own topography, the fabric stretched thin at the elbows, smelling faintly of cigarettes and stale beer. His posture slumps forward—the posture of a man who's given up.

There are moments—rare, flickering things—when the man he used to be peeks through. A softness at the corner of his mouth. A flash of humor. A memory in his eyes that hasn't drowned completely. Moments where I can almost imagine what my life would've looked like if Mom hadn't died, if the fire hadn't hollowed him out, if he hadn't been touched by something evil long before either of us understood what that meant.

But those moments burn out fast.

Now, he just looks... tired. Broken. Like a man forever apologizing, but never speaking the words. And even though I know how grief used him, made him what he is—I can't decide if that makes this version of him easier or harder to forgive.

For a heartbeat, pity stirs. But it curdles fast, burned away by the familiar knot of resentment coiled tight in my chest.

No matter how small he looks now, I can't forget the bottles. The silence. The nights he left me alone in the dark, listening for monsters and realizing I wasn't imagining them.

"You heading out tonight?" he asks finally, his voice flat, more habit than care. The kind of question people ask just to fill the air.

"Yeah," I say, sliding the eggs onto a plate. I grab a second one and divide the food between us, pushing a plate across the table to him. "Got things to do."

He blinks at the offering, almost startled, like he doesn't remember the last time someone made him breakfast. "You didn't have to."

I shrug, keeping my eyes on the pan. "You've got work later, right? Figured you'd need something in your stomach."

He lets out a humorless snort. "Work." The word comes out bitter, sour. He stabs at the eggs with his fork, his movements sharp. "Ten

46

bucks an hour to load pallets until my back gives out. Real dream come true."

"At least it's something," I say carefully, trying for encouragement but hearing the edge of challenge in my own voice.

His eyes flick up, sudden and sharp, cutting into mine like broken glass. "Don't lecture me, Evelyn. You think I don't know how pathetic it looks? You think I don't hear what people in this town say about me?"

The words aren't aimed like knives, but they cut all the same. I grip the edge of the counter, grounding myself against the sting. "I wasn't lecturing," I say, quieter this time.

He exhales through his nose, shakes his head once, and drops his gaze back to the plate. The eggs disappear bite by bite, and for a fleeting second, the kitchen feels almost like it used to—two people sharing breakfast in the morning light, nothing jagged between them.

But the moment doesn't hold.

"Always out," he mutters under his breath, not quite looking at me. "Always got things to do." The words land like a slap.

I don't answer. I can't.

He doesn't know about the demons, the blood, the nights JP and I spend hunting things that shouldn't exist. He doesn't know how close I've come to dying, or how many things in this world wear human faces until they don't. To him, I'm just the daughter who stays out too late, who dodges questions, who keeps secrets he's too tired—or too scared—to uncover.

He sees a stranger at his table, not the little girl my mother left behind.

We eat in a silence packed with every conversation we've avoided for years. The air feels heavy, as if the house itself is bracing for a truth neither of us is willing to speak.

Every scrape of his fork against the chipped porcelain plate is too loud, echoing through the kitchen like a warning shot. Every swallow feels like a countdown, ticking toward a moment where one of us finally breaks and says something we can't take back.

But neither of us does.

We just sit there, going through the motions of a family we no longer are, pretending our ghosts aren't crowding into the empty seats at the table.

When the last bite is gone, he pushes back from the table, chair legs shrieking against the worn linoleum. The sound makes me flinch. Without a word, he shuffles to the fridge, moving heavy, slow, like every step costs him. The door creaks open, the cool light spilling out, and then—*clink*. Glass against glass. A second later, he's pulling free another beer.

Eleven in the morning.

I roll my eyes and look away, refusing to watch him tip what's left of himself down another bottle. Once, he'd been someone I looked up to. My father. The man who carried me on his shoulders so I could "touch the sky." Who laughed loud and easy, telling me stories about constellations, swearing the stars were ancient guardians watching over us. I even used to believe him.

Now, he's just a hollow shell wearing my father's face.

I carry my plate to the sink, rinsing it clean, the hiss of running water filling the silence he left in his wake. It almost feels defiant, the small act of tidying something he won't. Behind me, the sharp fizzing of a bottle cap cracking open cuts through the quiet, followed by a long pull, then the sound of his footsteps dragging down the hall.

A door creaks. Shuts. And just like that, he's gone again.

The knot in my chest loosens—not much, but enough. Enough to breathe. Enough to remind myself I'm still here, even if he's not.

I head upstairs and grab my backpack from its spot near the bed. The familiar weight of it grounds me as I pull it open, laying the contents out across the blanket one by one. It's almost a ritual by now—measured, methodical. In a way, it's the only ritual I believe in.

First, the knife. Always the knife. My favorite, because it isn't just mine—it was hers. My mother's blade. Forged from steel mixed with powdered silver and something rarer still: meteor iron, JP once told me. He never explained where it came from or how he got it; just that it was older than both of us and stubborn enough to outlast us. The alloy makes it deadly to anything born of Hell, but the handle is what matters to me. Smooth from years of use, worn perfectly to fit my grip. Familiar. Trustworthy.

It's stained from last night's fight, black streaks dried along its edge like a reminder. I wrap the cloth around the blade, and drag it slow, careful, until the steel gleams sharp enough to split a shadow. The motion is steadying, almost meditative. The knife hums faintly in my hand, as though it knows its purpose and resents being idle. My aim with a gun will never match JP's, but a blade? A blade is honest. When steel and skin meet, there's no hesitation.

Next, the Glock. Not the .45 JP started me on, but a 10mm—a heavier kick, more stopping power. The kind of weapon you don't carry unless you mean business. I rack the slide back, check the magazine, count the rounds without needing to. The bullets glint under the bedroom light, ordinary at first glance, but I know better. Ordinary rounds don't matter against demons. You could empty a clip into one and it would only grin before tearing you apart.

These are different. Each casing etched with sigils, burned in one by one with a soldering iron, so small they'd vanish if you weren't looking close. Inside, the powder's been mixed with silver dust and a pinch of sanctified salt—JP's concoction. "Prayer powder," he calls it. Not perfect, he warned me, but enough to tip the odds. One round won't drop a demon clean, but a few well-placed shots can even make monsters remember what pain feels like.

The magazine clicks back into place, the sound oddly comforting, a punctuation mark on the ritual. Cold metal. Steady weight. My knife will always be my first choice, but the Glock is insurance. A voice in the dark when my blade isn't enough.

I pack them both carefully into the bag alongside my training clothes and sneakers. No clutter. No extras. Every item has to earn its place. Everything I carry is tailored for survival.

And survival is all that matters.

The house presses in around me as I zip the bag shut. JP said we wouldn't be heading out until tonight, but the thought of wasting the day here makes my skin crawl. I need out.

Outside, my motorcycle waits like a faithful hound. Black paint chipped and scarred, chrome dulled by rain and time. The engine's too loud, the seat worn thin, but she's mine. Always has been. Always will be.

I swing onto the seat, tug my helmet down, and turn the key. The ignition snarls awake, the engine roaring low and guttural, rattling through my chest like a second heartbeat. The sound shakes something loose inside me, breaking the last grip this house has on me.

Without another glance back, I twist the throttle and tear down the street.

The ride is a blur of motion and wind, the world rushing by in streaks of gray and green. Asphalt hums under my tires, steady and familiar, while I lean into each turn with muscle memory built by hours on these roads. The cold air whips against my face, sharp enough to sting through the helmet vents, but I welcome it. Pain means I'm here. Movement means I'm not trapped.

The town passes in fragments: cracked sidewalks buckling from decades of frost, shuttered shops with sun-bleached "Coming Soon" signs that fooled no one, the rusted water tower leaning just enough to make you wonder which storm will finally finish the job. Ashford isn't big—just a scattering of tired streets and peeling paint clinging to the edges of a forest that's always felt a little too close. A place where everyone knows everyone, and no one knows me at all.

It's a town stitched together by memories and scars, some older than its residents, some sewn into me alone. I ride through it like a ghost, untouched and unseen—just another blur in a place that's forgotten how to look closely.

And then, finally, the roads carry me to the only other place where I can feel like me: JP's office. More specifically, the basement beneath it. Our training room. Our battleground. The crucible where he's hammered me into someone capable of standing toe-to-toe with the things that stalk the dark.

If tonight is going to be as bad as I think, I can't sit still. I can't wait for nightfall.

I need to fight. To sweat. To push until every muscle screams.

It's the only way I know to drown out the noise inside me.

Chapter 4

Restless

The basement smells like sweat, leather, and the faint chemical bite of disinfectant. Familiar. Comforting, in its own strange way. The scent of work, of repetition, of blood scrubbed away but never truly forgotten.

The walls are bare concrete, cool and damp to the touch, mottled with old scuffs from boots and palms and bodies thrown harder than intended. The overhead bulbs buzz with a tired hum, casting a harsh, yellowed glow that exaggerates every shadow and makes the air feel dense with heat. A patchwork of training mats covers most of the floor—some new, some worn thin, edges fraying from years of impact.

In the corner sits the heavy bag, its surface cracked in some places, patched in others. JP's done that—stitched up the bag, like it's a soldier that he refuses to allow to retire. Resistance bands hang from a metal hook, curving like sleeping snakes. Dumbbells and weight plates lie in uneven stacks against the wall, their metal faces smeared with years of chalk dust.

The old stereo still rests on its milk crate near the stairs, one speaker rattling whenever the bass hits too hard. A towel rack sits beside it, perpetually stocked and perpetually ignored.

It's a room built for grit, not comfort. For fighting, not feeling.

And yet, standing here, the air thick with the phantoms of every punch I've ever thrown, it feels more like home than the house I left this morning.

I drop my bag by the wall, peel out of my jeans and T-shirt, and tug on my training clothes: leggings, sports bra, tank. My hands move automatically, wrapping cloth around my knuckles and palms until they're tight, secure, ready. Ritual.

The heavy bag waits in the far corner, suspended from a ceiling beam scarred with old impact marks. It sways faintly in the draft from the rattling vents—like it already senses I'm coming for it. Up close, its canvas is even more worn and cracked, patched in places where my knuckles and JP's boots have torn into it too many times. Sweat stains shadow its surface—ghosts of every fight we've rehearsed.

I plant my feet on the mats, fists raised, shoulders squeezed tight. Then, I drive a jab into the bag. Then another. Then a third, harder, enough to jolt the chain overhead and send a sharp vibration up through my wrists.

Each dull thud reverberates through the low-ceilinged room, bouncing off concrete walls and humming back into my bones. The metal chain groans but holds, like it always does.

This is what steadies me. Not silence. Not sleep. Not pretending I'm someone normal. This.

I cross to the old stereo perched crookedly on its milk crate. The plastic casing is cracked, knobs worn smooth from years of JP's rough hands and mine. The speaker that rattles when the bass hits too hard has a back panel that's held on by a strip of duct tape older than I am. Still—it turns on. That's enough.

I twist the dial until the music slams into the room, loud and raw. Bass thrums through the training mats, rattles the exposed pipes overhead, and sends a familiar buzz through the broken speaker. It's loud enough to nearly drown out the sound of my heartbeat— exactly how I want it.

If I can't hear myself think, maybe the thoughts won't catch me.

I roll my shoulders, step back onto the mats, and settle into my stance. It's muscle memory now—feet light, fists up, weight balanced. The beat drops. And then, I move.

My breath syncs with the rhythm—jab, cross, hook, pivot. Leather smacks against canvas, each *thud* swallowed by the music reverberating through the walls. Sweat prickles at my temples, sliding down the curve of my jaw before dropping onto the mat in dark splatters. My arms ache, shoulders burn, but I don't stop. Every punch feels like I'm trying to knock something loose from my chest, some weight wedged so deep it's impossible to move.

But the memories don't care about the noise. They crowd in anyway, slipping between the bass beats, clawing their way up from the dark corners of my head.

I was thirteen the first time JP told me the truth: that monsters weren't stories. That demons didn't lurk under the bed or hide in nightmares. That they walked the same streets we did—passed us in grocery store aisles, held open doors, smiled with borrowed mouths. They wore human faces until the moment they didn't. And they fed on fear, on weakness, on humanity itself.

I remember the sound of his voice when he said it—low, steady, unflinching. There was no dramatic pause, no gentleness. Just a simple, brutal fact delivered as casually as saying *the sky is blue* or *don't forget your jacket*.

And I hated it. Hated how calm he was. Hated how easily he shattered the fragile version of the world I'd scraped together after the fire.

I remember staring at him across the basement mats, fury and disbelief twisting through me. My fists were clenched so tight my nails carved crescents into my palms, grounding me in a reality I refused to accept. My pulse roared in my ears. He couldn't be right. He couldn't be telling me the truth. Monsters weren't real. They couldn't be.

Because if they were... then everything wrong with my life suddenly had a shape. A name. A face.

I refused to believe him.

And then, he dragged me into it. Not violently, but inevitably.

One night, he said "Suit up," and I didn't understand what I was agreeing to until he took me out into the dark, past the town limits, down roads I'd never driven, and into a world that didn't care I was only a kid clinging to her last scraps of normalcy. I felt the cold bite of fear in my throat.

And he showed me. He showed me exactly what hunted us. Exactly what hunted *me*. And from that moment on, I never got my old world back.

My fists slam harder now, rhythm breaking—*jab, cross, hook, hook, hook*. The bag swings wide, rattling the chain above, my knuckles throbbing inside the wraps. My breath grows ragged, tearing out of me in harsh bursts.

But no matter how hard I hit, the truth doesn't go away.

The world isn't safe. It never was.

And I'm not normal. I never will be.

Monsters were supposed to stay in stories—warnings whispered to scare kids into behaving, shadows explained away by imagination. Even after JP showed me one, dragged me to the cliff of that first truth, some part of me held onto the hope that it was a fluke. A nightmare. A one-time crack in reality that would seal itself if I just looked away long enough.

Then, he took me on a hunt. And there was no pretending after that.

I'll never forget the sound that split the night open: a guttural snarl that didn't belong to this world. It wasn't just an animal's growl; it was layered with something human and twisted, like two voices speaking through the same throat. The hair on my arms stood up. My stomach dropped.

And then, I saw its eyes.

Two burning coals floating in the dark, locking onto us with a hunger so sharp it whisked the breath right out from my lungs. My legs turned to stone—frozen, useless—while every instinct I had screamed *run* so loudly I could barely hear myself think.

But JP didn't run.

He stood his ground—calm, steady, like this was just another job. His hands moved with practiced precision, not a flicker of hesitation in his eyes as he raised his weapon and faced it head-on.

"Someone has to fight them," he told me afterward, when it was over, when the snarls had faded and the thing lay broken and burning. My legs were still shaking so badly I could barely stand. My palms stung from where I'd clawed them shut with my own nails.

"They'll never stop coming," he said, his voice low, unshaken. "But we can keep them from taking everything."

I wanted to believe him. Hell, I wanted to believe that someone—*anyone*—could stand against the dark and win. That the world wasn't as terrifying as the thing we'd faced. That JP wasn't dragging me into a nightmare I'd never wake up from.

But that night, when he drove me home and left me standing in the doorway with shaking hands and a heart that felt too big for my chest, I didn't feel braver. I didn't feel chosen or special or strong.

I felt hollow. I felt thirteen. I felt small.

I crawled into the hallway outside my father's bedroom, back pressed against peeling, yellowed wallpaper, knees hugged tight to my chest. The floorboards were icy under my feet. Everything in the house felt cold. JP had told me I couldn't tell my dad about monsters—said he wouldn't believe me, said it would just make things worse.

And maybe JP was right. My dad was already drowning, already looking at the world through a fog too thick for anyone to pierce.

But that night, I needed him anyway. So I stayed outside his door. Listening. To the uneven rhythm of his breathing. To the occasional snore that broke through the wood. To the fragile evidence that he was still there, still alive, still something resembling a parent, even if neither of us knew how to say the word out loud anymore.

It wasn't comfort, not really. But it was familiar. And somehow, it was enough to trick my terrified little heart into slowing down. Enough to make the shadows feel a little less menacing. Enough to let my eyes close for a while, even if sleep was just another kind of escape.

I didn't feel brave, but I didn't feel alone either. Not completely.

But nothing could stop the nightmares.

For weeks after, they stalked me every time I drifted off—red eyes burning in the dark, claws scraping against walls that felt too close, the weight of something inhuman pressing into my chest, until I woke up gasping, choking on shadow. Some nights I screamed, some nights I didn't. But every morning, I woke knowing the same thing:

The monsters were real. And they weren't going away.

The memory fades as my fist slams into the bag again—harder this time. The impact rattles bone, and I welcome it. Pain is simple. Pain makes sense. Pain keeps me here.

I pivot and launch a kick, the strike jarring up my leg, the heavy bag swinging wide on its chain. Sweat slicks every inch of me, dripping into my eyes, burning down my spine. My lungs seize and scream for air, but I don't stop. I *can't* stop. Because if I stop moving, the questions catch me.

Why me?

Why do I heal like this?

Why am I stronger than kids twice my size?

The worst thought lingers—quiet, unwanted—what if the danger isn't where I think it is?

The thought gnaws, chewing through the fragile barrier I've built, so I hit harder. Faster. Until my arms tremble, my breath comes ragged, and my chest feels like it's about to cave.

The music thunders from the old speaker, bass rattling the pipes, a wall of sound that drowns everything else. Until suddenly, it cuts.

The silence is violent in the way it startles me.

The heavy bag sways from the impact of my last strike, creaking on its chain. I stumble back, fists loose, every nerve firing like an alarm. My chest heaves as my gaze snaps to the doorway.

JP leans against the doorframe, arms folded across his chest, the posture of a man built from equal parts discipline and exhaustion. The dim basement light catches in his dirty-blonde hair—trimmed short, threaded with early streaks of gray that don't belong on someone his age, but somehow still suit him. His jaw is shadowed with stubble, the kind that appears not as a result of laziness, but because he's always too busy—or too tired—to bother shaving.

His blue eyes lock on me, steady and unblinking. He doesn't say anything at first. He just watches. Measures. Calculates.

His gaze is cutting enough to peel me apart layer by layer, searching for cracks, for weakness, for whatever storm I'm still holding in my chest. It's the same look he's given me a thousand times: the soldier's assessment mixed with something quieter, heavier. Something like worry he refuses to name.

But mostly, it's the look of someone who's already lost too much and refuses to risk losing more.

"Thought you'd be home resting," he says finally, his voice even but edged with that familiar note of judgment.

I grab the bag to still its swing, wiping sweat from my forehead with the back of my arm. "When do I ever just rest?" I shoot back, forcing the words between ragged breaths. To prove the point, I snap another jab at the bag, leather thudding under my fist.

One of his eyebrows ticks upward. The corner of his mouth twitches, like he's fighting off a smile. "Fair. But most people don't make exhaustion a lifestyle."

"I'm not most people," I mutter, eyes fixed on the bag, refusing to give him the satisfaction of looking at him.

"You can say that again," he murmurs, stepping fully into the room. His boots thud against the mats, steady and deliberate, as he circles me. He moves quietly but watchfully, like a wolf pacing its territory, eyes pressing down on me with the weight of expectation. The pressure makes me straighten my shoulders, makes me force the tremor out of my arms. The last thing I'll ever give him is weakness.

"Form's sloppy," he says bluntly. "Your guard drops after every hook. That'll get you killed."

"Not if I hit hard enough first," I snap back.

JP tilts his head, narrowing his eyes, searching for the thing I won't say out loud. "That why you're here?" he asks. "Beating the bag until it stops reminding you of last night?"

My chest tightens, breath stalling for a beat. I press my palm against the swaying bag, grounding myself, jaw clamped tight. "Better than sitting at home staring at the walls."

For a moment, he studies me in silence, his gaze unreadable. Then, his voice softens, quiet but steady, stripped of its usual bite. "Yeah. I get that."

He steps closer, gripping the heavy bag without asking, steadying it like it's nothing. "Again."

I give him a look, part glare, part plea. He doesn't flinch. He just nods at the bag, jaw set, face solidified in that stubborn way that says he's not moving until I do what he wants. So I plant my feet and jab.

"Too stiff," he says instantly, voice sharp as a blade. "Loosen your shoulder. Again."

I grit my teeth and throw it sharper.

"Better. Now add the cross. Hip into it." He slaps the bag with the flat of his palm where I should aim, eyes locked on my form.

I follow his direction—jab, cross, hook. The bag shudders under the impact.

"Guard up," he snaps. "You're telegraphing your hook. Don't waste your weight. Again."

Minutes bleed into an hour, sweat dripping from my chin, blinding my eyes, stinging every cut on my skin. My arms burn and my lungs scrape raw, but I keep going. Because stopping feels like failing. And I can't fail—not here. Not with him watching.

Through it all, JP doesn't budge. His boots stay planted, his grip steady on the bag, his presence immovable. His voice cuts through every strike—sometimes sharp, sometimes approving, but never wavering.

Finally, when my arms give out and my fists fall limp at my sides, I stagger back and collapse onto the mat, gulping air like I've just crawled out of the ocean. Sweat soaks through my shirt, dripping down my spine, pooling at the base of my neck.

JP tosses me a towel and a water bottle. No lecture. No smug smile. Just the necessities.

"Better," he says after a sip from his canteen. "You're getting faster."

I wipe my face with the towel, smirking despite the ache in every muscle. "What, no lecture about my sloppy hooks?"

He cracks a grin, dry as sandpaper. "Don't worry. I'll save that for tomorrow."

"Wow. Can't wait," I mutter, rolling my eyes.

"You should," he shoots back without missing a beat. "Means you're still alive to get yelled at."

I groan and toss the towel at him. He catches it one-handed, effortless, the smirk tugging at his mouth deepening for just a second before he hides it.

"You know," he adds after a beat, leaning back against the wall, "you could make this easier on yourself if you actually listened the first time I corrected you."

"I *did* listen."

"If you listened, you wouldn't be telegraphing your hook like you're waving for a cab in New York."

"You're impossible."

"And you're stubborn," he says, almost fondly. Then, softer, quieter, "Good thing stubborn keeps you alive."

The room hums with the overhead lights, the silence that follows settling warm around us. My body aches in that bone-deep way that almost feels good—proof that I'm stronger than yesterday. And sitting here beside him, JP doesn't feel like a mentor barking orders, or the soldier who dragged me into a war I never asked for; he feels like something closer. The father I lost. Or maybe the one I never really had.

JP glances at his watch, sighs through his nose, and pushes to his feet. "Come on. We've got a long night ahead. My contact won't wait forever."

The reminder knots my stomach, nerves and adrenaline tangling sharp and hot. I snatch the towel from the floor and wipe the sweat from my face before hauling myself off the mat. My muscles ache, but not enough to stop me.

"Give me a minute," I mutter, heading to the far corner where my bag waits. I dig out my jeans and jacket, peeling the damp workout clothes off my skin. The cold air aches after the heat of training, goosebumps rising along my arms as I tug on my T-shirt and jacket. My boots thud against the floor as I lace them tight, each knot a small act of readiness. By the time I sling the bag over my shoulder, I feel less like a kid dripping sweat on a mat, and more like someone bracing for whatever's coming. Almost.

JP is pacing near his desk, phone pressed to his ear, voice low. He doesn't notice me at first, nodding to whatever voice is on the other end, scowling like he's already assembling the battlefield in his head, like he's calculating six moves ahead and deciding which one will keep me alive.

When he finally hangs up, he scrubs a hand down his face and exhales, the edge in him easing but not gone. "Got it. Meeting spot's about three hours out. A mall parking lot just off the highway near Ridgefield. Neutral ground."

"Three hours?" I echo, frowning. "That's not exactly close."

"It's not supposed to be," he says, grabbing his jacket from the chair. "Guy's skittish. Doesn't want anyone knowing where he lives. This is as good as we're gonna get."

I cross my arms and lean into the wall. "And we're just supposed to trust him? Meet in the middle of nowhere like some spy movie?"

JP levels a look at me, steady and unreadable. "I've worked with him before. He's solid."

"Solid doesn't mean safe."

"Neither does standing still," he says flatly, pulling on his jacket. The leather creaks as he shrugs into it—a worn, weather-beaten thing that's seen more miles and more nights than I probably ever will. The edges are scuffed into a dull gray, the sleeves creased from years of use, and one shoulder bears a faint, long-healed slash that wasn't made by anything human. The jacket hangs on him like a second skin, heavy with the history he never talks about.

JP's tone dips slightly—softer than steel, but still unyielding. "I wouldn't take you if I didn't trust him."

That quiets me. I bite the inside of my cheek, fingers brushing the knife clipped to my belt. It's not the contact I need to trust; it's JP— and I trust him with my life.

Still, the unease gnaws at me. "Fine," I say at last, pushing off the wall. "But if this guy's shady, I'm not above putting a blade in his gut."

JP's smirk doesn't quite reach his eyes. "Good. Stay sharp." He checks the desk one last time, scanning the space with precision, making sure nothing gets left behind. Satisfied, he grabs his keys. "Let's move."

By the time we step outside, the fading sunlight has bled into dusk. The sky bruises purple at the horizon, the edges of town fading into shadow. Darkness stretches across the pavement, night's fingers reaching for our heels as we cross the lot.

JP's old truck waits by the curb. He unlocks it with a click, the sound disruptive in the quiet street.

We climb inside, the truck's worn seats groaning under our weight. The cab smells faintly of old leather and gun oil—sharp, metallic, familiar. The dashboard is cluttered with old maps, half-crushed protein bar wrappers, and a dented thermos that's probably older than me. JP slides the key into the ignition, and the engine awakens, shuddering once before settling into a low, steady rumble.

The office shrinks in the rearview mirror as we pull away, its warm glow quickly swallowed by the expanding dark. The road unfurls ahead in thin, weather-beaten lines, streetlights flickering by in uneven intervals, each one buzzing like it's struggling to hold on.

I lean my temple against the cool glass of the window, letting it ground me. Every mile seems to reinforce the air, turning the ride heavier, denser, like we're driving deeper into something we can't see.

Something in my gut twists, tight and insistent.

The night feels different. Charged in a way that makes the hairs on my arms prickle.

And no matter what JP says—no matter how much I trust him—something inside me knows the truth:

The real fight hasn't even started.

Chapter 5

Ashen Veil

JP's truck rattles down the two-lane highway, every bump in the road reverberating through its worn frame. Its headlights spear the dark, twin beams cutting through the deepening dusk. The engine hums a steady growl that fills the silence stretching between us.

Outside, the sky bleeds from purple to black, the last smear of orange fading at the horizon. The trees crowd close at the edges of the road, their bony shadows sprawling across the asphalt.

Dusk always unsettles me. It feels like the whole world is holding its breath, like something's waiting in that pause, just beyond what the headlights touch.

I shift in my seat, restless energy alive under my skin. My body aches from training, but it isn't enough to quiet the storm inside me. My hands bury deeper into the pockets of my jacket, fingers drumming against the lining, searching for a rhythm that doesn't exist. JP is all stillness beside me, steady as stone, eyes fixed on the road. That calm should anchor me, but tonight it only makes me itch.

Finally, I pull out my phone to distract myself, my thumb swiping the screen awake. A new message flashes at the top.

Maya: *Girl, you missed it!! Bonfire at Sam's! Half the town showed!!! Even the football idiots weren't that bad.*

Another text follows instantly:

Maya: *You've got to stop ditching. You're nineteen, not a ghost. Come be alive with us!!*

I bite my lip, staring at the glow of the screen, at words that feel like they're from another life.

I type back: *Sorry. Busy. Maybe next time.*

The three dots flash, like she's about to push back, but then they vanish. No reply. The screen goes dark, and with it, the little window into a world I can't seem to reach.

I sigh and lock the phone.

JP glances at me out of the corner of his eye, the kind of look that somehow manages to be both casual and prying at the same time. He's reading me—more than I want him to. More than I ever give him permission to. "Maya again?"

"Yeah." I shove the phone back into my pocket a little harder than necessary. "She thinks I should be out there living it up instead of..." I wave vaguely at the truck, at the endless strip of asphalt unraveling ahead of us, at the knives tucked under the seats, the dried flecks of old demon ash in the air vents. "...this."

He makes a sound somewhere between a grunt and a laugh. "She's not wrong."

My head snaps toward him so fast my neck cracks. "Excuse me?"

"You're nineteen," he says, eyes fixed on the dark road. The glow from the dashboard paints the side of his face in soft blue, smoothing over all those years written into him. "You should be at bonfires, sneaking into concerts, wasting your paycheck on shoes you'll regret in a week. Not cleaning blood off knives in my office."

There's something almost wistful in the way he says it. Almost.

"Wow. Thanks for the pep talk." I fold my arms tight across my chest, glaring out the window like the passing trees had personally offended me. "What do you want me to do? Pretend I'm normal? Play beer pong while demons rip through the edges of town?"

"I don't want you to pretend anything," he says. "I want you to remember you're still a kid. That's all."

"I'm not a kid," I snap, sharper than I mean to. My voice lands so hard it surprises even me.

"Could've fooled me." His mouth twitches, something dangerously close to a smirk tugging at the corner. "You still pout like one."

My jaw drops. "I do not pout."

"You're pouting right now," he says, the smirk widening just enough that I know he's doing it on purpose.

Heat flares across my cheeks, irritatingly noticeable. "You are infuriating."

"And you're still here," he replies, deadpan—and underneath the dryness, there's something warmer. "Which means you haven't given up on having something outside of all this."

I blink, caught off guard.

Then, he adds—too casually, too quickly—"Maya seems good for you. That's all I'm saying."

My heart stutters, because hearing it said out loud makes it feel real. Wanting to be normal isn't just a thought anymore, but a truth I can't ignore.

JP keeps his eyes on the road, pretending he didn't just drop a grenade into the cab.

"And before you ask," he continues, calm as if he's discussing weather, "no, I'm not suggesting beer pong. I'm saying she reminds you what you're fighting to keep."

I look away again, throat tight. He's not wrong. That's the problem.

I groan and turn toward the window, letting the cool glass press again against my forehead. Outside, the darkness deepens, headlights painting fleeting stripes of light across the trees. His words still hang in the cab, irritating and yet... I know they come from someplace real. He wants me safe. He wants me to have more than this. But I don't know how to explain that I can't. Normal isn't mine to have. So I change the subject.

"So... this contact of yours. Who is he?"

JP's smirk fades, his jaw working like the question is a pebble in his boot he can't shake loose. "Someone who owes me."

"That's vague." I arch a brow. "You've got to give me more than that. You said he recognized the symbol. Great. But how do you know him? How do you know he's legit?"

His grip tightens on the wheel, the leather creaking under his fingers. "Because I've bled beside him. That's all you need to know."

I study his profile in the dashboard glow. The scar near his temple catches the light, a pale line etched into tanned skin. I've known him long enough to see when he's dodging.

"You mean from the military," I press.

He exhales slow through his nose, not denying it.

"I know you were in," I continue, "but you've never told me what you actually did."

His lips twitch—almost a smile, but not quite. "That's because you don't want the details."

"Try me."

"Evelyn..." His voice carries that warning edge, low and sharp, the one that usually shuts me down.

68

But I don't back off. "You train me to fight demons. You drag me into this world where things wear human faces until they don't. But when it comes to you—you're some mystery. Doesn't seem fair."

His eyes flick toward me for the briefest second before snapping back to the road. "Fair's not something I've had the luxury of in a long time."

I lean back, arms crossed tight across my chest. "You weren't always this grumpy, right? At least, I hope not. What happened? Did the military beat the sense of humor out of you?"

"Maybe." He almost smirks, just a flicker, gone as soon as it appears. His gaze hardens again, fixed on the ribbon of highway ahead. "Or maybe life did."

The words hang heavy in the cab, heavier than his earlier silence, and for a moment, I wonder if I've finally pushed against a wall that won't move.

My voice softens, careful, like stepping onto thin ice. "You mean Selene."

JP's hands tighten on the wheel instantly, knuckles bleaching white against the worn leather. The truck drifts half a foot towards the grass before he corrects it with a sharp flick of his wrist. His jaw locks so hard, I hear the faint grind of teeth. That muscle in his cheek twitches—one of the few tells he hasn't managed to bury.

He doesn't respond, but he doesn't have to. I've seen the photo.

The one tucked into the corner of his desk frame, half-hidden behind a stack of files he pretends he hasn't reread a thousand times. JP and Selene side by side, both younger, both smiling in a way I've never seen from him. She leans into him slightly, like it's the most natural thing in the world. His arm is around her waist— not possessive, not performative, just easy. Familiar.

And every time I catch sight of it, something in his expression makes sense. The loneliness. The walls. The way his eyes go distant when certain memories brush too close.

"You don't talk about her," I add quietly, "but I know she mattered. I know she changed you."

For a long stretch of road, he says nothing. The hum of the engine fills the space between us, steady and low. The darkness outside thickens, pressing close to the windows, headlights carving narrow tunnels through its heft.

Finally, his voice comes—quiet, scraped raw by time. "She mattered more than I deserved."

The words ache. They sink heavy in my chest, pressing against bone and breath until it hurts to sit still. For a moment, I want to reach across the console—to touch his arm, to say something that loosens his grief. To tell him he's wrong.

But the wall he throws up is iron. Unmovable. I've learned which parts of him are battle scars, and which parts are locked doors.

So instead, I settle for the truth that won't crush me if I leave it unsaid. "I wish you'd tell me about her."

"Not tonight," he says with a finality that slices the thought clean at the root.

The cab sinks back into silence, heavier now with all the things he won't say and all the things I'm not brave enough to ask.

I clear my throat, forcing the tension down before it chokes me. "So... This guy of yours. You trust him?"

JP exhales slow, some of the steel in his shoulders easing, though not enough to fool me. "Maybe trust is a strong word. But he's good at digging where others can't. If anyone knows what that symbol means, it's him."

"And if he's lying?"

JP's mouth curves, but it's not a smile. It's too harsh for that. "Then we'll make him regret wasting our time."

That steel in his voice comforts and unsettles me. Sometimes I wonder which edge of him is sharper: the man who wants to keep me alive, or the soldier who won't hesitate to break anyone who gets in the way.

I lean my head back against the window, watching night swallow the horizon, mile by mile. The truck hums on, carrying us closer to answers I'm not sure either of us is ready for.

The hours pass in silence, broken only by the steady rumble of JP's old truck and the occasional squeak of its tired shocks. My phone buzzes a few times, but I ignore it. Whoever it is belongs to another world.

Outside, the landscape retreats deeper into shadow, moonlight spilling silver over treetops while the road stretches into an endless tunnel of black.

By the time JP steers us off the highway, the night has fully claimed the sky. The stars are smothered beneath the moon's cold glow, thin clouds drifting like smoke across its face. Ridgefield greets us not as a town, but as a grave—its welcome sign half-collapsed, its streetlights flickering like dying pulse points.

The strip mall sprawls ahead of us, abandoned. Cracked pavement stretches in every direction, split into jagged sections where weeds force their way through, like veins trying to revive a dead body. The storefronts loom with boarded-up windows, each one signaling years of neglect. Faded lettering clings to the glass where businesses once pretended to thrive: Electronics, Nails & Spa, Dollar Value. Nothing more than tombstones.

A single streetlamp buzzes overhead, its bulb struggling to stay alive. Its sickly light flickers, casting warped, twitching shadows that make the empty lot feel restless—like it might shift under our feet if we looked away.

Perfect for a clandestine meeting.

At the far end of the lot, a lone car waits: an old, dark sedan with chipped paint and tinted windows. Its engine idles low, a quiet, steady hum that vibrates through the stillness. No lights. No movement. No attempt to look casual.

Just a presence. Something out of place.

The strange car sits too perfectly centered between the faded parking lines, too deliberate in its stillness, like a predator pretending to be harmless. My stomach knots the second I see it, tension coiling tight beneath my ribs.

JP kills the engine beside it.

"Stay sharp," he mutters, voice low.

"When am I not?" I shoot back, though my hand drifts toward the knife tucked inside my jacket all the same.

The driver's-side door creaks open, echoing across the empty lot. A man steps out—wiry frame wrapped in a dark coat, posture taut as a drawn wire. Mid-forties, maybe older. His face is all sharp edges: cheekbones like blades, a hooked nose, lines sunken deep around his mouth. The kind of face that's seen too much and trusts too little. His accent colors his words even before he speaks, thick and Russian, his eyes darting across the shadows like he expects one to open up and swallow him whole.

"Pierce," he says, his voice cautious. "It's been a long time."

"Volkov." JP's tone is flat, carrying the weight of old history. "Let's keep it short."

I fall into step beside him, arms crossed tight against my chest. Volkov's eyes find me immediately, narrowing in suspicion.

"This your apprentice?" he asks, his voice tinged with distaste, as though I'm a liability.

"Something like that," JP replies. His tone makes it clear that's all he'll say.

Volkov frowns, unease rolling off him in waves, heavy enough I can almost feel it. He glances over his shoulder, scanning the empty lot again before leaning forward slightly. "You said you had questions. Then ask. But quickly—before I regret showing up."

JP doesn't waste time. He reaches into his jacket, pulls out the folded sketch—the symbol I drew from memory—and passes it over.

"Seen this?"

Volkov takes the sketch, but his gaze doesn't linger on the paper. It keeps darting back to me, sharp and suspicious, like he's trying to measure my presence here. Finally, he shakes his head, sharp and abrupt. "Not here. Not with her." His finger jabs toward me like a knife. "You should know better, Pierce. She's not cleared."

I bristle instantly, heat flaring in my chest. "Excuse me?"

JP doesn't flinch. Doesn't even shift. His voice stays even, but steel underpins every word. "She's with me. If you've got something to say, you say it in front of her."

Volkov sneers, lip curling back. "You're letting a child sit at the table? Since when did you start recruiting?"

My fists clench at my sides, words ready to bite out, but JP cuts in before I can unleash them. His tone sharpens, his presence commanding the air between them. "Since I found someone worth protecting."

He takes a step closer, boots scraping asphalt, and their eyes lock—two blades meeting mid-strike. The silence vibrates with

73

something old and dangerous, a history neither of them wants to speak aloud.

"If you don't trust her," JP continues, voice quiet but deadly, "you don't trust me. And if you don't trust me, you wouldn't be here."

The words hang like a hammer about to fall. Volkov's jaw works, but he doesn't move away.

Curiosity buzzes hot in my chest, impossible to ignore. "How do you two even know each other?"

Volkov's smirk is humorless as a scar. "Your mentor was once the army's favorite blunt instrument. They dropped him into warzones, shadows, pits you'll never read about. If it crawled, if it bled, he tracked it. I was the one who made sure his targets were worth killing."

My stomach knots tight. "So... you were his boss?"

"Handler," JP corrects flatly. His eyes don't leave Volkov's. "He pointed me at monsters and expected me to bring back pieces."

Volkov's lips twist into something that might have been a smile once. "And he always did."

The way he says it makes something cold coil in my gut. I turn to JP, searching his face for anything—regret, anger, humanity—but his expression is stone.

"Enough," JP says at last. "The mark. Tell us."

Volkov hesitates, fingers tightening on the paper. His gaze cuts back to me again, suspicion deepening, his words slow and deliberate. "She doesn't understand what she's walking into. If she knew what that symbol meant—"

"She'll learn," JP interrupts. His tone softens just slightly, but it carries the weight of finality, of choice already made. His eyes never leave Volkov's. "With me. Not without."

For a beat, the parking lot holds its breath. Even the night feels still, as though it's listening. Then, Volkov exhales sharply, muttering something in Russian under his breath before focusing on the paper.

"The symbol belongs to the Ashen Veil," he says finally. The words seem to curdle the air. "Old faction. Ruthless. They believed demons shouldn't be scattered, but bound. Controlled. *Used*. They branded themselves. They were thought to be gone. Dead. But if you saw this…" His eyes flick between us. "They are rising again."

A chill spiders down my spine. "And what do they want?"

Volkov's gaze cuts to me, sharp as broken glass. "Power. Always power. To tip the balance. To rebuild the world in their own image. And if they're back…" He leans closer, voice dropping. "…they won't stop until they find what they're looking for."

My pulse jumps, erratic. "And what's that supposed to mean?"

He stares at me for a long, unsettling moment. His silence feels heavier than words. When he finally speaks, his voice is like a knife slipping under the skin. "It means nothing good for you, girl."

The words are ice sinking into my skin. Before I can respond, JP steps forward, reclaiming the space between us. "Where are they operating?"

Volkov shakes his head, paranoia flickering across every tense movement. His eyes flick to the shadows around us, like he half-expects the Veil to crawl out from them. "You think they'll let me live if I give you names? No. I've already said too much."

"Anton," JP says, voice dropping colder still. "You owe me. Remember Sarajevo? You'd be bones under rubble if I hadn't dragged you out."

Something flickers across Volkov's face—shame, regret, maybe both. His shoulders hunch as he looks away, voice clipped when he finally answers.

"Look for the fires. Where the ash lingers, the Veil gathers. That's all you'll get."

"You'll give more when I ask," JP warns, but Volkov is already retreating, the moment fraying. He shoves the sketch back into JP's chest, his hands trembling despite his best effort to hide it.

One last glance—his eyes settle on me, dark and unblinking. "She will be your undoing, Pierce. Mark my words."

Then, his car door slams. Headlights flare bright, swallowing the lot in harsh white. An instant later, his taillights vanish into the night, leaving only the echo of his warning behind.

The silence that follows presses against my chest like a weight.

And for the first time, I wonder if Volkov's fear isn't of the Veil at all, but of me.

I try to break the silence with a weak exhale. "Well... He's charming."

JP folds the paper meticulously, sliding it back into his jacket pocket. "That was Volkov on a good night."

But the weight in his eyes says he's turning over every word, cataloging the danger in each of them.

"And what he said—about me—"

"Forget it." His tone is sharp, final, like a door slamming shut. "He doesn't know you like I do."

I nod, but the reassurance doesn't settle the gnawing in my chest. Because the way Volkov looked at me—the way his eyes lingered like he already knew something I didn't—sticks like an invisible thorn.

The road back stretches empty, endless yellow lines blurring under the headlights. The trees crowd closer to the highway, their shadows merging into a wall of black. JP drives in silence, knuckles clenched white around the wheel, jaw locked tight as a steel trap. I stare at him, heat bubbling in my chest until it finally spills. "So, are you going to tell me what he meant?"

JP doesn't look at me. "Which part?"

I throw my hands up. "Oh, I don't know—the part where he basically said I'm going to get you killed? That part."

His knuckles flex tighter around the wheel, leather creaking. "Volkov's paranoid. Always has been. Don't take his words too seriously."

"That didn't sound like paranoia," I press, sharper now. "He looked right at me when he said it. Like he *knew* something."

JP exhales hard through his nose, eyes never leaving the road. "Volkov sees ghosts everywhere. That's why he's still alive. Doesn't make him right."

"Doesn't make him wrong either." My pulse is pounding in my ears. "So what aren't you telling me, JP? What do you know that I don't?"

Finally, he glances at me. Just a second, but it's enough. His eyes are steady, heavy, carrying something he won't hand over. "You don't need to carry every burden, Evelyn. That's why I'm here."

I cross my arms, glaring daggers at the windshield. "That's not an answer."

"Maybe not." His voice softens, dropping into that infuriatingly fatherly cadence that makes me want to scream. "But sometimes answers do more harm than questions. You have to trust me."

"Trust you," I repeat bitterly. "That's all you ever say. *Trust you.* Meanwhile, I'm the one being hunted. I'm the one throwing punches at things nobody else even believes exist. And you want me to just smile and nod because you don't want to talk about it?"

His silence is worse than a fight. Worse than yelling. Silence means he's shutting me out. Silence means he's choosing the wall over me again.

I press my forehead against the window, the glass biting into my skin. The world outside passes in a smear of shadow and motion, but none of it registers.

All I see is Volkov's face. All I hear is his voice, low and certain, echoing in the cab like a curse: *She will be your undoing.*

The words replay over and over, cementing themselves in my body. They shouldn't matter—he's a stranger, a man drenched in fear and paranoia. But they stick. They cling to the raw places JP won't talk about. The ones I've only guessed at.

By the time JP turns onto the road leading back into Ashford, my chest feels tight, bound in wire. Frustration burns hot beneath my ribs, anger simmering in a way that makes my hands shake. He thinks he's protecting me. He thinks secrets keep me safe.

But from where I'm sitting, pressed against the cold glass in a truck full of things left unsaid, it feels a lot like betrayal.

And I don't know how many more secrets I can swallow—how many half-truths, how many closed doors—before something inside me finally fractures.

Breaks.

And once it breaks, I'm not sure either of us will know how to fix it.

Chapter 6

A Taste of Normal

The alarm blares far too early for the scraps of restless sleep I managed to get. I slap at my phone until the noise dies, groaning as I drag myself upright. My body protests, sore in the usual places, but not nearly as bad as it should be. Healing fast doesn't erase exhaustion—it just means I'm vertical when anyone else would still be buried under the covers.

I shuffle to the bathroom and flick on the light. The mirror greets me with bedhead in about six different directions, hazel-gold eyes still rimmed with shadow, and skin pale from too many late nights. "Cute," I mutter, but the smile tugging at my mouth softens the jab. A quick ponytail tames the chaos, and a sweep of mascara brightens me up enough to pass for awake. It's not glamour, but it'll do. Bag over my shoulder, I'm out the door before I can talk myself into crawling back under the blankets.

Work doesn't pause for demons. Rent doesn't take rain checks. And, honestly, the thought of coffee I don't have to brew myself almost feels like a reward.

By the time I push open the door to Ashford's Bean & Gone Coffee and the little bell overhead jingles cheerfully, a sound I've heard a thousand times but never quite gotten tired of, the morning rush has thinned, leaving only a handful of stragglers hunched over laptops, their cups half-empty but still steaming. The air is rich with the scent of espresso, caramel, and toasted bagels. Steam hisses from the machine behind the counter, harmonizing with the gentle indie playlist coming from the speakers.

The warmth hits me first and, for a second, it's easy to imagine this is all there is. No hunts. No scars. Just the buzz of grinders, the glow of warm bulbs against worn wood, and the low chatter of regulars debating whether oat milk actually tastes different from almond.

I shrug into my apron and knot it at my back, letting the familiar fabric ground me. The weight of last night—the fight, JP's frustration, Volkov's warning—lingers at the edges of my mind, but here it's easier to push away. Easier to tuck those pieces somewhere out of reach, at least for a few hours.

Here, I'm not a weapon or a mystery. I'm just Evelyn, another tired barista sliding lattes across the counter with a crooked smile.

And for now, that's enough.

Maya's already behind the counter when I walk in, her dark curls piled into a messy bun. A few rebellious strands frame her face, catching the early light and giving her a kind of chaotic halo that matches her personality a little too well. She's in her usual mismatched apron covered in marker doodles and coffee stains, hands flying between the register and the espresso machine like she's been awake for hours.

The second she spots me, her whole face brightens. "Evie! Finally. Thought you died in your sleep or something."

"Thanks for the concern," I mutter, stifling a yawn as I clock in. My voice comes out flat, but the corners of my mouth tug upward, despite myself. With Maya, it's hard not to smile.

She steps back, eyes narrowing, studying me with all the subtlety of a spotlight. "You look like crap. What did you even do last night?"

I grab a rag and start wiping down the counter, desperate for something to keep my hands busy. "Not much. Just... couldn't sleep."

Maya gasps dramatically, one hand flying to her chest as if I've confessed to murder. She leans over the counter, lowering her voice to a conspiratorial whisper. "Please don't tell me you were out with that older man again." Her eyebrows shoot up, dark and expressive. "He's, like, ancient. That's not cute."

I nearly snort coffee foam up my nose. "He's not ancient," I protest, trying—and failing—to hide my laugh. "And it's not like that. I've told you a million times—he's my uncle."

The word feels clumsy. Wrong. A Band-Aid slapped over a wound too deep to cover. But it's easier than explaining the truth. Easier than saying he's the only reason I'm still breathing.

Maya's smirk spreads slowly, the kind she pulls out when she knows she's winning. "Mm-hmm. Sure. Your *uncle*. That's what they're calling it these days?"

She wiggles her brows, eyes sparkling with mischief. She's relentless, dramatic, nosy in a way that should be annoying but somehow isn't. Maybe because she's one of the only people in my life who cares enough to pry, even if she has absolutely no idea what she's prying into.

I roll my eyes, but the corners of my mouth twitch. "You're ridiculous."

"Ridiculously right, maybe." She props her elbows on the counter, chin in her hands, studying me like I'm the juiciest piece of gossip she's had all week. "I mean, come on. Mysterious older guy? Dark and broody? Total bad-boy vibes? That's basically every girl's fantasy."

"He's not my fantasy," I mutter, fiddling with the milk frother just to give my hands something to do. My cheeks are hotter than they should be, which only makes Maya's grin widen.

"Whatever you say, Evie." She drags out the words in a singsong, savoring every syllable.

I groan, but the teasing makes something in my chest loosen. It's nice, this banter. No blades, no demons.

Maya wiggles her brows at me, relentless. "So, what's his deal, then? Does he live here? Does he have, like, a tragic past he tells you about over whiskey?"

I snort. "Wow, you've been reading *way* too many romance novels."

"Answer the question, Cross." She taps the counter for emphasis. "You disappear half the time, roll into work looking like you fought a bear, and then drop the uncle excuse. I call suspicious."

The smile slides off my face a little. If only she knew. If only I could tell her that the other night it wasn't a bear—it was four demons and one of them had a blade pressed to my throat. But the words stick in my chest like glass, impossible to spit out.

So instead, I shrug, forcing a casual grin. "He's just... complicated, okay? And no, we don't drink whiskey together. Coffee, maybe. He doesn't exactly scream 'fun at parties.'"

Maya laughs and reaches up to tighten her bun, dark curls springing loose around her face no matter how many times she tries to tame them. Her eyes sparkle with mischief as she says, "So mysterious. Honestly, I'd have a crush too."

I groan, dragging a hand down my face. "You're ridiculous."

"Yep," she chirps, turning back to the espresso machine with a little flourish. "And I'm still your favorite. You're welcome."

Before she can pry further into the disaster that is my personal life, the bell over the door jingles. Two guys swagger in—locals, maybe a year or two older than me, all ball caps, cheap cologne, and overinflated confidence. One of them lets out a low whistle, his eyes sweeping the counter.

"Well, morning just got a whole lot prettier."

Maya beams instantly, slipping into her favorite role: entertainer. "Flattery will get you a discount... sometimes."

The taller one leans against the counter, flashing me a grin that's too confident by half. "What about you? Think a guy's got a chance to win your number with a large latte?"

I blink at him, caught between irritation and surprise. Normal girls probably blush or giggle right now. Me? My brain instantly supplies about five different ways to snap his wrist if he leans in any closer. But then, I catch Maya's look—expectant, playful, daring me to roll with it.

So I plaster on a half-smile, sliding a cup under the machine. "Depends," I say evenly. "You tip well?"

Maya snorts into her sleeve, and the guy grins wider, like he thinks he's winning. His friend elbows him, muttering something about striking out, which only makes Maya laugh harder. For a few minutes, the banter bounces easily between us, the espresso machine hissing in the background, and it almost feels normal. Like I could just be Evelyn Cross, barista, nineteen, joking with her best friend while serving lattes to idiots.

But I'll never get to tell Maya the truth about the nights I vanish into shadows, how my bruises fade faster than they should, how I'm fighting a war under my skin, while she's deciding which TikTok dance to learn next.

Standing here, her giggles bubbling over and the guys fumbling for their wallets, I let myself lean into the moment anyway. Pretend, just for now. Pretend I belong.

The guys leave a few minutes later, drinks in hand, tossing one last wink over their shoulders as the bell jingles above the door. Then, it's just us and the espresso machine again.

Maya props her chin on her hand, eyes glittering with mischief. "Okay. That one was *totally* into you."

I roll my eyes, grabbing a rag to wipe down the counter. "He was into his own reflection in the pastry case. Big difference."

Maya laughs so hard she nearly drops her pen, her joy filling the shop like sunlight. And, despite myself, I laugh with her.

The smile softens into something else—something searching. "You know... you don't even try, and guys trip over themselves for your attention. But you always shut it down. Like you don't even see them."

I shrug, scrubbing at a stubborn coffee ring on the counter. "Maybe I just have higher standards."

"Or maybe you're hiding."

The rag stills in my hand. I glance up at her, and the look on her face makes my chest tighten. Maya's not teasing now; she's serious.

"I mean, you've got this whole..." She waves her hand at me, searching for the right words. "...mysterious, lone-wolf vibe going on. And I let it slide because you're my girl, but sometimes it feels like you're living in two different worlds. Like I only get to see the version of you that works shifts and cracks jokes with me."

Her words scrape something raw inside me. If only she knew how right she was.

I force a laugh, but it rings thin. "Wow. Deep analysis for a Tuesday morning."

Maya narrows her eyes, not letting me off the hook so easily. "I'm serious, Evelyn. You disappear. You come back with bruises. And you've got that look in your eyes sometimes—like you've seen things I couldn't even dream up."

The sting in my throat is sudden, sharp, but I mask it with a smirk. "Maybe I just need more sleep."

She doesn't buy it. I can see it in the crease between her brows, the little furrow she gets when she's worried and trying not to show it. Still, she doesn't push. Instead, she bumps her shoulder against mine, playful but steady, grounding in a way that makes something tight in my chest relax a little.

"Whatever it is... just remember you don't have to carry it alone, okay? You've got me."

She gives me a pointed look, then adds with a grin, "Like, for real. If you ever need backup—crying at 2 a.m., ditching work to run away and join a circus, hiding a body—I'm your girl. No questions asked."

Despite everything, a small laugh escapes me. Maya beams, satisfied.

"And I mean it," she says, softer this time. "You're not alone, Evie. Not ever."

For a second, I can't speak. The lump in my chest is too heavy, pressing up into my throat. All I can do is nod, pretending the tightness is just exhaustion and not the aching weight of knowing she can never really know.

But I reach out anyway, nudging her shoulder with mine—a small gesture, but the closest I get to unguarded.

"Same goes for you," I manage, voice softer than I intend. "If you ever need anything—anything at all—I'm there. No circus required. No body hiding necessary."

Maya grins at that, bright and warm in the way people only get when they believe the world is kinder than it is.

I hold her gaze for a beat longer. "I mean it," I add, quiet but solid. "You've got me, too."

The register dings with another order, shattering the moment in half. Maya flashes a grin, slipping back into her usual rhythm as if

85

nothing happened, the steam of the espresso machine curling around her like it's part of the performance.

But her words linger in the air. *You've got me.*

I watch her laugh with a customer, the lightness in her voice filling the shop, and it hits me—hard. The truth is, I've never had a friend like her before. Not really.

After the fire that took my mom, everything changed.

In junior high, the kids I used to laugh with at lunch stopped sitting next to me. At first, it was hesitation—like maybe they didn't know what to say, like they were waiting for me to snap back into the person I'd been before everything burned.

Jana was the hardest.

We'd been inseparable since kindergarten—matching friendship bracelets, sleepovers every weekend, whispered secrets under blankets with flashlights. She was the kind of friend you planned a future with: same high school, same college dorm, maybe even the same crappy apartment with mismatched furniture.

But after the fire, she couldn't even look at me. She'd pass me in the halls with her eyes locked on the floor, shoulders shrinking like my presence hurt. And I didn't blame her; grief made me strange, sharp-edged, unpredictable. But it still felt like losing a second family. A second home.

One day, she just stopped talking to me. No fight. No explanation. Just distance. Like losing my mom had made *me* dangerous. Like grief was something she could catch if she stood too close.

Everyone else followed her lead. The pity came next—soft smiles, careful voices, awkward silences that felt like knives. And finally... the space. The empty tables. The way people's conversations fizzled whenever I got too near.

Teachers weren't much better. They didn't whisper or tease, but their eyes betrayed them every time—they'd soften when they called my name, their voices dipping into that cautious, tender tone people use for broken things they're scared to touch.

Like I was fragile glass. Like one wrong word would shatter me. I hated it.

And when the pity faded, something worse took its place.

By high school, the whispers started. *There's the fire girl. She's cursed.* Some kids got meaner than others—a pack that fed on weakness. They shoved me in the hallways, knocked books out of my arms, hissed insults under their breath as I passed. *Freak. Weirdo. Pyro.* Like I'd struck the match myself.

The more I pulled away, the more the isolation hardened around me. Friends I'd once had didn't come back. The teachers stopped looking. The bullies didn't stop.

The thing is, I could've fought back.

Even before I understood what I was, I knew I was stronger than them. When one of the guys slammed me into a locker so hard my shoulder cracked against the metal, I wanted to snap. My instincts screamed at me to push back like I had before—just that once, when I realized what I was capable of—to show this guy exactly how much damage I could do, too.

But I couldn't do it. Because deep down, I knew if I let go—if I gave in—I wouldn't just shove him. I'd break him. And then I really would be the freak they whispered about. So instead, I bit my tongue, clenched my fists in my pockets, and took it. Every shove, every cruel laugh, every hissed *pyro*. I buried the fire instead of lighting it.

I learned how to disappear into the background, slip between the cracks. I'd hole up in the art room during lunch, hiding behind sketchpads, while the noise of the cafeteria raged on without me.

87

Drawing became the only way I could let everything out without hurting anyone. Anger, grief, loneliness—they bled onto paper in pencil and ink, where they couldn't destroy me—anyone else.

And when I wasn't sketching, I was training with JP. He never asked about school, never pushed me to explain the bruises I came home with. He just drilled me harder. Punches, kicks, footwork, discipline. He gave me an outlet where I didn't have to hold back— where my strength wasn't something to hide, but something to sharpen.

I think that's what saved me. Not the drawings, not even the training, but the balance between the two. One kept me from exploding; the other taught me how to control the explosion if it ever came.

So I stayed quiet. I stayed small. And even when my knuckles itched and my chest burned with the urge to fight back, I never gave the bullies what they wanted. I let them think I was weak. Better that than showing them the truth.

I learned to live without anyone. To walk alone. To fight alone. To *be* alone.

That's why Maya's different. She doesn't treat me like a tragedy, or a freak, or someone already halfway gone. She teases me. She drags me into her world whether I want to go or not. She reminds me, over and over, that maybe I can still belong to something normal.

And that scares me more than any demon ever could. Because she's the first proof I've had in years that I don't always have to be alone.

By the time my shift ends, my body feels like it's been running on fumes. The last customer drifts out with their caramel macchiato, and Maya sends me off with a hug that nearly knocks the breath out of me.

"Don't ghost me, Evie!" she calls, sing-song as ever. "Party next week. Non-negotiable."

I promise her a maybe—my usual lie—but the warmth of her grin follows me out the door.

Outside, the sky over Ashford is the kind of purple that makes the clouds look painted on. The first stars flicker faintly through the haze, stubborn against the creeping dark. For a heartbeat, I let myself enjoy the quiet: no growling engines, no claws scraping concrete, no shadows whispering my name. Just the hum of crickets in the grass and the distant bark of a neighbor's Beagle. Almost normal.

The ride home is short, familiar turns blurring past, but the weight settles in before I even hit my street. When I finally pull into the driveway, the porch light is still dead, the house sagging like it's tired of standing. My father's truck is gone—probably parked at the warehouse job or already outside O'Malley's Bar, the only place he keeps his promises.

I push inside, the familiar stench of stale beer and dust curling around me like a bad memory, and drop my bag by the door. Boots half-untied, I barely make it two steps before my phone buzzes in my pocket.

JP.

I swipe it up, answering before the second ring. "Hey."

"Evelyn." His voice is low, clipped, carrying that edge he only gets when the news is bad. "I made some calls. That symbol you drew? Volkov was right. It's the Ashen Veil."

The name alone makes my stomach twist, the syllables heavy with something that doesn't belong in the air. "And?"

"They're organized. They don't move unless it's deliberate." A pause stretches long, weighted. "They've been quiet for years.

Everyone thought they'd scattered. If they're back..." His voice trails off, rough with something unspoken.

I think about the sinking feeling I had deep in my stomach after last time, the awful realization that maybe I'm the one they're after. I sink onto the couch, fingers tightening around the phone. "JP... what if this isn't about Ashford? What if it's not about random demons crawling through cracks?" My throat locks, but I force the words through.

"What if they're coming after me?"

The silence that follows is its own terrifying answer. Finally, JP exhales. "Don't go there."

"But it makes sense," I press, words tumbling fast now. "Three times this month. And the other night—they weren't just looking for blood. They were waiting. Like they knew I'd show up."

"Evelyn—" His voice sharpens, almost a growl, but then softens. "You're not alone in this. Do you hear me? Whatever they want, whatever they think they know—you're not alone. I won't let them touch you."

The words should comfort me, but they don't. Because the way his voice cracks on *won't* tells me he's already picturing the worst. Already imagining the moment he can't get there in time. Already preparing himself for a failure he won't survive.

Maya's voice echoes in my memory—warm, bright, unwavering: *You're not alone, Evie. Not ever.* Her hand on my shoulder. Her grin. That stubborn sincerity that refuses to let me sink.

Two people. Two promises. Two lifelines I don't know how to hold without breaking.

But standing here, listening to JP's breath hitch like he's choking on fear he won't acknowledge, it hits me how fragile all of this is. How easily promises snap under the weight of what hunts us.

90

Maya said I wasn't alone. JP is saying it now. So why do I still feel like the ground is opening beneath my feet?

I curl tighter into myself on the couch, phone pressed hard to my ear. "Then I guess we better figure out what they're after. Before they find it first."

There's a pause—long, heavy. I can almost see him, pacing with that restless energy that fills a room like static.

Finally, he says, "Get some sleep tonight. We'll talk tomorrow."

The line clicks dead before I can argue.

I'm left staring at my phone, the screen going dark in my hand while the silence of the house folds in around me. It's the kind of quiet that feels alive. Even the floorboards seem to be holding still, waiting.

Sleep feels impossible, but JP's voice lingers anyway, floating through the dark like a buoy I don't quite trust.

You're not alone.

It should be enough. It should settle the shaking in my chest, quiet the panic clawing at the edges of my thoughts. But it doesn't.

Because deep down—far beneath the reassurances and the stubborn hope—I feel something gnawing. A hollow, sharp-edged fear burrowed under my ribs, chewing slow and steady.

Whatever the Ashen Veil wants, it isn't random. It isn't coincidence. It isn't going to pass me by if I pretend hard enough.

The pattern is tightening. Their circles, their symbols, their whispers in the dark—they're all pointing in one direction: toward me.

And standing alone in the silent house, phone still warm in my hand, the truth settles cold and certain: Something is circling closer. And somehow, impossibly, I'm standing at the center of it.

Chapter 7

Hunt in Ashford

The past several days have been quiet. Too quiet. No attacks, no leads. Just... waiting.

JP and I have still been keeping our eyes and ears sharp—checking patrol routes, tracking odd reports, scanning every shadow—but there's been nothing to fight, nothing to chase, nothing to bleed the tension out of my bones. People say silence means safety, but to me it feels like a held breath before something breaks.

It's morning, and JP and I are sitting in his office, two mugs of stale coffee going cold on the desk, weapons half-cleaned and abandoned beside them. The room smells like paper, leather, and the faint ozone tang of runes inked into old files. JP tosses a folded newspaper onto the desk between us, the pages creased from someone gripping them too hard.

I don't need him to say anything. One look at his face—the clenched jaw, the furrowed brow, the exhaustion settling beneath his eyes—tells me enough.

I pull the paper closer, smoothing the crumpled edge with my thumb. The headline knocks the exhaustion—and the breath—from my body.

LOCAL TEEN MISSING. POLICE HAVE NO LEADS.

The words sit stark and heavy on the page, swallowing the room's thin sliver of calm. A familiar cold washes over me—sharp, instinctual, laced with dread.

Quiet never means safe. Quiet means something is hunting... and it finally found its opening.

The words glare up at me in bold black print, each letter sinking like lead in my stomach. My throat tightens as I stare at the missing girl's face—blonde hair spilling just past her shoulders, a wide smile frozen in the kind of awkward school photo pose every teenager hates, braces catching the flash. Seventeen. Two years younger than me.

And gone.

Gone without a trace.

I force myself to read the caption, but the details blur together in a slurry of dread: *Last seen leaving her friend's house... never made it home... parents desperate for answers.* The same script I've seen too many times already—one that never ends with the truth.

"She's not the first," I whisper, the words scraping my throat raw. My voice comes out thinner than I mean it to, almost brittle.

JP's hand darts in, snatching the paper from me. His eyes rake the lines faster than mine ever could. A second later, the paper slaps against his desk with a sharp crack, the sound like a gunshot in the stillness.

His jaw clenches hard, muscle jumping at the hinge. "That makes three this month."

Three.

The number echoes in my head, louder than the tick of the office clock. Three girls. Three families waiting for a door to open that never will. Three shadows swallowed whole by something I can't see yet, but know too well.

Three girls. Almost my age. Plucked from the same streets I walk every day. Girls who probably bought coffee from me, who probably sat two rows over in math before graduating. Girls who thought they were safe.

I fold my arms tight across my chest in a weak attempt to hide the shiver crawling over my skin. "Same number as the demon attacks."

JP's eyes flick up to me, sharp and knowing. "Exactly."

For a beat, neither of us speaks. The silence in his office feels heavier than air should allow, pressing down until my lungs ache. The missing kids. The demons that weren't wandering aimlessly anymore. The symbol carved into flesh. Threads weaving together into something far beyond coincidence.

The Ashen Veil. Not a rumor. Not a ghost story. Not gone. Here. Circling closer.

JP pushes away from the desk so abruptly, his chair skids back and slams against the wall. The sudden movement jolts the office's stale air. He grabs his leather jacket from the hook, shrugging into it with quick, clipped motions that signal he's already halfway out the door in his mind. "Police found her trail cut off near the old lumber mill."

My stomach twists, a sour knot pulling tighter. The mill claws its way out of my memory, its skeletal beams jutting against the sky like broken ribs, shattered windows staring empty and hollow. Rust creeping through every seam, bleeding into the wood and metal as if the whole place were rotting from the inside out.

It's where JP took me for my first hunt.

I can still feel the cold bite of the air that night, hear the creak of warped lumber beneath our feet, see the moonlight cutting through the busted slats in thin, ghostly blades. I remember the stink of mold and old blood, the way shadows crawled along the floorboards like they had intentions of their own.

94

I remember gripping JP's sleeve so tightly my knuckles ached. I remember the sound the demon made when it realized I was there—the moment I understood monsters weren't the stuff of bedtime stories, but were instead real enough to breathe on me.

After that night, I avoided the mill for years. At thirteen, I'd dared myself to ride past it, heart hammering, convinced that just looking at it too long might curse me. Forgotten. Crumbling. Waiting for something hungry enough to claim it.

Now it's waiting again.

"You think that's where they took her?" My voice feels small, thin under the weight of the thought—like the mill's shadow had reached all the way into the office, curling around my ankles.

"I think it's where we'll find something," he says flatly. His tone is all steel now, all soldier. "And I'm not waiting for the cops to catch up."

Five minutes later, we're in his truck. The engine growls low, headlights spearing through the rising dusk as he steers us toward the edge of Ashford. The town slips away behind us, swallowed by shadows. Ahead, the road narrows, lined with trees like sentinels, their branches reaching toward the fading sky.

Each mile drags me closer to the truth I don't want to face: the Veil isn't just circling anymore. They're hunting.

JP pulls off the road, killing the headlights, and eases the truck into the shadow of rusted machinery and broken fencing. The lumber mill looms against the moonlight like a cadaver, its hollow windows staring down at us like gaping eye sockets, its walls sinking inward.

I swallow hard and grab my pack. The familiar weight of the knife at my hip steadies me, grounding me in a way the Glock never does. The pistol sits heavy, tucked tight in my waistband, insurance for when things go bad. But tonight, as always, I want the knife in my hand. I want to prove—to JP, to myself—that I can stand on my own two feet.

"Stay sharp," JP murmurs as we step out. The way his eyes cut across the shadows, scanning every movement, makes my stomach knot.

"Always do," I whisper back, though my pulse is hammering in my throat so hard I'm sure he can hear it.

We slip through a gap in the fencing, boots crunching over broken glass and gravel. The air is full of rot and mold, fierce with the sting of rust and the ghost of sawdust. The smell clings to the back of my throat, sour and heavy.

My pulse pounds louder the deeper we move, each inhale catching hard against the cold in my chest. Then, I hear it: a voice. Low. Rhythmic. Chanting in a language I don't recognize.

The syllables drag themselves across my bones like knives. The sounds are wrong, twisted, scraping against something deep inside me that doesn't want to be touched.

I stiffen and raise a hand. JP halts immediately, dropping into a crouch as his eyes flick forward. He nods once. We move as one, slow and silent, creeping toward the source.

Shadows shift ahead, firelight flickering through a jagged hole in the wall. The glow spills across the floor in broken patterns, and the smoke curls upward.

When we peer inside, the scene twists my stomach into knots.

The cavernous center of the mill is lit by a single bonfire that burns low and strange, its flames licking green and orange as if they've been feeding on something they shouldn't. Figures circle, hoods pulled low, their bodies swaying in time to the chant that grates against my body.

And at the center—drawn in chalk and ash across the split concrete—is a symbol whose lines bend in directions they shouldn't, whose angles refuse to sit flat in reality. The same as the one etched into the demon's skin, only bigger. Alive. Glowing faintly, pulsing with every syllable spoken.

Four figures in black robes kneel on the floor, circling a crude symbol painted in blood.

The symbol.

Even from here, the sight of it makes my skin crawl, a cold prickle that ripples from my scalp to my fingertips.

Flames gutter in rusted oil drums shoved into the corners, their light stuttering unevenly as the wind finds its way through broken windowpanes. Smoke spills upward, staining the rafters a deeper black. Each flicker of fire casts the robed figures into monstrous silhouettes—heads bowed, shadows stretching long and ragged across the floor, not just shifting but *writhing*. The shadows twist over the bowed bodies as if alive, doubling them, tripling them, making it look like a hundred cloaked forms are swaying in unison.

Then, their chanting continues.

Their voices rise together, guttural and discordant, scraping against each other in a way that shouldn't be possible. It's not a language so much as a sound forced out of torn throats—too deep, too warped to belong to anything human. The noise tears through the mill.

Each syllable hooks under my skin like barbed wire. The vibrations rattle my teeth. My stomach churns, twisting hard enough to make bile burn the back of my throat.

The air tastes like metal, and with every breath, the temperature seems to drop another degree.

Whatever they're calling... it's listening.

"They're summoning," JP mutters, his hand tightening on my shoulder. "Trying to open a crack."

My throat is sandpaper, but I manage a whisper. "And if they succeed?"

He glances at me, blue eyes hard as ice. "We don't let them."

Before I can answer, one of the robed figures stops mid-chant, head tilting like a predator catching a sound no one else hears. Slowly, he lifts his face from the shadows. Black eyes lock onto mine.

A jolt of cold shoots straight down my spine, snapping every nerve taut. "Shit," I breathe.

The chanting halts, the silence excruciatingly quiet.

The figures surge to their feet. Robes snap like wings as they lunge toward us, the symbol behind them pulsing once, bright and hungry, before dimming again.

Not demons this time—no glowing eyes, no monstrous faces. Just humans, flesh and blood. But their eyes... black, fanatical, empty of fear. They move like men already dead, fighting with reckless abandon, as though their only purpose is to spill blood until someone stops them.

And I fight like I have no choice.

One charges me head-on, curved blade catching the firelight, steel flashing sharp enough to blind. I don't think; my body takes over, instincts screaming louder than my brain. I drop low under the swing, my knife already flashing upward. The silvered edge kisses flesh, splitting across his forearm. Hot blood sprays, warm against my cheek, metallic in my nose. He howls, stumbling, but doesn't stop.

Another slams into me from behind, arm locking around my throat like a steel band. Panic spikes—white-hot, suffocating. My vision tunnels, edges fraying, every sound muffled under the pounding of blood in my ears.

Instinct explodes. I drive my elbow back once, twice—hard enough to feel ribs give beneath the blows. A grunt bursts out of him, his grip loosening for a split second. I wrench free, twisting hard, and snap my skull backward.

Bone meets bone. The crunch is sickening, wet, his nose collapsing under the impact. Bile surges hot in my throat, but there's no time to gag, no time to flinch.

They keep coming.

More robes closing in, blades flashing, voices rising in snarled fragments of that same guttural chant, as if they're trying to rip the words back into being even as they fight.

And the symbol on the floor pulses again, brighter, hungrier.

Every move JP drilled into me comes back in flashes—pivot, guard, weight in the hips. My arms ache, lungs burn, but I grit my teeth and swing anyway.

Steel clashes, sparks flying in the flickering firelight. My knife glances off a blade, the shock jolting up my arm. Blood spatters the rotting floorboards, the iron tang thick in the air. I drive my knife deep into one man's shoulder, twist hard, then shove him back with all my weight. His scream rattles the rafters as he crumples.

Another rushes me, roaring like an animal. I sidestep, slam my boot against his knee sideways. The sickening crack echoes in the hollow room as he collapses, howling.

The last one lunges, eyes wild, blade raised high. I catch his wrist mid-swing, adrenaline turning my grip into iron. I twist—bones grind, his scream tearing raw from his throat as the blade clatters to the floor. My knife finds his throat in the same motion, edge biting just deep enough to freeze him where he stands.

99

He gasps, chest heaving, those black eyes locked on mine. And for one heartbeat, I see it: fear. But not fear *of* me. Fear *for* me.

"You don't understand," he rasps, blood bubbling at his lips. His voice is raw, desperate. "They don't want the town." His gaze flicks over me, sharp and deliberate. "They want *you*."

My stomach drops, the ground tilting beneath me.

"What?" My voice is a whisper, torn from me like a plea.

Before I can push, before I can demand more, JP's gun barks. The cultist's head snaps back, and he crumples—dead before he hits the floor.

The silence afterward is deafening. The chanting gone, only the crackle of guttering flames remains. The symbol smeared in blood pulses faintly once, then dims into nothing. The air stinks of smoke, sweat, and copper.

I spin, chest heaving, eyes snapping to JP. He lowers his weapon slowly, smoke curling from the barrel. His expression looks carved from stone: his jaw is tight, his eyes hard, scanning the room like the threat still lingers.

"Evelyn," he says, steady but rough, "don't listen to him."

But it's too late. The words are already lodged in me, repeating like a curse. *They want you.*

JP's gaze flicks to me, scanning for wounds, for blood, the way he always does after a fight. "Evelyn—are you—?"

"I'm fine," I cut in quickly, though my chest is heaving and my hands won't stop trembling. The lie tastes bitter on my tongue. My voice cracks anyway, betraying me. I swallow hard, forcing the words out before I lose my nerve. "JP... he said it. Out loud. The Ashen Veil—they're not after Ashford." My throat tightens, but I push through.

"They're after me."

The words hang between us in the stale air, heavier than the blood on the floor, heavier than the bodies cooling at our feet.

JP's jaw tightens. His silence stretches too long, saying more than words ever could. He doesn't argue. He doesn't deny it.

And that's when I know; I can see it in his eyes. That flicker of recognition, of dread, not surprise. He already knew.

A hot rush of anger scorches through me, mixing with the adrenaline still screaming in my veins. My voice comes out sharp, too loud in the cavernous mill, echoing off rusted beams and broken walls. "You knew! All this time, and you didn't tell me?"

"Evelyn—" He takes a step closer, his voice dropping into that steady, grounding register he always uses when I'm spiraling. The tone meant to calm me, to keep me tethered. "Now's not the time."

"No, JP." My grip tightens on the knife until my knuckles ache, the blade trembling in my hand with a rage I can't contain. "If they're after me, if I'm the reason people are disappearing, then I deserve to know!"

His shoulders rise and fall in a slow, heavy breath, his chest expanding like he's holding back the whole damn world. For a second, I think he's going to snap, to shout back, to let the soldier in him finally break free. But when he speaks, his voice is controlled, steady as ever.

"You don't need to carry that weight. Not tonight."

The words scrape raw. My chest twists, half with fear, half with fury. I want to scream, to demand more, to make him spit out every secret he's been choking on. But the way his eyes lock onto mine—hard, unyielding, and maybe even scared—stops me cold.

Because I've seen JP angry. I've seen him deadly calm. But scared? This is new.

I drop my gaze, the truth crashing over me like cold water. Whatever the Ashen Veil wants... it's tied to me. And JP has been trying to shield me from it all along.

JP's jaw clenches once more, the muscle ticking, and then he exhales hard, decision settling over him like armor being strapped into place. He glances toward the open doorway, toward the dark halls beyond where the chanting had been.

"We're done here," he says, voice leaving no room for argument.

I blink at him, stunned. "What? No— We should keep looking. The girl—"

"Evelyn." My name cracks through the air like a command. He steps closer, lowering his voice, but the weight behind it only sharpens. "This wasn't the whole pack. You think four cultists were enough to hold this place? You think they wouldn't have posted others outside? Reinforcements could be here any minute."

"But if she's here—"

"She's not," he cuts in firmly. His hand comes down on my shoulder, steady but insistent, anchoring me in place. "If she was, we would've found her already. What we did find is proof that the Veil is operating in Ashford. And now they know you're onto them. That makes this place a death trap."

I swallow hard, gaze dragging back to the bloodstained floor, to the unfinished symbol glistening wet in the firelight. My chest twists painfully. Every part of me wants to keep fighting, to rip through every corridor until I find something—anything—that makes sense. But the cold weight in JP's eyes tells me he's right. Staying is suicide.

He gives the room one last sweep with his eyes, then squeezes my shoulder once, firm. "We move. Now."

My feet feel heavy, like walking away now is an act of betrayal, but I force them forward. Together, we retrace our steps, boots crunching glass, shadows stretching long behind us in the flicker of dying firelight. Every creak in the rafters sounds like claws. Every gust through the broken windows feels like breath on my neck.

By the time we step outside, the night air slams into me and I suck it in greedily, though it doesn't chase the tightness from my chest. JP's gaze sweeps the tree line, restless, sharp, his hand hovering close to his gun. The way his shoulders stay tense tells me he's expecting something to follow us out.

We climb into the truck, and the engine roars awake, gravel spitting under the tires as JP jerks the wheel hard, tearing us away from the mill.

Only when the broken silhouette of the building is fully swallowed in the rearview mirror does he finally speak. "They're moving faster than I thought," he mutters, more to himself than to me.

I sink back into the seat, fingers still locked around the knife. My reflection stares back from the window—pale, hollow-eyed, tight-jawed. And beneath it, Volkov's warning and the cultist's last words keep circling, clearer every time I hear them.

They don't want the town. They want you.

The words burrow.

The road back to Ashford is a dark blur of trees and broken fences. JP drives in silence, his hands locked on the wheel, jaw set in that way that says his thoughts are already miles ahead of us, planning, calculating, bracing for the next hit.

I can't stand it. The silence, the unanswered questions, the weight of what that cultist said.

Finally, I break. "JP... you knew."

His eyes stay pinned to the road. "Evelyn—"

"No. Don't brush me off. Back there, when he said it, you didn't even look surprised. You knew the Veil wasn't after Ashford. You knew they were after me."

The only sound for a long moment is the hum of the engine, loud in the cramped cab. JP's knuckles flex tight around the wheel, white in the glow of the dash.

When he finally speaks, his voice is low. Controlled. "I knew there was a chance."

"A chance?" Heat rushes up my neck, filling my face. "People are missing. People are dead. And you thought maybe—just maybe— they were coming for me? You should've told me!"

His gaze flicks toward me, then back to the road. "And what would you have done with that, Evelyn? What would it have changed, except made you more reckless?"

"I'm already in this!" My hands slam against my knees, my heart pounding hard enough to shake my ribs. "Every fight, every night— we both know I don't get to walk away. If I'm the reason this is happening, then I deserve to know. Don't you dare keep me in the dark."

For a moment, his face softens in the wash of dashboard light, the hard lines loosening just enough to show the man beneath the warrior.

"You think I want this for you?" His voice cracks. "You think I don't wish you had a normal life? That I could take this weight off your shoulders?" He swallows, and when he speaks again, his voice is quieter, almost breaking. "I'd burn the whole damn world before I let them take you."

The words slam into me, cutting through my anger like a knife. For a moment, everything inside me stops—air, thought, even the ache in my ribs. My throat tightens, my chest contracts around something too big, too complicated to name. Love. Fear. The spirit of every loss we've survived together. All of it tangling in the space between his promise and the truth neither of us can outrun.

But then, the fear creeps back in—slow, deliberate—curling through the cracks like smoke searching for a place to burn. Because beneath all his bravado, beneath the steel in his voice, I saw it. The flicker. The moment his mask slipped.

The dread he couldn't hide. The dread that's been gnawing at me ever since Volkov said I would be his undoing.

I turn toward the window, the glass vibrating faintly with the movement of the engine. My reflection stares back at me—pale, fractured by motion, eyes shimmering with a fear I refuse to let win.

"Then you better figure out why they want me," I whisper, the words scraping out of a throat too tight. "Because I'm not going to sit here waiting to be taken."

JP doesn't answer.

It tells me everything. He already *is* trying to figure it out. Trying, and failing, and fearing the moment he won't be fast enough.

And for the first time since this all began, I realize: He's not just afraid *for* me. He's afraid *of what happens if he loses me.*

Chapter 8

Fires in the Night

Sleep has become a stranger. Every time I close my eyes, the fire is waiting.

It always begins the same way—a spark, a hiss, the faint curl of smoke threading through the darkness like a warning. Then, the world ignites. Flames lick up the wallpaper, devouring color and shape in hungry strokes. Heat blooms against my skin as the fire crawls across the ceiling, branching like veins of molten light. The walls inhale and exhale, breathing a heat blistering and alive.

My mother's voice cuts through the crackle—soft at first, then hardened by terror.

"Evelyn!"

The sound bends, then warps, swallowed by rising smoke. I try to run toward her, but the air thickens, choking me. Every breath burns. Somewhere deeper in the house, through the roar of collapsing beams, my father shouts my name—rough, panicked, desperate.

I push forward—or I try to—but the hallway stretches away from me, twisting like it's made of rubber and shadow. The floorboards melt under my feet, turning into a river of glowing embers that pulse orange and red. The heat gnaws at my legs, searing through skin that refuses to blister, refuses to burn.

Their voices fade, one by one, leaving only the roar. Only the fire. Only the terrible emptiness where they used to be.

And that's when I see *it*. A figure stands inside the inferno. Still. Unmoving. Untouched.

The flames curve toward it, bowing, bending, as if even the fire recognizes something older, something stronger. The silhouette is tall—human yet not—shoulders squared, posture calm amid the chaos. But it's the eyes that freeze me in place.

Glowing red. Not reflections of the fire, but something deeper altogether. Something alive. Burning like coals in a furnace, fixed on me with a hunger that stops my heart.

They watch. They always watch.

The ceiling gives way with a deafening crack. The world collapses in on itself. The roar becomes a scream—maybe my mother's, maybe my father's, maybe mine. I can't tell. I never can.

I jolt awake, heart hammering against my ribs, breath ripping in and out of my lungs. Sweat slicks my neck, my back, the sheets twisted around my legs like bindings I can't fight off. For a moment, the smell of smoke lingers before I remember it isn't real.

Not the fire. Not the house burning again. But the eyes? Those feel real. Too real.

The clock on the nightstand glows a dull, merciless 3:14 a.m. Another night gone. Another morning where I feel more ghost than girl.

For a long time, I sit in the dark. The house is silent except for the faint groan of old pipes, the hum of the fridge downstairs. My chest still heaves like I've been running, but there's nowhere to go, no one to wake. I pull my knees up, wrapping my arms around them, trying to slow the tremor in my hands.

When I was little, nights like this meant tiptoeing down the hall, crawling into my parents' bed between them. My mom would smooth my hair and whisper that fire couldn't touch dreams, that

107

I was safe. My dad would grumble about early mornings but hold me tight anyway.

For a moment, I almost move, almost swing my legs over the edge of the bed, go to him like I used to. But I stop. Because even if I did, he wouldn't wake up. Or if he did, he wouldn't recognize the girl sitting there in the dark.

The girl who smells like smoke and blood. The girl who kills monsters that look too much like men. So I stay where I am. Alone in the quiet, counting my breaths until the hammering eases in my chest.

Outside, the wind rattles the siding—an empty, hollow sound that scrapes along the walls like fingernails. The kind of noise that makes old houses feel like they're whispering secrets they can't quite speak aloud. I close my eyes again, not to sleep, but to listen.

To the faint creak of the floorboards settling. To the groan of pipes cooling behind thin walls. To the dark breathing around me, shifting with each gust of wind.

Everything feels tuned to a frequency just beneath hearing, the house holding still, waiting with me. The silence isn't peaceful; it's watchful, like something unseen is crouched and hungry just beyond the edge of the light.

Waiting. Waiting for the next spark. The next scream. The next fire to start.

By the time I drag myself into JP's office, the world feels washed-out and hollow—like someone drained all the color out of it while I wasn't looking. My head throbs from lack of sleep, and the bitter tang of old coffee hits me before I even step through the door.

JP's already here, hunched behind his desk, the glow from his monitors splashing his face in shades of blue. He's typing something into one of his encrypted systems, the soft clack of the keys filling the silence. He doesn't look up when I enter.

"You look like hell," he says flatly.

"Gee, thanks." I drop into the chair across from him, slumping into it with all the grace of a corpse. "Remind me why we're pretending this coffee fixes trauma?"

That gets him to look up—barely. His eyes flick from the dark circles under mine to the coffee cup in my hand, then back to the screen. "You need rest."

"I need answers," I shoot back.

He sighs, a slow exhale that says he's already too tired for this conversation. "Answers don't mean much if you're too exhausted to stand."

"Yeah? Funny how that never stopped you."

That earns me a glance—one of those long, measuring looks that always makes me feel like he's trying to read more than I'm saying. "You're not me," he says finally.

"Thank heavens," I mutter, rubbing my temples.

The tension between us hums like a live wire. Ever since the night at the mill, it's been like this—every conversation a minefield. Every question I ask runs straight into the same brick wall. And every time he dodges, every time he looks away instead of answering, I feel that distance stretch a little farther.

I lean forward, elbows on my knees, staring at the floor just to keep from saying something I'll regret. "You can't keep shutting me out, JP."

His hands pause over the keyboard. "I'm not."

I bark out a humorless laugh. "You really believe that?"

He meets my eyes then, and for a second, I see it: the flicker of guilt, the shadow of something heavy. "There are things you don't need to carry," he says quietly. "Not yet."

"Not yet," I repeat, shaking my head. "That's what you said last time. And the time before that."

"I'm protecting you," he insists, voice rising just enough .

"From what?" I snap. "The truth?"

The question hangs there, too sharp to take back. He exhales slowly, leaning back in his chair, the leather creaking. He looks older in this moment than I've ever seen him—like the weight of it all finally caught up.

"From everything that comes with it," he says at last.

It's not the answer I want. But it's honest, and somehow, that's worse.

Before either of us can push it, JP's phone buzzes against the desk. The sharp sound slices through the heavy quiet between us. He checks the screen, and his expression shifts—his shoulders stiffen, his mouth flattening into that grim line that always means something's gone wrong.

"What is it?" I ask, my voice catching on the edge of dread.

He doesn't answer right away. His eyes flick across the message once, twice. Then, he exhales slowly through his nose. "Reports of a fire," he says at last, voice low, measured. "Old textile factory in Briar Hollow. Fire crews can't get close."

The word *fire* hits like a physical blow. My pulse stutters. For a second, the air in the office thickens—hot, suffocating—pressing against my lungs like the room itself has been set alight. I smell smoke that isn't there, phantom and acrid. I hear the faint roar of flames behind my eyelids.

My dream surges back in jagged pieces: my mother's voice screaming through the haze, the blistering heat crawling up my arms, the ceiling cracking open in molten lines—and the figure standing untouched in the blaze. Tall. Still. Unburned.

And those eyes. Two glowing red embers staring through the inferno, locked on me like they'd found what they were searching for.

Alive. Hungry. Following me out of the dream and into the waking world. A chill races down my spine, violent and cold enough to cut through the phantom heat.

I blink hard, forcing myself back into the present. "Fire crews can't get close?" My voice sounds distant even to myself.

JP nods, already standing, his hand reaching for his jacket. "Locals say they saw people—hooded, chanting—before it went up."

The world tilts. *Hooded. Chanting.* Like the mill.

My stomach sinks, cold taking over where the heat had been. "The Veil."

He meets my eyes, grim and certain. "Yeah." His voice is quieter now, almost a whisper. "They're sending a message."

He shrugs into his jacket and grabs his keys in one practiced motion. "Let's move."

For a heartbeat, I just sit frozen in my chair. The world around me feels dim, distant—like I'm looking at JP through a sheet of heat-warped glass. The smell of phantom smoke still clings to the back of my throat. My tongue tastes like ash. My skin prickles with the memory of heat.

I can almost hear the chanting slithering beneath the crackle of flames. The echoes move through my nerves, tightening them until it hurts. Red eyes flicker behind my eyelids, those same unblinking embers from the fire, watching me.

The nightmare wasn't just a dream. It wasn't random. It was a warning. And whatever it's warning me about is getting closer.

I push up from the chair, the legs scraping against the floor. "I'm right behind you."

As we head for the door, I can't shake the feeling that we're walking straight into the fire I saw last night.

By the time we reach Briar Hollow, the night sky glows orange—an unnatural dawn burning on the horizon. Flames tower above the tree line, devouring the old factory in waves of heat and smoke, and the stench of it stings my eyes.

Sirens wail in the distance, lights flashing like dying stars through the haze, but the fire is already too far gone. The whole structure crackles and moans, metal twisting in protest as the roof caves inward. It sounds alive—a monster feeding on everything it touches.

"Stay close," JP orders as we pull up beside a cluster of fire trucks. His voice is low but sharp, the soldier in him cutting through the chaos. But I barely hear him. The heat presses against my skin, pulsing. People swarm the perimeter—firefighters shouting commands, paramedics rushing stretchers—but my world narrows to one terrible sound.

Screams.

They cut through the roar of the blaze, raw and unmistakably human.

"JP..." My voice cracks. "Someone's still in there."

He's already scanning the flames, jaw tight. The reflection of firelight flickers in his eyes, making him look carved from steel and shadow. "No one could've survived that," he says, but even he doesn't sound convinced.

Then, from behind us, a firefighter's voice shouts over the chaos. "We've still got people inside! Two, maybe three! Can't reach them—the floor's caving!"

The words hit me like a punch. My stomach twists, adrenaline spiking hard and fast. I can hear the screams again—faint but real, begging for help—and suddenly, standing here feels like suffocating.

"JP, we can't just—!"

"Evelyn!" His hand clamps around my arm, firm, commanding. "We don't know what's in there. The Veil could've set this—"

"I don't care!" The words tear out of me before I can stop them. I yank free, the movement rough enough to sting. "Those people need help!"

He curses under his breath, stepping after me, but I'm already moving. The world blurs into noise and heat and motion. The fire's glow swells brighter with every step, painting everything in shades of blood and gold.

The heat hits like a forcefield the moment I cross the threshold. My jacket does nothing to stop it—my skin prickles, lungs burning as I drag in a breath thick with smoke. The roar of the flames drowns out everything else—sirens, shouting, even JP's voice calling after me.

The factory is a maze of collapsing beams and molten shadows. Sparks rain from the ceiling like fiery snowfall. I throw my arm up to shield my face and push deeper into the inferno.

Somewhere ahead, through the crackle and the smoke, I hear it again: screams, closer this time. Desperate. Human. And I run toward them.

The air inside the factory is a furnace. Heat rolls over me in waves so intense it feels like my skin is peeling away. Every breath sears my throat, thick with smoke and the bitter taste of melting plastic. I can barely see through the haze—just shifting shapes and tongues of fire licking up the walls.

Then, I spot him. A man slumped near a shattered window, his body half-covered in debris. His coughing is ragged, wet. Blood streaks his chin as he tries to breathe.

"Hey!" I drop beside him, my knees hitting scorched concrete. "Hey, stay with me."

He blinks up at me, eyes glazed from smoke and fear. "Please..." he chokes, voice raw.

"I've got you." I hook an arm under his shoulders and haul him upright. He's heavy—dead weight from exhaustion—but adrenaline floods my veins, burning through the pain. The world narrows to movement: one step, then another, dragging him toward the faint glow of daylight bleeding through the wrecked doorway.

Each breath is agony. The fire roars like a beast behind us, hungry and furious. I can feel it chasing me, the heat clawing up my back.

"Go!" I shout as we reach the threshold, giving him one last shove into the cool night air. He stumbles, collapsing into the arms of a firefighter rushing forward.

I double over, coughing hard enough that stars burst across my vision. Every breath scorches my throat. My lungs feel shredded, raw, like the fire has crawled inside me and decided to stay. The taste of ash coats my tongue, thick and bitter.

But then—a voice. Faint. Somewhere deeper in the factory.

"Help! Please!"

My head snaps up. I blink through the smoke, eyes watering, vision swimming. Past the collapsed beams and the screaming machinery, another voice rises—a woman this time, fragile and terrified, the sound fading into the roar of the flames.

I should leave. I *know* I should. The fire's closing in, beams sagging overhead, the floor groaning under the strain of collapse. This place is seconds away from becoming a tomb.

But that voice—that desperate plea—reaches something in me that refuses to yield.

"I'm coming!" I shout back, my voice cracking hard in the heat.

"Evelyn!" JP's bellow cuts through the blaze, muffled by distance but sharp enough to slice through bone. "Get out of there!"

I don't answer. I can't.

I push forward, arm over my face, ducking under a fallen beam as embers rain down like burning insects. One catches my sleeve—fabric flaring, curling—before I slap it out with a hiss of pain. The

115

air vibrates around me, alive with the roar of the flames, with the cracking and snapping of wood giving way—and then, with something else.

A pulse. Low. Rhythmic. Chanting.

My heart stumbles. The cadence slithers under the roar of the fire, threading through the crackle of burning machinery. It's the same guttural pattern that haunts my dreams—the same sick rhythm that crawls beneath my skin when I sleep.

For a moment, the flames part and I see them: red eyes. Staring at me through the fire. Unblinking. Hungry. The same eyes from my nightmares, glowing like coals in the heart of the blaze.

I freeze, terror lancing up my spine. The world narrows to a pinpoint of heat and fear. The flames swell, smoke billows—I blink. The eyes are gone.

Just fire now. Just smoke. Just the burning frame of the factory collapsing inward. But the chanting remains, echoing deeper inside the inferno, layered beneath the screams, beneath the groan of metal warping in the heat.

I know. This wasn't an accident. This fire wasn't random. This entire place—the heat, the chaos, the screams—it's all a staging ground. A ritual.

The Veil set this fire for a reason. And somewhere inside this inferno, they're still here.

I turn, heart hammering so loud it drowns out the roar of the fire, and push through the smoke. My eyes sting, watering so badly the world blurs in flashes of orange and black. I can barely breathe. Every inhale scorches my throat. But then, I see her:

A woman, maybe mid-thirties, pinned beneath a fallen support beam. The flames dance along it, eating through the wood, creeping dangerously close to her. Her hair is matted with soot, her cheeks streaked with ash and tears.

"Please," she chokes out, reaching a trembling hand toward me. Her voice cracks, desperate, small. "Please, help me."

I drop to my knees beside her, coughing so hard my lungs ache, the heat pressing down on me like a physical weight. Sweat sliding down my temples in scalding rivulets. The fallen beam pinning her leg is massive—easily twice my width—and its edges glow a furious, molten red. I press my palms against it and feel the burn instantly, heat searing through skin and muscle. I grit my teeth and push.

My muscles lock tight, seizing under the brutal strain. My arms tremble violently, every tendon burning like it's about to snap. The steel groans beneath my grip but refuses to budge. Smoke curls around my face in choking ribbons, stinging my eyes, clawing down my throat. I grit my teeth, widen my stance on the shaking floor, and throw everything I have into one more heave.

"Come on!" The words rip out of me, half-sob, half-command. "Come on, MOVE!"

The beam doesn't budge. My shoulder wrenches hard, pain tearing through me, white-hot and sharp enough to make me gasp. My vision spots. Still, I don't stop. I pull until I feel something give— not the beam, but me.

My shoulder pops. The sound is sickening.

I stumble forward, the air shuddering with her screams. The flames lick higher, crawling toward her like they can smell her fear. The scent hits next—burning hair, seared flesh, thick and nauseating.

"Please!" she sobs again, voice breaking.

I try one last time. I throw everything I have at it—strength, rage, grief. My body shakes with the effort, my boots sliding against the floor slick with ash and melted plastic. But it's not enough. The beam won't move.

The heat swallows her cries until they twist into something terrible, high and raw. The fire catches her clothes, and her body arches once before she goes still.

And all I can do is stare, horror locking me in place while the flames consume what's left of her. Her screams echo inside my head long after they stop. I fall back, my knees hitting the floor hard, lungs gasping for air that won't come. The smell, the sound—it's everywhere. It's my nightmare come to life.

Somewhere behind me, I hear JP shouting my name, his voice cutting through the roar of the inferno. But it's already too late. Because this time, I didn't save her. This time, I was too late.

JP bursts through the smoke, his silhouette cutting through the haze like a phantom. He doesn't hesitate—his hand snatches the back of my collar, yanking me off the floor just as the ceiling gives way.

The world *erupts*.

A blinding wave of heat slams into us, throwing sparks and debris in every direction. The air becomes fire. The sound—damn, the sound—is deafening. Wood splinters. Steel screams. For a heartbeat, everything disappears in a wash of orange and white.

When the roar finally fades, I'm on the ground outside, coughing so hard it feels like my lungs are turning inside out. JP drags me farther from the inferno, his arm locked around me as if I might run back in. Ash drifts through the air like snow, settling in my hair, clinging to the sweat on my skin. The factory is nothing but a cage of fire now, its frame collapsing in on itself, sparks leaping into the night.

I can barely feel my legs. My throat is raw, every breath scraping like sandpaper. My hands shake uncontrollably—blood, soot, and smoke blending into something dark and unrecognizable.

JP crouches beside me, his chest heaving, face streaked with soot. His voice is steady but rough, the gravel of it crumbling at its edges. "You did what you could."

I stare at the flames devouring the building—the place where her screams ended—and a laugh claws out of my throat, brittle and hollow. "It wasn't enough."

The words hang there between us, swallowed by the crackle of fire.

For a long moment, neither of us moves. The firefighters' shouts fade into the background, distant and meaningless. Somewhere deep in the wreckage, something groans, a final death rattle of twisted steel.

And then, I hear it. Faint under the chaos. A sound that doesn't belong. A whisper. Low. Rhythmic. Familiar. The chanting.

My head snaps toward the building, eyes scanning the blazing ruins. No figures. No movement. Just flame. But the sound is there, slithering beneath the crackle and roar, echoing from somewhere unseen.

JP hears it too. I can tell by the way his expression hardens, eyes zeroing in on the fire. "They're gone," he mutters, half to himself. "They set the fire, but they were never inside."

My skin crawls. "Then who—?"

"The Veil," he says grimly. "They wanted us here. Wanted *you* here."

The chanting rises one last time, lifted by the wind—a warped, mocking echo that fades into the night. I clutch at the dirt, trying to ground myself, but the sound lingers in my head like an infection. They're out there. Watching. Waiting. And this fire wasn't the end. It was the beginning.

JP doesn't say a word the entire drive home. His jaw stays locked, muscles ticking in a rhythm that matches the tension in his hands on the wheel. His eyes are glued to the road, like if he looks away for even a second, everything will come crashing down.

I sit rigid in the passenger seat, the world outside flashing by in smeared streaks. I can still smell the smoke on my skin, in my clothes, clinging to me like it has no intention of letting go. The phantom heat burns behind my eyes.

I press my hands hard against my thighs, trying to steady their shaking, trying to breathe, trying to pretend I didn't see what I saw. *If* I even saw it.

Red eyes. Watching through the fire. But maybe it *was* the fire. Maybe it was the smoke. Maybe it was my brain misfiring in all that chaos, stitching nightmares into reality. Because who sees eyes like that and lives?

A shiver crawls up my spine. I watch my reflection in the window and whisper a truth I'm not ready to say aloud:

I don't know if they were real.

But the fear lodged under my ribs tells me they were. And that scares me worse than the fire ever could.

By the time we make it back to the office, dawn is bleeding into the horizon. The world outside looks muted and gray, like even the sun doesn't have the heart to rise.

When we step inside, the familiar scent of coffee and dust should feel grounding, but it doesn't. The silence presses too heavy. The walls feel closer. My chest feels too small.

JP shrugs out of his jacket and drops it on the desk, running a hand over his face. He looks like hell—soot streaked across his cheek, shirt torn at the sleeve—but his eyes are all sharp edges and movement, scanning me, assessing damage the way he always does after a fight.

I stand there in the middle of the room, trying to breathe, but the moment I close my eyes, I hear it again: the fire, the screams, the woman's voice begging for help.

Something in me cracks.

My knees buckle before I realize I'm moving, and I'm on the floor, gasping, the sobs leaving my body before I can stop them. My hands dig into the rug, trying to anchor myself in something solid, but all I can see is the fire. All I can hear is her voice. The smell of burning flesh.

JP is there in an instant, dropping to a crouch beside me. "Evelyn." His voice is low, careful—like he's talking to a wounded animal. "Breathe. Look at me."

"I couldn't save her." My voice breaks. "She was right there, and I couldn't—"

"Hey." His hand hovers near my shoulder, not quite touching. "You did what you could."

I shake my head, choking on the words. "That's what you said before. It doesn't help."

His face tightens, and for a long moment, he doesn't say anything. Just watches me, the weight of something unreadable in his eyes. Then, he exhales slowly, like coming to a decision he doesn't like. "Come on."

Before I can ask what he means, he stands and pulls me to my feet. His grip is firm, steady. He doesn't say where we're going, but I already know. Downstairs. The training room.

The smell of disinfectant and leather hits me the moment we step inside. The air is cool, the concrete floor rough beneath my boots. It's the one place that's always felt predictable. Controlled.

"JP, I don't—"

He cuts me off. "You need this. You can't hold it in. You'll drown."

"I don't want to fight."

"Then hit something until you do."

He tosses me my gloves and points at the heavy bag. I hesitate—torn between anger and exhaustion—but the look in his eyes leaves no room for argument.

So I start to hit. Slow at first. Then harder. Each strike rattles through me and echoes in the empty room.

"Again," he says, voice sharp.

I hit harder.

"Harder!"

"I am!" I snap, slamming my fist into the leather until my knuckles split.

He steps closer, eyes blazing. "Then why are you still holding back?"

My chest heaves. "I'm not!"

"You are. You freeze when it counts. You hesitate when it matters—"

"I'm not a soldier!" I explode, spinning toward him. "I'm not you! I can't just shut everything off when someone dies!"

His eyes flash. "You think I can?"

For a moment, I see it—the guilt buried beneath his armor, the ghosts he carries behind every command, every scar. He's pushing me because he's terrified. Terrified I'll die before he can save me.

The fire inside me flickers, the rage collapsing into something smaller but heavier. I wipe my bloodied knuckles on my shirt, the sting grounding me. My throat tightens.

"She was pleading with me to save her," I whisper, voice trembling. "That women in the fire. I tried. They burned her alive, JP. They're doing this for me."

"Then we make them regret it."

He tosses me a towel and turns toward the door. "Clean up. You're not done yet."

I stare down at my hands. Blood slicks my knuckles, mixing with the grime and sweat. My fingers tremble, my skin still reeking faintly of smoke. I can feel it in my hair, my clothes, my lungs. The fire hasn't left me.

It's under my skin now. And in a way, it's still burning.

When I finally collapse into bed, exhaustion drags me under so fast it feels like falling through water. My body sinks into the mattress, muscles trembling, lungs still carrying the phantom taste of smoke. But sleep doesn't bring peace.

The flames are waiting.

They rise around me in an instant—no spark, no warning—just a world already burning. Heat washes over my skin, blistering-hot yet somehow distant, as if I'm standing in the memory of a fire instead of the fire itself. Ash swirls in the air like black snow, settling on my shoulders, clinging to my hair.

And there, at the center of it, stands my mother.

Her silhouette wavers in the heat shimmer, but her face is clear—gentle, steady. Her hair glows like molten copper in the firelight, every strand dancing with light the flames can't consume. Her eyes, the same warm hazel as mine, burn bright and calm, untouched by the chaos that devours everything else.

She doesn't scream this time. She doesn't reach for me. She just *looks* at me, soft and sad and knowing.

For a moment, the roaring of the blaze dulls to a low hum, like the fire itself is holding its breath to hear her. She opens her mouth. One word. Barely a whisper. Barely a breath.

Run.

Then, the world erupts. The flames surge upward like a living thing, swallowing her whole, the heat slamming into me with a force that knocks the air from my lungs. Her face dissolves into smoke, into embers, into nothing.

Chapter 9

Fractures

The morning after the fire smells like smoke and metal. Even in my own room.

It clings to everything—to my clothes draped over the chair, to the tangled sheets twisted around my ankles, to my hair and skin. It's as if whatever burned last night left its fingerprints on me, invisible but impossible to ignore. I lie there for a long moment, staring up at the ceiling, wishing I could stay empty, numb, just a little longer. But the second I close my eyes, she's there again.

The woman trapped under the beam. Her screams echo through my skull, raw and tearing.

Her fingers clawing, desperate, slipping against mine as the fire crawled closer. The way the flames lit her eyes—not with reflection, but with terror, bright and alive—just before the ceiling groaned and—

I jerk upright so fast the room tilts. My heart slams against my ribs, and sweat beads across my forehead despite the cool morning air.

My body feels stiff. Heavy. Like I fought all night instead of slept. My arms ache with phantom strain, my palms sting where blistered skin used to be in the dream, and a deep, otherworldly exhaustion wraps around my bones.

Maybe nightmares are a different kind of battle. And judging by the way I feel, I lost.

I finally peel myself out of bed and drag myself toward the bathroom. The hallway creaks under my steps, the same familiar groans I've heard for years, but today it feels like the house is echoing my exhaustion.

In the mirror, I look like something hollowed out. Dark circles bruise the skin beneath my eyes, stark against the light brown. My face looks sallow, drawn tight in ways it never used to be. My eyes—normally too bright, too alive—seem dull today, glassy from lack of sleep, reflecting back a version of myself I barely recognize.

I peel off my clothes and step into the shower, twisting the knob all the way to hot. The pipes rattle before releasing a rush of scalding water. Steam fills the room instantly, thick and swirling, climbing the walls and swallowing the edges of the world. The mirror fogs over until my reflection disappears completely, which feels like mercy.

The water hits me harder than I expect, a pounding rhythm against tired muscles. Heat blossoms across my skin, spreading in waves that almost mimic the fire's touch. My shoulder flares first—an old ache I pretend doesn't bother me. Then my arms prickle, tiny sparks of pain where smoke licked along them last night. My knuckles twinge next, stiff and tender in a way they shouldn't be.

They should've healed. I should've healed. I always do. But today, even my body feels unsure of that truth.

I press my palms against the tile, head bowed as the spray washes over me. I pretend the water will strip everything away—the nightmares, the fear, the memory of her screams. But the heat only loosens my muscles, not the knot in my chest.

No matter how long I stand there, it feels like the fire followed me home. And it doesn't intend to leave.

If I'd been stronger... If I'd gotten there sooner... maybe she'd still be alive.

"Stop," I whisper to myself, pressing my palms against my eyes. "Stop thinking like that." But the voice in my head doesn't listen.

When I finally shut off the water, my chest feels tight as ever, like the smoke is still heavy in my lungs. I towel off slowly, mechanically, and pull on jeans and a clean shirt—anything to make me feel normal, as far from the truth as that may be.

Downstairs, I shove some bread into the toaster and spread peanut butter with a knife that needs sharpening. The small, mundane ritual feels foreign in my hands.

Footsteps creak behind me. I freeze.

My father shuffles through the kitchen doorway, hair once again sticking up like he slept on concrete, eyes bloodshot, shirt wrinkled and stained. He stops when he sees me, blinking slowly before continuing to enter the kitchen.

We don't speak.

He opens the fridge. The clink of bottles shifts something ugly in my chest. 8:14 in the morning. He grabs a beer anyway.

He walks past me, not even looking my way, and disappears into the living room. The TV flicks on. A sitcom laugh track erupts, painfully bright against the grey morning.

I swallow the lump in my throat and force down my toast, the peanut butter sticking like glue. Everything tastes like ash.

He didn't ask where I was last night. He didn't notice I didn't come home until after dawn. He didn't notice the smoke still clinging to my hair. He didn't notice me, like he hasn't in years.

After I throw my plate in the sink, I grab my jacket and head for the door before the silence suffocates me completely. But as I step out onto the porch, I catch myself gripping the railing to steady my shaking hand.

I survived a fire. A summoning. A cultist whispering my name like a prophecy. But the worst part? I'm not sure I survived the guilt.

Not because I'm weak. Not because I'm useless. But because JP refuses to tell me. And today, something in me is done being kept in the dark.

JP's already in the training room when I arrive downstairs. The air smells like sweat, rubber mats, and old leather. His sleeves are rolled up to his elbows, gloves strapped tight around his fists. Every punch he throws into the heavy bag sounds like he's trying to beat the guilt out of himself.

Thud. Thud. THUD. Each hit shakes dust loose from the rafters.

"Couldn't sleep?" I ask, my voice rough, bare from hours of replaying the fire in my head.

He doesn't look at me. Doesn't even pause. "You should be resting."

I cross my arms, leaning against the doorframe. "Yeah, because that's working out great for me lately."

JP's fists hammer on, steady and relentless. He knows exactly what I'm saying. He's just choosing to ignore it. The silence stretches until my skin feels too tight, until the thudding starts to sync with the pulse pounding behind my eyes.

Finally, he stops mid-swing. The bag sways between us like a pendulum.

"What happened last night—" he says without turning around, "—it can't happen again."

My jaw tightens. "You mean me running into a burning building to save someone?"

That gets him. He turns, slow and deliberate, blue eyes burning with fear, anger, maybe both. "I mean losing control."

Sweat glistens along his jawline, dripping from his temple. He pulls one glove off with his teeth, tosses it aside. "You can't save everyone, Evelyn. Not yet." His voice softens just barely, but it's not for comfort—it's a warning. "Not when you don't even understand what you're fighting."

The words hit harder than any blow he's ever thrown. My throat tightens, heat rising like I've been slapped.

"Then teach me!" The shout rips out of me before I can cage it. My hands are shaking, fingers curling into fists. "Stop giving me half-truths and riddles! You keep saying you're preparing me, but for what, JP? Demons? Cultists? Hell itself?" I take a step closer, heart hammering. "Because right now, it feels like I'm fighting blind!"

When he speaks, his voice stays infuriatingly calm. Almost detached. "You're not ready for the truth."

"Bullshit."

His nostrils flare, gaze shifting like he's considering saying something honest—then, he shuts it down. Locks it away.

And that—*that*—makes my frustration burn even hotter.

My stomach twists so hard it hurts. "You sound just like my father when he was drunk and trying to explain why Mom died," I snap. "*'You're too young to understand, Evie. It's better if you don't know.*'" The words spill out in a warped, mocking imitation—my voice bending into something ugly, something sharp enough to draw blood. It tastes like poison on my tongue, but I can't swallow it back.

I step closer, heat crawling up my neck, fury buzzing under my skin like a live wire.

"Guess what, Jacob Pierce?" I draw his name out, every syllable slow and deliberate. I *never* say his full name. No one does. It lands in the air like a slap, like I'm daring him to pretend this isn't serious. I want him to feel how angry I am.

His eyes flick toward me at the sound of it, and something in his expression tightens—surprise, hurt, maybe even guilt—before he shutters it away.

"I'm not twelve anymore."

A tick pulses near his temple, but he doesn't flinch. "You think I enjoy keeping things from you?" His voice isn't raised, but it strikes like a blade. "You think I haven't seen what happens when people learn too much, too fast?"

"Stop acting like you're protecting me!" The words tear out of me, sharp and cracking at the edges. "You're not my dad, JP! You don't get to decide what I can or can't handle!"

Silence detonates between us.

JP goes perfectly still. His chest rises and falls in slow, controlled breaths, like he's wrestling down something that wants to break free. My own breathing is uneven, ragged in my ears.

When he finally speaks, it's barely above a whisper.

"You're right." He strips off his remaining glove, ripping the Velcro like it offended him. "I'm not your father."

The glove hits the mat with a soft thud that, in our silence, feels stronger than a gunshot.

"But," he adds, stepping toward me, his blue eyes cutting straight through whatever defenses I have left, "I promised him I'd keep you alive. And that means I don't get the luxury of telling you everything—not until I know you can survive it."

My heart stops. Actually *stops*—a painful stutter in my chest that steals the breath from my lungs. "You *promised him*?" The words barely come out. Small. Thin. Fragile. Nothing like the fire raging in me seconds ago.

His eyes flick toward me, and for the briefest moment, I see it: regret. Raw and unguarded. He didn't mean to say that. He didn't mean for *that* piece to slip. The look vanishes the instant I recognize it.

"Drop it," he mutters, already retreating behind that wall I've learned to hate.

"No." My voice trembles, but my feet stay planted. Something inside me won't let this go. Can't. "You said you promised *him*. My dad. What did you mean? Before all this?" My breath shakes. "Before the fire? Or after?"

"Evelyn." His entire posture shifts, everything locking tight. It's the tone he uses when danger is stalking close. "Enough."

But I push anyway. I have to. I've lived too long in the dark to turn away from a scrap of truth now.

"Did you know my dad before the fire?" My throat feels tight. "Did you know him before my mom died?"

He flinches. Actually flinches. Something flickers across his face—pain, guilt, memory—all tangled into one expression I've never seen on him before. It guts me, knocks the breath right out of my chest.

131

And then, he turns away. "This conversation's over," he says, his voice a steel door slamming in my face.

I stare at him, anger and confusion boiling until I feel like I'm going to crack open. I don't know which feeling is winning: rage or heartbreak. "You can't keep shutting me out," I say, my voice shaking. "You can't keep treating me like some kid who doesn't deserve the truth."

He looks back at me then, and his expression is stoic. Unshakeable. "You don't have to like what I'm doing," he says. "You just have to listen."

And that's it. That's the moment something in me fractures— quietly, invisibly, but enough that I feel it. Enough that I know things won't go back to the way they were.

I grab my bag from the chair and sling it over my shoulder. The weight of it knocks against my hip.

"Fine," I snap, heat burning behind my eyes. "You want to be the one with all the answers? Keep them. I'm done waiting."

"Evelyn—"

There's a warning in his voice, thick with emotion, but I refuse to hear it. If I listen, I'll crack. And I will not let him see me break again.

"I'm done," I repeat, voice shaking. It makes me furious that he can probably hear it.

I shove past him. My shoulder bumps his arm, and he reaches out like he might stop me, might grab my sleeve and try to fix everything with one of those frustrating, cryptic reassurances, but I'm already moving. Boots thudding across the mats. Across the concrete floor. Up the stairs two at a time.

His voice follows me, deep and steady and maddeningly calm— like smoke slipping under a closed door.

"Evelyn. Don't walk away like this."

I don't stop. Don't slow. Don't breathe.

The office above the training room is dim, lit only by the muted glow of the desk lamp JP always forgets to turn off. Papers are scattered across the table—maps, notes, photos of missing kids—and for a second, the sight makes the ache in my chest sharper, deeper.

I'm part of this mess. I'm drowning in it. And he still won't tell me why.

Before I can talk myself out of it, I yank my phone out and call the one person in my life who isn't made of secrets and warnings.

Maya picks up on the second ring. "Yo, Evie—did you just pocket-dial me again? Please tell me this isn't another incident with the espresso machine."

"You still going to that party tonight?" I blurt. The words come out fast, half anger, half desperation.

There's a beat of silence. Then, she gasps dramatically. "Evie Cross willingly attending a social gathering? I need to sit down. I need a witness. I need a diary to log this historic moment."

Despite the fire roiling in my chest, a small, shaky laugh escapes me. "Don't push it," I mutter, scrubbing my hand over my face. "Just... Yeah. I'll come."

"Hell yes you will!" Maya cheers. "I'll save you from awkward small talk. And from Matt trying to impress you with his single push-up."

I hang up and let the phone slip from my fingers, leaning back against the desk. The cold edge digs into my spine, grounding me in a way nothing else seems to. My hands are still trembling—from anger, from exhaustion, and from the crushing, suffocating weight of not knowing what I am.

Not knowing why a cult would carve symbols meant for monsters and then try to burn a woman alive just to get to me. Not knowing why JP looked genuinely terrified—*not angry, not annoyed, terrified*—when I asked about my dad. Not knowing why every question about my past feels like it's brushing up against something with teeth.

The uncertainty wraps around me like fog.

Maybe a party is exactly what I need. Noise. Heat. Music too loud to think over. People who don't know that my name means anything more than what's on my apron at Bean & Gone. Maybe I need something normal. Something human. Even if it only lasts an hour. Even if it's a lie. Even if the moment I step back outside, the world tilts off-balance again.

Right now, I'll take anything that isn't the truth JP refuses to give me. Anything that lets me breathe without feeling like the dark is waiting to swallow the next piece of me.

By the time I pull into Maya's driveway, the sun has fully dipped behind the hills, taking its warmth with it. Porch lights glow against the dark, and somewhere down the street, bass thumps hard enough to vibrate through the still evening air.

Before I even lift my hand to knock, Maya yanks the door open.

"There she is!" She grabs my wrist and pulls me inside like she's been waiting all night. "Evelyn Cross stepping into my house willingly? Hold on, let me go write this down in my gratitude journal."

"Maya," I warn, though a tiny smile threatens. "If you make a big deal out of this—"

"I make big deals out of everything," she declares. "And tonight? We're making you look cute. Because you are *not* going to this party dressed like..." She gestures up and down at me. "Like you're about to mop the floors at Bean & Gone."

I look down at my black T-shirt and jeans—the only things that feel like mine. "What's wrong with this?"

"It's adorable," she assures me, patting my shoulder. "But tonight we're aiming for *fun,* not 'I've been awake for three days and life is pain.'"

She drags me to her bedroom, which looks like it's been decorated by a minor hurricane. Clothes are everywhere—tank tops draped over lamps, jeans tossed across chairs, sparkly dresses half-hanging out of drawers.

She points at the bed. "Sit."

I sigh dramatically, planting myself on the comforter. "I didn't agree to a makeover."

Her eyes go wide. "Evie. Sweetie. Love of my retail life. You absolutely did."

She starts throwing tops in my direction. I dodge one that's particularly glittery. "Maya, I'm not wearing sequins."

"Fine," she huffs. "We'll save the sequins for New Year's."

Eventually, I find something that feels... acceptable. A fitted dark red tank top and a pair of high-waisted jeans that hug just enough to be flattering without being "look at me" loud.

"Oh, hell yes," Maya breathes, clapping. "That's the vibe. Casual hot. Effortless danger."

"Maya."

"What? Accuracy matters." She ushers me into the bathroom to change, and when I come out, she literally gasps.

"Girl. You have a body, and you didn't tell me."

I snort. "Stop."

"I will not. Now sit. Hair."

"Maya, no—"

But she's already behind me, tugging out my ponytail and letting my hair fall loose around my shoulders. She fluffs it gently, stepping back like an artist judging her masterpiece.

"And makeup," she says triumphantly, grabbing her makeup bag.

"Oh hell—"

"Oh hush. I'm not putting you on magazine cover mode. Just a little something to make you glow."

I give her a deadpan stare. "Maya, I don't glow."

"Watch me." Five minutes later, she steps back with a flourish. "Boom."

I look in the mirror. And I actually... don't hate it. A tiny sweep of eyeliner, a touch of highlighter catching the warm light, a gloss that makes my lips look slightly fuller. It's subtle. But it makes me look awake. Alive.

Like someone who didn't spend last night drowning in thoughts she can't share.

Maya beams. "Damn. If I weren't into dudes, I'd climb you like a tree."

"Please don't."

"No promises."

We weave through the neighborhood sidewalks toward the party, Maya walking beside me with the energy of a caffeinated hummingbird. I can already hear the music from a block away—a heavy bass that makes the pavement buzz beneath my boots.

"Okay, serious question," Maya says, glancing back at me. "On a scale of one to ten, how mad are you going to be if someone spills beer on your shoes?"

"Eleven," I deadpan.

She laughs and bumps her shoulder into mine. "You're in a mood. It's perfect. Parties love moody girls."

Before I can retort, we step through the open gate into the backyard and—

The music *hits* us. Big. Bold. Loud enough to vibrate the wooden fence. String lights crisscross overhead in messy zigzags, glowing warm and golden. A bonfire roars in the center of the yard, sparks spiraling up into the night sky.

Maya's grip on my arm tightens as she practically bounces.

We step deeper into the yard, drawn into the ebb and flow of bodies moving, laughing, shouting. The air is thick with the smell of cheap beer, sweet cider, and bonfire smoke—but not the kind that suffocates me. Not the heavy, choking kind that claws up old memories.

This smoke is different. Warm. Human.

137

A group of kids from Ashford High attempt a chaotic dance circle near the fire pit, limbs flailing with more enthusiasm than rhythm. Someone's blasting throwback pop like it's a religious experience. On the deck, a couple poses for dramatic selfies under the string lights, contorting like they're auditioning for a reality show.

Near the fence, Matt from work is trying—and failing spectacularly—to impress a group of girls with his "one perfect push-up." He drops to the ground with a grunt, manages half of one, and immediately collapses. The girls blink. Maya physically cringes, like she's witnessing a small tragedy in slow motion.

It's ridiculous. Messy. Chaotic. And for the first time in weeks... I feel almost human. Almost like I could belong here, just another girl at a party, instead of someone being hunted in the dark.

Then, I see them—the guys from the coffee shop. The same ones who lean on the counter, flashing crooked smiles and tossing out bargain-bin flirtations just to score a discount. The ones who treat the tip jar like it's optional, but winks like they're currency.

They're clustered near the bonfire now, red plastic cups in hand, laughing way too loudly at something that's definitely not that funny. The flames throw their shadows long across the grass, stretching them into smirking, swaggering silhouettes.

The tall, blond one—Travis, I'm pretty sure—spots me first. His grin spreads instantly, slow and wide, like the universe just handed him the plot twist he'd been waiting for all night.

"Well, well," he says, weaving through the crowd with exaggerated confidence. "Look who decided to join the living!"

I roll my eyes, but there's a tug at the corner of my mouth I can't quite fight. "Don't get used to it."

"Oh, I won't," he says, though his smirk says otherwise. He holds something out to me—a cup beaded with cold condensation. "Here. Liquid courage. Or liquid regret. Dealer's choice."

"I don't drink," I say automatically.

He shrugs. "Then live a little."

The cup is cold against my palm, condensation slipping between my fingers. There's something disarming about how casual it all is—just a boy, a cup, a party. Normal. Easy. Something I haven't had in... ever.

For a heartbeat, I let myself imagine it. Being that girl. The one who can flirt and laugh and not wake up smelling smoke or blood. The one who doesn't see demons in every shadow or danger in every stranger.

But then—like smoke sliding across my mind—the memory hits. The fire. The woman trapped beneath the beam. Her scream cutting off like someone silenced the world. JP's face when I demanded answers he refused to give. And the cultist's voice echoing, low and certain: *They want you.*

My stomach twists, warning me off. I lift the cup to my lips anyway—and tip the whole thing back in one go.

The drink scorches down my throat immediately, sweet for a second before the burn hits. It makes my eyes water, heat blooming in my chest, but at least it's a pain I *choose*. Something I control.

"See?" Maya's voice chirps beside me as she bumps her shoulder against mine. "Not so bad, right?"

I exhale slowly, letting the warmth spread through my chest. "Yeah," I say softly. "Not so bad."

But even as I smile, something tight curls in my gut—an ache that reminds me normalcy is temporary. And tonight, it feels dangerously fragile. As laughter echoes around me and the firelight flickers across faces that don't know what danger looks like, something inside me twists.

They're all so carefree. So careless. So *unbreakable* in their own ignorance.

A girl shrieks with laughter near the fire, spilling cider on her shoes. A guy pretends to shove his friend into the flames. Someone starts chanting *chug!* like it's a battle cry. Their biggest fear tonight is a hangover or a bad hookup story.

They don't know what it's like to run for your life. To smell burning flesh. To feel blood drying on your hands. To be hunted.

And suddenly, it hits me all at once—I don't belong here.

The music pulses through the ground, vibrating against my boots, but it feels distant, like it's meant for someone else. Someone lighter. Someone whole.

I swallow hard, forcing a smile when Maya catches my eye, waving at me like she's trying to anchor me to Earth. But the feeling doesn't let go. The hairs on the back of my neck lift. A cold prickle crawls down my spine. The voices around me blur together, muted, as if the world has begun to shift.

Because still, beneath the thrum of music, beneath the laughter, beneath the illusion of normal, I swear I can *feel* eyes on me. Watching. Waiting. Hungry.

A cold ripple crawls up my spine. I force myself to turn—slowly—toward the bonfire. The flames snap and spit, shadows jerking across the grass, stretching long and warped. For a split second, my chest locks tight as I brace for that terrible glow... those red eyes staring back through the blaze.

But there's nothing. Just fire. Just normal shadows. Just the heat licking upward into the night like it has better things to burn.

Still, the feeling doesn't leave. It sits inside my ribs, coiled and certain. Something is out there. And it knows exactly where I am.

A shadow flickers at the edge of the crowd, near the tree line. Too quick. Too deliberate. Gone before I can fully register it.

My breath catches. No one else notices—of course they don't. They're too busy drinking, dancing, living. But me? My heart knows better. The Veil hasn't forgotten me. They never will.

And suddenly, the party feels less like an escape and more like a trap. A cold shiver ripples up my spine. The shadow near the tree line. The feeling of being watched. The instinctive twist in my stomach telling me *you're not safe*.

For a heartbeat, I almost drop the cup. But then, Travis appears at my side like a golden retriever, grinning wide and oblivious. "Evie! Ready for round two?"

He gently bumps my shoulder with his. "C'mon, you promised you'd give this party a real chance."

"I don't remember promising anything," I mutter, but my voice is tired, not sharp.

Maya slings an arm around me from behind, nearly knocking the cup out of my hand. "She's being dramatic," she tells Travis, loud enough for half the yard to hear. "She's actually having a great time."

I shoot her a glare. She shoots me one back. Hers wins.

"Drink," she commands as she hands me another cup. I roll my eyes... and drink.

Warmth spreads through my chest, loosening muscles I didn't realize were clenched. The noise blurs just enough to feel distant. Manageable. The fire crackles. Someone turns up the music. Maya drags us toward a dancing crowd, shaking her hips like she doesn't care who's watching.

Travis leans in close so I can hear him over the speakers. "You dance?"

"Not really."

"Good," he says, already taking my hand. "Because neither do I."

I let him pull me into the crowd. A mess of limbs and laughter and terrible rhythm. Maya cheers like she's hosting a game show. Someone spins her until she shrieks with laughter. I laugh too. It sounds strange in my own ears—like it belongs to someone lighter, someone with fewer scars. But the sound is real, and it feels wrong and good all at once.

Every time I feel eyes on me, I take another drink. Every time a memory creeps in, I let the music drown it out. Every time the world tilts in that familiar, dangerous way, I lean into the dancing instead.

And for a little while, I let myself be nineteen. Just a girl at a party. Just Evelyn. Not hunted. Not chosen. Not broken. Just... here.

A cold prickle still lingers under my skin from earlier, but the music and the fire and the crowd press against it, smothering the worst of it.

Travis spins me one more time—badly, off-beat, almost making me trip—and I burst out laughing despite myself. He laughs too, head thrown back, blond hair catching the string lights.

"Okay, okay," he gasps, hands raised in surrender. "I accept defeat. I am officially the worst dancer at this party."

"Pretty sure that guy by the cooler has you beat," I say, nodding toward someone doing something that can only be described as interpretive seizure dancing.

Travis snorts. "Fair point. But I still suck."

"Yeah," I tease lightly. "But it's kind of charming."

His grin softens. "You're kind of charming."

Heat rushes to my cheeks—part embarrassment, part alcohol humming in my veins. I try to blame it all on the drink, but that's a lie. It's been a long, long time since anyone looked at me like this. Like I wasn't a problem to solve, a responsibility to guard, or a mystery to decode. Just… a girl.

Travis steps closer, his voice a little quieter. "I'm glad you came, Evelyn."

Something in my chest stutters.

Maya dances past us, hollering, "Get it, Evie!" before disappearing into the crowd again, cackling like she planned this. I roll my eyes, but the smile stays on my lips.

Travis reaches up, hesitating just enough for me to pull away if I want to. "Can I…?"

I should say no. I should remember the shadows watching me. I should remember the woman in the fire. I should remember JP's face when I walked away.

But tonight, I don't want *should*s. I want something simple. Something human. Something mine.

I nod.

He leans in, slow enough that I feel the question in the space between us before our mouths ever touch. His lips brush mine— barely there at first, soft and cautious, like he's afraid I'll shatter if he pushes too hard.

But something inside me loosens, unspools. So I kiss him back.

The world rushes in warm and dizzy—music thumping through the ground, laughter rising around us, the sweet burn of alcohol still humming in my bloodstream. His lips taste faintly of beer and mint gum, new but familiar, and the heat of him chases away the cold coil of fear that's lived inside my chest for days.

His hand slides to my waist, fingers curving gently, almost reverently, like he's discovering the shape of something he's only imagined until now. The touch sends a spark up my spine—unexpected, electric, terrifying in the best and worst ways.

In this moment, the world holds still. No demons. No nightmares. No cult whispering my name from the shadows. Just the warmth of his mouth against mine and the way my heart stutters like it's remembering how to beat.

When we finally pull apart, he looks stunned—eyes wide, breath caught, lips parted like he's scared to move in case the moment snaps. I probably look exactly the same.

"Wow," he says breathlessly.

"Yeah." My voice comes out small. "Wow."

We stand there for a heartbeat—a single suspended moment—while the party swirls around us like a kaleidoscope. Music thumps through the ground, bass vibrating up my legs. Maya is somewhere behind me, shouting something completely unintelligible but certainly chaotic. The bonfire crackles so fiercely its sparks lift into the air, drifting high enough to make the stars look like they're flickering in response.

The night feels alive—louder, brighter, bigger than the fear that's lived inside me for so long.

And for the first time in... hell, I don't even know how long, I feel—not whole, not fixed, not safe—but something almost like free.

Because tonight, just for this sliver of time, I get to pretend I'm normal. Pretend I'm just a girl at a party. Pretend the darkness isn't narrowing in on me with every breath. Pretend the world isn't burning in the corners of my mind.

Tonight, I get to pretend. And it feels dangerous. And it feels good.

Chapter 10

The Mark of the Veil

My phone won't stop vibrating.

At first, I think it's just my nerves again—phantom buzzing, the kind that's been haunting me. The past two days have been a smear of half-slept nights and showers that run too hot in hopes that the steam will wash away things I can't unsee. I spend hours staring at the cracks in my ceiling, pretending I'm fine. Pretending I'm not thinking about the fire. Pretending I'm not thinking about Travis.

But the buzzing doesn't fade. It gets louder. Sharper. Needling under my skin until I can't ignore it anymore.

I groan and roll onto my side, burying my face into the pillow to muffle the world. My head throbs—leftover ache from too little sleep and too many thoughts. The phone vibrates again, rattling against the nightstand, demanding my attention.

The screen lights up, bright enough to stab straight through my eyelids. JP. Of course it is.

He's already called five times. Maybe six. I lost count somewhere between ignoring him purposely and being too exhausted to care.

We haven't spoken since the fight—since I told him I was done waiting for answers he refused to give. Since I walked out on him.

Now the phone buzzes again, angry I haven't picked up yet. I swear under my breath and swipe to answer, more out of annoyance than anything.

"What?" I mumble, voice thick with sleep and days of pretending I'm not actively avoiding him.

"Well, good morning to you, too," JP snaps back. His tone is clipped—no patience, no warmth. "What took you so long? I've been calling for twenty minutes."

I sit up slowly, rubbing grit from my eyes. "Some of us enjoy sleeping," I mutter. "You should try it sometime."

"You haven't returned a single message in three days," he fires back immediately. "Don't pretend I'm the one being unreasonable. I was two seconds from kicking down your door."

"Would've saved me the trouble of answering," I mumble—just quiet enough that he might not hear. But he does.

There's a pause. Not a soft one. A tense, heavy, *I know you're still mad but I'm going to ignore it* kind of pause. He chooses the easy route—the one where he can pretend emotions don't exist.

"We have another missing person," he says flatly, all business.

My breath stalls mid-inhale. "...What? Who?"

A beat. Then: "Travis Reed."

Everything inside me freezes. Travis.

Laughing under the string lights. His hand warm at my waist. His lips brushing mine, soft and hesitant, like he wasn't sure I'd want it. All of it slams through me so hard I can't breathe.

I grip the phone so tightly my knuckles crack. "When?" I whisper. The word scrapes out like it's cutting my throat.

"Two days ago," JP says. "He never made it home on Saturday night."

Saturday. The night he kissed me. The night I left him smiling. My stomach lurches, hot and sick. The room tilts sideways like I'm

146

falling off the bed. I press a hand to my forehead, squeezing my eyes shut until stars burst behind my eyelids.

No. No, no, no.

"Evie?" JP says, his tone shifting, softening in a way he rarely allows. "You okay?"

I swallow hard, steadying my breathing just enough to force the lie. "Yeah. Yeah, I'm— I'm fine."

He doesn't buy it. I can hear it in the pause that follows, in the subtle change in his breathing, in the instinctive tension he gets when something isn't adding up. But he doesn't push. Not yet.

"I picked up a lead," he says, sliding back into mission mode like flipping a switch. "Possible Veil activity on the outskirts of Briar Hollow. I need you ready in twenty minutes."

My vision blurs. "Twenty—? JP, hold on—"

"Evelyn," he cuts in, dropping his voice to that low, urgent tone he only uses when something is terribly wrong. "This one might be bad."

A chill crawls up my spine. Before I can speak, before I can ask anything, before I can react, he hangs up. I sit in the silence of my dim, cluttered room, phone still pressed to my ear, heart beating too fast, too loud.

Travis is missing. Two days. No one saw him after the party. No one saw him leave.

And I... I'd kissed him.

And now the only thing louder than the pounding in my chest is the truth I wish I didn't know: The Veil took him. And I don't even know if it's because of something he did... or because of me.

I'd allowed myself to feel something rare—something warm and stupid and normal—and now he's gone. The universe always seems to punish me for wanting anything beyond bare survival. Like joy is a luxury I was never meant to touch.

Guilt slams into me so hard my knees almost buckle. How dare I flirt, or drink, or kiss someone while women are burning, while cults whisper my name, while people disappear in the dark because of *me*.

My throat tightens until I can barely breathe. Heat prickles behind my eyes, sharp and humiliating. I press both hands over my face, willing myself not to cry. Not over this. Not now. Not when everything else in my life is already spiraling.

Crying feels selfish. Weak. Like giving in to something I don't deserve. So I force myself forward.

I move on autopilot, body working even while my mind fractures. I splash cold water on my cheeks until they sting, hoping it'll shock the emotion out of me. I shove my hair into a messy knot that screams *I'm fine*. I dig through drawers for clothes that don't smell like sleep and guilt and nightmares I can't outrun.

I keep my breath even. I keep my hands from shaking. I make my face blank, smoothing over every crack threatening to show.

Hold it together. Hold it together. Hold it together. Because if I don't... I'm afraid of what might come spilling out.

By the time I'm at JP's office twenty minutes later, the mask is in place. Barely.

He's standing outside by the truck, arms crossed, pacing like he's been rewinding and replaying information in his head. He turns when he hears my footsteps and does a double take.

"You look like hell," he says.

I shrug, keeping my voice even. "Didn't sleep much."

"Yeah, no kidding."

He studies me—eyes narrowed, jaw clenched, reading me deeper than I want him to. I look away before he sees anything real.

A beat passes. He exhales hard through his nose, shoving a hand through his hair. "Whatever. We don't have time for this."

I stiffen. "For what?"

"For mood swings," he mutters, grabbing the truck door. "And you walking around like a zombie."

My teeth grind. "Thanks for the empathy."

He pauses, glancing back at me with a flicker of guilt, or maybe recognition that he pushed too far. But instead of apologizing, he hides it behind that stone expression of his. "Get in, Evelyn," he says quietly. "We have work to do."

I climb into the truck, forcing my breathing steady, even as my heart aches in a way he can't see—and can never know. Because if JP finds out I knew Travis... that I kissed him... I don't think I could live through his disappointment and the truth all at once.

I strap myself in, swallow every feeling clawing at my chest, and force the words out evenly: "I'm ready."

The silence between us settles in immediately. Three days of not speaking. Three days of avoiding each other. Three days of replaying the fight in my head, wishing I'd said less... or more.

The engine rumbles to life, and JP pulls onto the main road without a word.

I stare out the window, watching Ashford blur by. Houses. Trees. Streetlights. All of it feels distant, unreal. Finally, I can't take the silence anymore.

"Why didn't you call me sooner?" I ask, my voice sharper than I intend. I keep my eyes glued to the passing scenery. "If there was another missing person."

149

He drums his fingers on the steering wheel. "You weren't answering." A beat. "And I didn't think you wanted to talk."

He's not wrong, but the truth lands heavy and sour in my throat. "You should've called anyway," I mutter.

JP glances at me—quick, assessing. "Would you have picked up?"

I clamp my lips shut. He hums under his breath, a sound that says *exactly*. But he doesn't push. He never pushes. He just lets the distance stretch between us, like it doesn't bother him that it's there.

The drive drags on—long, winding, tense. Every mile feels heavier than the last. My leg bounces in agitation. JP notices. His jaw ticks, but he keeps his focus on the road.

Eventually, the pavement dissolves into dirt, and the trees grow thicker, swallowing the sky. The air feels colder here—damp and heavy, like the woods know something is wrong.

After what feels like forever, JP eases the truck to a stop on an unmarked dirt road. The trees around us loom tall and ancient, twisted together so tightly they form a canopy that blocks out most of the light.

A thin strip of faded police tape hangs crookedly between two branches, flapping weakly in the breeze, barely holding on.

"We're here," JP says, pushing open his door.

I step out, pulling my jacket tighter around me. The woods smell like wet earth and old leaves, but underneath, something else lurks—something metallic and sour that makes my stomach twist.

"Forest Service guy tipped me off," JP says, circling to the back of the truck to grab his gear. "Said he saw strange activity out here the past few nights. Figures moving through the trees. Symbols carved into the bark."

150

A chill snakes down my spine. "Symbols?"

"Ashen symbols," JP says, his tone hardening.

My blood runs cold. Images flash in my mind: the tattoo carved into the cultist's arm, the sigil drawn in blood on the warehouse floor, the flames consuming the factory, Travis's laugh beneath the string lights.

My throat tightens. "So... the Veil was here."

"Still is," JP says, grabbing a flashlight. "Come on."

He doesn't see me flinch. Thank heavens he doesn't, because if he looks too closely he might see the truth written all over my face. The truth I can't let him know: that Travis isn't just another missing person. He was mine. If only for a moment.

We walk deeper into the woods, each step sinking into damp earth. Fallen leaves cling to my boots, sticking like the memories I've been trying to scrub off for days. The air grows colder, tighter... wrong.

Then, the smell hits. Rotten. Sour-sweet. My stomach flips violently. "Shit..." I whisper, covering my mouth.

JP's flashlight swings ahead in a tight arc. "Stay close," he warns, voice low.

"I know." The words tremble like they're barely holding themselves together.

We push through a final tangle of brush, branches snagging my jacket, scratching my skin—and then, everything stops. Everything.

A body is slumped against the roots of a massive tree, head tilted at an unnatural angle. Pale skin. Torn clothes. Eyes open—far too open—staring upward at nothing.

My heart stutters. The world tilts dangerously. Travis. For a second, I think I've said his name out loud. I haven't. Not yet.

My knees buckle, and I grab the nearest tree trunk, nails digging deep into the bark until my fingers sting. The rough wood bites into my skin, grounding me just enough that I don't collapse.

His face is still. So still.

His blond hair is matted with dirt and leaves, stuck to his forehead in dried streaks. His lips—blue, horribly blue—hang slightly parted like he had been trying to say something. His shirt is torn across the chest, revealing bruises that bloom dark across his ribs.

"Evelyn." JP's voice is softer now, gentler than I've heard it in months. "Don't go closer."

I can't move anyway. My gaze drops to Travis's wrist. Blood caked thick and dark. Skin carved open in deep, jagged lines. The Ashen sigil. Crescent. Flame. Broken line. The same symbol I drew for JP. The same symbol the cultist wore like a badge.

My breath catches in my throat, sharp and painful.

Travis. Travis. *Oh shit.*

I force myself to stand straighter, swallowing hard—pushing down the sob clawing its way up my chest. I wipe my face quickly, pretending it's just sweat. Pretending I'm not breaking.

JP steps beside me, arms folding across his chest. He studies the scene with a grim familiarity that makes me want to scream. "This is their work," he says quietly. "No doubt about it."

I nod stiffly, keeping my jaw clenched so tightly my teeth ache. "They marked him. He wasn't just taken... They wanted us to find this."

JP crouches, examining the symbols carved into the tree roots behind Travis—more of them, etched into the bark like warnings.

His voice drops into something colder. "Something worse is coming."

Worse. Worse than cultists. Worse than demons. Worse than whatever took Travis. I bite my lip until I taste blood. Anything to keep the emotion from spilling over. Because Travis's empty eyes are still staring upward, lifeless, wide open. Staring at the sky like he's searching for answers he'll never get.

My heart quietly shatters in my chest. Silent. Painful. Shards slicing me from the inside out. And JP can't know a single piece of it. Not ever.

I climb in the truck first, shutting the door a little harder than I mean to. I stare straight ahead, blinking fast so the tears gathering at the corners of my eyes don't spill over. The smell of the woods— damp soil, rotting leaves, decay—clings to me.

JP climbs in beside me, but he doesn't start the engine. Instead, he just sits there, staring at the steering wheel like maybe whatever answers he's looking for are carved into the plastic.

After a moment, he exhales—long, slow, heavy. "Evelyn... talk to me."

My fingers twist into my jacket. "About what?" My voice comes out flat, foreign.

"You've been distracted for days," he says carefully. "Quiet. Off. Something's bothering you. If you'd just—"

"I said I'm fine." The lie burns like swallowing fire.

JP's eyes flick toward me, clouded with worry. He studies my face, reading every twitch, every tremor. His lips press into a thin line. "Don't shut me out," he says, voice quieter. "Not like this."

A bitter laugh rips out of me before I can stop it—sharp, humorless, ugly. "You have *no right* to say that."

JP's jaw clenches. He looks away first.

"Evelyn…" He rakes a hand through his hair, fingers trembling faintly. "There's a reason I can't tell you everything yet."

"Then *start explaining*," I snap, turning toward him. My hands shake in my lap, but I don't hide them. "Why do they want me? Why are they back? What the hell do they see in me that I can't see? What am I missing? What aren't you telling me?"

He flinches—not from anger but from something else. Pain. Guilt. Fear.

He closes his eyes, inhaling slowly like he's bracing himself. When he opens them again, something shutters behind them. He retreats. Emotion gone. Walls up. Stone. Steel. Unmovable.

"I can't," he says quietly.

My breath catches. "Can't… or *won't*?"

"That doesn't matter right now."

"It matters to *me*! I'm the one they're hunting. I'm the one they carved symbols for. I'm the one who—" My voice breaks, and I snap my mouth shut before the truth spills out.

He watches me. Something in his eyes softens, but he doesn't move, doesn't reach out, doesn't let his mask slip further.

154

"I'm trying to protect you," he says softly.

"That's the problem," I whisper, voice hoarse. "You're so busy protecting me, you won't even tell me what I'm supposed to be protected *from*."

JP looks away again, jaw flexing like he's grinding down words he refuses to say. He's keeping secrets. Even after this. Even after Travis.

Something inside me fractures. "Then I guess we're done talking," I whisper.

JP swallows hard, throat bobbing. For a moment, his hand hovers over the ignition, frozen like he's fighting himself, trying to find something—anything—to say.

Instead, he turns the key and the engine roars to life, harsh in the tense silence.

As JP pulls away from Briar Hollow, the woods disappear behind us, swallowed by the darkness. I keep my eyes glued to the window, watching the blur of trees and road and shadows slipping past like ghosts.

Nobody speaks. We don't even breathe in sync anymore.

There's a pressure sitting on my chest like someone's stacked bricks there, one by one. Travis's face won't leave my mind. His eyes open, staring. His wrist carved.

The Ashen sigil.

My fault. Because I let myself get close. Because I let myself feel anything. I dig my nails into my palms until pain shoots up my arms.

"You're doing that thing again," JP mutters suddenly.

I blink. "What thing?"

155

He keeps his gaze forward, knuckles white on the wheel. "The thing where you go quiet and start blaming yourself for everything that goes wrong within a ten-mile radius."

I clench my jaw. "Maybe if you told me what I am—why they want me—I wouldn't have to guess."

"I told you," he says, voice low. "You're not ready."

I whisper it before I can stop myself: "Travis wasn't ready either. He didn't deserve this."

JP freezes. The shift is instant. "You knew him?" he asks carefully.

Shit. I swallow hard. "No—I mean, not really. Just... seen him around town." My voice cracks on the lie. I hate that it does.

JP studies me harder now, intently. "Evie."

"I said I'm fine." I force steel into my tone. "Can we not do this right now?"

He lets out a slow breath, like he knows I'm lying and hates it, but also knows pressing will just push me further away.

He turns onto Main Street and I stare out the window, blinking against the tears I refuse to let fall.

After a while, he speaks again. "You should've told me if you knew him."

I stiffen. "I said I didn't."

"You're lying," he says softly. Not accusatory—hurt. "You don't lie to me."

I look straight ahead. "You lie to me all the time."

The truck falls silent again. By the time we pull into the lot near the office, I can't tell if I'm angry or heartbroken or just empty. JP puts the truck in park but keeps his hand on the key. "Evelyn... I'm trying to protect you."

"From what?" I whisper. "From the truth? From myself?"

He hesitates. "No. From everything else."

I open the door, not wanting to hear more. Not wanting him to see the cracks.

"Goodnight, JP."

"Evie—"

I shut the door before he can say another word. I turn away from JP and head toward my bike, refusing to look back.

The night air is sharp against my cheeks and my hands shake slightly when I fit the helmet on, but I hide it, even from myself. The engine growls to life beneath me—familiar, grounding—but tonight even that comfort feels thin.

Ashford at night is quiet—too quiet. Houses dim. Stores dark. The kind of stillness that feels less like peace and more like waiting.

A few blocks out, the feeling hits me. A prickle at the base of my skull. A shift in the air. Like a gaze pressing into the back of my spine. I slow just a little, scanning my mirrors. Nothing. Just empty road. Just shadows. Still, my pulse skitters.

The sensation deepens—something unseen pacing me from the dark, just out of sight. Not following on foot, not following in a car. Just... *there*. Watching.

I tighten my grip on the handlebars. "If someone's out there," I mutter into my helmet, "knock it the hell off."

The night answers with silence.

The chill creeps in deeper, crawling under my jacket. I twist the throttle and speed up, the engine screaming beneath me. The wind stings my eyes, tears threatening to spill.

But the feeling that I'm being watched doesn't leave. Not until I turn onto my street. Not until my house comes into view. Not until I pull into the driveway and kill the engine. Then—like someone flipping a switch—it's gone.

I sit for a moment in the quiet, the ticking of the cooling engine the only sound. My breath shudders. My hands shake as I pull off my helmet.

Inside, the house is dim. Dad's uneven snores rumble from his room. The smell of stale beer clings to the walls. I head upstairs without turning on a light, each step heavier than the last. As soon as I reach my room, I shut the door behind me. And everything breaks.

My knees buckle, and I slide down the wood until I'm sitting on the floor, back pressed to the door like I'm trying to keep the whole world out. My breath comes out in ragged gasps, too fast, too shallow. I press my hands to my face, but the tears slip through my fingers anyway.

Travis's empty eyes. The sigil carved into his wrist. The shadows in the woods. The feeling of being watched. And JP's voice in the truck: *I'm trying to protect you.*

I choke on a sob, burying my face in my knees, trying to smother the sounds before they reach anyone—before they reach Dad and wake him up.

But the tears won't stop, not this time. Not after Travis's body in the forest. Not after the kiss I'll never get back. Not after the secrets JP carries like anchors around my neck. Not after feeling hunted all the way home.

For the first time in a long time, I don't feel strong. Or fast. Or special. I feel small. Breakable. Alone.

I curl in on myself on the floor as the tears keep falling, quieter and quieter, until exhaustion finally drags me under.

And even then, the fear follows me into sleep.

Chapter 11

Close Calls

The woods are quiet in the dream—too quiet. Moonlight filters through the trees in thin silver blades, slicing across the forest floor. My boots sink into wet moss, each step swallowed by silence. I know this place—recognize the gnarled roots, the sharp bend in the creek—but something's wrong. The air feels heavy, still.

And then, I see him: Travis.

He's sprawled against a tree, head tilted in a way that makes my stomach twist. His skin is ash-pale, his lips cracked open like he tried to speak but couldn't. There's blood at the corner of his mouth—dry, dark, too much.

"Travis?" My voice sounds small, childlike. "Hey. Hey, wake up."

No response.

I kneel beside him. The air smells of copper and rot and something sweet—like burning flowers. His arm lies across his chest, sleeve torn. That's when I see it: a mark carved into his wrist.

The same one I saw on the demons. The same twisting lines. The same impossible geometry that seems to move when I look too long.

The mark pulses—once, twice—like it's alive. Then, his eyes snap open, and they're black.

I scream.

Smoke explodes from his mouth, filling the woods, rushing down my throat. The trees catch fire. Flames lick up the bark, the world collapsing into heat and screaming metal. Travis's voice echoes through it all, not his own anymore.

"They want you, Evelyn."

The fire surges, and I wake up choking on smoke that isn't there.

The sound of crackling wood fades. The scream of bending steel, the burned-skin smell—it all fades when my eyes open, leaving only the stale air of my bedroom and my heart hammering, trying to escape from my chest.

Another nightmare.

My pillow is damp, sticking to my cheek. My hands won't stop trembling as I shove my hair out of my face, fingers catching in sweaty tangles. Sleep stopped being restful weeks ago—now, it's another warzone. Every night, I'm dragged back into the same hell: fire and shadows and my mother's hand slipping from mine as the world around us collapses.

Some nights it's worse. Some nights it's Travis slumped against a tree in the woods, carved open and lifeless, eyes empty in a way that feels like a warning meant for me.

But today feels different. The fear doesn't just sit heavy—it coils. Tighter. Smaller. Meaner.

Like something is circling closer, aware of me now in a way it wasn't before. Watching from the edges of sleep, waiting for the moment I'm too tired to fight back. The Veil doesn't want Ashford. They don't want power. They don't want chaos for the sake of chaos. They want *me*.

And whatever they're planning—whatever they're preparing for—they're getting closer.

The nightmares aren't dreams anymore; they're warnings. And I'm running out of time to ignore them.

Morning light leaks through the blinds, cutting my room into gold and gray. I push out of bed, every muscle stiff like I fought someone in my sleep. My reflection in the mirror looks worse than I feel— dark circles, hair wild, a thin red mark where I must've clawed at my own neck in the dream.

I splash cold water on my face until my skin tingles. For a second, I can almost pretend the circles under my eyes are from long shifts at the café; not from the monsters that stalk my subconscious.

The faucet creaks when I turn it off. Silence again. Just the soft hum of the refrigerator downstairs, and the old pipes complaining through the walls.

I grab a towel and stare at myself in the mirror. "You're fine," I whisper. "You're fine." The lie feels thinner every morning.

I pull on jeans, a black T-shirt, and my Bean & Gone apron. Routine helps. Pretending helps. Anything helps.

My hair goes up into a ponytail, fingers moving on muscle memory even though my hands are unsteady. The necklace my mother gave me goes on last—cool against my skin, settling just above my collarbone. One of the few things that still makes me feel human. Or reminds me I once was.

For a second, I imagine walking into work and telling Maya everything. Telling her about the nightmare. About the fire. About Travis—what I saw, what I *think* I saw, the way guilt keeps dragging me underwater every time I think about him.

But the thought of saying it out loud makes my throat close. How do you tell someone your biggest fear is that you didn't just imagine a boy dead in the woods—but that it was a message? How do you admit you kissed someone who might now be dead because of you?

I want to talk to her. I just... don't know how.

Downstairs, the air smells like old wood and coffee grounds. My dad's still asleep—or passed out. I don't check which. The quiet around him has become its own kind of caution.

Sunlight hits my eyes when I step outside, almost mockingly bright. It's the kind of morning that dares you to believe things are normal. That dares you to let your guard down.

I force a smile I don't feel, grab my keys, and head for the door. If the Veil is coming, they won't find me hiding in bed.

By the time I reach the coffee shop, the morning rush is already in full chaos mode. The line snakes from the counter all the way to the door. People are talking over each other, tapping feet, scrolling on phones, barking out orders like caffeine is oxygen and they're suffocating without it.

The espresso machine screams like it's dying. The grinder whirs nonstop. Someone's already spilled something sticky on the floor and tracked it halfway across the shop.

Typical Monday.

I drop my bag under the counter, cinch my apron tight, and smooth a few stray strands behind my ear. Then, I look at the schedule pinned beside the espresso machine.

Maya should've clocked in ten minutes ago. She's never late.

I pull out my phone, thumb hovering over her name. Call. Text. Repeat.

Nothing. Not even a half-asleep "brb" or one of her chaotic sunrise selfies with captions like *"why am I awake pls end me."*

I check the screen again—no response. Read receipts off. My stomach dips hard.

Maya always texts back. Even when she's hungover and swearing she'll "never drink again (lies)." Even when she's mad at me for stealing her favorite mug at work. Even when she's being dramatic and insisting she's "dying of heartbreak because Brad didn't text back so obviously he's in love with someone else and she needs to move to France." Especially then.

But now? Silence.

A cold thread slips through my ribs, tightening with every passing second. I glance at the door. At the empty parking spot where her beat-up red hatchback should be. At the counter where she'd normally be shoving pastries at customers while narrating her morning like she's hosting a podcast.

Nothing. Something is wrong.

But the shop doesn't care about my anxiety—it keeps moving. Milk steaming, grinders whirring, orders piling up. Like the world hasn't just shifted once again under my feet.

"Order for Carson!"

"Where's my oat latte?"

"Miss, I ordered this extra hot—this is only medium hot."

"Uh, sure, Karen." Maya usually mutters that part. Today it escapes my mouth under my breath.

I shove the unease down like espresso grounds and push through the rush, slinging drinks left and right. Lattes, americanos, mochas, macchiatos—my hands fall into autopilot even though my brain is miles away. The steam burns my wrist. Milk splatters my apron. Someone snaps at me for mixing up their drink when they definitely ordered it wrong.

We're short-handed, and it shows. We're behind on every order. The pastry case is nearly empty. A line of mobile orders keeps blinking angrily on the tablet.

164

I'm doing the job of three people, and all I can think about is: Where is Maya? Why isn't she answering?

Every time the door opens, I look up, expecting to see her bright curls bouncing through the crowd, that sunbeam grin lighting up the room as she apologizes for oversleeping or forgetting her phone.

But she never walks in.

The bell rings. Another customer enters. A cold, sour feeling creeps deeper into my chest.

By the time the rush finally slows and the line dwindles to two bored teens arguing over frappé flavors, I'm sweating, shaking, and barely holding onto the fake-smile mask I plastered on.

Maya's absence isn't just inconvenient; it's terrifying. Maya doesn't go missing. Not in Ashford. And definitely not without telling me.

By the time my shift ends, I'm barely holding myself together. My hands shake as I untie my apron. My stomach is one huge, tight knot. I keep replaying the moment I looked down at the schedule and saw Maya's name, empty. The silence on the other end of the phone. The unread messages.

And beneath all of it, Travis's dead eyes staring at me from the dream, black and bottomless.

What if the same thing happened to her?

What if she's lying in the woods somewhere?

What if I'm already too late?

Nausea bubbles up my throat. I call Maya again as I walk to my bike. Straight to voicemail. "Pick up, pick up, pick up—"

It clicks to her recorded greeting. My heart drops.

"Maya, it's me," I whisper. "Call me, okay? Please. Just... call." My voice cracks on the last word. I end the call before it can break more.

I don't go home. I don't think. I rev the engine and tear out of the parking lot. The wind slams against me as I speed through Ashford's narrow streets, tears forcing themselves from my eyes even as I pretend they're from the cold. Houses blur by. Storefronts whir past in streaks of color. Everything feels too slow and too fast at the same time.

Travis's lifeless body flashes in my mind. His wrist. That mark. Burning. Moving.

"No," I breathe, shaking my head hard. "No, no, no—she's fine. She has to be." But the panic in my chest only grows.

I skid into Maya's neighborhood, gravel spitting under my tires. Her house is small and cute—white shutters, flower boxes her mom redoes every season. It should feel warm. Lived in.

Today it looks dead. The curtains are drawn tight. No music drifts through the windows. No shoes have been kicked off by the porch steps. No laughter. No Maya singing off-key like she always does when she's bored.

My heart slams painfully as I knock. "Maya?"

Silence tightly wraps the house. I knock harder. "Maya, it's me. Open the door."

Nothing.

I press my ear to the wood. No footsteps. No movement. Not even the hum of the TV. The air feels wrong. Too still. My pulse spikes. Something claws at my insides.

I circle around the house, slipping through the side gate. The latch sticks, like it hasn't been opened in hours. Maybe longer.

The backyard looks painfully normal—garden pots lined in neat rows, a faded hammock swaying lazily even though there's no wind. It should comfort me. It doesn't. Not even a little.

I step toward the back porch—and something glints in the corner of my eye. A scorch mark. Burned into the wooden step. A symbol. No—*the* symbol. Jagged, looping lines. Half-circle. Radiating slashes. Exactly like the one on Travis's wrist.

My blood runs ice-cold. I can't breathe. The Ashen Veil was here.

I stumble back, shaking so hard my teeth click. The smell of burned wood creeps into my nose, and suddenly I'm in the woods again—Travis's corpse, the mark pulsing, his dead mouth whispering my name.

They found her. They took her. Because of me.

"Oh no," I whisper, gripping the porch railing. "Maya..." The edges of my vision pulse. My knees threaten to give out. *This is my fault. They're coming after her because of me.*

The symbol sits on the step like a brand. A promise. They're closing in.

I crouch low, heart hammering, the scorched Veil mark still glowing faintly against the porch step. I don't dare touch it again—my fingertips still buzz from the heat.

My phone is already in my hand. JP's contact stares back at me. I should call him. I should call him right now. He would know what to do. He always—

A flicker at the edge of the yard freezes me mid-breath. Something moves between the hedges. My thumb hovers over JP's name, but instinct screams louder. I don't call him. I look up.

A hooded figure stands half-shadowed beneath the trees, robes black as oil, face swallowed by darkness. No features. No eyes. No humanity. A void wearing the shape of a man.

A cold, crawling chill spiders up my spine—but before I can even breathe, the void moves, and Maya steps into view.

Her wrists are bound with rough cord, skin reddened where she's fought against it. A gag cuts across her mouth, too tight, biting into her cheeks. Her eyes are wide—wet, terrified, pleading. Her hair, usually a wild halo of curls, hangs tangled and dirty, plastered to her face. She stumbles when the cultist yanks her closer, knees buckling like she's barely conscious.

My blood turns to fire.

"MAYA!" The scream rips out of me raw, cracking in the cold air.

She jerks toward the sound, muffled cries shredding through the gag, her whole body straining just to reach me. The cultist snarls—a guttural, rattling sound far too deep, too broken to be human—and drags her backward into the line of trees.

A trap. I know it's a trap. Everything about this is wrong—too perfect, too deliberate, too pointed. Maya isn't bait by accident. She's bait because of me. But the thought barely flashes before adrenaline detonates in my veins, turning fear into something sharp and blinding.

I move.

I vault the fence in one violent surge—the wood scraping deep grooves into my palms—but I barely feel it. I hit the ground hard, but momentum shoves me forward into a sprint.

My knife is in my hand before I even register drawing it, metal glinting with the promise of violence.

Trap or not, I'm going in. Because Maya is screaming for me. Because she trusted me. Because I will burn the whole world down before I let them take someone else.

"Let her GO!" I snarl.

The cultist whips around, a curved blade materializing in his grip as if pulled straight from the shadows themselves. His head snaps toward me, and for one fractured second, the void where a face should be tilts—aware, locked on me, like I'm the only thing in the clearing that matters.

Then, with a vicious, effortless motion, he throws Maya aside. She hits the ground hard, skidding across dead leaves and dirt, her shoulder slamming into a fallen log. She cries out, her bound wrists tangling beneath her as she tries to push herself up. The sound punches the air from my lungs.

Rage explodes inside me.

The cultist doesn't hesitate. Doesn't pause. Doesn't even look at her again. He lowers into a predator's stance, blade catching the faint moonlight. Then, he charges.

I slide low across the grass—feel it tear beneath my palms—and duck under his first swipe. The blade slices a lock of my hair, glinting in the afternoon light.

He swings again, vicious and wild. This time I'm ready. I catch his wrist mid-arc, yank him forward, and drive my knee into his ribs— once, twice, *three times*. The crack is loud, sickening, vibrating up my thigh.

He hisses, staggering, but he doesn't go down. Fanatics never do. He lunges again, blade flashing. I twist sideways, feel the steel graze my shoulder—a burning line of pain—and drive my elbow into his temple. The impact rattles up my arm hard enough to numb my fingers.

Maya screams into her gag, the sound strangled and terrified.

I pivot toward her, breath tearing from my throat. She's sprawled in the dirt where he threw her, wrists bound, hair plastered to her cheeks with tears and sweat. Her eyes lock onto mine—panicked, pleading.

I drop to one knee beside her for half a heartbeat, hands shaking as I grip her arms. "Hey—hey, I've got you." I haul her upright, shoving her behind me with one arm while my other hand snaps up to block the cultist's next strike.

"Maya, GO!" I shout, forcing every ounce of command into the word.

She stumbles back, nearly face-planting, catches herself on trembling legs, then scrambles toward the yard—half-running, half-falling, terror turning her steps clumsy and desperate.

The cultist shrieks—a raw, animal sound that curdles the air—and throws his entire body at me with wild, murderous force.

I pivot, gripping his robe and using his momentum to hurl him over my hip. He crashes into the dirt, breath whooshing out of him.

Before he can recover, I drop low and sweep his legs. He collapses sideways. I grab the side of his hood, slam my palm into his jaw as hard as I can. The snap echoes. He goes limp, writhing in the grass, clutching his jaw.

I stand over him, chest heaving, knife poised. One more strike. One thrust to the throat, and he'd never hurt Maya again.

But Maya is watching. Terrified. Confused. Her hands shaking uncontrollably. And suddenly, I can't. I lower the knife, my own breath trembling.

"Stay down," I warn the cultist—though he's barely conscious. My voice shakes with adrenaline and something darker: the knowledge that he wanted Maya only because they want me.

I turn towards her. "Maya," I breathe, rushing back into her yard to untie the gag. "It's okay. You're okay. I've got you." But even as I say it, even as she sobs into my shoulder, I know it's a lie. Maya's cries shake both of us, her fingers clutching my shirt like she's terrified I'll vanish if she lets go. And maybe she's right. Maybe she should be terrified. But I can't help her yet. Not until I'm sure the man is down. Not until I know he can't follow.

"Maya, stay right here," I whisper, forcing a calm I absolutely don't feel. "Don't move." She nods, trembling violently, tears streaking down her dirt-smeared cheeks.

I step back into the tree line, toward the cultist, knife still clenched so tightly in my fist my knuckles ache. He's trying to push himself up—slowly, clumsily—one arm shaking beneath him. His jaw hangs crooked, like its hinge has snapped. Each breath comes out in a wet, rasping wheeze that curls sickeningly in my stomach.

He's alive, but barely. And it's not good enough. If he gets up—if he calls for the others—Maya is dead. I'm dead. We don't get second chances with people like this.

I tighten my grip and drive the heel of my boot into his temple with everything I have left. There's a crack. A shudder. Then, nothing. His body collapses into the grass with a dull thud, limbs slack, head rolling slightly to the side.

My hands start shaking immediately.

A wave of nausea rises hard and fast, bile burning the back of my throat. I swallow it down. Hard. I can't afford guilt. Not now. Not when the shadows are still alive with danger. Not when Maya is somewhere out there alone and terrified.

I force myself to breathe: one sharp inhale, one ragged exhale.

Then, I yank out my phone with trembling fingers, nearly dropping it. My thumb fumbles across the screen, smearing dirt and sweat. No time. No room for panic. I need help. I need someone to pick up before the world falls apart again. I need JP. I quickly send a text.

Evelyn: *Found Veil at Maya's house. Handled it. Come NOW.*

I tuck the phone away and turn back to Maya. She's pressed against the porch railing, knees drawn up, eyes blown wide with terror. My throat closes. She's my normal. My last thread to anything human. If I lose her… If the Veil takes her because of me…

No. I can't let that happen.

I kneel in front of her, lifting her chin gently, forcing my voice soft even though my pulse is a jackhammer.

"What—what the hell was that?" she gasps, breath hitching. "Evelyn, he—he came out of nowhere, and his face—his face wasn't—"

Think, Evelyn. Think fast. Lie. Lie beautifully. "Probably just a drugged-out creep," I say, steadying my tone.

Her eyes widen more. "Drugged-out? He tried to *kidnap* me!"

"Yeah." I swallow. "I heard Ashford's been seeing more break-ins lately. He probably thought no one was home." It's flimsy. Weak. The worst lie I've ever told her. But it's all I have.

She shakes her head frantically. "But his face—it wasn't even human. It was just… black. Like a void."

Shit.

"Shock," I say quickly. "Fear messes with your head. I bet you'll remember more clearly later."

She trembles harder, clutching my arm. "He whispered something," she breathes. "Before he grabbed me. I don't know what language it was, but I did understand one thing and it—it felt like it was meant for you."

Ice knifes straight through my spine. My lungs seize. "What did he say?" My voice is almost soundless.

Maya squeezes her eyes shut, tears falling. Then she whispers, voice breaking: "Forsaken."

The word hangs between us like a plate of glass catching the light. I blink. "Forsaken?" The syllables feel foreign on my tongue. Heavy. Ominous. "I... I've never heard that before."

Maya's eyes snap open, wet and frantic. "He said it like—like he knew you. Or like you were supposed to know what it meant."

A cold weight settles low in my stomach. Why would a cultist say that to *her*? Why would he say it about *me*? "Maybe..." I swallow hard. "Maybe you misheard."

She flinches. "I didn't mishear, Evelyn! He looked right at me when he said it. Like it was aimed at you." Her voice cracks. "Like... a warning."

My pulse skitters. I force the panic down, bury it deep. "We need to get you inside," I say, reaching for her hand. But she jerks back. Not from fear of what *he* did. From fear of *me*.

"Evelyn—what the hell is going on?" she demands, voice trembling. "Who *was* that guy? Why does he know who you are? And—and how did you...?" Her breath hitches. "How did you fight like that?"

My heart stutters painfully.

Maya swallows, eyes wide. "You moved like—like someone in a movie. You flipped him. You broke his—" She clamps a hand over her mouth, gagging at the memory. "You were so fast. Strong. Like you knew exactly what to do."

I freeze. She saw too much. Way too much. "Maya—" I start, but she cuts me off.

"No. No, Evelyn, what aren't you telling me?" Her voice rises, shaky but insistent. "You work at a coffee shop! You bail on plans, you say you're tired, you disappear for hours—fine, whatever. But *that*?" She points toward the yard, toward the unconscious cultist hidden behind the garden pots. "That wasn't normal. That wasn't even close."

Her chin trembles, and seeing the way I've wounded her hurts more than any blade I've taken. "Maya," I whisper, stepping closer. "Please. Listen to me."

Her eyes soften just barely—a tiny crack in her fear—but she doesn't move. I take a shaky breath. I have to lie. I *have* to.

"I've been taking self-defense classes for years. You know that." It's flimsy. Weak. Her expression crumples with disbelief.

"Evelyn, that wasn't self-defense." She wipes at her face with trembling fingers. "That was like... like you were trained. Or like this has happened before."

I swallow the guilt. Hard. My throat aches with everything I can't tell her. Everything that would drag her deeper into the darkness already reaching for her. "I'm not... anything special," I lie softly. "I just... reacted."

The hurt in her eyes twists deeper. Then, she whispers, voice barely audible: "Why would he say that word to me? *Forsaken*... Why me?"

I shake my head slowly, heart pounding. "I don't know," I whisper honestly. "I swear, I don't know." And that's the truth that terrifies me most.

Because if *I* don't know, if JP never told me, if the Veil knows words for me I can't even recognize, then everything is shifting faster than I'll be able to survive.

I reach out again, gentler this time. "Come inside. Please. You're shaking. We'll figure it out. I won't let anything happen to you."

Maya hesitates, then finally, slowly, she lets me touch her hand. But the trust there is fractured. And the fear in her eyes isn't just about the man who grabbed her. It's about me, too.

I pull Maya inside, locking the back door behind us. She's still shaking, fingers twisting in the hem of her shirt as she tries to breathe through the terror.

"Sit," I murmur softly, guiding her to the kitchen stool. She obeys like she's sleepwalking, eyes glazed and distant. I grab a glass of water, but she can barely hold it, her hands trembling too hard.

Her voice cracks. "He—he would've dragged me into the woods. Evelyn, I—" A sob cuts her off.

"I know." My own throat tightens. "You're safe now. I promise." But the promise feels like a lie as soon as it leaves my tongue. I hover beside her, trying to calm her, trying to pretend I have this under control. But my gaze keeps dragging toward the back window.

I can still feel the cultist's presence out there. Still smell the smoke from the burned sigil. Still taste the panic in the back of my throat.

A flicker of movement flashes across the yard. My breath catches. A figure slips along the fence. Large. Broad-shouldered. Moving with deadly, quiet precision. JP.

I see the outline of him only for a second—his profile in half-shadow, the practiced crouch as he kneels beside the unconscious cultist, the glint of metal in his hand from some tool or blade.

He doesn't look toward the house. Doesn't hesitate. Doesn't need instructions. He's already doing what he came to do—getting rid of the threat, the evidence, the mess I caused by existing. My stomach buckles painfully.

In the next heartbeat, he drags the cultist behind the shed, disappearing from view. Moments later, another faint movement—he's wiping the scorch mark. Erasing the truth as efficiently as the Veil had carved it.

175

Maya doesn't notice. She can't even lift her head. Her whole body shudders like she's freezing. "Evelyn?" she whispers hoarsely. "Why—why did he say that word? Why me?"

I force myself away from the window, away from the familiar shadow cleaning up the carnage. "I don't know," I lie.

Her eyes search mine, desperate and afraid. "And how did you— how did you fight him? You moved like you—like you've done this before."

My breath stutters. I can see the suspicion in her eyes. The hurt. "Maya," I whisper, kneeling in front of her. "Listen to me. I just reacted. That's all."

She looks like she wants to believe me, like believing me might be the only thing keeping her from falling apart completely.

"Okay," she finally whispers, though her voice is thin and fractured. Before I can say anything else, I hear car tires screech to a halt outside. Maya's mom. Maya must have texted her while I was messaging JP.

We both jerk our heads toward the front window as the front door bursts open and her mom rushes in, panic splashed across her face.

"Maya! Oh my goodness—Maya!" Her mother wraps her up, sobbing into her hair. Maya collapses into her arms, a trembling mess of tears and gasps. I stand back, hands shaking, heart pounding. I'm relieved for her. But the guilt slams into me harder. Because if the Veil wanted Maya today, it's only because they couldn't get to me.

The next minutes blur together. Sirens. Police boots pounding up the walkway. Officers fanning through the house, asking questions that I lie my way through.

"Yes, he jumped the fence."

"No, I didn't see his face."

"Yes, he had a knife."

"Yes, I fought him off."

"No, I don't think he followed us inside."

Each lie feels like broken glass in my mouth.

Maya's mom clutches her daughter's trembling hands, insisting they go to the hospital "just to make sure she wasn't hurt." Maya nods weakly, her gaze flicking to me one last time. "You'll come by?" she whispers. "Promise?"

My chest aches. "I promise."

She gives a small, broken nod before her mom leads her out the door, officers escorting them to the car. The instant the engine starts and they pull away, the street goes quiet. Too quiet. I step outside. The afternoon light feels wrong—dim, heavy, like it's pressing on my lungs.

I grab the railing to steady myself. My fingers shake uncontrollably. My normal life is gone. Burned. Ash under my boots. They took Travis. They almost took Maya. And they said something—some word—meant for me. *Forsaken*. Whatever that means. Whatever I am.

I swing my leg over my bike. The engine roars to life beneath me, vibrating up through my bones. I'm done being kept in the dark. Done pretending everything's fine. Done letting people get hurt because of secrets I'm not allowed to know.

I grip the handlebars. My reflection stares back at me in the mirror—tired, angry, afraid, determined. If the Veil wants me, they can come get me. But next time, I won't be running.

I tear out of the driveway, the wind swallowing the last of my fear.

When I pull up outside JP's office, my bike sputters to a stop. The building is dark, silent.

His truck isn't here. The lights are off and the air feels abandoned. My chest tightens. "Great," I mutter under my breath. "Perfect timing."

I unlock the side door and head downstairs into the training room. The moment I flick the lights on, the old fluorescents hum awake, casting cold, clinical light across the mats. The emptiness hits me like a punch.

No JP pacing. No weight of his stare. No anchor to grab onto. Just me. And the echoes of everything going wrong.

I walk to the center of the mats, staring down at my bruised knuckles. They throb in time with my heart, each pulse reminding me of Maya's terrified face: her wide eyes, her trembling voice, the word that spilled from her mouth like poison.

Forsaken.

I still don't know what it means. I still don't know why the cultist said it. I still don't know why the Veil marked *her house instead of mine*. Nothing makes sense.

"If I don't figure out why they're after me..." My voice shakes. "If I don't figure out what they want..."

My throat tightens. "Maya could've died today." My hand curls into a fist, my nails biting into my palms.

I step in front of the heavy bag and press my forehead against the leather. "I don't even know what I am to them," I whisper. "I don't even know why this is happening."

I pull back and punch the bag.

Once. Twice. A third time so hard the chains rattle.

I hit it again. Harder. Faster. I hit until my knuckles scream, until the bag swings wildly, until my breath shreds in my throat.

"You almost took her," I snarl through my teeth, slamming my fist into the bag. *THUD.*

"You won't touch her again!" *THUD.*

"You won't touch anyone I care about!" *THUD.*

Sweat drips down my face. My arms ache. My whole body trembles with leftover fear and rage and confusion.

Finally, I stop, chest heaving, the bag swaying slowly like it's mocking me. "I'm done being hunted," I whisper, voice splintering. "I'm done not knowing."

But the words don't comfort me. They don't settle anything. They just hang there, heavy and hollow. I stare at my reflection in the mirror across the room—red-eyed, exhausted, fists raw and trembling.

"I'm strong," I murmur weakly. "Fast. Better trained than most." But even saying it, I feel smaller.

Forsaken.

A word that means nothing to me. And yet it terrifies me anyway.

I may be tougher than yesterday, sharper, more determined than ever—but I am still blind. Still clueless. Still exactly where the Veil wants me: off-balance, desperate, and grasping in the dark.

For now, this doesn't end in triumph. It ends with a single, brutal truth: If I don't figure out who I am and why they want me, everyone I love will suffer for it.

Chapter 12

Forsaken Echoes

The training room smells like old sweat and metal, and beneath it lingers the faint sting of disinfectant, sharp and chemical, trying and failing to mask the ghosts of fists and bodies that stained these mats long before I ever stepped foot in here.

The air flashes cold against my skin, each exhale forming a thin fog that hovers for a moment before dissolving into nothing.

It's the same as always, but tonight the room feels tighter. Smaller. Like the walls are leaning in, listening. Like the air itself is waiting for something to break. Like it knows something I don't— something it's trying to warn me about.

The heavy bag hangs in the corner of the room, swaying almost imperceptibly. Its chains groan softly each time the vent rattles overhead, a metal whisper that echoes in the back of my skull. The fluorescent lights above me hum and glitch, one bulb in the center flickering like it's struggling to cling to life.

The rubber of the mats is cold and unforgiving against my bare arches. My hands are wrapped, knuckles throbbing from earlier rounds—small pulses of pain that work like anchors, pulling me back from the edge of my spiraling thoughts. Every dull throb keeps me here in this moment, instead of drowning in the fear gnawing steadily at me.

If I stand still long enough, I swear I can feel the dark pressing right up against the windows.

I draw back my fist—*thud*.

The bag shudders backward. My shoulder stings as my arm recoils. Again. *THUD.*

My pulse picks up. The bruise deep in my ribs pulses with each breath, sharp and mean, reminding me I'm human.

Again. *THUD.*

My voice cracks between breaths. "Why?" My throat burns. "Why me? Why now? Why Maya?" The bag absorbs the hit, but the backlash runs up my arm like a shock—sharp, grounding, real.

I keep trying to put it all together, but the pieces won't fit. Travis's lifeless body. The demons. Those marks burned into walls and floors. The cultists whispering my name like they own it. Maya—tied, terrified, almost gone.

I punch again, harder, breath tearing in my lungs.

"Is it because I heal fast?" Another hit. "Or because I'm stronger than most?" Hit. "Is that it?" I slam my fist into the canvas, harder this time, and the chains rattle above me.

"That's not enough to make a demon cult drag a girl out of her backyard," I growl. *THUD.*

Sweat drips down my spine, sliding under my shirt. My breath shakes. The bag swings wildly before I catch it with both hands, steadying it. I lean my forehead against the rough canvas that smells like leather and salt and something old.

My voice drops to a whisper. "What do you want from me?" My fingers curl around the bag. "Why won't anyone just say it?"

Silence fills the room, thick and suffocating. The kind of silence that feels alive. Waiting. Then:

"Evelyn."

The voice cracks through the air like a whip. I spin, heart lurching into my throat.

JP stands in the doorway like a storm bottled inside a man. His shoulders are rigid, broad frame blocking out half the hall behind him. The dim light spills around him, casting his silhouette in hard lines, making him look larger, heavier, carved out of fury and restraint.

His eyes sweep over me—quick, precise, clinical. My stance. My breathing. The sweat dripping down my jaw. The raw, angry swelling blooming across my knuckles. Then, his gaze lifts and locks on my face.

The shift is small, but I feel it like a punch. His expression settles into something weighted, expectant, bracing—like he already knows what's coming. Like he's been waiting for this moment, this fight, this fracture between us. Like he knows we're about to blow each other apart, and he's already choosing which pieces he's willing to lose.

"We need to talk," he says quietly, but there's iron threaded through the softness.

I wipe sweat from my forehead with the back of my wrist, not breaking eye contact. "Thought you were busy cleaning up bodies."

His jaw twitches. A flash of something—annoyance, maybe hurt—cuts across his face before he smothers it.

"We need to talk," he repeats, stepping into the room. "Now."

I turn away, grabbing the bag like it might steady me. It doesn't. "I'm not talking until you do."

His boots thud once against the mats before stopping just at the edge: an invisible line drawn between us. "Evelyn—"

"No." My voice breaks—not from weakness, but from pressure. A fragile thing finally splitting.

"I'm done," I say, breath shaking. "I'm done being left in the dark. I'm done waking up every day wondering why demons know my name. I'm done watching people I care about get dragged into this shit—or hurt—because *you* think I'm too fragile to handle the truth."

The words spill out fast and fierce. I shove a few loose strands of hair back with my forearm, the gesture quick and impatient, anything to keep my hands from giving away my fear.

JP inhales sharply. His nostrils flare. "You think I'm doing this because I think you're fragile?"

"You won't tell me anything," I snap back instantly, the words spilling out hotter than I intend. "You dodge every question I ask. You shut down every conversation. You act like I'm going to break if you tell me the truth, like I'm still twelve." My voice cracks with anger I can't swallow. "So tell me—what else am I supposed to think?"

His composure fractures. A small crack, but enough. He steps fully onto the mats, closing the distance between us with slow, deliberate steps. "You think I want any of this?" he fires back. His voice isn't quiet anymore. It echoes off the concrete walls. "You think I enjoy watching you walk into the same nightmare that destroyed—?"

He cuts himself off. Not because he wants to. Because he has to. Because he almost said something he's spent years burying. His face flickers with emotion: fear, guilt, grief so deep it sucks the breath from the room.

He looks away for the briefest second, and in that moment, I see all of it. The weight. The history. The secret he refuses to give me.

It hits me like a punch to the ribs. Maya's terrified face flashes behind my eyes: her trembling hands, the bruise on her cheek, the way she whispered that horrible word. And suddenly everything inside me tilts.

My voice drops to a cracked whisper. "Destroyed *who*, JP?"

His eyes close, just for a heartbeat, but it's enough. Enough to see how the question hits him like a physical blow, how it knocks something loose from inside him. A flicker of pain crosses his face so quickly, I almost think I imagined it.

But he still doesn't answer. And the silence between us sharpens—thin, brittle, dangerous—like if either of us moves wrong, it'll slice us open.

I drag in a shaky breath, chest tight, lungs scraping for air that suddenly feels too heavy. I force myself to shift gears, to pull back before I corner him into shutting down completely. I know this look—I know it too well.

That locked-steel stare. The one where the shutters slam down behind his eyes. Where every emotion, every truth, every memory gets sealed away so deep, no one—not even me—can reach it.

When he looks like that, nothing gets in. Nothing gets out. And if I keep pushing... he'll disappear behind those walls again, leaving me in the dark with questions that burn holes in my chest.

I can't let that happen. Not when everything feels like it's unraveling at once.

So I change the subject. The only one that matters. "JP..." My voice softens before I can stop it. "She almost died today."

His eyes flicker. He closes them for a second, long enough to draw a breath that sounds heavier than his body should be able to hold. When he opens them, he looks... worn. Like someone scraped years off him all at once.

He nods. "Tell me everything," he says quietly. "All of it."

My throat tightens. I swallow hard. "Maya said the cultist, the one who grabbed her, he said a word."

JP's posture changes instantly—shoulders tightening, spine straightening, attention snapping into focus with military quickness. "What word?" he asks.

"Forsaken."

JP freezes. Not a flinch, not a twitch, but a full-body stillness. Like someone hit the pause button on him. My stomach twists. "What does it mean?" I whisper.

He looks away. Actually looks away. JP never looks away. "Nothing," he says softly. Too softly. "It's just a scare tactic—"

"Bullshit." The word erupts from me before I even think. "You flinched."

"I didn't—"

"JP." I step in front of him, blocking his exit, forcing him to look at me. "Tell me the truth."

He stares at me like I'm a door he's been standing in front of for years, hand on the handle, afraid of what comes out if he opens it. His eyes soften. Harden. Soften again. Finally, he exhales.

"I can't," he says, voice barely above a whisper. "Not yet."

Something inside me splits clean down the middle. "So, Maya almost dies," I breathe, "and you still won't tell me why?"

His voice cracks. Just slightly, but enough to gut me. "I'm trying to protect you," he says.

"That didn't protect *her*." My voice shakes with anger and hurt. "It didn't protect Travis. Or the woman from the factory. Or any of them."

His expression falters enough to reveal the fear tucked beneath the frustration, the panic he's trying so damn hard to hide. It flickers across his features like a shadow rippling through light— there and gone, but unmistakable.

185

Then, the silence falls between us. Thin. Dangerous. Neither of us moves. Neither of us breathes.

The silence says everything we can't.

JP is terrified—of losing control, of losing me, of truths he can't drag into the light. I'm furious—at the lies, at the secrets, at how he still treats me like I'm breakable when I've already been broken and remade in fire.

Both of us are standing on a line that won't hold forever. A fault line. A breaking point. And I can feel it trembling beneath our feet.

Finally, he exhales—long, rough, defeated. "One of my old contacts called," he says. "There's another victim. Two hours north. Same M.O. Same timing." His eyes are tired. "We need to go."

A scream begins to claw up the back of my throat—at him, for the secrets; at myself, for caring anyway; at the Veil, for tearing my life apart piece by piece.

But I stifle it and instead, I grab my jacket with fingers that won't stop shaking. "Fine," I mutter. "Let's go."

The truck hums softly as we pull onto the highway, the engine vibrating through the floorboards. Headlights stretch into the deepening fog, cutting a narrow, pale tunnel through the night. The road ahead looks endless.

I settle against the cold window, tapping my fingers against my thigh in a restless rhythm. I can't sit still, not when my mind is sprinting in circles I can't escape.

JP hasn't said a word in twenty minutes. Neither have I. But inside my head? A storm.

Why me?

Why the sigils?

Why the word "Forsaken"?

Why do the Veil speak like they've known me my entire life?

I steal a glance at JP. His knuckles are bone-white on the steering wheel, tendons standing out like ropes under his skin. His jaw flexes every few seconds—tight, grinding—like he's chewing down a memory he doesn't want surfacing. He has that look again... The one he gets right before a fight, or when something from the past forces its way too close.

The silence is thick enough to choke on. Heavy enough to smother both of us. It presses against my ribs until the pressure becomes unbearable.

"Why won't you tell me what you know?" The words barely make it out of my mouth.

He doesn't look at me. Not even a flicker of his eyes. His attention stays glued to the road ahead, jaw locked so tight I'm afraid it might crack.

"Because once I do..." He swallows hard. "...you can't come back from it."

A chill curls down my spine and settles low, spreading like ice through my stomach.

"That doesn't tell me anything," I whisper. My voice feels too small in the confined space of the truck. "That's not an answer."

It's an omen. And it terrifies me more than the truth he's withholding.

"It's the only one I have right now."

"That's not good enough."

His jaw tenses. "I'm trying, Evelyn."

I turn back to the window, bitterness burning at the edges of my eyes. "Try harder."

The words hit him. I see it in the flick of his eyebrow, the way his grip tightens even more. But he doesn't fire back. He just drives.

The fog thickens outside, blanketing the world in muted gray. The trees blur into shadowy streaks, bending under the weight of the wind.

I press my forehead against the window, feeling the vibration buzz through my skull. I don't want to be mad at him. I need him. I know that. But it's unbearable, the pain of needing someone who won't be honest with me.

"JP?" I try again, quieter this time. "Am I... in danger?"

He exhales through his nose. Not an answer. Not denial. Just a sound full of tension.

My chest tightens. "You know I can't do this alone."

For a second, just a second, his eyes soften. Then the wall slams back into place. "We'll handle it," he says. "Together." It sounds like a promise he doesn't know if he can keep.

By the time we turn down the old service road, night has swallowed everything. The truck's headlights sweep over trees sagging with moisture. Pine needles drip in steady rhythms, glistening like glass shards. Mud slicks the ground in thick ribbons, shining wet under the beams.

The police are long gone. What's left behind feels abandoned, like a scene the world has already turned its back on.

Deep tire tracks scar the mud, leading straight toward the clearing before veering away. Yellow caution tape sags between two warped posts, snapping weakly in the wind. It looks tired. Defeated. Like it knows it won't keep anything dangerous out.

The air smells like damp earth and pine sap. It stings a little, familiar and unsettling all at once.

JP kills the engine. The sudden quiet rings in my ears, leaving me painfully aware of every breath I take. We step out. My boots sink half an inch into the mud, cold water seeping through the seams. The trees around us are tall and silent, their branches dripping like they're shedding tears.

The air feels like the whole forest is holding its breath, waiting for us to step farther in. Waiting for whatever comes next.

And I can't shake the feeling that something is already watching.

I wrap my arms around myself against the chill, trying to steady my breath. "Where was the body found?" I ask, stepping beside JP.

He gestures with his flashlight, its beam cutting a pale circle in the darkness. "Just up ahead. Near the tree line."

I swallow hard. Another victim. Another one we couldn't save. And deep down, the creeping, icy fear whispers: *What if all of this is my fault?*

JP moves ahead, boots squelching softly in the mud. The beam of his flashlight catches on damp leaves, tangled roots, patches of disturbed soil. I trail close behind, trying to match the careful precision of his steps.

The woods are quiet. Too quiet. Even the insects seem to know not to move.

A cool breeze brushes against my face, and I tilt my head back instinctively, eyes drawn to the open sky above the treetops. The stars look impossibly bright tonight—scattered diamonds across an endless black sea. I exhale, the breath tight in my chest. *At least something looks normal.*

Then, JP stops so abruptly I slam into his shoulder.

189

"Warn me," I mutter, steadying myself.

But he doesn't reply. He crouches low, angling the flashlight toward the ground with slow, deliberate movement.

My stomach drops. Carved into the dirt—clean, perfect, impossible—is a sigil. Not scratched. Not smeared. Not hurried. Sliced into the ground with surgical exactness.

Concentric circles. Interlocking lines like veins. Sharp angles that fold into themselves. It hums with an energy I can't feel, but somehow *sense*.

"What the hell..." I whisper, crouching beside him.

JP doesn't answer. His face has gone pale—ghost-pale. The beam trembles in his hand. He reaches out with his gloved fingers and brushes the outer ring. He flinches.

"JP?" My voice pitches higher.

"This..." he mutters, throat tight, "is the same pattern we saw weeks ago. The door marking. The ritual circle." His jaw clenches. "It's identical."

A cold pressure blooms in my chest. *Identical.* The same symbol they chanted over. The same one that glowed like blood and fire.

JP exhales through his nose, slow and controlled, like he's bracing himself. "Volkov reached out this morning," he says, eyes scanning the tree line instead of me. "He finally told me what the symbols mean."

My pulse stutters. "And?"

He hesitates—just long enough to make my skin crawl—before answering.

"A locator glyph," he says quietly. "Used to find something." His gaze shifts to me, sharp and heavy. "Or someone."

The words punch the air out of my lungs.

"JP..." I swallow hard. "What were they tracking?"

He doesn't answer right away. His eyes dart to the trees.

"JP." I grab his sleeve. "What were they—?" A noise echoes through the air behind us. A wet, rattling inhale. We spin, weapons raised, but find nothing but darkness.

But that sound— We follow the trail deeper into the trees—broken branches, deep gouges in the mud, something dragged through the underbrush. The forest is unnervingly still. No distant birds. No rustling leaves.

JP raises his flashlight. The beam swings across trunks, briars, wet earth—then snags on something pale. At first, it looks like a body caught in the roots of a fallen tree. A deer, maybe. Or a person.

But then, the shape shifts. The skin is too gray. The limbs too long. The angles all wrong. JP lifts the light higher. And the creature comes into full view.

A demon is slumped against the fallen trunk like a broken marionette abandoned mid-performance. Its chest is split open, ribs cracked outward like snapped branches. Thick, tar-like blood oozes down its torso in slow, glistening rivulets, pooling black into the dirt. Flies cling to the wounds, but even they seem hesitant.

It's dying. Slowly. Horribly.

But its eyes—milky, luminous, glowing faintly like moons underwater—drag upward. And lock onto me.

Not JP. Me.

A shiver slices down my spine so sharp it steals my breath.

JP steps in front of me instantly, one arm sweeping out, protective and tense, his stance dropping into the familiar coil of someone ready to kill or die in the next heartbeat.

The demon's jaw twitches. Then, its lips peel back in a grotesque imitation of a smile—skin splitting, teeth cracked and jutting at unnatural angles. It lifts one mangled arm—bones exposed, flesh hanging. Shakily, spasming, the finger extends. Pointing. At me.

"Evelyn... Cross..." it croaks.

My lungs stop working. The forest tilts.

"Don't move," JP murmurs, voice low and lethal.

The demon gurgles a laugh, choking on its own blood. Its words slip out like poison: "The Key that breathes..."

My pulse stammers.

"The Forsaken Flame..."

My skin crawls.

"The doorway's... child..."

"No," I whisper, backing up a step. "No—what does that mean? What are you talking about?"

JP tenses beside me, blade angled down, gaze flicking between me and the creature like he's weighing whether to kill it or cover my ears.

The demon's eyes widen as it stares at me—like it's seeing something *in* me, something I don't know exists. "Yours..." it hisses, voice dissolving into a wet rattle, "...is the blood... that opens..."

It convulses violently, limbs jerking in unnatural spasms. Then, it collapses forward, black ichor spilling across the leaves. Dead. The forest goes still. Completely, utterly still. The silence presses against my ears until they ring.

My throat tightens. "JP...?" It comes out tiny. Childlike.

He doesn't answer. He doesn't even seem to hear me. Because he's staring—first toward the direction of the sigil burned into the forest floor, then at the demon, then at me.

His gaze flicks between the three like he's tracing invisible threads, threads that were separate until this moment, threads that now form a picture he's been terrified to see. A picture with me standing dead center.

A cold weight drops into my stomach. I can't breathe. Can't blink. Can't think. The world contracts into a suffocating tunnel where the only thing I can hear is the demon's last words echoing inside my skull:

The blood that opens...

And the way it said my name. Not like it had learned it. Like it *owned* it.

My skin prickles, heat and cold colliding under my ribs. Slowly—very slowly—I turn to JP.

His face is the color of bone, every ounce of warmth drained out of him. His eyes are blown wide, locked on me like I'm a threat he never trained for. His mouth is pressed into a bloodless line, lips tight, jaw working as if he's shredding words before he can speak them.

He's trying to hide it. Trying to hold the pieces together. Trying to stay strong for both of us, but I see it anyway: *fear.*

Not of the demon. Not of the sigil. Of *me.*

"JP..." My voice barely makes it past my throat. It comes out thin, trembling, like someone else is speaking through me. "Why did it know my name? Why did it... know *me*?"

He opens his mouth. For a fraction of a second, I swear he's going to tell me. Really tell me. All the things he's buried since the night he dragged me out of the fire.

193

His eyes soften—just once—like he knows he's standing on the edge of a truth so heavy it could crush both of us. But then, he swallows hard and shutters himself behind that soldier's mask again.

"We're leaving," he says abruptly, his voice tight. He grabs my arm—not roughly, but urgently. "Now."

"JP—" My voice cracks. I don't even know what I'm asking.

"Now, Evelyn." His voice *shakes*. JP's voice never shakes. The terror that grips me now has nothing to do with demons. Nothing to do with the dead body in the trees. Nothing to do with the glyph carved into the earth.

It's him. JP. The man who never cracks, never hesitates, never fears. And he's shaking.

Oh hell.

Volkov's voice slams into my mind like a fist: *She will be your undoing.*

Back then, I thought it was paranoia. I thought it was just Volkov being Volkov—dramatic and unhinged. But now... now the words wrap around my ribcage like barbed wire. What if I'm not just in danger? What if I' *am* the danger? To JP. To Maya. To everyone.

My breath hitches. "JP..." I whisper again, "Tell me what's happening to me."

Instead of answering, he pulls me toward the truck, eyes scanning the trees like something else might crawl out at any second. Something worse.

We walk back toward the truck in silence, if it can even be called silence. My heartbeat roars in my ears. JP's boots crunch too loud in the mud. The trees whisper in the wind like they're warning us away. The night feels wrong now. Crowded.

Every step we take feels watched.

The sigil behind us keeps pulsing in my mind, and the demon's last words echo in my body. *"Forsaken Flame... Doorway's child... Yours is the blood..."*

My breath catches, and I force myself to look around, to check the tree line, the branches, the shadows shifting in the fog.

Nothing moves. But I feel it: a prickle along my neck. Like cold fingers dragging lightly over my spine. Like eyes. So many eyes. "JP..." I whisper. "Do you feel that?"

"Yeah." His voice is low, clipped, the kind of calm that only comes right before everything goes to hell. He grips my elbow—not gently this time, but firm, grounding.

"Stay close," he murmurs.

We keep walking. Every crack of a twig makes my stomach twist. Every rustle of leaves tightens my throat. The fog thickens, curling around our legs, swallowing the path behind us. The truck is only twenty feet away, but it feels like a mile. JP unlocks it fast, scanning the shadows over his shoulder.

I swear I see movement—something dark slipping between the trees—but when I blink, there's nothing. Just the sky bleeding starlight through the fog.

"Get in," JP orders.

I climb in, shutting the door hard enough to rattle the frame. JP circles to the driver's side, every muscle coiled like he's expecting something to lunge out of the dark. He slides in, slams the door, and locks the truck instantly.

He starts the engine and the truck's headlights illuminate the woods. Nothing. No figures. No demons. No cultists. Just fog and trees. But the sense of being watched doesn't fade. If anything, it gets stronger.

JP grips the wheel, knuckles white. A muscle jumps in his jaw. "We're not alone out here."

"I know." But the worst part is I don't think whatever's watching us wants to kill us; I think it's waiting. For me.

JP throws the truck into gear. Gravel spits under the tires as we speed down the service road, leaving the sigil—and the dead demon—behind.

But the feeling stays. Heavy. Cold. Something out there knows my name. Knows my face. Knows what I don't. And it's getting closer.

Chapter 13

Ashen Assault

JP and I patrol near downtown as dusk bleeds into night, turning the sky a heavy, bruised purple that sinks low over the rooftops. The streetlamps blink awake one by one, shaky halos sputtering through the thinning branches overhead. The air carries the first real bite of early fall—cold enough that each breath slices a little on the inhale, crisp enough to sting down deep into my lungs.

Leaves, brittle and copper-bright, skitter along the pavement dragged by short, jittery gusts of wind. Their dry scraping trails behind us, between brick buildings and shuttered storefronts, a chorus of tiny claws scratching at the concrete.

Somewhere nearby, a chimney coughs woodsmoke into the air. The warm, nostalgic scent mingles with the damp, earthy smell of rain-soaked gutters and decaying leaves. It should feel comforting, this quintessential small-town autumn. But tonight, nothing about Ashford feels comforting.

The whole town feels brittle, like it's waiting for something to snap.

Shadows extend beneath flickering lamps. Shop windows reflect us back in distorted smears, warping our silhouettes with every ripple of light. Streetlights hum overhead, buzzing with a nervy, uneven rhythm. Every few steps, their glow dips—just slightly— like something unseen is crossing before the bulbs, dimming them in a single sweeping motion.

JP notices it too. I can feel him go rigid beside me, posture shifting, senses sharpening. Something is out there. Watching. Learning.

And the town, wrapped in its autumn shell of dying leaves and haunted quiet, feels one breath away from breaking.

I rub my chilled hands together, huffing out a dramatic sigh. "So, Maya keeps asking if I'm dead. I feel like I might actually be close."

JP nudges me with his elbow—the closest he ever gets to affectionate teasing. "You look alive enough."

"Oh wow," I deadpan. "Be still, my heart. Such flattery."

He snorts under his breath. "If you wanted flattery, you should've brought someone else."

"Trust me," I say, bumping his shoulder with mine, "if I had options, you'd be the last person I'd call."

"Liar," he mutters, but there's the faintest twitch at the corner of his mouth. Almost a smile.

"Maybe," I concede. "But we're pretending tonight, remember? Play along."

He shakes his head, but the tension in his shoulders eases just a hair. "Right. Pretending."

"Exactly. I'm thriving. Warm. Rested. Emotionally stable."

JP actually huffs a quiet, surprised laugh. "Now *that's* a lie."

I start to smile—a real one, small but genuine—

CLATTER.

Metal crashes behind us. Sudden. Violent. A trash can slams onto its side at the mouth of the alley, the echo knifing down the narrow brick corridor. The sound reverberates off the walls, slicing straight through the easy moment we'd managed to build.

The night goes still. Too still. JP's hand goes to his sidearm without a word, and my smile dies in my throat.

198

My pulse spikes instantly. "JP—"

He's already turning, already pulling out his Colt 1911 that he keeps holstered beneath his jacket. Then, movement explodes all around us.

Shadows peel off the walls in the form of three demons, lean and feral, their limbs sharp as snapped branches. They hit the pavement in lunges that look both too smooth and too broken for anything human.

The smell hits next—rot, demon ichor, cold earth, like something dug itself out from under a cemetery and hasn't stopped rotting.

They don't waste a breath. They rush us.

JP spins, his Colt flashing under the streetlight, a streak of polished steel catching the frigid night air. The gun's weight looks like an extension of his arm, steady and sure. I pivot beside him, knife drawn, adrenaline flooding my veins with a heat that clashes instantly with the cold.

The first demon lunges at me, all snapping jaws and spidery limbs. Its claws scythe toward my throat in a blur of motion. I duck just in time. The wind of its strike brushes my skin, like a gust of air pulled from a grave.

I drive my knee up into its ribs. There's a crack—bone, cartilage, something—and the demon staggers with a wet hiss, frosty breath bursting across my cheek. But it doesn't fall.

The second one drops from a stack of crates, landing with a metallic thud that rattles the alley. It slams me back against the wall hard enough to shake leaves loose from the gutters above. Pain arcs across my spine, sharp and electric.

It swipes, claws screeching across brick, sparks spitting off the wall. I slash upward, blade slicing across its forearm. Its blood splatters the wall—black, steaming, foul.

The demon shrieks, but instead of finishing the attack, it steps back. Circling. Watching.

"What the hell...?" I pant.

Behind me, the third demon lunges at JP. He dodges left and fires—*BANG*. The crack echoes down the alley, silver-etched round slamming into the demon's shoulder. Black ichor sprays across the pavement, sizzling in the cold.

The demon snarls, staggering—but not dead.

It could've followed up. It could've ripped into JP right then, but it doesn't. Instead, it leaps back, landing low, its body coiled like a tightened spring. Its gaze shifts—not to JP, not to the gun pointed steadily at its chest—but to me.

My stomach twists.

The first demon charges again. I pivot right, slash deep across its torso, and it collapses, choking on its own breath. But even dying, its gaze stays locked on me. Studying. Learning. Tracking.

JP fires again—*BANG. BANG.* Two crisp shots echo through the cold air.

But the last demon still doesn't fall. It dodges, fast and eerily fluid, as if it knew exactly when JP would shoot, like it was anticipating his timing. A cold dread sinks low in my gut.

They're observing. Collecting data. Running tests. On me.

We finish the last one together. JP grabs the demon's arm, twisting it sharply behind its back. The creature snarls, spine bending at an unnatural angle as it thrashes. JP drives it forward—straight into my waiting blade. The steel sinks in deep.

The demon screeches, the sound sharp enough to split the air. Its body convulses once, twice, then collapses. Black smoke pours from the wound, curling around our feet before disappearing into the cracked asphalt with a hiss.

The alley falls silent. My breath fogs in the air—ragged, sharp, shaking. My ribs ache with every inhale, and my pulse thrums against the inside of my throat.

JP wipes a smear of blood from his cheek with the back of his sleeve, his exhale steaming into the cold.

"They're sloppy," he pants. "Too sloppy."

I shake my head slowly, heart still hammering. "No." The word scrapes out, brittle. "Not sloppy. They had openings—plenty of them. They could've taken me out so many times but didn't." The chill in my voice has nothing to do with the temperature.

JP frowns, turning toward me fully now. "Then why didn't they?"

The wind whistles down the alley, cold enough to sting my eyes. I grip my knife harder, my fingers trembling. "They're not trying to kill us," I whisper. "They're trying to... *test* us."

JP's expression tightens, something dangerous flickering behind his eyes. His breath slows in realization. He shakes his head once.

"Not *us*," he says quietly.

A truth he doesn't want to say out loud, but can't hold back anymore: "Test *you*, Evelyn."

The words drop like ice into my stomach.

A gust of cold wind tears through the alley, whipping my hair around my face. It numbs my fingers, bites into my skin, but the chill running down my spine comes from somewhere deeper—somewhere instinct knows what my mind doesn't want to admit.

They weren't here to win. They were here to *learn me*. Every tell. Every weakness. Every instinct.

At night, I lie awake in the freezing dark, staring at the ceiling until the shadows start to shift. The leaves scrape across the windows like claws, and each whispering drag feels like breath on the back of my neck.

I don't sleep. Not even for a second. Because for the first time, I'm not afraid of the monsters in the dark. I'm afraid of what they think I am.

It's dusk. The old churchyard sits at the end of a narrow, crooked street—the kind where dead leaves gather in piles and never seem to blow away. The air is colder here, colder than the rest of town, colder even than it should be, biting clean through my jacket and threading ice along my spine.

The heavy stone chapel rises against the dimming sky, its silhouette jagged and severe. The stained-glass windows are dark, colorless in the failing light, like the irises of something long dead and still watching.

As we cross through the yard, our boots crunch against frost-tipped grass. The smell of damp earth clings to everything—rich and old and vaguely metallic, like the ground remembers too many burials. Moss crawls along the headstones of the chapel's cemetery, their carved names half-devoured by time.

The wind gusts through the trees, bending them just enough that their branches creak like old bones shifting in their graves.

CREEEAAAK.

The bell tower groans above us, a rusty hinge twisting in the wind. JP freezes mid-step and his hand drifts toward his holster. I look up. A shadow detaches from the steeple.

For a split second, it clings to the stone, suspended like some grotesque bat. Then, it lets go. *THUD—CRACK.*

Taloned feet slam into the pavement below with enough force to spiderweb the concrete. Chips of stone shoot across the ground and pepper my boots and the shock hits my legs like a jolt of electricity, rattling upwards.

My heart lurches.

"Go!" JP barks, already lunging forward, Colt flashing in the dim light.

The demon is on us in an instant.

It's impossibly tall, its limbs stretched thin like someone pulled its bones apart and let them heal wrong. Joints bend at angles that shouldn't exist. Its spine hunches, vertebrae jutting beneath grayish skin that looks pulled taut over something starving.

Its breath clouds in white puffs, each exhale ragged and steaming despite the creature's unnatural heat. Fangs drip with thick, black spit that hits the frozen ground and sizzles instantly, burning tiny pits into the stone.

Its eyes: Hell. They lock onto me with that same awful, hungry calculation I've seen all week.

We dodge. Move. Strike.

The demon sweeps at me with a clawed hand, a blur of jagged fingers slicing through the air. I duck under it, feeling the rush of freezing wind skim the top of my head like a blade shaved past my skull. My heart slams against my ribs.

I surge up from my crouch and drive my knife into its arm. The blade bites deep. Cold ichor explodes across the ground, splattering dead leaves that curl inward as if the black blood burns them.

The demon howls—ragged, high, eerily close to human—but instead of retaliating, it jerks backward, posture snapping straight. Its eyes lock on me, glinting with a strange, awful intelligence.

JP slashes across its back with brutal efficiency, carving a deep line from shoulder to hip. The creature bucks forward, stumbling on elongated limbs. But even then—even wounded, even staggering—it pivots back toward me, ignoring JP entirely.

Its eyes gleam, reflecting the twilight like shards of obsidian. My pulse spikes hard. My lungs cinch tight.

It lunges again, claws outstretched, coming straight for my throat. And then, it hesitates. Just a fraction of a second. A hitch in its movement. A glitch in its killing instinct.

It could've taken me out. It didn't. Instead, it circles me in a slow, deliberate arc. Measured. Methodical. Not like I'm a threat, not like I'm prey. But like I'm a specimen under glass.

My skin crawls so violently I swear every hair on my body lifts at once. "JP!" I shout, stumbling back, my boots sliding on a carpet of wet leaves.

JP reacts instantly. He charges the demon from behind, his knife flashing silver. The blade drives straight through the creature's spine with a sickening crack, icy black blood spilling down the steel and onto his hand.

The demon jerks, spasming, limbs quivering in sharp, unnatural angles. But it doesn't scream. It doesn't thrash. It doesn't fight. Instead—

It turns its head toward me, vertebrae grinding as its neck twists far past anything human. The movement is slow, deliberate, obscene. Its lips peel back revealing teeth like splintered bone. And it smiles.

Cold. Curious. Almost... pleased.

My entire body goes rigid, the air trapped in my lungs like ice. Then, finally, the demon collapses. Its body folds inward like a puppet with cut strings, steaming black blood pooling across the frost-tipped ground.

The air goes still. Too still. Not a breeze. Not a creak. Not a rustle from the trees above.

Only the pounding of my own heart and the echo of that impossible smile burned into my memory like frostbite. And as I stand here shaking in the gathering twilight, I know with absolute certainty: This wasn't about winning. It wasn't about killing. It was another test.

And I don't know how many more I can survive.

Ashford feels... wrong.

A cold front swept in overnight, and every gust of wind feels sharper now—thin, slicing right through my jacket and settling deep into my bones. The sky hangs low and swollen with steel-gray clouds, the kind that smother the sun and make dusk arrive early. The streets look dim even with the lamps on, their halos trembling in the wind.

People whisper about shadows moving where shadows shouldn't be. Dogs snarl at empty sidewalks, hackles rising at nothing. Porch lights flicker like the whole town is breathing too shallow, too fasts.

Everyone feels it, even if they can't name it. Something is out there. Something watching. Something waiting.

The Veil has been keeping their attacks small. Precise. Contained. Never enough for the news stations to care. Never enough for the town to panic. Just enough for us. Just enough for me.

It is night now, and JP and I are cutting through the narrow alley behind the hardware store, brick walls pressing close on either side, dumpsters stacked like hulking shadows. The air is sharp with the smell of paint thinner and frost.

That's when it happens. A brittle ping of metal overhead, then the rusted fire escape groans: *CRASH!*

A demon drops straight in front of us, metal shrapnel raining around its landing. It hits the pavement in a crouch that cracks the concrete, a burst of frozen air blasting outward. The stench rolls off it in waves—rotting demon ichor mixed with wet rust and something sour.

Slowly, it lifts its head. A snarl unfurls from deep in its throat. Its eyes glow with recognition.

"Move!" JP barks. Before the order fully leaves his mouth, the demon lunges.

I dodge left, boots skidding on the icy asphalt. JP meets the demon head-on, Colt already in his hands. *BANG! BANG!*

Two quick shots. Sparks erupt as demon claws slam against the metal frame of the gun, ricocheting off the brick walls with a metallic screech that echoes down the alley like a warning bell. The demon twists away—unnaturally fast—and swipes at me.

I drop under the arc, but my shoe catches on the uneven pavement. My foot slips. My breath seizes. And for half a second, I fall. Panic spikes like lightning through my veins.

In that heartbeat, the demon stops *mid-attack*. Frozen. Still. Head cocked. It turns toward me. Not toward my knife. Not toward my exposed flank. Toward my panic.

Its nostrils flare. Its pupils expand. Its body leans in, not to strike, but to *listen*. To measure. I feel its focus like cold fingers settling around my throat.

My blood chills. "JP—something's wrong!" I gasp, scrambling back. "They're not fighting normal. They're—they're tracking something!"

"Focus!" JP snaps. But beneath the command is fear. Real fear.

The demon lunges again, faster this time, deliberate. Its claws graze my arm—a whisper of contact—just enough to slice through the fabric of my jacket, but not enough to cut skin.

It could've ripped my arm off. It chose not to. Why?

I slash back, blade catching its jaw, tearing a ragged line across its face. It recoils with a wet, guttural hiss—more animal than monster.

JP uses the opening. He fires point blank: *BANG.* The round punches straight through its chest.

The demon jerks, limbs spasming. Black blood splatters the alley, sizzling on the cold ground. The sour fumes hit my nose, thick and suffocating.

But even as its body convulses, even as its knees buckle, even as JP steps in to put another clean shot between its eyes, the demon doesn't look at him. Not once. Its dying gaze stays locked on me.

I feel the weight of its stare burrow under my skin, like it's memorizing me—recording me—even as the last flicker of light drains from its eyes and it collapses at my feet.

The alley goes silent. My heartbeat thunders against my ribs, refusing to slow, refusing to let me forget how that thing looked at me.

The flickering streetlights don't feel like broken wiring; they feel like blinking eyes. Watching.

I'm running on fumes. Little sleep. Too many bruises. Bandages that never stay clean. And questions—sharp, relentless questions—grind at me harder than any demon's claws.

My limbs feel heavy, like someone filled my bones with wet cement. Every step drags. But my nerves buzz like exposed wires, sparking at every sound. Every whisper of wind feels like breath on my neck. Every shadow looks like a warning crouched low and waiting.

I can't tell if it's paranoia or instinct. Or both.

JP isn't doing much better. He's wound tight as a bowstring, pacing constantly, jaw locked so tight, the muscle jumps near his temple. His hand never strays far from his Colt. His eyes flick over every alley, every rooftop, every rustle of dead leaves skittering across asphalt.

Twice as alert as usual. Twice as quiet. He can sense it, too: the pressure building around us. The Veil tightening their net.

We're halfway down a narrow service street behind the abandoned rail yard. Then, I hear it: a faint scrape of claws against metal, almost lost in the whistle of the cold wind. JP stiffens, head snapping to the side. "Left—!"

They come all at once. Two demons erupt from the alley to our left, their jagged claws gleaming, breath billowing in the frigid air like smoke. Another bursts from behind a dumpster on the right, shoving it aside like it weighs nothing. The fourth drops from the rooftop above with a thunderous crash—*THUD—CRACK*—landing in a crouch that opens the pavement beneath it.

A perfect formation. A coordinated strike. A trap sliding shut. We're surrounded before either of us can react.

The air tastes like iron and cold stone. The walls feel too close. The darkness feels personal.

The first demon lunges at my throat—a blur of claws and snapping teeth. I twist away, pain flaring through my ribs where old bruises scream in protest.

A second demon's foot slams into my side: a brutal, jarring kick that sends me spinning into the brick wall. My shoulder crunches against the cold stone with a grunt. It hurts—white-hot and deep— but not enough to break bone. Not enough to kill.

Because they're not trying to kill me—not right away.

JP fires—*BANG! BANG!*—the Colt's muzzle flash lighting the alley in bursts of orange. One demon recoils, ichor spraying, but it doesn't fall. It doesn't make a sound.

They move in eerie unison—a coordinated advance, forcing us back into the narrowing choke of the alley, turning it into a cage of violence. The demons' claws scrape against asphalt in shrill, metallic shrieks, metal dumpsters groaning under heavy impacts, the wet rasp of demon breath fogging the frozen air.

Frosty night wind sears my lungs each time I suck in a breath. I dodge, strike, kick stagger, moving on instinct more than training.

Blood slicks my arm, hot against the freezing night. Every inhale tastes like copper and cold. Every twist of my torso sends pain radiating through my ribs—sharp, splintering, like cracked glass grinding inside my chest.

But something's wrong. Horribly wrong.

Their blows land with precision, but never with full force. Every slash grazes my skin instead of ripping straight through it. Every kick sends me stumbling, not shattering. Every clawed swipe drives me back, back, back—cornering me, spiking my heartrate—then easing just enough to keep me conscious.

My mind races. My stomach drops.

They're pacing me. Pushing my limits. Tracking how fast I bleed. How quickly I heal. How I move when I'm hurt. What I do when I'm desperate.

And, the worst of it: This time, they're tracking my fear.

My panic spikes as one demon slams me against the cold brick wall. Its body pins me like a vice, blocking off my escape. I shove against it, breath tearing from my throat, pulse hammering.

Its eyes widen to show dilated pupils, shining wet and black. Its nostrils flare sharply. It leans in and inhales a slow, deliberate breath, like it's smelling something intoxicating.

"JP!" I choke, voice cracking as another demon swipes in an attack perfectly timed to the exact moment my pulse surges.

JP's fighting two at once, sweat streaking through the dirt and blood on his face. His Colt flashes, each blast echoing like thunder in the narrow alley.

"Stay low! Don't let them—!" But he doesn't have to finish; the demons already know what they're looking for.

It's like my fear is calling to them. Like it's lighting up some invisible signal only they can see. My panic rises, and the demons respond so fast it makes my vision blur.

Their eyes widen and their chests heave in sync, breathing deeper. Their claws flex, scraping the asphalt. Their heads tilt toward me like I'm singing a song only they can hear.

They're feeling it, feeding off it, measuring it. Using the resonance of my fear like a tuning fork. Like every emotion in my body is a data point they're collecting. Like I'm not their target; I'm their test subject.

JP crashes into one of the demons with a force that rattles straight through my teeth. "Back off!" he snarls, a sound pulled from somewhere deep and dangerous inside him. I've heard it maybe twice in my life, and both times death was close enough to taste.

He slams his shoulder into the creature, hitting it with enough power to shake the bricks behind me. The demon skids across the pavement—claws dragging, throwing sparks and tearing long, jagged scrapes into the asphalt.

Before the demon can recover, JP's Colt barks—a deafening crack that shreds the cold night. The demon convulses, ichor spraying from the impact. With one final shot, its body drops with a wet, sickening thud that echoes down the alley.

A second demon lunges for me, its jagged teeth dripping. I meet it with a desperate slash across the throat. My knife bites deep—skin, sinew, vein—and black ichor explodes across the frost-tipped ground, hissing as it burns through leaves and ice.

The demon gurgles, choking on its own blood. Its limbs jerk once, twice—then collapse beside the first. Two down. But the alley doesn't relax. The other two demons freeze—not in fear, but in recognition.

They tilt their heads in eerie unison, eyes gleaming with something too intelligent, too calculating, as if they've reached the end of their invisible checklist, the last box filled, the final number collected. As if now, we've delivered the exact reaction they'd come for.

Then—in near-perfect synchronicity—they retreat. Not flee, not panic, but withdraw. As if to say, *experiment: complete*.

My legs buckle. I stagger back and slap a hand against the cold brick to keep from falling. My lungs drag in freezing, jagged breaths that burn all the way down. My heartbeat thrashes against my ribs like it wants out.

"That wasn't a fight," I manage, my voice thin, "It was a test."

JP wipes demon blood from his Colt with slow, deliberate movements—movements that tell me he already knew. I hear the faint grind of his teeth. "I know," he says, quiet. Haunted.

My pulse becomes a war drum—pounding, frantic, uneven—every beat stoking the dread clawing up my spine.

"They want something from me," I whisper. My voice shakes. It's not a guess anymore. Not a theory. The truth feels heavy enough to crush bone. "They've been pushing me. Watching me. Tracking me."

JP doesn't argue. He doesn't try to soften it. He doesn't lie. He just looks away, because the truth on his face is too dangerous to aim at me.

"Yeah," he murmurs. "They do."

Cold slithers through my gut. Thick. Icy. We stagger out of the alley, our steps uneven, the cold wind slicing at our wounds. My side throbs—warm blood trickling through my shirt, soaking into the waistband of my jeans. Even with my healing, the wound burns deep, hotter than it should. Intentional. Too precise.

Not meant to kill. Just enough to hurt. Just enough to push. Just enough to see how long it takes me to recover. Another data point. Another piece of the experiment.

The Veil is getting closer to whatever answer they want. They're getting closer to me.

We head toward the truck, boots crunching through glass scattered across the pavement like frozen lightning, reminders of the violence we just survived.

My skin prickles before my mind even understands why. "JP—" I whisper, breath fogging in the freezing night air.

"I feel it," he murmurs tightly.

Those three words—the tension in them—slice fear straight through my stomach. JP always senses danger before I do. The fact that I felt it first means something is off. Deeply, horribly off.

Slowly, like the night itself is lifting my chin, I raise my gaze toward the rooftops. And then, I see him.

A figure stands on the edge of the old hardware store roof, framed by the thin wash of moonlight. Tall. Still. Cloaked in a long coat that

213

moves subtly with the wind, like fabric that remembers how a heartbeat feels.

His silhouette is too sharp. Too perfectly shaped. Unnervingly motionless. As if carved out of the night itself.

He doesn't shift. He doesn't hide. He simply watches. Not like a hunter studying prey. More like a scientist observing a reaction. Running diagnostics. Calibrating variables. Checking off boxes on a list only he understands.

My breath stutters. My bones go cold. "Do you know him?" I whisper. My voice trembles like it's afraid to leave my mouth.

JP follows my line of sight. The moment his eyes find the silhouette, something in the air changes. A ripple. Faint as frost cracking on a windowpane. Even the shadows seem to bow away from the figure, like they're obeying some inaudible command.

The figure tilts his head. Just slightly. As if acknowledging us. As if acknowledging me. Then, not a jump, not a step, not a blur, but one blink—and he's gone. Like someone sliced his shape cleanly out of the world.

I stumble forward instinctively and grab JP's sleeve, my knuckles bone-white. "Who was that?"

JP's face drains of color. He scans the rooftop again, but the emptiness only tightens his expression. His jaw clenches hard enough to crack. "Someone worse than demons," he says, voice low, haunted. "A hell of a lot worse."

The fear in his voice—real fear—makes my stomach twist so violently I swear I might be sick. The cold night presses in around us, heavy and suffocating. The streetlights seem dimmer. The air tighter.

Tonight wasn't random. None of the attacks this week were. They weren't testing Ashford. They weren't testing the town's defenses.

They were testing me. My limits. My panic. My strength. My healing. My heartbeat.

And somewhere out there—in the spaces between the buildings, in the fractures of shadow too narrow for light—that man, whoever he is, is still watching. Still waiting. Still counting. Counting down to something I don't understand.

Something coming for me. Whether I'm ready or not.

Chapter 14

The Breaking Point

JP's office feels colder than usual. Maybe it's the flickering fluorescent lights overhead, buzzing like dying insects trapped in their own repetitive death rattle. Maybe it's the cement floor—stained, cracked, and cold enough to creep through the soles of my boots. Maybe it's the shadows pooling in the corners, darker than they should be, like they're leaning in to hear every word.

Or maybe it's me.

My nerves are stretched so thin it feels like my own heartbeat might snap them. Every breath sounds too loud. Too fast. Too shallow. The office has always been my safe place. Concrete walls. Metal filing cabinets. The old corkboard cluttered with maps, strings, scribbled notes. JP's desk—scarred oak, battered and stubborn, like the man himself.

But tonight the room feels off-kilter in a way I can't shake. It doesn't have its usual comfort—the familiar safety of sweat and routine and muscle memory. Instead it feels shrunken, claustrophobic, like the walls crept closer when I wasn't looking. The air feels tight, dense with things unsaid, with secrets JP hasn't told me. Like every inch of the room knows something I don't, and it's leaning in, waiting for the moment I finally notice.

JP sits behind his desk, elbows braced against the scarred wood, hands clasped under his mouth. His shoulders are hunched—not just with exhaustion, but with the weight of the last week finally settling in like concrete. His eyes are rimmed red, hollowed out by nights without sleep and days spent patching wounds he pretends don't hurt. A dark bruise shadows his left temple, half-hidden under his hair, and the cut along his jaw—still raw from the demon in the alley—pulls tight each time he clenches his teeth.

He looks exhausted. He looks haunted. He looks like he's trying to solve an equation with half its numbers missing—and he knows the wrong answer could get us both killed.

I'm not doing much better.

I pace back and forth across the concrete floor, boots stomping out sharp, angry echoes that snap through the stillness. My ribs ache with every twist, the bruises from the last ambush pulsing in stubborn, rhythmic reminders. A shallow cut across my forearm stings each time I move, reopening just enough to smear red along the wrap covering it. My knuckles throb—half from training, half from the adrenaline of punching demons in the face all week.

My thoughts chase each other in frantic circles—messy, tangled, impossible to catch or quiet.

Rooftop. Figure. Gone in one blink.

And the worst part wasn't even the vanishing; it was the way it *looked at me first.*

My breath comes in uneven bursts—part fury, part panic, part something I don't have a name for yet. My hands won't stay still; they open and close compulsively, as if I need to fight something just to make the buzzing in my blood stop.

The office hums around us. A distant heater rattles in the vents. A loose ceiling tile taps rhythmically as the wind shifts outside. The buzzing light flickers again, casting the room in a momentary strobe of shadow and glare.

I can feel JP's eyes following me, assessing me, measuring me—the way the demons had. The realization makes my throat close.

"Evelyn," he says finally.

Hearing my name only makes my chest tighten more. I can hear in his tone the fear he won't name, the truth he won't say. And I'm not sure which scares me more: the monsters hunting me outside, or the secrets waiting for me in this room.

"Tell me," I snap, the words slicing through the room like glass. "Tell me what's happening to me."

JP doesn't move. Doesn't look away. Doesn't even blink. "Evelyn—"

"No." The word detonates out of me, sharp and raw. "No, you don't get to do that. You don't get to say my name like I'm a terrified little kid and you're the wise adult who gets to decide what I can handle."

He inhales slow, controlled, like he's trying to swallow every emotion threatening to break loose. "I'm protecting you," he says.

"From what?" My voice spikes upward. "From the truth? From myself? From the demons who already know my name, JP? Because *they're* not the ones leaving me in the dark."

He flinches. It's tiny—barely a twitch—but I see it. A crack in his armor, proof the words hit somewhere deep. He drags a shaking hand down his face, rubbing hard, like he might scrub the exhaustion off, or maybe the guilt. "You're not ready for the answers."

Something inside me burns. Hotter than fear. Hotter than rage. "Who decides that?" I demand. "*You*?"

He opens his eyes and looks at me—really looks at me. For a second, he doesn't look like the unshakeable soldier or the hardened hunter. He looks wrecked. Like he's standing on a landmine and knows one wrong word will set it off.

He swallows, the movement tight. His voice drops to a frayed murmur. "You don't understand," he says. "Knowing will put you in more danger than you already—"

"More danger than being hunted?" I cut in. My voice trembles, breath hitching. "More danger than demons sniffing out my panic like it's blood in the water? More danger than whatever the hell that thing on the rooftop was?"

JP closes his eyes like he can't stand the image in my words. Like he's afraid because I'm right.

I step closer, the space between us charged, electric, painful. "Every time you tell me nothing, you make me weaker," I say, breath shaking. "Every time you hide something, you make me vulnerable. You think you're protecting me?" I jab a finger at his chest. "You're not. You're protecting your secrets."

His eyes snap open—sharp, wounded. "That's not fair," he says hoarsely.

"No." My voice softens into something hollow. "But it's true."

He doesn't deny it. He can't. The guilt in his eyes answers for him.

I throw my hands up so hard my wrists ache. "I'm already in danger!" I shout, voice splintering at the edges. "You think I don't know that? You think I didn't see those things practically sampling my heartbeat? Sniffing my fear like it was— Like it was some kind of beacon?"

JP opens his mouth, but I don't let him speak.

"You think I didn't hear the demon call me—" The memory hits like a punch. Twisting. Coiling. Dragging breath from my lungs. My throat closes around the word, strangling it. "Whatever the hell it called me?" I whisper, voice fracturing.

JP stands so abruptly, his chair slams into the wall. The crash makes me jump. "There are things you can't unkn—"

"Stop." This time the word comes out broken. Small. So much smaller than I want to be. My voice shakes. "Stop treating me like I'm breakable."

The silence that follows is thick and suffocating. JP's breathing is uneven, like he's fighting every instinct he has. And my own heart hammers so violently it hurts, every beat a reminder that time is running out, and that ignorance is killing me.

And for a moment—one brief, unguarded heartbeat—I see everything he's been trying to hide. Guilt. Fear. Love, raw and terrified. Loss carved into the posture of a man barely holding himself together. All of it tangled into one expression he never lets me see.

The sight of it hits me like a blow. I *hate* seeing him like this. JP isn't supposed to look breakable. He's supposed to be my constant— my rock, my anchor when everything else in my life tilts sideways. The one person who doesn't flinch when demons scream, or when I do. The one who always knows what to do next.

But right now, he looks human. And it hurts. It hurts worse than any demon wound, worse than claws in my skin or fire in my lungs— because those things are monsters. I can fight monsters.

This? This is JP breaking.

And that terrifies me more than anything hunting us in the dark. It hurts because it's real. Because it's human. Because it's *him*.

But then—like a door slammed shut—his face blanks. His shoulders lock. His eyes harden into steel. The soldier returns. "I'm doing what I have to," he says, voice controlled to the point of strangling itself.

"And I'm doing what *I* have to," I bite back, "which is getting answers."

His hands curl into fists at his sides, knuckles straining white, tendons standing out like cords. "Not like this," he grinds out.

"Then *how*, JP?" My voice spikes before I can stop it, tears burning sharp behind my eyes. "How am I supposed to do any of this when you won't trust me with anything?"

He steps toward me—one step only—but it feels like a chasm closing. When he speaks, his voice is rough, frayed like something ripping. "Because I'm trying to keep you alive, Evelyn." He swallows. Hard. "Even if it means you hate me for it."

The words punch the air out of my lungs. The room goes still. I stare at him. This man who raised me more than my own father ever did. Who taught me how to throw a punch, how to steady my breath, how to survive in a world built to break people like me. And right now, he feels like a stranger. A stranger holding all the missing pieces of who I am and refusing to let me see even one.

My throat tightens. My voice drops into something small, shaking. "You don't get to make that choice for me."

For a long moment, he says nothing. His jaw works, his fists clench, his breath trembles just enough for me to notice. Then, quietly—so quietly I almost miss it—he says, "I don't want to lose you."

The words land like a punch to the gut. Not loud. Not dramatic. Just raw. True. He doesn't look at me when he says it. Can't. His eyes stay fixed on the floor, like if he meets mine, he'll shatter right through.

"You think I'm doing this to control you?" His voice cracks, just once. "Evelyn... I'm doing this because I can't—" He breaks off, breathing hard, swallowing whatever comes next. "I can't lose you too."

And somehow that hurts worse. More than yelling. More than anger. More than all the secrets he's been burying for years, because in it, I hear the truth. The fear. The desperation. The past he won't talk about, tightening around his throat.

Something inside me cracks open. I shake my head slowly, each motion heavy, weighted with everything we're not saying. "You already lost me," I whisper. "You just don't want to admit it."

JP's face twists—pain flashing first, sharp and unfiltered. Then, something heavier follows: regret. Terror. A man crushed under the weight of the truth he kept private for too long.

For a breath, I think he might move, might reach for me, say my name, stop me. But he doesn't. He stands there, silent, letting me walk out. Letting me leave him.

That hurts more than any word between us.

My hands shake as I grab my helmet off the counter. My fingers fumble around the strap. I shove open the office door harder than I need to, and the cold autumn air hits me like a slap. It steals my breath. It steals my heat. It steals whatever composure I had left.

Tears sting hot against my cheeks, blurring the hard yellow glow of the parking lot lights. Anger burns under my skin so bright it feels feverish, like something boiling over, too big for my chest to contain.

I don't look back. I can't. Because if I do, I'll break in half. And I have been broken enough. So I step into the night alone, for a moment not caring if shadows are shifting, if someone is watching from the rooftops as I walk away.

The ride home is a blur of motion and noise, but none of it reaches me. The engine roars beneath me, vibrating through my bones, but it feels distant, like I'm hearing it from underwater, or from behind a wall I didn't realize I'd built just to keep myself upright.

Streetlights smear past in long streaks of gold and white, bending and blurring with the speed. I tear through town like a ghost with nowhere left to haunt. The wind slashes across my cheeks, numbing them until the drying tears feel like shards of ice clinging to my skin.

My hands shake around the handlebars. At first from anger—hot, sharp, explosive, something that could've set the whole night ablaze.

But mile by mile, the fire gutters and drains into something heavier. Something softer. Something that hurts more: grief.

My chest aches, hollow and scraped clean, like something vital has been torn out of me and left behind on the office floor I just walked away from. Every inhale feels too big. Every exhale, too thin. My ribs feel cracked open, bruised from the inside out.

The wind whips strands of hair free from my helmet, snapping them against my neck like stinging lashes. The night smells like dead leaves, cold pavement, and distant woodsmoke curling from chimneys—autumn scents that should feel familiar, grounding.

But nothing grounds me. The deeper I ride into Ashford, the more familiar everything looks, and the less any of it feels like home. The streets, the houses, the rusted-over stop signs—every piece of this town feels like it belongs to a life I'm no longer part of. A life I've already outgrown.

And with every turn, every mile, every heartbeat, one truth settles heavier in me: I don't know where I belong anymore.

By the time I turn onto my street, my fingers are stiff from clutching the handles too tight—white-knuckled, desperate, as if letting go might mean falling apart. My heart feels heavier than my jacket. My whole body trembles with leftover adrenaline, leftover rage, leftover fear.

I pull into the driveway and kill the engine. Silence crashes down. Not peaceful. Not comforting. Suffocating. The quiet presses around me like a vacuum—no roaring engine to hide behind, no wind to drown out my thoughts. Just the cold, heavy truth settling in my bones.

My breath fogs in the air as I sit on the bike, letting the cold seep into me, trying to feel something other than the twisting, splintering ache inside. Slowly, I tilt my head back.

Above the roofline of the tired little house—its dead porch light, its peeling siding, its dark windows—the sky stretches wide and endless. The stars flicker faintly through thin clouds. Distant. Eternal.

I stare up at them, throat tight. My mom used to tell me the stars always watched over us. That if I ever felt lost, all I had to do was look up, and I'd find her in the spaces between the constellations, in the quiet places where light refuses to die.

Right now, I wish harder than I have in years that she were here. That she could sit behind me on this stupid motorcycle, arms around me, whispering that everything will be okay. That she could tell me who I am. What I'm becoming. Why all of this is happening. Why I'm so scared.

But the stars don't answer. They just glow, distant and indifferent. My breath trembles as I exhale, watching the fog fade into nothing.

I finally climb off the bike, feeling more alone than I have since the night everything in my life burned.

I swallow hard, wiping under my eyes with the heel of my palm. Then, I open the door, bracing myself for the usual scene: Dad passed out, bottle on the floor, TV flickering through static. A shadow of the man he used to be.

But he's awake. Sitting on the sagging couch, TV humming a low, bluish glow over his face. His eyes—tired, red-rimmed, but open—shift toward me when the door creaks. For a moment, surprise flickers across him like he forgot anyone else existed in the world.

"Evie?" His voice cracks around my name. "You're... home early."

I don't answer. I can't. I stand there in the doorway, helmet dangling from numb fingers, and suddenly I feel nineteen and nine all at once. Small. Overwhelmed. One breath away from collapsing in on myself.

My dad blinks like he's trying to focus, confusion pulling his brows together. He rubs a hand over his face, wiping sleep or exhaustion—or something deeper—away.

"Everything alright?" he asks, voice hoarse. It's the most he's said to me in days.

The question hits harder than anything JP threw at me tonight. My throat tightens, something fragile inside me finally cracked open. "I don't..." My voice comes out as barely more than breath. "I don't want to be alone right now."

He freezes. Just... freezes. Like time stops with him.

For a moment, he just stares at me—eyes wide, uncertainty etched into every line of his face. Like he can't believe I'm asking him for anything after all the distance, all the silence, all the nights we've spent pretending the other doesn't hurt.

Then, slowly, carefully, he nods and pats the cushion beside him. "Yeah," he murmurs. "Okay. Come sit."

The living room is the same disaster as always—beer cans on the coffee table, a half-eaten bag of chips on the floor, a blanket slumped over the armchair like a sleeping animal. The smell of stale cigarettes and old memories clings to the walls.

Usually, it suffocates me. Tonight, I walk toward the couch anyway.

I sit stiffly, shoulders tight, fingers knotted together in my lap. Dad keeps his eyes on the TV a little too long, like I'm some skittish thing he doesn't want to scare away. Like he's afraid looking at me will spook me. Silence stretches—awkward, fragile, alive with

225

everything we're not saying. Then, something in me breaks. Not loudly. Not dramatically. Just... gives way.

I lean sideways until my shoulder brushes his arm. My breath catches in my chest as I wait—hope and fear tangled into one painful knot.

He doesn't pull back. So I let myself lean in more. Closer. Curling into him like I did when I was small and the world felt too sharp.

He hesitates—just long enough for my heart to crack—then makes a choice. Carefully, shakily, he wraps his arm around my shoulders. His hand settles there awkwardly at first, like he's forgotten how. Then, slowly, it relaxes—like some old instinct that hasn't entirely died.

"Hey..." His voice is barely a whisper. "It's okay, kiddo."

Kiddo. I haven't heard him say that in years. The word hits me like a punch and a hug at the same time. Just warmth. Just presence. No questions. No judgment. Just... him.

I close my eyes, breathing in the scent of him—soap, old leather, a faint sting of alcohol, but underneath it all, something familiar. Something I thought I'd lost.

And for one small, precious moment, I don't feel like I'm falling apart. Only when the tears start to fall—soft, silent, soaking into his shirt—do I realize how alone I've been. How afraid I am of what I'm becoming. How much I needed someone—anyone—to stay.

He doesn't ask why I'm crying. He doesn't move away. He doesn't make excuses or disappear into another beer. He just holds on.

And tonight—just tonight—I let myself be small. Let myself be held.

And for the first time in years, I let my dad be my dad.

Chapter 15

A Cage Made of Secrets

I haven't been back to JP's office in two days. We text about patrol schedules. Leads. Logistics. Nothing human, nothing real. Nothing about what I am or why demons speak my name like it's prophecy.

I tell myself I'm giving him space. That he needs time to cool off, to think, to breathe. But deep down, I know the truth:

I'm avoiding him. Avoiding the look I saw in his eyes. Avoiding the fear that wasn't for the demons, but for me. Avoiding the crack growing wider between us, a fault I'm afraid might split open if I touch it.

Ashford feels heavier tonight. Like the whole town has shifted a few degrees off center. The air is cold and thin, like winter is gnawing its way in early, chewing through what's left of autumn. The wind snakes down the streets, carrying with it the scent of rain and rusted metal.

Clouds mark the sky, thick and low, blotting out the stars completely. The streetlights flicker under the weight of the fog, casting the sidewalks in a sickly, uneven glow. Houses hunch behind skeletal trees, their windows dark, their porches bare, the town pulled back into shadow.

I should go home. I should sleep. I should pretend—if just for one more night—that I'm normal. Instead, I walk.

Down past the shuttered shops. Past the sagging water tower. Past the places that used to feel familiar.

My boots crunch through drifts of dead leaves, each step reverberating in the empty street. The silence presses in on me, dense and watchful, like the town knows a secret I haven't caught on to yet.

I don't know where I'm going; I just know I can't go back. Not yet. Not until I can breathe without feeling like the world is about to close its jaws around me.

I let the cold bite at my cheeks until they go numb. I drift down side streets and empty lots, taking the long way back from the shop. Leaves flutter across the pavement like they're trying to run from something. The old sodium streetlights buzz and spill sick orange halos onto the cracked sidewalks.

My thoughts are too loud—too sharp—echoing JP's words on a loop I can't seem to shut off.

You're not ready.

I'm protecting you.

Once you know, there's no going back.

Each one hits like a stone dropped into my chest, sending ripples of anger and fear outward until I can barely breathe.

I shake my head hard, like I might be able to jostle his voice loose, knock it out of my skull and onto the pavement. My hair whips against my cheeks, stinging, but the words stay. They dig in deeper, like they always do.

His voice clings like smoke—familiar, heavy, impossible to escape.

I think about calling Maya. Maybe she's okay now. Maybe we could talk about stupid things, drink iced caramel lattes, laugh about customers who can't pronounce *macchiato*. Pretend we're normal girls with normal problems and not whatever we actually are.

But I haven't seen her since the attack. I promised I'd visit her in the hospital. Told JP I would. Told myself I would.

But, when the time came, I couldn't. I couldn't walk into that sterile room and see the bruises around her wrists, the bandage on her cheek, the IV in her arm. I couldn't stand the thought of looking into her eyes and seeing it again: that fear. That confusion. That moment where she stared at me like she didn't recognize me at all, like she'd seen a stranger wearing my skin.

The image flashes behind my eyes. Maya trembling. Maya crying. Maya shrinking away from me. I grimace and shove the memory back where it came from, burying my hands deeper into my jacket pockets. The cold air slips between my fingers, but it doesn't prick the way it should.

It never does anymore. I don't know if that's comforting, or terrifying.

I cut through the small park three blocks from my street. Frost crackles under my boots, brittle and sharp. The swings creak in the wind, their chains clinking like bones knocking together. The slide has a thin glaze of ice, reflecting the streetlamp in warped, shivering lines.

It's late enough that even the drunks have stumbled home. No laughter. No footsteps. Just me and the hollow sound of the wind. I'm alone. Or—I *think* I am.

"Evelyn."

The voice lands right behind me, too close. I freeze mid-step. My breath catches in my throat as the sound of my name crawls up my spine—calm, deliberate, from the voice of a man who chooses every syllable with care—not because he said it, but because I recognize the *tone*.

Smooth. Velvet edged with knives. I turn slowly. He stands under the crooked streetlamp at the far edge of the park, the light flickering above him like it's afraid to fully illuminate him.

The coat is the first thing I notice—long, dark wool, tailored and expensive, the collar turned up slightly against the cold. One hand tucked in a pocket, the other relaxed at his side. He looks like he walked straight out of a London alley after cutting a deal with the devil, and then stopped here for a breath of fresh, American chaos.

But he's not a demon. Not like the ones I fight. There's no monstrousness in his posture. No hunger. Just calculation. A sharp mind wearing human skin.

Up close, I see more—late twenties, maybe early thirties. Cheekbones refined, hair dark and slightly tousled, artfully careless. His eyes are the strangest part—gray, but deep, layered, like storm clouds reflecting distant lightning. Familiar. Too familiar.

"You," I breathe, fog curling from my lips. "The roof."

He smiles, just barely—more a suggestion of amusement tugging at one corner of his mouth. Not kind. Not cruel. Just entertained.

"Good," he says, tone low and silk-slick, confident in a way that makes my skin crawl. "You remember." His voice isn't loud—it doesn't need to be. It carries the easy cruelty of someone who always gets what he wants.

He steps forward, unhurried, hands still in his pockets, as if approaching someone at a cocktail party. His boots make almost no sound against the frost-stiff grass.

He circles me. Not like a predator sizing up prey—worse. Like a historian studying a rare artifact. A collector evaluating authenticity.

My heartbeat spikes, thudding painfully against my ribs. Every instinct in my body screams at me: *Move. Run. Grab the knife.*

230

Fight. Something. But I can't. My feet stay planted, locked into the earth like the cold has already claimed them.

His presence presses in close—not physically, but like the air bends around him, drawn toward him in subtle, invisible ripples.

"How are you sleeping, Evelyn?" he asks lightly, conversationally, like we're chatting over tea instead of standing alone in a freezing park at midnight. He drifts behind me again, his coat brushing the air with a soft whisper. "Nightmares. Tremors in your hands. Heat under your skin for no reason." A pause. "*Yes?*"

The bottom drops out of my stomach. I stiffen, fists curling at my sides. "Who are you?"

He gives a soft hum, amused, the sound rich in a way that makes my skin crawl.

"Your spark is dormant," he murmurs, half to himself, tone almost clinical. "But your blood remembers the fire."

The words hit me like a misfired punch, off-balance and disorienting.

Spark?

Dormant?

My blood... *remembers?*

A pulse thuds beneath my ribs and echoes in my ears like a warning I can't decipher. My breath fogs in a shaky plume, the cold suddenly sharper, cutting.

I whip toward him, confusion snapping through my fear. "I asked who you are." My voice sounds strained, thin, like it's trying to carry more weight than my body can hold.

He stops directly in front of me, hands still tucked casually in his coat pockets, head tilted just a fraction. His posture is maddening—relaxed, unguarded, comfortable in a way that makes my skin crawl. As if this whole moment belongs to him. As if *I* do.

His eyes flick over my face—measuring, evaluating, pleased by something he sees.

But all I can think is: *What spark? What fire? What the hell is he talking about?*

And why does part of me—some deep, instinctive part I don't understand—react like the words aren't new at all, but something I've been running from for years?

"Someone who knows what you are," he says. His voice curls around the words like smoke—smooth, deliberate, unsettlingly certain. "And what you're not."

I clench my fists harder, nails biting into my palms. The sting helps me stay grounded. "I don't know what I am. No one will tell me. So start talking."

Something flickers across his eyes—approval, or interest, or maybe just the thrill of a game he's finally getting to play. The faintest smile touches his mouth, a quiet curve that feels more like a provocation than anything warm.

"You're not afraid of me," he notes, almost pleased.

"I'm done being afraid of shadows," I snap. "I've spent my whole life being lied to, shoved into the dark, treated like I can't handle who I am. If you know something—*say it.*"

The wind picks up, rustling leaves across the pavement, whispering through the empty swings behind us. The air feels colder, exposed, as if the whole world is listening.

He studies me, eyes bright with a sharpness that cuts right through my defenses. "You're angry," he says softly. "*Good.* Anger loosens things." He steps closer, voice lowering to something intimate and dangerous. "Fear cracks them." Another step. "Pain opens them."

My heartbeat reacts instantly—faster, louder, slamming against my ribs like it's trying to answer him. The heat under my skin flares, crawling up my spine in a warning signal I don't understand.

I hate that he notices.

His smile widens slightly.

"You feel it, don't you?" he murmurs. "The shift. The stir. The little whisper under your ribs that says you're not what you pretend to be."

"Shut up," I manage, voice shaking despite how hard I try to steady it.

He laughs softly, like I've just confirmed a hypothesis. Then, he steps closer again, close enough that I can see the faint silver scar near his lip, like a hint of something from another time.

"Let's see," he says, "how much truth you're ready for." He circles me again before continuing. "Tell me, Evelyn," he murmurs, voice wrapping around my name like silk pulled tight. "How did it *feel* when the Veil dragged your little friend toward the trees? When you saw the mark burned into her steps? When you realized," he leans in just slightly, "they weren't after her at all... but *you*?"

My chest locks up so hard it hurts. "Shut up."

He smiles, not wide—just a small, knowing tilt of his mouth that makes something ugly stir in my stomach. "And when your mentor stood in front of you the other night," he continues, voice dropping to a soft, amused purr, "and chose *silence* over truth? When he chose his fear over your understanding?"

My throat burns, the cold air slicing at the back of it. "You don't know anything about JP."

He arches a brow, unbothered, like I've just told him the weather. "Oh, I know Pierce rather well. Painfully well." His smile widens a fraction. "And I know what he does when he's cornered."

My blood runs cold.

"Pierce kept the truth from you," the man says, voice silky and lethal, "because he fears your awakening."

The sentence hits like a blade—quiet, deep, unavoidable. I take a step toward him before I realize I'm moving. "That's not—"

"He hears it," he cuts in, the amused edge sharpening. "He feels it every time you walk into a room. The pressure. The potential. The shift in the air." He taps his chest lightly. "And it terrifies him."

My hands start to tremble. I want to take a swing at him. I want to knock that arrogant smirk clean off his face. I want him to keep JP's name out of his mouth—but he isn't finished.

"He's hoping," the man goes on, stepping in just close enough to violate my space, "that he can train it out of you. File you down into something manageable. Containable. Something *small enough* to protect."

The words scrape something raw inside me. "He doesn't want to contain me," I snap, even as doubt flickers in my chest.

The stranger sees it. He *drinks it in*. "My dear girl," he says softly, "you have no idea what he's trying to contain."

A cold shiver crawls up my spine, sharp as ice. "What do you want from me? Who are you?" The question slips out too thin, too breathless—too *afraid*—and I hate myself for letting him hear it.

He notices. Of course he does. The stranger tilts his head and studies me with the calm, meticulous interest of someone inspecting a rare artifact, turning it over, searching for cracks, deciding where it will break first. There's no urgency in him. No threat of violence. Just a patient, razor-edged curiosity that makes my skin crawl.

"You may call me Dane," he says at last, offering the name like a gift.

But it feels like a verdict. Like a door closing. Like a trap snapping shut with my name engraved in the steel.

It feels like he's been waiting for this moment, waiting for me to demand his name, waiting for the exact second he could deliver it.

And every instinct in my body screams that, whatever Dane is, he is absolutely not the kind of man whose name you want to know.

"What I want," he says, voice smooth as silk over glass, "is quite simple." His eyes never leave mine—sharp, gray, consuming. "I want you to stop pretending you're just a very strong, very fast girl with a healing quirk and a tragic past."

He steps closer. The wind rattles the swings behind us, chains clinking like bells of warning. "You," he says softly, "are not an accident, Evelyn Cross."

My breath stutters. "Don't—"

He closes the distance entirely until we're toe-to-toe, barely inches apart. His presence feels colder and heavier than the October air around us.

"You are your mother's daughter," he murmurs, and something inside me fractures at the mention of her. "You are a Key... pretending to be a girl."

Something deep inside me lurches—like a cord pulled taut suddenly snapping. My breath catches, sharp and painful. Heat flares under my skin. Not normal heat—unnatural, blistering, crawling over my collarbones and down my arms like liquid fire. Pressure builds behind my ribs, swelling outward, like something inside me is expanding, stretching, waking.

"I—" I choke, fighting the sensation. "You're insane."

Dane smiles with quiet satisfaction, as if my reaction is a predictable stage of his favorite play. "Go on," he says lightly. "Tell yourself that. It will hold... for now."

My vision ripples at the edges: a subtle shimmer, colors bending, the world warping for half a second before snapping back hard enough to make me sway.

The air feels thick, pushing against me, curling around me. Anger claws at my chest. Fear answers it. Desperation devours them both.

"I don't care what you think I am," I say, voice trembling despite my attempt to steady it. "Tell me what it means. What is a Key? What do the Veil want? Why are they after me?"

He exhales a soft laugh—dark, amused. "You're asking the wrong man, darling." His gaze sharpens to something cold and deadly. "Ask Jacob Pierce."

My stomach drops.

Dane steps even closer, his voice dropping to a dangerous whisper: "After all, he's the one who survived this the first time."

The park tilts. Or maybe I do. My throat tightens. "What?"

Dane watches my reaction with hungry fascination. "Oh yes," he purrs. "The last time he stood between the Key and the Door, the world burned."

My breath becomes needles.

"You were there," he says, "even if you don't remember all of it."

Images flash—firelit smoke, sirens wailing, my mother's scream. I flinch, shaking harder. "Stop," I whisper, "You don't get to use her."

But he doesn't stop. If anything, the cruelty in his smile deepens. "You're angry," he murmurs. "Good. Anger loosens the Lock. Pain turns it." He circles me again—slow, deliberate—as if tasting the emotion emanating off me.

"Pierce trained your body. Taught you to punch, kick, run, bleed." He shrugs. "Useful tricks." He leans in, breath ghosting my ear,

236

voice a razor's edge. "But your power—" His tone drops lower still, "doesn't answer to his drills."

I swallow hard. "Power? I don't—"

"It answers," Dane whispers, "to pain. Not his training."

A tremor rips through me—heat, pressure, rising fast like a tidal pulse. And Dane... Dane smiles like he's finally hearing the music he's been waiting for.

My control snaps. I don't think; I just *move*. I lunge at him with everything in me—every sleepless night, every lie JP fed me "for my own good," every demon, every scream, every unanswered question and every crack in my chest—all of it funnels into my fist.

I swing at Dane's jaw with enough force to break bone. For once, I want something to *hurt*. I want something to *feel* it. But Dane—

Dane doesn't block. He just *shifts*. Not fast. Not flashy. Not supernatural. Just a slight, elegant adjustment of his body, like he's sidestepping a spilled cup of coffee, not a full-force punch meant to drive his teeth through the back of his skull.

My fist misses his face by a breath. My body jolts past him, thrown off balance by my own momentum. The ground moves, my shoulder twists, and rage ricochets through my chest—hard, violent, like a physical blow that rebounds inside me with nowhere to go.

And then he touches me. Only once. A single palm brushing my shoulder. Not a shove. Not a strike. Not even pressure. Just a guide. A redirection. A suggestion my body obeys before my brain can process it.

But the hate, the fury, the panic—they don't drain out of me, they don't ebb. They bounce.

Straight.
Back.
In.

It's like slamming my fist into a mirror that refuses to break—one that throws the impact back tenfold, crashing into the hollow of my chest.

My breath explodes out of me in a jagged, shocked gasp. The heat under my skin spikes so fast it's dizzying, racing down my arms, pooling in my palms, burning in my ribs like someone struck a match inside me.

My hands tremble. The edges of my vision blur. The air tastes metallic, sharp, electric. Something is happening. Something I can't stop. Something I've felt before in nightmares and fire and moments I never dared question.

The spark he spoke of—the one he said was dormant—it's waking.

"You attack me," Dane says mildly, as if discussing weather, "because you think *I'm* the problem." His eyes lock with mine, storm-gray and knowing.

"The problem is the cage you've built inside yourself," he says softly. "The cage they built. The cage they locked. The cage they never explained."

My pulse is a drumline. My hands shake. The air around us vibrates—just a shimmer at first, like heat over asphalt on a summer road. Except it's freezing.

I stagger back a step, clutching my chest. "What... what is happening?"

His smile is small. Pleased. Patient. "Cracks."

The pressure behind my ribs tightens, growing hotter, brighter, like something ancient and furious is pounding on the inside of my chest, begging to be let out. I drop to one knee, palms braced on the cold pavement, sucking in winter air that does nothing—*nothing*—to cool the burn under my skin.

Dane watches like a scientist observing his specimen finally reacting. "That's it," he murmurs, delighted. "You feel it, don't you? The spark scraping against your bones, the Door rattling in its frame, the blood remembering—"

"Stop," I gasp. "I'm not—I don't—" The words crumble in my mouth. I can't breathe right. Can't think right. "You're messing with my head," I choke out.

He chuckles once, like he finds the whole thing charming. "I don't have to mess with your head, darling." He steps closer, hands still in his pockets. "You've done most of the work yourself simply by surviving this long."

His head tilts, studying the trembling air around me. "And the rest?" Another soft smile. "That's just your blood waking up."

Dane lifts his right hand with casual elegance, like he's reaching for a pen instead of something lethal. A small blade slips from inside his coat—narrow, curved, perfectly clean. The metal catches the streetlight and flashes cold.

I tense, bracing. But he doesn't come toward me. Instead, with a bored little sigh—like he's doing paperwork—he drags the blade across his own palm. Blood wells up instantly. Too dark to be red. Almost black. And in the freezing air, it steams.

My breath catches.

He crouches, slow and deliberate, pressing his bleeding hand to the pavement between us. The concrete is cracked, uneven, frost-bitten. His blood spreads across it like ink spilled across parchment.

Then, he drags his palm across the dirt in a deliberate pattern: circles, lines, angles that knot together in ways the mind doesn't want to follow—shapes that seem to bend the air around them, tugging at something just behind my eyes. It's the pattern from the woods. From the warehouse. From the nightmares.

"Do you know what this is?" he asks without looking up.

My throat works around a tight swallow. "A sigil."

He gives a small, almost pitying hum. "Not just a sigil." His fingers press into the final curve, smearing a thin streak of blood into the dirt. "It is a Door."

The word hits me like a shove.

Door.

Door.

My pulse stutters violently. The demon in the woods—its ruined mouth leaking black blood—*Doorway's child...*

"To open a door," Dane continues softly, "one only needs a key." He looks at me as he says it.

When he finishes the sigil, the pattern gleams wetly—unnatural, iridescent—before the blood begins to sink into the ground. It doesn't soak in like normal liquid. It pulls downward, spiraling, dragged into the earth as if the ground itself I were thirsty, starving for it.

The air hums. The trees groan. Something shifts beneath us, and I can't tell if the ground is opening, or if something on the other side is pushing to get out.

"Stop," I rasp, throat raw. "Don't—"

"Watch," he murmurs, soft enough to sound harmless. Then, his gaze lifts to mine—sharp, dissecting—like he's studying the architecture of my soul.

"Think about the fire, Evelyn," Dane whispers. "Think about your mother's scream."

Pain lances through my chest.

"Think about Pierce standing over you while the world burned."

My heart seizes.

"Think about how he looked at you afterward."

Images slam into me so fast, so violently, I choke on them: my mother laughing in the kitchen, her hand smoothing my hair; waking up choking on smoke; the heat, the terror, the world splitting apart; JP's silhouette in the doorway; my father yelling; sirens screaming; the ceiling collapsing inward like a dying star.

A crack tears through my chest. The heat under my skin surges, violent, uncontrollable.

The air around us shimmers, trembling harder now, as if the entire park is holding its breath. The edges of my vision go white, bleeding outward in a halo of light. My heart pounds so hard, I feel it in my teeth.

Then, something moves inside me. A pressure. A push. A force trying to break outward from my ribcage. And the sigil responds. The blood lines glow.

Faint at first, an ember in the dark. Then, pulsing slow and steady, in time with my heartbeat. I gasp, stumbling back. The glow flickers. Then dies. The sigil goes dark again, only blood soaking into concrete.

I sway, dizzy. "What did I—? What was that?"

Dane rises smoothly, wiping his bloody palm on a pristine white handkerchief, leaving a perfect streak of blackish red. He folds the cloth neatly, as if finishing a business transaction rather than bleeding onto the path.

"You," he says simply.

"I... I don't understand," I choke, breath shaking. "What did I just do?"

His smile sharpens like a blade sliding out of a sheath. "You don't have to understand. Not yet."

My hands won't stop trembling. The heat under my skin settles into a simmering ache, glowing low and threatening, like coals beneath ash waiting for air. "You were there that night," I whisper. "The fire. My mom. You were there... weren't you?"

Dane meets my gaze and nods once. No elaboration.

My stomach drops like I've stepped off a cliff. My eyes fall to the sigil again, the blood smeared into perfect lines.

"Door... to what?" I whisper, voice thin as thread.

Dane smiles in a way that makes the cold feel colder. "To what waits for you," he replies softly, "and to what waits *because* of you."

He steps back once, boots crunching frost. "You're opening it piece by piece, Evelyn Cross." He taps his temple lightly. "Whether you understand it or not."

A familiar sound slices through the night, low, rumbling, aggressive:

JP's truck.

I turn as headlights carve through the park, flooding the swings and pavement with blinding white. The truck pulls up so fast it fishtails slightly, tires grinding over gravel and dead leaves. The engine cuts. The door slams. Boots hit pavement—fast, hard, urgent.

"Evelyn!" JP's voice snaps across the park like a whip, tight with panic I've never heard from him before.

He jogs toward us, Colt in hand, eyes locked on Dane like he's staring down a ghost from a nightmare he never escaped.

Dane doesn't even flinch. He barely acknowledges JP—just turns his head with a lazy, mildly annoyed glance, as though someone interrupted him during a chess match.

"Careful, Pierce," Dane drawls, tone smooth and unbothered. "Last time you stood between the Key and the Door, we both buried someone."

The words hit like a punch to the chest. Cold shock floods through me. I whip my head toward JP, and he stops dead. All the color drains from his face. His grip around the gun trembles. His jaw clenches so violently, a vein jumps in his temple. He looks like he's going to throw up.

Something cold and sharp sinks into my gut. He knows. He knows exactly what Dane is. Exactly what *I* am. Exactly what the fire really was. And he never told me.

"You..." My voice comes out small. Thin. "You know him."

JP doesn't answer. He doesn't look at me. His eyes stay locked on Dane with a mixture of dread and rage and something older— something like grief.

"Relax," Dane says, sounding thoroughly unimpressed with JP's theatrics. "If I wanted her dead, she'd be ash by now."

JP takes a furious step forward, shoulders coiled tight like a bowstring. "You're not touching her."

"I don't need to," Dane replies, bored. His gaze slides back to me, and something deep in my chest tightens painfully. "She's already waking up. All I did was knock."

"Stay away from her," JP growls, and the sound is pure desperation—raw in a way I've never heard from him.

243

Dane's mouth curves into a smirk. "You said that last time, too."

The wind picks up—cold, biting. It tugs at Dane's coat, rippling the fabric. For a moment, it looks like the air bends, refusing to touch him.

He steps backward, away from the drying sigil. Away from us. "You're almost ready, Evelyn," he says, calm as a man giving weather predictions. "Don't run from what waits inside you. The Veil won't."

Then, he turns. He doesn't disappear in a flash of light. Doesn't dissolve into smoke. Doesn't leap away with supernatural speed. He simply walks. And somehow, that's worse.

By the time JP moves—by the time he remembers he *can* move— Dane is already swallowed by the night, like a shadow returning to the dark.

We're left alone in the park. Me, JP., and the faint outline of a blood sigil drying on the cracked sidewalk.

My heart is a wild drum. My skin still hums with leftover heat. The pressure behind my ribs lingers, like something massive and asleep rolled over inside me, and is one breath away from waking up.

"Evelyn—" JP starts.

I step back instantly. "Don't," I rasp. My voice is shredded and shaking. "Don't you dare."

JP looks wrecked. "Evelyn, it's not what you think—"

I laugh once—short, hollow, ugly. "Really? Because it *sounds* like you and that psycho set my life on fire once already."

The hurt in his eyes makes it worse. Not better. "I was trying to—"

"To protect me," I snap. "Yeah. I've heard that one." The wind whips merciless and cold between us. My thoughts spiral. *Key. Door.*

244

Spark. Fire under my skin. Your power answers to pain. You were there the night it burned.

I don't know what any of it means. All I know is this: Something inside me is changing. Something I can't control. Something I don't understand. And JP—the one person I trusted—has known more than he's ever said.

Fear coils tight in my gut. Not fear of demons. Not fear of Dane. Fear of myself.

JP takes one careful step toward me. "Evelyn. Please. Just—just let me explain."

But I'm already backing away, arms wrapped around my torso like they're the only thing holding me together. Dane's words twist through my mind like barbed wire: *You are a Key pretending to be a girl.*

And I'm not sure he's wrong. The truth terrifies me more than anything the Veil has ever done.

The cold presses in from every direction. My breath fogs in broken bursts. My chest aches like something inside is splitting right down the center.

JP reaches for me again, one single hand lifted from his side. "Evelyn," he says, voice frayed. "Please. Don't walk away angry. Just let me—"

"No." The word is quiet. Final. It hangs between us like frost in the air.

His shoulders drop, and I see it: the moment he realizes he's losing me. The moment he realizes I'm stepping somewhere he can't follow... or won't let himself.

The swings creak again behind us. The blood sigil on the pavement is already drying, turning to a dark stain against the concrete. A reminder. A warning. My throat tightens. "I can't do this," I whisper.

"Not with you keeping secrets. Not when I'm the one paying for them."

"Evelyn—"

"I need space," I murmur. "And you're not giving me answers. So I'm done standing here hoping you will."

His jaw clenches. Pain flashes behind his eyes—vulnerable, exposed—but he doesn't move after me. He doesn't chase. That hurts worst of all.

The wind curls around us, cold and sharp, piercing through my jacket. I take a step backward, away from him. Then another. He stays where he is, standing beside the fading sigil, swallowed in shadow. Blade still in his hand. Fear still in his eyes.

I turn away before he can say anything else. Before I can break. My boots crunch on frost as I walk toward the edge of the park, leaving him behind—leaving the lies, the half-truths, the fire inside my chest that I don't understand.

I don't look back. I can't. By the time I reach the street, JP is just a dark shape in the distance—alone in the cold, the world around him silent and heavy.

And for the first time in my life... I feel truly, terrifyingly alone.

Chapter 16

Convergence

Ashford feels different in the morning. Not calmer. Not safer. Just... *hollow*. Like the whole town has been scooped out and left with nothing but shells of what used to be.

A thin fog clings low to the cracked sidewalks, coiling around mailboxes and porch railings like ghost fingers too tired to fully reach. It shifts in slow, unnatural ripples, as if the air itself is still reeling from whatever touched it in the night. Sirens wail somewhere on the east side of town—sharp, frantic, too frequent for a place where the emergency dispatch usually handles car accidents and bar fights. The sound cuts through the morning quiet like a warning bell no one knows how to answer.

People stand in loose clusters on their porches, flannel robes wrapped tight around their trembling bodies. Coffee mugs shiver in their hands. They whisper behind closed palms, voices hushed but frantic, eyes darting to every rustle of leaves, every shifting shadow. Like they're all waiting for something to step out of the fog.

Even the dogs know something is wrong. They pace fenced yards with restless energy, ears pinned back, barking at nothing I can see, but something I can *feel*.

A streetlight hums, flickers, then dies with a soft pop. The silence it leaves behind is worse.

An uneasy sting crawls up the back of my neck. The air feels wrong—charged with a static that doesn't belong to the weather.

It vibrates against my skin, creeping under my jacket, settling heavy in the hollow of my lungs. Each inhale feels like brushing against unseen sparks.

And underneath all that noise? Beneath the sirens and fog and the distant, desperate barking? A pulse. A faint thrum low in my chest, like someone plucking a violin string tied directly to my ribs. *Twang.*

I press my palm hard against my sternum and suck in a breath. *Ignore it.* But the vibration only spreads, crawling outward like something inside me is waking up, and it won't let me ignore anything anymore.

I pull out my phone. My thumb hovers over Maya's name. I've typed a dozen different messages over the last two days and erased them all. What am I supposed to say?

Hey, sorry you were kidnapped by demon cultists because of me. How's your week going?

And I can't dump the truth on her—not the *real* truth. Not the nightmares or the sigils or the blood or the way the world keeps tilting under my feet. She doesn't deserve the weight of that. She doesn't deserve *me.*

So instead, I type something small. Safe. Too normal for everything that's happened.

Me: *Hey. Just checking in. How are you?*

I hit send before I can overthink it again—before guilt worms its way into my fingertips and makes me delete what I've written for the thirteenth time.

For a moment, I stand there on the sidewalk, staring at my phone like I can force it to light up. The town hums around me—a car door slamming, a crow screaming overhead, its call echoing down the empty street. Fog clings low to the road, nuzzling against my ankles.

Then, my phone vibrates. Just once. My breath catches mid-inhale.

Maya's reply pops up on the screen. Short. Flat. Nothing like her usual chaotic, emoji-stuffed paragraphs that read like she's narrating her own soap opera.

Maya: *I'm okay. How are you?*

Just that. No jokes. No dramatic flair. No heart emojis or seventeen exclamation points. But she answered. And it's enough to make something in my chest unclench—just a little, just enough to breathe again.

I type back quickly, before I lose my nerve.

Me: *Hanging in. Talk soon?*

A second later, she likes the message. No words. No follow-up. But she saw it. She responded. She didn't shut me out completely. It's more than I deserve, and it puts the smallest, aching smile on my face—thin, fragile, but real.

I tuck the phone into my pocket and swing onto my motorcycle. The engine rumbles to life beneath me—familiar, grounding, loud enough to drown out the buzzing panic in my head. I back out of the driveway and roll down my street, letting the fog swallow me whole.

If only everything were as easy to start as this engine.

As I roll through the streets, Ashford looks different, wrong in a way I can feel more than see.

Shops that always open early have their lights off. The bakery's door is still locked—and Mrs. Harper is never late. A police cruiser rolls slowly past the corner like it's patrolling a war zone. People walk faster, huddled close, glancing over their shoulders like they expect something to leap from the alleys.

The air smells like the moment before lightning strikes.

As I ride toward JP's office, the world blurs around me—rusted lampposts, faded storefronts, the autumn fog clinging to the pavement. Trees on both sides of the road shed brittle leaves that scatter across the asphalt like tiny fleeing creatures.

Something is happening here. Something the town feels even if they can't name it. The pulse in my chest beats once harder, echoing deeper. I gun the engine. The office comes into view.

Whatever waits inside, I know one thing for sure: The Veil's shadow is spreading. And Ashford is starting to feel the weight of it.

I sit on my motorcycle long enough for the engine to tick as it cools, long enough for my breath to fog the visor, long enough to debate turning around and driving until Ashford is nothing but a smear behind me.

Because I don't know what waits inside that office. Not after last night. Not after Dane. JP's face when he saw him... It wasn't fear of a man—it was fear of a memory.

And I don't know which version of JP I'm walking into now: the exhausted mentor, or the stranger who let silence shatter what was left of our trust.

The pulse in my chest gives a faint, unwelcome thrum. I swallow hard and force myself off the bike. The office looks different in daylight, exposed.

Sunlight leaks through the grimy blinds in thin, dusty stripes, bleeding across the maps and files spread over JP's desk like crime scene tape. It's late morning—almost noon—and the air inside is stale with old coffee and sleepless nights.

I stand just inside the doorway, helmet still in hand, staring at the man I used to trust more than anyone. He doesn't look up. JP is hunched over his laptop, shoulders tight, hair a mess, hands trembling just slightly on the keys. He looks like he hasn't slept in days—and guilt twists my stomach, because I haven't either. Finally, he mutters without lifting his head: "Sit."

Not a greeting. Not a question. An order.

My jaw tightens. "Oh, now you want to talk?" I spit out. "Should I feel honored?"

I hear the tone—sharp, petty, childish—and part of me knows I'm being a brat. Knows I sound like a teenager slamming her door and screaming *you're not my real dad!* But I'm tired. I'm hurt. And right now, I don't care how it comes out.

JP freezes for a fraction of a second, the muscles in his shoulders coiling tight. Then, he closes the laptop—hard—like he's slamming a door in my face.

"Don't start with me today," he warns, his voice fraying at the edges.

I bark a humorless laugh that sounds more like a crack than a joke. "Why? Afraid you'll have to answer something honestly for once?"

His eyes are blue, hardened, exhausted, and brimming with a frustration that's been building between us for days.

"Really?" I step forward, heat rising in my throat, words spilling faster than I can shape them. "Because from where I'm standing, you're the one who knows everything. Dane. The fire. My mom. What I am. What the Veil wants. Your past."

My hands clench. My voice trembles. "And all the things you pretend never happened."

His eyes narrow, but he doesn't interrupt. I shouldn't say it. I *know* I shouldn't. There are lines you don't cross with JP, names you don't touch. But I'm tired of being shut out. Tired of secrets. Tired of him treating me like I'm still the girl he pulled out of a burning house.

"Like what happened to Selene Pryce."

The name hits the air like a gunshot. JP's whole body goes rigid. His breath stops. His eyes go flat and cold.

There it is. The name he never says. The shadow he never faces. The wound that never healed.

"Don't," he growls.

"You don't get to tell me *don't*," I snap, my voice cracking in the middle. "Not when you won't tell me *anything*. You keep my entire life under lock and key, and then get mad when I try to open the door."

His jaw clenches so hard I hear a faint grind. "I'm not doing this with you," he mutters, standing abruptly. "Not today."

"Then when?" I demand. "When another demon calls me by name? When Dane shows up again and reminds me he knows more about me than I do? When I wake up on fire? Tell me, JP— when exactly am I allowed to know what the hell I am?"

My voice echoes off the concrete walls. For a long, painful moment, neither of us moves. Then, JP drags a shaky hand down his face and sinks back into his chair.

"Evelyn..." His voice is rough. "I'm not hiding things to hurt you. I'm trying to keep you alive."

"Funny," I say quietly. "That's exactly what Dane said you were trying to do before my house burned down."

The words hit him like a punch. His shoulders slump. His eyes close.

"And Selene?" I push, softer now, but it still lands hard. "Was that you trying to save her too?"

His eyes open. Haunted. "Don't bring her into this," he whispers.

"Then don't keep shutting me out," I whisper back. Silence settles between us—thick, heavy, hurting both of us.

Finally, JP exhales, shaky. "I can tell you some things. But not everything. Not yet."

It's not enough. It'll never be enough. But it's more than I expected.

"Fine," I say, dropping into the chair across from him. "Start talking."

He hesitates, then nods—just once. "Dane was at the fire," JP begins. "He started it. That part he told you is true."

My throat tightens. I don't interrupt.

"I was there to stop him," JP continues quietly. "To get you out. That's all you need to know right now."

"Why was he there?" I ask. "What did he want with us?"

JP looks away. "That's the part I won't—can't—explain yet."

Anger flares in me, but so does fear. If JP won't say it, it must be something big enough to break me.

"So you'll give me half-answers?" I ask. "Is that the deal?"

He meets my eyes again. "For now."

I look away, swallowing everything I want to scream. He studies me for a moment, then asks, "What did Dane say to you?"

I tense. "Nothing important."

"Evelyn—"

"Nothing," I repeat, too fast.

How am I supposed to explain the way the air trembled around me? The heat blooming under my skin? The way something inside my ribs *shifted*—slow and deliberate—like it was waking up after a long sleep?

How am I supposed to tell him that Dane looked at me like he already knew, like he'd been waiting for that reaction?

How am I supposed to explain that Dane said I'm a *key*—to a door carved from blood and nightmares?

No. No, I'm not telling him that. Not when opening up to him means handing him more pieces he refuses to give back.

Some truths—especially Dane's truths—feel too dangerous to trust him with.

Not yet. Maybe not ever.

JP studies me, suspicion tightening his features, but I stare him down. Neither of us breaks. Eventually, he exhales through his nose—sharp, frustrated, defeated. A fragile truce forms between us, born of exhaustion, adrenaline, and the knowledge that we can't afford another fight.

Finally, JP reaches for a stack of photos. "Then, let's get to work."

And though it doesn't fix anything, I sit beside him. Because the alternative is facing all of this alone.

He finally turns the laptop toward me. My stomach tightens. The screen is crowded with photographs—nighttime shots washed in the blue haze of police floodlights, grainy phone pictures, and close-ups of carved lines illuminated by JP's flashlight.

Three images dominate the center of the page: a symbol burned into the asphalt behind the hardware store; another gouged into the bark of an ancient oak by the old church—deep enough to bleed sap like a wound; and a third splashed across the side of the abandoned train depot, the paint so black it looks wet.

I inhale sharply. They're the same. Not similar. Not variations. Exactly the same. Down to the last curve, the last angle—like they were stamped into the world by something that doesn't make mistakes.

But these aren't the small locator sigils we've seen before. They're larger—each one several feet across—and the lines don't sit flat. They ripple, rising and falling subtly as if the symbols don't just *lie* on the surface, but rest inside it. Alive.

I lean closer to the screen, pulse picking up. "These... look different."

"They are," JP mutters, rubbing at his temple. His voice is paper-thin, worn-down. "They're Ashen, but not the simple marks we've been dealing with."

His eyes flick sideways at me just enough to make my skin crawl.

"They're part of a structure," he continues.

My heart bumps against my ribs. "A structure like... what? A pattern? A map?"

He exhales, long and tired. "Like a ritual."

The word hollows out my lungs. I swallow hard. "They're trying to summon something?"

His stare meets mine—haunted, heavy, telling me more than his words ever could. "Or *open* something," he says quietly.

A cold tremor snakes through me, settling under my skin like frost.

He turns the laptop back toward himself, switches to another tab, zooms in on the symbol behind the church, its lines crisp, deep, impossibly perfect.

"Evelyn," he says, fully turning toward me for the first time today. "We need to check out the new one. It was found this morning behind the old textile plant, before the police even knew what they were looking at."

I'm already standing. "Then, let's go."

But JP doesn't move. He doesn't even breathe. Instead, he just stares at the keys on the desk—jaw tight, shoulders rigid, as if something in him is trying not to crack.

"What?" I ask, pulse skittering. "Just say it."

He finally lifts his gaze. And what I see there—fear, guilt, recognition—roots me in place. "These symbols..." His voice is barely above a whisper. "They're tied to you."

My stomach drops like a stone. "Tied to me *how*?"

The silence that follows is suffocating. He doesn't answer. He just picks up his keys with a shaky hand, closes the laptop, and heads for the door—leaving the question hanging between us like a noose.

The drive to the plant feels like holding my breath for miles. Not just because JP and I aren't talking—but because the whole town isn't either.

Ashford unfolds outside the truck windows like a place bracing for impact. Storefronts with half-drawn blinds. People stepping outside only long enough to grab mail, then slamming doors. A kid's bike lying abandoned on a lawn. Something big is coming. The tension outside matches the tension inside the cab—silent, suffocating twins.

The leather of the wheel creaks under JP's fingers. He hasn't looked at me since we left the office. Every muscle in his jaw ticks, working through thoughts he'll never share. Every few seconds I catch him checking the mirrors—not for traffic, but for threats.

Finally, we leave the residential streets behind and slip into the industrial outskirts of Ashford. Out here, the buildings are bigger and emptier. Fog clings to the ground in pale sheets. The sky hangs low, dotted with storm clouds. The air feels thick, like we're driving into a pressure cooker.

I hug my arms around myself. "This place feels..."

"Wrong," JP finishes. His voice is a low rasp.

We pass rusted machinery slowly sinking into weeds, an overturned forklift, and piles of scrap metal that look like twisted bones. The textile plant rises up in the distance—huge, hulking, and silent. Its broken windows gape like dark, hungry mouths.

JP kills the engine near a sagging chain-link fence. After the motor dies, something keeps humming—not the truck, but the *air*.

A faint vibration, almost too soft to notice, like the ground is trying to contain a shiver. JP steps out first, shutting his door quietly, like loud noises might wake something. I follow, boots crunching on gravel.

The cold hits immediately—a deep, unforgiving cold that sinks into me. Every instinct I have tries to pull me back into the truck. The pressure in my chest—the faint thrum I've been trying to ignore all morning—tightens. Like a string being tugged from somewhere ahead of me.

JP notices me freeze for half a second. "You okay?"

"Yeah," I lie. "Just cold."

He doesn't believe me. I don't believe me. But neither of us says anything else. We move together toward the plant, every step heavier than the last.

Something is waiting for us. And I'm not sure I want to know what.

We round the corner and I stop so fast, JP nearly crashes into me.

"Evelyn?" he mutters, hand lifting instinctively toward his gun. "What—?"

I can't speak. The ground behind the textile plant looks like it's been gutted. Sprawled across nearly the entire back lot is a sigil: twenty feet wide, carved so deep into the asphalt it looks like the earth itself was peeled open. Gouged with the precision of a surgeon and the brutality of a monster.

It's beautiful in the worst possible way. Circles within circles. A map and a wound. A warning and an invitation. Razor-sharp angles locking into one another like teeth. Lines branching outward like veins—or chains.

JP exhales slowly. "Bigger than the others."

My throat feels tight. "JP... this thing could swallow a car."

He steps forward, scanning the edges, every move tense but controlled. "Size means intention. They're escalating."

A cold ripple crawls down my spine.

"You okay?" he asks, softer this time. I nod, even though he knows I'm lying. Neither of us addresses it. There's too much else hanging between us.

"Go closer," he says. Normally I'd snap something back—something sharp, something angry. But not now; whatever this thing is, we need to face it together.

I swallow hard and step forward. The moment my foot crosses some invisible threshold, the ground hums. A vibration more than a sound. A distant engine turning over. A heartbeat underneath my own.

My chest tightens instantly. "JP..." I whisper.

The sigil reacts. The carved lines begin to glow—faint, pulsing, like embers revived under a breath of wind.

A tremor runs through the asphalt, subtle but undeniable, and the vibration climbs up my boots, my calves, my spine. My pulse syncs with it. One beat. Then another. A perfect, terrifying mirror.

Heat flickers under my skin—the same heat Dane teased awake last night—and I take a shaky breath as the sigil brightens just a fraction more. It's alive. It's responding. To me.

JP moves up beside me, his expression carved from stone. "Step back."

I don't.

"I've got you," he murmurs. The words are low. Rough. And despite everything between us, I believe him.

"What... what is this?" My voice sounds small.

"A resonance mark," he answers quietly. "Ashen design. Rare. Dangerous."

I shake my head. "And it reacts to... what? My heartbeat?"

"Your blood," he says. "Your presence. Your—" He stops himself.

My stomach twists. "My what?"

259

JP looks at me—really looks—and the worry in his eyes nearly guts me. "Evelyn... this is for you."

A cold gust of wind scrapes across the lot, and for a second I swear the sigil brightens again, like it's listening.

"What does that mean?" I whisper. "JP, if this thing reacts to me... then what *am* I?"

He presses his lips together.

"Dane's building something," he finally says. "And he's using you as the trigger."

I take another step back, breath shaking, but my pulse remains locked with the sigil, like it has a hook in my chest.

Before I can ask anything else: a crunch of gravel, rustling, a hiss of whispered voices.

We spin in unison, adrenaline detonating through both of us. JP's hand goes straight to his side—the Colt clears its holster with a sharp, metallic snap, barrel steady, both hands on the grip. The muzzle glints under the weak daylight.

The anger between us vanishes instantly, burned away by instinct. By training. By the fact that we've survived a hundred fights side by side.

I drop into a low stance, knife in hand, pulse still synced with the sigil behind me. The whispers sharpen. Multiply.

Four Veil cultists slip from behind the building like spilled ink, robes dragging over gravel, masks smooth and expressionless. They move fast—too fast for anything human—not toward JP, but toward me.

JP reacts instantly, stepping in front of me with his Colt up, stance wide and protective. His arm brushes mine, solid and grounding, but his voice is all panic. "Stay behind me."

But the cultists don't rush. They fan out, forming a half-circle, cutting off every escape route with eerie precision. They don't even look at JP. Their bodies pivot around *me*, their attention locked on my heartbeat like they can hear it hammering.

Dust swirls at their feet. One whispers. Another joins. Then another. Low. Layered. Chanting.

"The Key stirs…"

"The blood hums…"

"The Door is listening…"

A cold sweat breaks across my spine. "No," I whisper. "Stop—no—"

One lunges. JP fires—a deafening crack—and the figure jerks back, robes tearing, stumbling. But the shot only buys one second, maybe two. The others glide around him, sliding past him, as if he's just background noise to whatever they're here for. Like *I'm* the gravity in the room, and JP doesn't matter.

My breath stutters. I stumble back toward the sigil.

JP's voice breaks as he fights the closest cultist. "Evelyn—move! Get away from the circle!"

I try. But they close in tighter. Pushing me, guiding me, steering me like I'm a piece on a board they've manipulated a thousand times.

Their whispers rise, overlapping into something that vibrates in my teeth.

"The Key is stirring… the Key is waking…"

"Her breath feeds the flame…"

"She is the spark…"

My veins burn. Heat crawls up my arms, down my chest, pooling under my ribs. My vision blurs at the edges—bright, pulsing halos like I'm looking through a fever.

The sigil behind me glows. Faint at first, then stronger. Something inside me—some pressure I've been trying to ignore—pushes back. My knees wobble.

"JP—something's wrong—!" I choke.

"I know!" he snaps, terrified. He shoots another cultist point-blank, voice hoarse. "Evelyn, don't let them touch you!"

But one does. His hand clamps around my wrist. The moment skin touches skin, a sound like a crack of electricity splits the air.

The cultist screams—a raw, inhuman shriek—and rips his hand away as if he'd grabbed molten metal. His palm smokes. He falls backward, writhing.

I stare at my wrist. Unmarked. Normal. But I felt it: that heat, that spark, that *something* that hit him instead of me.

JP doesn't hesitate. He barrels into the cultist, knocking him out cold before he can crawl away.

The others freeze. Then, like a signal reaches them all at once, they retreat, slipping backward into the shadows, robes disappearing between broken machinery, leaving no footsteps, no taunts, no fight.

Just silence. Silence and a circle of still-glowing bloodlines behind me.

JP lowers his gun with shaking hands. "Evelyn... What did they do? Did they hurt you?"

I shake my head, panting. "No. No, I— JP, I think I hurt *him*."

His face drains of color. "What?" he breathes. "How?"

I look at the sigil. The faint shimmer. The way the glow slowly fades as my heartbeat levels. I don't know how to answer. I don't know anything—except one thing, the whisper that clings to the cold air long after the cultists vanish:. *The Key is stirring.*

Back at the truck, the cold air still vibrating with the echo of the sigil. JP's phone buzzes violently in his pocket, and he snatches it up like he's been waiting for this call.

"Volkov?" His voice dips into that clipped military register. "Slow down. I can't understand you."

The voice on the other end fires off frantic Russian—fast, panicked, almost choking on fear. I can't make out the words, but the edge in it makes the hairs on my arms rise.

Volkov was skittish when I met him. Paranoid, jumpy. The type of man who checks every shadow twice. Hearing him *panicked* feels wrong.

JP's jaw grinds. "Repeat that. How sure are you?"

A pause. Wind cuts through the lot, sharp and metallic.

"...Shit."

JP ends the call harder than necessary, thumb slamming the screen. He stands there for a moment, exhaling through his nose like he's trying to steady something breaking inside him.

"JP?" My voice wavers.

He finally looks at me, and inside the dread in his eyes, there's something new. Something heavy. "The Veil," he says slowly, "Their movements... They're not random anymore. Every attack, every sigil—every damn thing—they're all pointing to the same location."

My pulse spikes. "Where?"

He hesitates. "Ridgefield."

I blink. "Ridgefield? That's... that's not even close. That's three hours north."

He nods once, grim. "Exactly."

My heart stutters. "So, the Veil isn't circling Ashford anymore. They're moving—?"

"Pulling," JP corrects, voice tight. "Everything they're doing, everything Dane's orchestrated... It's all dragging you in one direction."

I step back, breath fogging in the cold. "Why Ridgefield? Why that far?"

JP hesitates. And that's how I know it's bad. "That mall out there," he says finally. "The old one. The one that shut down before you were even born."

"The Ridgefield Commons?" I whisper. "That place is... dead."

"Yeah," JP mutters, swallowing hard. "And in a dead place, the Veil can work without eyes on them."

A cold tremor ripples through me. Ridgefield Commons—all shattered skylights dripping rust, empty escalators frozen mid-crawl, storefronts with charred mannequins and hollow glass eyes—is a concrete graveyard with a hundred places for shadows to breathe.

The same mall where we met Volkov. Where he told JP I'd be his undoing.

"I heard rumors back in the day," JP says, eyes narrowing at the map. He's not looking at me anymore—he's staring at some point just past the paper, like he's connecting dots he wishes he didn't recognize. "Whispers from units farther north. Ashen activity. Strange readings. Groups experimenting with symbols like these. Failed ops. Missing teams."

He goes quiet. My pulse kicks up. "You've seen this before?"

"Not *this*," he snaps a little too fast. "Never this concentrated. Never this close to home."

I step closer, chest tight. "Then what aren't you telling me?"

JP's jaw clenches. "This isn't about my past."

"Actually," I whisper, voice threading thin, "I think it's about what's coming."

He flinches—a tiny, sharp movement he doesn't realize I caught. Not guilt. Not memory. Fear.

Before he can respond, a pulse detonates inside my chest. I gasp and grab the truck door, knees buckling.

"Evelyn!" JP lunges toward me, Colt still in one hand, the other outstretched but trembling. "What is it? What's happening?"

"I—" The breath tears out of me. "I don't know. It's pulling. Harder than before. North. Toward—" My voice cracks. "—Ridgefield."

JP goes pale. He takes a small step back before catching himself.

"Evelyn," he says shakily, "this pull—does it feel like pain? Like pressure? Like heat?"

All of the above. And none of the above.

"It feels like... like something waking up," I whisper.

His breath stutters. The air between us feels heavier than the sky. Everything Dane warned, everything the Veil whispered, everything JP hasn't told me—it all collapses into one terrible truth: Whatever I am, the mall is calling to it.

JP swallows hard and looks north, into the dense forest that hides Ridgefield miles beyond the horizon.

"That's where Dane is," he says softly. Then, he looks at me. "That's where he wants you to go."

Chapter 17

Gathering Storm

Morning light slips through the blinds in thin, uneven slats, pale gold sliding across my room like lines on a map. The air carries a chill that sinks straight into my bones. Everything feels too quiet. Too still. Like the world is pausing before something breaks.

I move through my room slowly, methodically—the way people pack before leaving their home for war. Every motion feels deliberate, heavy with meaning I don't want to look at too closely. My hands won't stop shaking no matter how hard I flex them or clench my fists.

My knife. Holster. Ammo packs. Gauze rolls. Flashlight. A small med kit. Extra blades. The gear JP drilled into me to carry, the things that mean the difference between living and not.

All the pieces of a life I never asked for—tools that might keep me alive if tonight goes bad. Maybe even if it goes right.

Because tonight isn't just another patrol. It isn't another hunt or another ambush in the woods. Tonight, JP and I are going back to Ridgefield Mall, back to the place that feels like a wound in the center of a map.

We're going to see if we can end this—once and for all. I'm walking into something I might not walk out of.

I pause over each item, making sure it's what I need, then lower it into the duffel. The soft thuds stack up, one after another, each one tightening the air around me. By the time half the gear is inside, the room feels smaller—like every piece I add pushes the walls another inch closer.

The overhead light hums faintly, flickering once, just enough to raise the hairs on my arms. My breath catches. I wait. But nothing else happens.

Still, every few minutes, a tremor flickers under my skin—like someone striking a live wire inside me. Not painful—not exactly. Just wrong. A spark that doesn't belong, a pulse that seems to move with intention. Like something is brushing the inside of my ribs. Testing. Tapping. Waiting.

As if the thing Dane talked about—the spark, the fire, the Key—isn't dormant at all. It's here, pacing.

I exhale slowly, forcing the tremor down, pretending it doesn't scare me, and my fingers brush the necklace resting at my collarbones.

The chain is warm from my skin, the small silver charm smooth where years of touch have polished it. I curl my hand around it, thumb tracing the tiny engraving I could draw blindfolded.

Holding my mother's necklace tight, I close my eyes. For a heartbeat, the world isn't demons and sigils and whispers calling me something I don't understand. For a heartbeat, I'm twelve again, standing in the living room while she twirls to music, laughing like light.

"I wish you were here," I whisper, voice breaking in the empty room. "I wish you could tell me what's happening to me."

A spark tremor shivers up my spine, sharp and unexpected. I suck in a breath, unclench my hand, and tuck the necklace back under my shirt, letting it rest it against my heartbeat like a secret.

Then, I zip the duffel, sling it over my shoulder, and walk out of my room before fear convinces me to stay.

The stairs creak under my boots as I head down, each step heavier than the last. The house smells like stale radiator heat, cheap coffee, and burned toast. Home. Ordinary. Painfully, achingly ordinary.

It feels wrong for the world to smell this normal today.

In the kitchen, my dad stands hunched in his work jacket, lunchbox ready on the counter, a plate of half-eaten scrambled eggs cooling beside him. The overhead light washes him in pale yellow, softening the lines on his face.

He looks... normal. Too normal for a morning where I don't know if I'll make it back.

He glances up, fork pausing midair. His eyes widen just a little, surprised to see me before noon.

"You're up early," he says, voice gravelly.

"Yeah," I breathe. "Big day."

He nods slowly, really looking at me, like he's noticing the shadows under my eyes, the tension in my shoulders, the way I'm gripping my duffel so tightly my knuckles are white.

He hasn't looked at me like this in years. Not really. Not past the haze of grief and bottles.

He clears his throat, shifts his weight, and wipes his mouth with the back of his hand. Nervous. Almost shy. "I, uh..." He swallows hard, "wanted to say thanks."

It takes me a second to respond. "For what?"

His shoulders lift in a small, awkward shrug. "For... sitting with me. The other night." His voice cracks slightly, and he winces like it embarrasses him. "I—It meant more than you think, Eve."

A lump rises in my throat so fast it almost chokes me. Before I can talk myself out of it, I step forward and wrap my arms around him.

269

He freezes—for just a heartbeat. Then, his arms come around me in a slow, hesitant embrace. Careful. Gentle. Like he's holding something precious he thought he'd lost a long time ago.

"I love you, Dad," I whisper into the worn fabric of his jacket, voice trembling.

His breath stutters. His chest rises and falls against mine. "I love you too, kid," he murmurs, rough and honest.

For a moment, the kitchen is just quiet breathing, warm arms, and the illusion that everything might be okay. Just a father and daughter pretending the world isn't about to demand something terrible from one of them.

When I pull back, he cups my cheek with a work-roughened hand. His thumb brushes a shadow under my eye.

"You look tired," he says softly.

"I'll sleep after... work," I lie.

His brows pull together—he knows something's off, but he doesn't push. "Be safe."

"You too."

I sling the duffel over my shoulder before he can ask anything more—before he can see the fear in my eyes—and slip out the door. It closes behind me with a soft click that feels too much like goodbye.

The cold morning air hits me like a slap when I step outside. I straddle the bike, the leather seat stiff from the chill, and the engine rumbles to life beneath me. Nothing feels settled anymore.

I ease onto the street and let the town fall behind me, house by house, block by block. The road stretches ahead in a straight gray ribbon, lined with bare trees that claw at the sky like fingers.

Normally, riding clears my head. Not today. Today my thoughts cling to me like frost. *What if this is the last time I leave home? What if the pull in my chest is leading me somewhere I can't come back from? What if Dane was right about what's inside me?*

I tighten my grip on the handlebars until my fingers ache. Every so often, another flicker shivers under my skin—a little spark, a pulse of heat, that pressure behind my ribs whispering that something is changing, waking.

I swallow hard. I don't want to be dangerous. I don't want to be important. I just want to be... me. But I don't even know who *that* is anymore.

Wind rushes past the visor of my helmet, the world blurring into streaks of gray and brown in the weak autumn light. The familiar route to the office feels foreign, like I'm riding toward a place that won't exist the same way once I arrive.

Halfway there, the hairs on the back of my neck rise. That prickling awareness. That instinct. Someone is watching me.

I flick my eyes to the mirrors. Nothing. Just empty road. Bare trees. A lone parked truck gathering frost. No movement. No footsteps. No shadow slipping between buildings.

But the feeling doesn't fade. It presses between my shoulders, crawls down my arms, settles low in my gut. I swallow hard and push the bike faster, letting the roar of the engine drown my thoughts.

By the time I pull into the alley beside JP's office, my pulse is racing and my breath fogs the inside of my helmet. I cut the engine and sit there for a moment, heart hammering, waiting for the sensation of being watched to fade.

It doesn't. Not until I step inside the building and shut the door behind me. And even then, I'm not sure it leaves.

The office feels different today, charged. The air hums with a low, static pressure, like the walls are bracing for something.

I take the stairs two at a time, boots thudding on the worn steps. The hallway is dim, old bulbs flickering and casting long shadows that tremble across the floorboards. The storage room door at the end hangs half-open, a bar of white fluorescent light slicing across the darkness.

I pause at the threshold.

Inside, JP stands hunched over the workbench, shoulders tight beneath his worn gray Henley, sleeves pushed to the elbows. His forearms flex as he works, loading magazines with slow, precise movements—click, slide, press, repeat. His stubble is thicker than usual dark circles bruise the skin beneath his eyes. He hasn't slept, not even a little.

Weapons are spread out across the table: blades, holsters, blessed rounds, demon-snare chains.

He still doesn't look up as I step in. "You're early," he mutters, voice rough.

I drop my duffel on the table beside him. "So are you."

A humorless huff escapes him—part laugh, part sigh. "Didn't sleep."

I lean a hip against the table. "Same."

His hands finally still. He lifts his head. Our eyes meet. For a moment, everything that's been twisting between us eases.

He nods toward the tools. "We need to prep. Grab the silver-coated blades. Check their edges. Tighten your holster straps, too. Tonight's going to be... heavy."

I snort softly. "That the technical term?"

"It's the one I've got," he says without smiling, but something about the line relaxes both of us.

I unzip my bag and pull out my knife. The metal catches the fluorescent light, reflecting a sharp, cold sheen. There are faint dark stains on the edge: old demon blood, crusted into the grooves. Cleaning it feels like washing off pieces of myself I'd rather forget.

JP watches me in the reflection of the blade. "Why didn't you tell me your hands were shaking?" he says quietly.

I freeze. My fingers tremble around the hilt—barely, but enough. I force them still. "Just tired."

He slides a freshly loaded magazine onto the counter with a soft *click*. "We're both tired," he says. "That doesn't answer my question."

I grit my teeth. "JP... can we not do this right now?"

Silence. Then, he nods once. A small surrender. "We'll talk upstairs," he says, "after prep."

We fall into rhythm. Not friends. Not enemies. Just two people who know how to move together, even when they're falling apart.

I sharpen and oil the knife. He counts rounds. I check the edges of the silver blades. He organizes gear into piles. Our motions sync without effort—years of training, arguing, and surviving translated into muscle memory.

We both reach for the same bundle of blessed rounds, and our fingers brush. Both of us jolt back like the metal burned. JP clears his throat, rubbing the back of his neck. "Blessed rounds... are in the top drawer. Take a set."

"You think we'll need them?" I ask.

He hesitates. That alone is terrifying. "We take them," he says finally. No elaboration.

When we finish, he shuts the weapons case with a soft, final *click*. The sound settles in my bones—heavy and inevitable.

"Upstairs," he murmurs.

I wipe my palms on my jeans, pretending the sweat isn't from fear. A tremor sparks under my ribs—hot, sudden, sharp. A pulse of pressure. I press a hand to my chest, breath catching, willing it to stop.

JP notices. His jaw flexes hard, but he stays quiet. The stairs groan under our boots as we climb—an old, tired sound that echoes up into the dim second floor. The office feels colder up here, the heater clicking uselessly in the corner. Papers litter the desk in messy stacks, the laptop screen glowing with a map of Ridgefield covered in red markings around the mall. Danger zones, patterns, ritual vectors.

JP closes the door quietly behind us, but the sound feels loud in the stillness.

I drop onto the edge of the couch near the window. He stays standing for a moment, arms crossed tight over his chest, staring at the floor like he's trying to piece together answers from the cracks in the wood. The distance between us feels like a continent.

My throat tightens. "We need to talk."

His jaw works once before he sighs, long and exhausted. "Yeah," he murmurs. "We do."

He drags a chair over but sets it *just* far enough away to feel deliberate—not intruding, not welcoming. Neutral ground. He sits, elbows on his knees, hands clasped loosely. Up close, he looks older than I've ever seen him, eyes dark from sleepless nights, stubble shadowing his jaw, weariness carved into the corners of his mouth.

And beneath it all: fear.

"Your turn," I say, voice low. "You've been keeping things from me since the night of the fire. Since before I even knew demons were real."

He winces. "Evelyn, I..." He swallows hard. "It wasn't lying. It was— Damn, I don't know. Survival. For both of us."

"That's not good enough."

His shoulders sag. "I didn't know how to tell you the truth without..." His voice cracks. "Without losing you."

Something sharp twists in my chest.

He looks down at his hands, the same hands that pulled me out of fire, trained me, dragged me through hell and back. "When I found you in that burning house... When I carried you out..." His voice thins. "You were just a kid. And what Dane was trying to do—what your mother died protecting you from— Evelyn, I swore I'd never let that happen again."

My breath stutters. "JP," I whisper, "what was she protecting me from?"

"Being used." His voice breaks. "Being turned into something you didn't get to choose."

A spark tremor hits—sharp, electric—flaring under my ribs. I clamp my arms tighter around myself, hiding it with a rigid breath.

But JP sees everything. His eyes narrow. "Evelyn... what was that?"

"What was *what*?" I deflect, too fast.

"The way you just tensed. The shake in your hands." He gestures gently—soft, careful. "Something's happening to you."

Panic spikes. "JP, don't—"

"Hey." His voice softens. "I'm not accusing you of anything. I'm asking you."

My throat closes. If I tell him the truth—the heat, the pressure, the way reality blurs at the edges—I don't know what he'll see when he looks at me. So I stay silent, just one beat too long.

JP watches me, jaw tightening. Then, he nods. "Okay," he says. "We'll talk about it when you're ready."

The relief and guilt tangle in my chest so fiercely they almost choke me.

He exhales, pinching the bridge of his nose. "For years, I've been terrified I'd fail you the same way I failed her."

"Her," I echo softly. "My mother?"

Pain flickers across his face. "Not just her."

My breath catches. "Selene."

He goes still—like the name hits a bruise that never healed.

"You won't talk about her," I press gently. "About what happened. About how she died."

He lifts his head, blue eyes raw and unguarded. "It's not because I don't want to." His voice is barely audible. "It's because some days, I still feel like I'm there, holding her lifeless body. I don't know how to carry that and protect you at the same time."

The room around us is suffocating.

"You don't have to protect me from your guilt," I whisper. "I'm strong enough to handle it."

He laughs softly—a broken, humorless sound. "Evelyn... I'm not trying to shield you from guilt. I'm trying to shield you from *me*."

My eyes burn. "JP... I'm scared."

He looks up sharply.

"I don't know what I am," I admit, voice trembling. "I don't know what Dane wants. I don't know if I'm dangerous, or useless, or—" My breath cracks. "Or both. I just know I'm changing, and it terrifies me."

JP moves before I register it, kneeling in front of me, palms braced on his thighs, head tilted just enough to catch my gaze.

"Evelyn." His voice is low, rough, breaking. "There is nothing— *nothing*—in this world that could make me afraid of you."

Something inside me shatters like thin glass.

"I need you," he says, voice shaking. "I need you to trust me enough to let me protect you, even if you never forgive me for what I kept hidden."

I blink back tears. "I do trust you. I'm just... tired of being lost."

He nods once—slow, sure. "Then I'll help you find your way. Whatever you become, whatever we face, I'm right here. Not leaving."

My vision blurs. I turn away before the tears fall. A sharp tremor ripples through my chest and I swallow it down. One thing at a time. "Okay," I whisper. "Let's... plan."

He squeezes my shoulder, then stands. Together, we move toward the desk. Maps. Weapons. Notes. Danger. Together. Not fully healed. Not fully okay. But together. For now.

Maps rustle across the desk as JP spreads them out— topographical layouts, old blueprints, satellite printouts of Ridgefield Mall. The paper smells like dust and toner, the edges frayed from handling. Outside, the late afternoon light leaks through the blinds in pale stripes, casting long shadows across the mess.

JP leans over the maps, tapping a pen against one of the highlighted entrances. "The west loading bay is the easiest access point, but it's also the most obvious. If the Veil is expecting us—which they are—it'll be watched."

I adjust the blade at my hip, sliding my thumb along the familiar grooves on the hilt. "So we don't use the obvious route."

"Exactly." He circles the edge of the main lot, his brow tightening. "We take the front parking area. It's obvious, which is why it works. The Veil's expecting shadows and back entrances, not two people walking straight up like they belong there."

I raise a brow. "Going through the front is our big plan?"

"It's the least fortified angle," JP says, voice low. "If the Veil expects anything, it's that we'll try sneaking in."

I huff out a humorless breath. "So we're betting on them underestimating us."

He cracks the ghost of a smile. "We're due for a little luck."

We both know that's a lie, but we let it slide. Some things are easier to pretend.

He moves to the next map, tracing a line through the mall's walkways with a tense finger. "Nothing lines up clean. No central locus. No clear pattern. Dane's either hiding his tracks or scattering them on purpose." His jaw ticks. "Which means we cover everything. Every wing. Every floor. No assumptions."

I nod slowly, the weight of it settling in my chest. "So we go in blind."

"Not blind," JP says. "Prepared."

"JP..." I meet his eyes. "We both know there's a difference."

His throat works, but he doesn't argue. Not this time.

A flicker of pain lances behind my ribs; the pull toward Ridgefield surges again, a deep, internal tug, like someone hooking a string behind my sternum and gently reeling me forward. I inhale sharply through my nose, forcing the tremor down.

"You okay?" JP asks quietly.

I nod too fast. "Just... tired."

He looks like he wants to push, but doesn't. Maybe he's too afraid of the answer. Maybe I am too.

We move wordlessly for a few minutes, slipping back into the rhythm we know best. I sort through the gear on the table while JP double-checks each item: blessed rounds stacked neatly beside silver-coated knives, extra magazines that snap into place with a familiar metallic click, flares, medical kits, and JP's homemade anti-possession sigils—little paper wards he tucks into ammo tins like secrets.

The room fills with the soft chorus of metal, leather, and quiet breath, a silent agreement that tonight will demand everything we have.

He hands me a pack of ammo. "Load up. You're faster with the ten-mil than I am."

"Only because your hands shake," I say before thinking.

He gives me a flat look, but there's tenderness buried under the exhaustion. "Thanks. Really needed the reminder."

Despite everything, my lips twitch. "Just being honest."

"Well," he says dryly, "we're having a lot of that today."

I slip a magazine into place, the metallic click sharp in the quiet. "JP... do you really think we can stop him? Dane?"

His eyes lift to mine. They're tired. Haunted. But steady. "We're going to try," he says. "And we're going to do it together."

Something hot stings the backs of my eyes. I look away, pretending to double-check the strap on my thigh holster.

After twenty more minutes of planning—entry routes, fallback plans, coded signals in case we're separated—we start hauling gear downstairs.

The cases thud against the asphalt as we load them into the truck bed one by one, heavy with steel and fear. The air outside smells like cold asphalt and woodsmoke drifting from a distant chimney.

The sun is sinking behind the tree line, bleeding purples and gold across the sky. It's the kind of sky that looks like a warning.

JP closes the tailgate with a soft clunk. We both stand there for a moment, side by side, staring at the truck like it's a lifeboat and a funeral hearse at the same time. Neither of us speaks. Neither of us has to. This might be the last sunset one—or both—of us sees.

Finally, JP turns toward me, expression soft in a way that guts me. "Ready?"

My throat tightens. I shake my head once. "No."

He nods, like he expected that. Like he feels the same.

"But let's go anyway," I whisper.

JP's jaw clenches. He opens the truck door, waiting for me to climb in first. I take a breath. Then, I do.

The truck rattles beneath us as JP pulls out of the parking lot, headlights slicing through the early dusk. I buckle myself in, fingers trembling just enough that I hide my hands in my jacket sleeves. The hum of the tires on cracked asphalt is steady—too steady—like the calm before a storm that doesn't care who it will destroy.

I stare out the window, watching Ashford blur by. Houses I grew up around. Streets I used to bike down. Roads where scraped knees and summer heat were my biggest problems. All of it feels small and distant now, like it belongs to someone else's life—some other girl who didn't have demons stalking her or fire under her skin.

We pass Bean & Gone, its neon "OPEN" sign flickering in the dimming light. Through the windows, I catch a glimpse of the bar counter, the clutter of mugs, the chalkboard menu I've memorized down to its smudged flourishes.

For half a second, I swear I see Maya behind the register, hair pulled back, rolling her eyes at one of the regulars. But it's not her—just another barista. Just another shift that I won't be there for. A pang hits me, sharp and unexpected.

I think of Maya's awkward text yesterday morning. Of her smile, quieter now. Of how she used to shove pastries at me when she thought I hadn't eaten. Of how normal she made me feel.

I think of my coworkers too: Tasha humming off-key when she's stressed, Jordan flirting with literally anything that breathes, the way they'd all tease me for being "mysteriously intense."

They don't know where I'm going tonight. They don't know what I'm about to face. I don't know if I'll see them again.

The coffee shop disappears behind us as JP turns onto the highway, and the ache in my chest settles deeper—something between grief and longing. The world I knew is slipping away in the rearview mirror.

My chest starts to tighten. Not from the spark tremors creeping deeper under my skin, not from the fear gnawing at the edges of my mind, but from the unknown waiting for me in Ridgefield.

Cold wind hisses along the seams of the truck. My breath ghosts against the window, fog blooming and fading as the last scraps of daylight slip away.

I try to focus on the road. On the hum of the engine. On anything except the fear simmering inside me.

But the quiet... The quiet drags me backward. Not to the fire. Not to the smoke, or the screaming, or the night everything went dark. To a week later, the night of my mother's funeral.

I remember the stiff black dress. The murmurs of strangers who didn't know her laugh. My father disappearing halfway through the reception, leaving me alone in a sea of pitying faces. The world felt too big, too empty, too ruined.

JP found me outside, sitting on the curb with my arms wrapped around my knees, trying not to cry but failing anyway. I remember the way he crouched beside me—not too close, not touching, just close enough that I didn't feel like I was drowning alone.

When he brought me to the truck, I slid into this exact seat. Smaller then. Lost. Silent. He didn't drive right away. He just sat there with me in the dark, hands braced on the steering wheel, head bowed like he was praying for the right words.

Finally, his voice—soft, rough, certain—broke the silence: "I won't let anything hurt you, Evelyn. Not while I'm alive. I will always protect you."

I remember how terrified I was of a future without my mother—of what had killed her, of the shadows I couldn't name. But sitting next to him, something inside me steadied. Even then.

Even now.

The memory dissolves as the truck hits the highway, merging north. JP glances at me, just once, just long enough for me to see the fear warring with determination in his eyes.

"Evelyn?" he asks softly.

"I'm okay," I lie, but the corner of my mouth lifts. "As okay as I can be."

He nods, understanding more than I say.

Outside, the sky darkens into deepening blues and steel-gray clouds. The wind howls across the road, beating against the truck like a warning. The hum in my ribs answers it—faint, but unmistakable.

Something is waiting for me in Ridgefield. Something I'm not ready for. But I'm not going alone.

The truck pushes north, headlights cutting a path through the coming night. JP's presence beside me—steady, grounding, unshakable—wraps around the fear pulsing under my skin.

And for the first time since Dane touched my life, since the sigils began glowing, since the Veil whispered my name, I don't feel entirely powerless.

Whatever waits for me—whatever waits inside me—I'll face it. Because JP is here.

And for tonight, that's enough.

Chapter 18

The Mall of Ash

Ridgefield's dead mall rises out of the dark like a carcass left behind by something older and hungrier than time. The parking lot unfurls in every direction, an abandoned black sea carved by the skeletal remains of rusted light poles. Some lean like drunks mid-collapse; others jut upward like broken ribs. Weeds claw through the asphalt in jagged veins, spreading outward from cracks like something beneath the surface has been trying to break through.

The storefronts stare back at us—dark, hollow-eyed, long-forgotten. Glass blown out. Plywood rotting. Every doorway, a mouth left open in a silent scream.

My pulse thumps harder with every foot we roll closer, a quiet hammering behind my ribs that grows more insistent, more alive, the nearer we get. JP eases to a stop near the far edge of the lot. The engine ticks heat away in soft metallic pops, each one swallowed instantly by the dead, dense hush pressing in from all sides.

JP kills the engine, and the night eats the silence whole.

A thin wind slithers across the cracked asphalt, tugging at loose debris, carrying the stale scent of rain that never came. Underneath it: the faint iron trill of rust and old oil. And beneath *that*—something low and patient. Something aware.

"Stay sharp," JP murmurs, eyes sweeping the lot. His voice is steady, but I hear tension threaded through it. He doesn't touch me—not really—but his hand grazes my arm. A small, grounding brush. A familiar warning: *Stay alive*.

He scans the darkness with the care of a man who's walked into burning buildings and expected not to walk out. Mapping exits. Counting shadows. Listening for ghosts.

I swallow, my mouth suddenly dry. "Always." I push the door open. The air outside is colder than it has any right to be. Gravel crunches beneath my boots—unnervingly loud—echoing across the empty expanse like we've trespassed into someone else's territory.

My fingers drift instinctively to the knife at my hip. My mother's knife. The steel is cool, steadying, a whisper of comfort against my palm. The Glock presses warm and solid against the small of my back, loaded with runed rounds capable of tearing through demon hide like wet paper.

I slide the knife free. Guns create distance; knives tell the truth.

JP moves to my side, shoulders squared, posture coiled with the kind of tension that only comes when a man senses a trap long before he sees it. His voice barely rises above the wind: "You feel that?"

I hesitate. "Yeah..." But it isn't just the chill biting under my jacket. It's the prickling pressure crawling up the back of my neck. The unmistakable sensation of eyes on us—watching, waiting, circling. *So much for going through the front unnoticed.*

The plan already feels naïve. Like we walked straight into a spotlight neither of us can see.

I turn, scanning the dark edges of the lot. The shadows lean inward. Watching. Waiting. Like the whole dead mall is breathing slow and deliberate, anticipating the first scream.

JP's hand hovers near his holster. "Talk to me."

"I don't know," I whisper. "It just—feels like something's... looking."

285

He nods once. "Good. Trust that."

JP circles the truck and falls into step beside me, every muscle in his body wound like wire. We move together toward the mall's outer walkway. At first, it's just emptiness, wind chasing an old paper bag across the asphalt. The hollow echo of our footsteps bouncing between concrete pillars.

No people. No cultists. No demons. But the air... The air feels *thick*. Heavy. Like the whole mall is waiting for us to enter.

The deeper we move into the lot, the more the world feels... wrong. Not dangerous, not overtly threatening, but misaligned. The air carries too much cold in it. Too much stillness. Too much quiet.

A breath like winter fingers drags down my spine, sinking straight into my bones.

"JP..." I murmur, struggling to keep my voice from betraying me. "Do you feel that?"

His jaw tightens, a twitch pulsing beneath his stubble. "Yeah. Been feeling it since we passed the old movie theater." He tries for steady, but the words are thin, like saying them any louder might wake something up.

We move through a scatter of abandoned shopping carts sitting at odd angles, their metal frames half-fused to the asphalt by rust and time. One lies on its side, wheels still rocking faintly, though the wind is barely reaching it.

A torn strip of faded caution tape flaps from a lamppost. Its whispering scrape against metal sounds almost like a voice—a warning too late to matter.

"Feels like we shouldn't be here," I murmur.

JP scans the rooftops, the shadows, the far corners of the lot—never lingering on one spot, always moving. "We shouldn't," he says quietly. "But here we are."

Another gust of wind crawls between us. This one, colder. Sharper. It cuts through my jacket, sinks into my ribs, and sits there like it's claiming space it doesn't deserve.

JP stops. I halt beside him, knife tightening instinctively in my hand. His eyes track the pavement ahead.

"Look," he whispers.

At first I see nothing but darkness, cracks in the asphalt, trash pinned to the ground by old rainwater stains. Then—beneath the grime, the dust, the weeds—a line. A faint curve at first, barely visible; then another, and another.

My breath catches. "Oh…" The word slips out before I can stop it. "JP."

Burned into the ground beside a cracked storm drain is a sigil. Ash clings thick around the grooves, as if the mark wasn't drawn but scorched there—recently.

JP drops to a crouch, his flashlight's beam cutting a thin, harsh line across the symbol. His mouth hardens into a grim slash. "This is fresh," he mutters. "A day old. Maybe less."

The wind dies completely, as if even the air is afraid to move. I step closer before I can stop myself, curiosity, dread, and something else—something deeper—pulling me in.

The moment my boot grazes the outer ring, the sigil hums. A soft, low vibration rattles under the sole of my shoe, rising through my ankle like the ground is drawing a breath. A faint orange glow flickers, ember-like, in the carved grooves. Pulsing. Waking.

I jerk back with a gasp. "JP."

"Back up," he snaps, standing so fast the gravel skitters. "Evelyn, get away from—!"

But it's already too late. A spark tremor ripples through my ribs, sharp and electric, matching the sigil's rhythm. My heartbeat stutters. Catches. Then falls into time with the glyph's pulse.

The glow brightens, slow and full of intent, like it's tasting my presence and finding it familiar. Like it's responding to my blood, to whatever the hell I am.

My throat tightens. The cold feels heavier, coiling around my lungs. "It— JP, it reacted to me." I step back, voice cracking. "That thing reacted to me."

JP stiffens, body going still in that controlled, disciplined way that says he's two breaths from fight mode. His gaze flicks from the sigil to me, and something inside him buckles—fear surfacing, tangled with regret he's spent years trying to bury.

"They're mapping the whole lot," he says finally, scanning the surrounding asphalt. "Ashen geometry. A full ritual spread."

Heat buzzes under my skin like someone struck a match in my chest. I swallow hard. "And I'm the what?" My voice is raw. "Say it."

JP's jaw flexes. He doesn't answer, not immediately. He looks at me in a way he never has before, as if seeing the outline of something he's been terrified to name. As if the truth he's been hiding is no longer willing to stay buried.

He swallows once, twice. Hard. "You're the variable they're building it around," he says.

His tone is steady. Like he rehearsed that lie a hundred times. And it is a lie—not the words anyway, but the substitution. *Variable*. Because that's not what he meant. That's not what almost slipped out. And we both know it.

The real word hangs between us in the cold air, heavy and suffocating: *Trigger*.

The sigil pulses again behind us. Stronger this time. Like it heard him and agreed. Like it just woke up hungry.

We push forward across the empty lot, heading toward the mall's main entrance. The glass doors hang crooked on broken hinges, one of them cracked down the center like something tried to claw its way out. Graffiti scorches the metal frames—warnings, symbols, slurs—none of them enough to chase away the wrongness seeping from inside.

The moment we step through, darkness swallows us whole.

Our footsteps echo off shattered tile, loud in the suffocating hush. The air drops ten degrees instantly, cold sinking into my bones like the mall is exhaling decades of rot. Overhead, the ceiling is a grid of warped metal, its missing tiles leaving exposed wires hanging like veins torn from flesh.

JP's flashlight shakes faintly—almost imperceptibly—as it slices through the dark and across hollow storefronts.

Abandoned stores gape open on either side: dust-coated mannequins frozen mid-pose, blank eyes catching the light; rejected clothing racks stripped bare; sale signs curled and yellowed with age; food wrappers fossilized in corners like offerings left for ghosts.

"This place is a graveyard," I whisper before I can stop myself.

JP's jaw ticks as he scans ahead. He doesn't disagree. His flashlight sweeps across a cracked concrete pillar—and freezes.

Painted on the column in thick, tar-black strokes is a sigil. Large. Violent. Complex. The lines overlap like tangled bones, that same raw geometry that feels *wrong* to look at. The paint still glistens, wet enough to drip.

"JP..." My voice breaks. "That's not old."

He steps closer, lowering the beam. "This wasn't here in any of the scouting photos," he mutters. "This is new. Hours. Maybe minutes."

Before I can respond, my own flashlight beam grazes the sigil, and the lines shimmer. Just a flicker, a pulse, following the exact rhythm of my heartbeat. Heat spikes under my sternum—sharp and sudden—like something inside me just lurched forward to answer.

I stumble back so fast my boot scrapes tile. "That's— That's not normal," I choke out. "JP— Did you see—?"

He grabs my hand in a single controlled squeeze meant to steady me. But his own skin is cold, tension wired through every tendon. "Yeah," he says. "I saw. Stay with me. Don't touch anything."

His voice stays low and measured, but it's stretched thin, like he's holding panic behind his teeth, refusing to let it loose. We keep moving.

The mall corridor stretches ahead in a long, black throat. Our flashlights barely scratch the surface of the darkness that seems to absorb the beams rather than scatter them.

A toppled kiosk blocks part of the walkway, its plastic display shattered, fake jewelry scattered across the tile like offerings on a broken altar. A single indoor plant—dead, brittle, leaves curled to nothing—sits on its side, dirt spilled in a soft mound.

The air grows heavier with every step. Thicker. Harder to breathe. Then, the hum returns. Faint at first. Underfoot. A quiet throb, like a heartbeat buried beneath concrete.

My own heart stutters, falls out of sync, then snaps back into rhythm with the pulse vibrating through the floor. I stiffen. JP notices instantly.

"What is it?" he asks, already scanning our flanks.

"I don't— JP, I think it's reacting again."

He moves in front of me, hand drifting toward his holster. "To what?"

"To me." The words scrape out of me. "It's... aligning with me. Like before. Like it knows me."

JP's breath hitches, confirming the thing I've been terrified to admit. We push deeper down the corridor.

Around the next bend, the mall opens into the wide central concourse where fountains used to roar and crowds once moved shoulder to shoulder.

Now it's nothing but an empty pit. A void. And carved into the center of the cracked tiles is another sigil. Bigger. Vast. A geometry of circles and lines so intricate, it hurts to look at it straight on.

The grooves glow faintly and pulse in the same slow, steady rhythm as my chest. The reaction is immediate. My ribs crush inward as if the air has thickened around my lungs. Heat crawls up my spine. My vision warps at the edges, tunneling around the glowing lines.

JP grabs my arm. Hard. "Hey— Evelyn— Look at me. Focus."

"I— JP— I can feel it pulling." My voice is barely a whisper. "This one's stronger."

The sigil brightens. Just a shade. Just enough to prove it heard me. JP's eyes flare in fury. "They're using these to triangulate you."

"Triangulate," I echo, breath trembling. "Like a signal."

He doesn't answer. He doesn't have to. The answer is already burning under my skin: a trigger, a key, a beacon.

Whatever word he won't say, the sigils already know it. We stand there in the dead center of the mall, the glow growing brighter, the hum deepening, the air vibrating around us like the walls are waking up.

And then, the shadows at the far edges of the concourse begin to move. JP's grip tightens. "We're not alone."

Up ahead, an escalator sits frozen mid-step, rust chewing at the rails. Food court chairs lie overturned like people ran from their meals mid-bite. Trays scattered. Straws crushed. A soda cup still half-full of something black and cemented with age.

Then, the smell hits: thick mold, old dust, and burnt copper, like a forge left to die centuries ago. It sticks to the back of my tongue. Sinks into my clothes. Into my skin.

Another hallway yawns open, swallowing the beam of JP's flashlight whole. On the far wall, another sigil. Not painted this time, not dripped or brushed. Carved.

The grooves gouged deep into brick, each stroke measured and powerful. Whoever made this didn't use tools; they used strength. Or claws. Or something worse. The lines pulse as we pass.

We turn a corner. Another sigil. Then another. Then another.

A whole web of symbols encircles the mall like a massive ritual nest, each one gleaming a little brighter when I come near. My skin prickles under the attention and every hair on my arms rises like static crawling across my bones.

"They're connected," I whisper, voice thin. "All of them. This is... this is a pattern."

JP's jaw hardens. "Yeah. A net."

"Built around me."

His silence confirms it. My spark trembles with every step—small, hot flickers under my ribs, embers trying to breathe, trying to rise. I press a hand to my chest as it stutters again, heat punching through me in an uneven rhythm.

Then, a sound, not ours. Footsteps. Soft. Synchronized. Measured. Shapes peel out of the shadows behind a row of dead kiosks—silhouettes stepping deliberately into the faint glow of JP's flashlight.

Four. Five. Seven. Veil cultists.

Their black robes trail over cracked tile, their masks carved with hollow eyes and long slit mouths. They tilt their heads toward us in perfect unison—animalistic and mechanical at the same time.

JP draws his Colt so fast the metal flashes white in the dark. "Stay behind me," he growls.

But I don't. I shift to his flank, knife already in my grip, the familiar weight grounding me even as my pulse spikes. My heart hammers, but my hands are steady.

The cultists don't attack—not right away. They expand outward forming a wide crescent around us, cutting off every exit except the one we came from. Herding, just like last time. Their breaths hiss behind their masks, and their voices slip out like thin, dying whispers:

"The Key walks the threshold..."

"The blood hums..."

"The Door... prepares..."

Their words crawl across my skin like frost. I grip the knife tighter, but the spark beneath my ribs pulses like it's answering them. A heavy creak echoes above us. Metal. Strained, like weight shifting

"JP," I whisper too late. The ceiling lattice groans and something huge dislodges. The cultists lift their heads.

A demon drops from the second-floor balcony with a bone-shaking *CRASH*, shattered tile exploding outward under its weight. The creature's stench hits instantly, and its skin ripples like oil poured over jagged rock. Its black eyes snap straight to me—never to JP. It doesn't speak my name, but the way it looks at me makes it spill across my mind anyway.

JP fires, muzzle flash shredding the dark, but the demon snaps sideways at the last millisecond, twisting unnaturally, anticipating the bullet. Like something forbade it from letting the shot hit. Then, it lunges.

"EVELYN! MOVE!"

I dive hard, rolling across broken tile. Glass slices my palm and the pain flares sharp and hot. I shove off the floor, popping to my feet just as the demon's claws carve through the air where my throat had been.

I slash upward, blessed steel grazing its shoulder. The demon shrieks—not in pain, but in recognition. It staggers back, head cocking, circling me low, predatory, calculating.

"Come on," I growl through clenched teeth, raising my knife. "Try it. Try me."

Its lips peel back in a grin fueled by hunger and prophecy. It lunges again. But this time, I'm ready.

I duck beneath its swing, slam my knee into its chest, feel ribs crunch under the impact. Before it recovers, I carve along its chest, the blade slicing a seam of black ichor that splatters across broken tile like tar.

It reels, eyes burning hotter. Then, it hesitates. Claws hover inches from my throat. Again, held back. Another killing blow denied. A cold ripple runs down my spine. *What are you waiting for?*

The demon lunges, but its angle is wrong. Not for my throat, not my chest. It slams into my side, shoving me, steering me, corralling me to the center of the court. Toward the massive sigil carved into the tile, huge enough to swallow a car. Lines spiral and hook like a trap waiting to snap shut.

"No," JP snarls behind me. He fires again—the gunshot cracking through the court. "GET AWAY FROM HER!"

A cultist aiming at my back jerks violently, mask splitting open. Another robed figure rushes JP from the left; he twists, parries, slams his demon-killing blade into the attacker's ribs, then fires point-blank over the collapsing body's shoulder. He moves with brutal precision, but he's outnumbered. He won't hold them alone.

The demon charges me again, wild and skittering. I pivot, letting its momentum overshoot me, and slice the back of its knee. Bone gives with a wet crack, and it crashes onto all fours, howling.

But it doesn't retreat. It crawls toward me—dragging itself, shaking—drawn to me like a moth to flame.

"STAY BACK!" I shout, kicking it in the chest with everything I have.

The demon slams into a broken pillar, stone fracturing on impact. For a second, I think it's done. Then, it rises. Trembling. Spasming. Drawn. Controlled. Bound.

Its claws hook my jacket and yank me forward so hard the air punches out of my lungs. My ribs scream. I slash its wrist, tearing through tendons, and black blood splatters the wall in a thick arc. It releases me with a ragged screech, shaking its hand like my touch burned it..

Heat erupts beneath my skin. Pressure surges outward, bursting behind my ribs like a detonating spark. And the demon, mid-snarl, freezes.

Its nostrils flare. Its pupils widen. Its breath rattles like it's inhaling something sacred and forbidden. Slowly, haltingly, it lowers itself... into a kneel.

My stomach drops. "What—?" The word tears out of me, shaking.

Around us, the cultists whisper louder, frenzied, trembling, reverent:

"She stirs—"

"The Key awakens—"

"The blood remembers—"

JP sees the kneel. Something breaks in him. "NO YOU DON'T!"

He's already moving, fury snapping off him like sparks. He tackles the demon off me so hard the impact echoes through the court. He slams it onto its back, tile spiderwebbing under the force. Before it can twist free, JP drives his blade straight into the base of its skull.

CRACK. A violent shudder. Stillness.

He grabs my arm—hard—dragging me upright. "MOVE!" His voice is raw, frantic. "More are coming! MOVE!"

Footsteps thunder from every hall—masks, claws, shadows multiplying like a tidal wave crashing inward. We are seconds from being drowned.

The sigils around us glow brighter, pulsing in perfect sync with my heartbeat. Calling. Urging. Commanding.

No. Not now. Not here.

"JP!" I gasp. "The Door— We need to move!"

He yanks me away from the burning symbol. "Don't—!" His voice cracks. "Don't even look at it! RUN!"

We sprint into a service hallway, boots slipping on broken glass. The roar rising behind us is deafening—either the demons tearing after us or the magic in the sigils spiraling to life. Or both.

My pulse hammers so hard it feels like it's trying to break out of my chest. Like the thing inside me is waking up, whether I want it to or not.

JP shoulders open the west exit door with a violent slam. Cold air smashes into us like a wall.

We stumble out into the mall's backside: a wide, empty loading lot scattered with rust-eaten dumpsters, cracked pavement, and dead light poles jutting from the ground like broken bones.

The door swings shut behind us with a metallic *clap* that ricochets across the concrete. And then, there is silence. Not relief, not calm. Something worse.

My breath fogs in the air, each exhale hanging too long before vanishing. Then, it starts. That feeling. A prickling, icy crawl up the back of my neck like fingers dragging across my skin.

My stomach tightens. Someone is watching us. Not the cultists. Not the demons. This is something else. Something higher. Something patient.

My eyes dart across the rooftops, the jagged edges of broken fire escapes, the dark mouths of vents lining the top of the mall. The wind doesn't even move. The night doesn't shift.

Nothing breathes. But the sensation stays—hot and cold at the same time—like a stare pressed between my shoulder blades, unblinking.

"JP..." I whisper. "We're not alone."

He doesn't look up. He doesn't turn his head. But his hand drifts—slow, subtle, instinctive—toward his Colt.

"Eyes forward," he murmurs. A command through clenched teeth. "Don't give them anything."

We descend cautiously into the center of the lot, boots crunching through weeds and fractured asphalt. The only sounds are our movement and the faint whistle of my own breath shaking.

We're halfway across the lot when the ground flickers. At first, I think it's the moonlight shifting. Then, the dirt beneath our boots glows: soft, faint, like embers under ash.

"JP..." I breathe.

He swings the flashlight downward, and the darkness drops away.

A giant glyph—hidden beneath years of grime, trash, and overgrowth—*IGNITES*. Lines swirl outward beneath our feet, circles within circles, spirals interlocking into a perfect geometric lattice. Each groove hums with deliberate purpose, pulsing like something alive has just opened its eyes.

I don't have to be told what it is. It's a Door. Not an exit. Not a portal. A Door. And it knows me.

The light pulses again, a long, slow beat—and my own heart slams into sync with it.

A pull gathers behind my sternum, sharp and hot. A hook embedded deep inside me yanks forward with invisible force. The pain steals my breath—hot, jagged, blooming outward like something trying to claw its way out of me.

"JP..." My voice cracks. "I can feel it. It's... calling me."

His head snaps toward me like he's been shot. The expression on his face—I've never seen it before. Horror stretches across his features like something tearing him open from the inside.

"I know," he whispers, voice shaking. "Evelyn, don't move. Don't step any closer."

But the pressure is rising, thrumming through the concrete, pulsing up my legs, racing through my bones. The sigil hums, awakening under my feet. My knees weaken.

Shadows shift at the far edges of the lot. Then, one by one—like figures peeling themselves free from ink—shapes detach from the darkness. Hooded figures. Cultists in heavy robes. Demons with glistening claws, their bodies rippling like oil. And other things—low, skittering shadows with too many joints and no faces at all.

Dozens. Maybe more. Emerging in a slow, deliberate ring. They don't charge. They don't growl. They simply stand—silent, reverent—as though bearing witness to a ceremony. Or a coronation.

The sigil beneath us brightens. The light burns up through the dirt. The air thickens into something syrupy and electric, sticking to my lungs.

I gasp. "I— JP— I can't—"

He steps in front of me, shoulders squared, planting his boots like a wall constructed by fury. Every muscle in him vibrates with protective violence. "It's a trap," he growls, voice low and shredded. "We walked right into it."

The sigil pulses again. Then again—faster, harder—until its light becomes blinding, washing the world in white fire. The ground vibrates. The hook in my chest pulls harder. My spark thrashes like it's being dragged awake by force.

And every shadow around the lot takes a single step forward.

Chapter 19

First Spark

JP and I stand our ground as the Veil circle us.

They move, separating from the dark like it's shedding them on purpose. One shape... then two... then four... until the shadows are crowded with bodies I can't count.

Robes drag like funeral cloth over the cracked concrete. Masks glint faintly under the Door's growing light. But it's the eyes behind the masks that twist my stomach: black, glassy, glowing, like the eyes of predators waiting by firelight.

Behind them, worse things crawl out.

Demons with spines jutting too far from their backs, ribs rising and falling in sharp, irregular jerks, their limbs bending in angles that should shatter any skeleton. Teeth glisten wet, as their mouths unhinge too wide, sucking in the cold air in slow, greedy breaths.

The temperature drops. The air thickens with pressure. Every inhale tastes like a storm.

"Stay behind me," JP murmurs, raising his Colt. The gun glints silver in the Door's glow, the etched sigils along the slide flickering like they're waking up too. His stance is pure muscle memory: feet braced, shoulders squared, ready to die before he lets anything touch me.

"On you," I whisper, though the knife is already in my hand, my grip so tight the hilt bites into my skin.

The nearest cultist steps forward, head tilting, inhaling deeply like he's savoring perfume.

"The Key stands in the circle," it murmurs, voice dripping reverence. "At last, she answers the call."

My jaw locks. I force my legs to move. JP moves with me, half a breath behind, always guarding my left side like instinct.

Suddenly, the sigil under our boots explodes into light: first, a faint pulse like a heartbeat testing itself; then, the lines flare. Circles within circles, angles sharp as fangs, latticework that shouldn't make sense.

Dirt shrivels. Weeds curl into ash. The grime burns away to reveal the full carved geometry beneath: a door.

Not metaphorical, not symbolic, but a thing built into the world. Waiting. Cold light bleeds upward through the cracks, crawling over our boots, licking up my spine.

The pull snaps tight. It yanks behind my sternum—hard—like a hook buried deep in my chest suddenly remembered why it was planted there.

I choke on a breath. "JP—!"

He's already turning toward me, face twisted with fear he doesn't have time to hide. "Evelyn," he warns, voice breaking. "Don't move. Don't you take one step."

"I'm not—" I gasp, stumbling as the pull drags again. "I'm not *trying* to!"

The cultists whisper louder, circling tighter. Their robes brush the asphalt in rhythm with the Door's pulse.

"She awakens—"

"Blood of the veiled flame—"

"The boundary parts—"

JP raises his gun toward them, voice thunder-low. "One more step and I drop every one of you."

A masked figure laughs—a dry, rattling sound like brittle leaves in wind. "You cannot protect her from what she is, soldier."

JP fires once—clean, controlled. The cultist's mask snaps in half, body collapsing in a heap.

For a moment, the circle halts. But the Door doesn't. Its light pulses. Strong. Faster. Brighter. The ground vibrates under us. My ribs vibrate with it. The hook inside me pulls again—violently this time. The force nearly knocks me to my knees.

"JP—" I gasp, reaching for him without meaning to. "It's inside me. The pull— It's—"

"I know." His voice is steel. And agony. And love. "I know, kid. Stay with me. I've got you."

But the ground shudders again, harder. The sigil brightens to blinding white. The air howls as if inhaling.

And every Veil figure around us takes one synchronized step forward. The first demon lunges. Then, the lot erupts. Claws scythe for my throat—fast, impossibly fast. I duck, feel the wind split over my head, and drive my knife up beneath its jaw. The blade bites deeper than steel should, the blessed alloy hissing as it meets corrupted flesh. The demon convulses, black veins spiderwebbing across its neck before it detonates into greasy ash that the wind scatters like burnt leaves.

A second comes from my left—low, too fast, jaws unhinging wide enough to swallow my face. I pivot hard, slam my heel into its ribs. *Crunch*. The impact rattles up my leg. It staggers just long enough for—

BANG. BANG.

JP's Colt spits twin flashes. The rounds punch through its skull, the runes along the casings flaring blue before the corpse collapses into smoke.

There's no flow. There's no rhythm. This isn't a battle—it's a street fight in hell, teeth and claws and shadows slamming in from every angle, leaving no space to breathe, no time to think.

My world narrows to blows and breath. Hook. Cross. Elbow. Knee. Steel. Blood.

A demon rakes its claws across my shoulder—hot pain bursts down my arm—but the agony dulls in seconds, the torn skin knitting even as I twist away to avoid a finishing bite.

Another grabs my jacket from behind, wrenching me backward. I react without thinking. I spin, slash blind. The blade catches something soft—flesh? throat?—and warm spray splatters my neck. The thing screeches and drops.

"LEFT!" JP barks.

I drop instantly. A demon barrels through the space where my head was a split-second before. Its claws rip sparks from the ground.

BANG.

JP's first shot takes out its left eye, snapping its head sideways.

BANG.

The second shot ends it. The demon folds to its knees, then collapses into cinders. But the next one is already coming.

Boots scrape behind me—JP, pivoting, gun smoke curling from his barrel as he fires point-blank into another robed figure reaching for his back. The mask fractures, its body going limp mid-lunge.

"On your right!" he shouts.

I spin too slow. A demon slams into me like a freight train, knocking the breath out of my lungs. We crash into the asphalt, rolling in a flurry of claws and limbs. I jam my forearm under its throat to keep its fangs off my face; the weight is crushing, breath hot and rotten.

I stab upward again and again—chest, neck, eye socket—the knife biting, tearing. The demon shrieks, its claws gouging asphalt on either side of my head. Then, its body crumbles over me, collapsing into powder.

I shove it off, panting. But there's no time to stand. Another shadow looms. Another claw arcs down. Another voice hisses my name like a curse.

"EVELYN, MOVE!" JP roars.

I roll instinctively, a demon's hand smashing into the ground where I'd been lying, splitting concrete like rotten wood. JP fires over my shoulder, the bullet tearing through the demon's jaw. It reels back screaming, just enough for me to drive my knife up into its gut. I rip sideways. The creature folds, dissolving.

"Stay close to me!" JP shouts, voice cracking under the strain.

"I'm trying!" I yell back, slashing at another set of claws.

"Try harder!"

He's terrified, and he hides it well, but I hear it in the ragged edge of his breathing. This isn't a battle he can control. This is a tide he can barely hold back.

And they keep coming.

Shapes peel out of the darkness, first from the left, shadows splitting into robed figures with blades glinting. Then, from the right, another wave surging forward, feet pounding the pavement in a sickening rhythm. Whispering voices swell behind us, rising out of the black like a chorus dragged from a nightmare.

We're surrounded. Pressed in on all sides. Hemmed in by bodies that move like they're part of one mind, one purpose.

The sigil beneath our feet pulses—once, twice—like a living heart beating under the concrete. Light seeps through cracks in the pavement, white-gold and hungry, as if it's pulling every cultist closer—and pulling *me* with them.

The air vibrates with their chanting, with the pounding footsteps, with the thrum building in my chest in perfect sync with the sigil's pulse.

JP steels himself, stance shifting, but even from here I can feel it: He's not enough for this. Not tonight. Not against *this many*. And the terror he thinks he's hiding bleeds into the air like smoke.

We give ground without meaning to—foot by bloody foot, breath by burning breath—pressed toward the glowing circle because every other direction is worse. Dead ends. Claws. Masks. Teeth. The dark itself turning hostile.

"As soon as we get an opening," JP grits out, blocking a clawed hand with the butt of his Colt, "we break for the truck."

"Got it," I say—though the words feel thick, strained, because the lines of the sigil tug at me like gravity trying to rewrite my orbit. Every pulse of that light digs hooks deeper into my ribs.

The demons attack again, but their ferocity is tempered, redirected. Claws that should slice my jugular veer at the last second, grazing my cheek instead. Jaws that should clamp onto my shoulder snap at empty air, herding me sideways. Even their kicks land strange—hard enough to bruise, to shock, to shove—but never enough to break.

They're still shoving me toward the burning center of the Door like sheepdogs pushing a lamb into a pen.

"Do not step in that circle," JP snaps, his voice a bark of command so sharp it jolts straight through my bones.

"Wouldn't dream of it," I shoot back—though my feet itch to move forward, though heat curls in my chest and whispers, *go, go, go*.

Then, all at once, the demons falter. They don't fall; they simply... stop. Like someone pressed pause on the world.

A single breath hangs suspended. The air thins, as if sucked inward. It gets colder—enough to sting my teeth, and my lungs seize for a beat. And then, I smell it: not demon rot, not brimstone, not blood—but smoke. Clean, faint, like candles blown out in a room where someone had been praying.

A ripple shudders through the cultists—shoulders bowing, heads tilting, bodies dropping a fraction lower in something like reverence or fear. I can't tell which.

My chest tightens. "JP..." I whisper. "What is—?"

"Don't," he says sharply. "Don't say a thing. Don't give him anything."

The shadows at the far edge of the lot are moving, making room.

He doesn't walk out of the dark; the dark simply decides to let him emerge. Like it's been holding him, shaping him, waiting for its cue.

Dane.

A black coat settles perfectly across his shoulders, untouched by wind or ash. His eyes—still cold as winter lightning—land on me with all the inevitability of doom.

A slow smile ghosts across his mouth. *Found you*.

JP inhales sharply beside me—the smallest sound—but in this silence, it's deafening.

"Evelyn Cross," Dane murmurs, voice soft but coiled with danger. "On time, for once. I'm touched." His tone drips with amusement, like we've stumbled into some twisted tea party instead of a ritual meant to tear the world open.

My grip tightens around my knife hilt. "You set all this up just to drag me back here?" My voice comes out raw. "Ever heard of texting?"

One corner of his mouth lifts, the smallest, cruelest smile. "Still hiding fear behind sarcasm," he murmurs. "You really do have his wit." His eyes flick briefly toward JP—gleaming, knowing. "And your mother's eyes," he adds softly. "Unmistakable."

My stomach drops. Heat and cold collide under my skin; my eyes—my hazel-gold, too-bright, too-aware eyes—have always betrayed me. They shimmer when my emotions surge, flicker like embers when something inside me stirs. And I feel that shimmer now. A faint glow blooming at the edges of my vision—unwanted, undeniable—like sparks catching dry tinder.

A tremor ripples through me—heat, cold, and something deeper. Something waking. I plant my feet anyway, refusing to give him the satisfaction of seeing me waver.

JP shifts half a step in front of me, Colt leveled at Dane's sternum. His stance is coiled, furious, ready to break everything to keep me alive.

"That's far enough," he growls. "You don't take another step toward her."

Dane gives the gun a lazy, uninterested look, as though JP's aim is a buzzing fly by his ear. "You brought salt and scripture to a bonfire," he sighs. "Adorable, Pierce. Truly."

"Back. Away." JP's voice vibrates with murder.

Dane lifts one hand—the gesture effortless, negligent.

A demon collapses to its knees beside him, spine bowing as if compelled by a command older than language.

"I'm not here for a brawl," Dane says, amusement sharpening into something colder. "I'm here for the girl."

"She's not a girl," JP snaps. "She's my responsibility."

The word lands in me like a weight—heavy, familiar, too much like a cage. Not JP's fault. Still, it stings. I step out from behind him.

I'm done being shielded. Done being spoken for.

"You want something?" I rasp. "Say it to me."

Dane studies me like a jeweler inspecting a rare gemstone, checking for fractures he already knows are there. His eyes gleam with satisfaction and coil sickeningly in my gut.

"I'm here," Dane says softly, "to keep my promise. To offer you what you've earned: a choice."

His voice drops lower, silk over steel. "It's time you stopped pretending ." His gaze sharpens like a blade. "You're not an accident, Evelyn. You are a Key trying very, very hard to pretend you're human."

Heat surges under my skin and crawls along my collarbones, threading down my arms, humming behind my ribs.

"You're wrong," I snap. "About all of it."

"No," Dane says mildly. "I'm not." He takes a single step closer.

The Door beneath us flares—bright, violent, eager—its lines pulsing in perfect harmony with his movement. Light crawls outward, chasing his shadow.

"You think your little tricks—your strength, your healing—are flukes?" His voice is quiet, intimate, like he's whispering truth into a wound. "That the way demons scent your fear and salivate at your heartbeat is random?"

His smile widens a fraction. "You're a doorway, Evelyn Cross." He leans his head slightly, studying me with predatory affection. "And doors," he whispers, "are not meant to stay shut forever."

"Enough," JP bites out, each syllable ground through his teeth.

Dane's eyes flick lazily toward him. His smile doesn't widen, but it sharpens. "Ah. Yes," he murmurs, voice soft enough to bruise. "The soldier who dragged you out of the first fire."

Then, he moves. Not a blur. Not a sprint. Just gone from where he stood.

One heartbeat, JP is beside me, gun steady—unshakeable, the human wall I've leaned on my whole life. The next heartbeat, he's gone. Yanked forward as if invisible hooks sank deep into his spine and ripped. His boots leave the ground.

The sound he makes—half grunt, half gasp—is swallowed by the violence of the motion. He hits the asphalt hard enough to rattle the air around us, a brutal, sickening thud that vibrates up my legs. He rolls with the impact, muscle memory kicking in faster than breath can return to his lungs.

And he comes up firing. Three shots—clean, controlled, lethal. Heart. Head. Heart. The pattern he drilled into me since I was old enough to hold a weapon.

Perfect. Unquestionable. And completely useless.

Because Dane simply isn't standing where the bullets arrive. He hasn't blurred. He hasn't vanished. He's just... not there.

As if he saw the trajectory half a second before JP pulled the trigger and casually stepped aside—no hurry, no strain, hands still tucked in his coat pockets. His expression is almost bored, like gravity, ballistics, and the laws of physics are all tedious inconveniences he outgrew long ago.

The blessed rounds slam into a rust-eaten light pole instead. Metal bursts in a spray of orange flakes. The runes etched along the bullets flare a dull, frustrated blue—sparking angrily before they fizzle out against cold steel.

Those bullets were meant for monsters. And the man standing in front of us just made them look slow.

JP doesn't pause. He surges forward in a burst of trained violence, closing the distance with military speed, shoulder low, elbow tight. He throws a short, vicious punch aimed at Dane's throat: a killing strike.

Dane catches his wrist mid-air, fingers curled almost delicately around bone. The *crack* is wrong. Wet. Like the cry of a snapped sapling branch.

JP's wrist folds at an angle it was never meant to. He grunts, pain shooting down his arm, but he doesn't stop. He rides the momentum, pivots, throws an elbow with his other arm. But Dane steps into it, not away. His elbow slams down across JP's clavicle with perfect, leisurely precision. Something gives—another sharp, brittle snap that makes bile rise in my throat.

"JP!" The scream tears out of me before I can stop it. Demons lunge to block my path. I go through them. Knife, heel, knee— movement blurring with instinct and rage. I parry a claw, jam my elbow into a temple, feel bone crunch under the impact. Another lunges, and I duck, sweep its leg, slit its hamstring, spin, and slice its throat in one fluid arc.

I'm fast. I'm strong. I'm bleeding and healing at the same time, wounds knitting mid-fight as if my body refuses to let me stop. But for every monster I drop, another shudders into its place—masks and claws and teeth forming a wall between me and JP.

Another second stolen. Another second Dane has his hands on him. Another second closer to losing the only person in this damn world who ever chose me.

"GET—OUT—OF—MY—WAY!" I snarl, slashing another cultist across the face, ichor spraying. But the circle tightens. My vision blurs with fury. My heartbeat pounds in my skull.

Ahead of me, Dane holds JP upright by a fistful of his jacket, studying him like a specimen. Like a thing he has already broken and is deciding whether or not to discard.

JP spits blood at his feet. "You touch her again," he growls, voice strained and ragged, "and I swear— I swear— I'll—"

Dane tilts his head, amused. "You'll try," he says. And his grip tightens before he lets go.

Dane sweeps JP's legs out with a casual flick of his heel—no force wasted. JP hits the asphalt hard, the impact knocking the breath from him in a sharp, agonized grunt. His back arches, air leaving him like it's been punched out of his lungs.

He rolls instantly—trained, automatic—hand reaching for the Colt lying inches away. Dane doesn't even look. He kicks the gun aside with one polished boot, sending it skidding across the concrete. It slides straight toward the edge of the Door, its glowing lines curling toward it like hungry, reaching fingers.

Then, the light recoils, rejecting the weapon, and fades back into its pulse.

JP swears under his breath. Pain turns the sound ragged. He shoves a hand under his jacket, fingers closing around the short silver blade sheathed against his ribs. He rips it free and slashes upward. No warning. No windup. No hesitation. A killing move.

But Dane catches his hand mid-strike. His fingers clamp around JP's wrist like a man closing a book mid-sentence—casual, bored,

311

unbothered by the blade's blessed edge trembling inches from his throat.

"You don't touch her," JP snarls through his teeth. Dane leans in slightly, as if sharing a secret across a dinner table. "I plan to do much more than that," he murmurs, voice soft enough to chill bone. "Just not tonight."

Then, without shifting his expression, without winding up, Dane drives his free hand straight into JP's torso. Just under the ribs. Angled up. The strike is brutal, practiced, and designed to break.

The sound is sickening: a thick, wet thud, like meat hitting stone and something inside it coming apart.

JP's breath leaves him in a choked, wheezing exhale and his body folds around the pain, his knife clattering from his hand.

Something tears open inside me. A hot, ripping surge under my sternum—as if the same place the Door is pulling from just got yanked in half.

"JP!" My scream cracks out of me—high, sharp, animal.

Dane turns his head fractionally toward my voice, grey eyes gleaming with a quiet, pleased recognition. Like he just struck the exact note he wanted. Like he knows the fracture he's carving open in me is the one he's been aiming for all along.

I'm on them before I even register moving—one heartbeat, I'm behind JP on the ground; the next breath, I'm in Dane's shadow, blade raised high.

I swing for his throat with everything inside me—every nightmare, every lie he forced me to live, every "you're not ready," every second JP spent breaking himself to protect me. All of it pours into the strike.

Dane turns—not fast, not startled—just a smooth, effortless pivot, like a door swinging on a well-oiled hinge.

My knife misses his throat by inches, skimming along his jaw instead. A thin line opens. Dark, molten blood spills and steams in the cold air. His eyes flare. Not with fury. With delight.

"Oh," he breathes, voice smooth and hungry, almost a laugh. "There you are."

His backhand hits before I even register the movement. It feels like a truck colliding with my skull. The world detonates sideways—light, sound, and air turning inside out. The asphalt slams into me, scraping skin. I roll, momentum carrying me until my palms skid across cracked concrete.

My vision splits into two overlapping worlds, both spinning. My cheek burns—sharp, electric—but the skin is already sewing itself back together in hot, healing.

"Evie—!" JP's voice—hoarse, torn—reaches me like a thread I'm about to lose.

I force myself upright, legs shaking, head ringing. I lunge at Dane again. He still doesn't meet me with effort. He steps aside, not even breaking rhythm. A lazy tap to the nerve cluster in my shoulder—my arm goes dead, knife nearly slipping. A casual nudge to my ankle, and my knee buckles for half a breath.

He's not trying to kill me. He's showing me how little it would take if he wanted to.

"Get away from him," I snarl, shaking with fury.

Dane's smile is soft, almost pitying. "Make me," he murmurs.

Movement flickers at the far edge of the lot. A figure. A silhouette where there wasn't one a second ago—slender, still, hair long enough to move with the faintest wind. Watching.

My heart lurches violently, a twist of shock and recognition I don't understand. Not now. Not here.

"Evelyn." JP's voice is barely a sound at all—just air shaped around pain.

I turn toward him instinctively, but Dane is already looking down at JP, head tilted with a disturbingly gentle curiosity. He touches two fingers to JP's temple. A mock blessing. A benediction twisted into a threat.

JP's eyes roll—once—then snap into focus past Dane's shoulder. They widen. Wider. Wider than I've ever seen. His lips part around a single word—one I've heard in whispers, in warnings, in the quiet grief he never let himself voice.

"Selene."

It's not a shout. It's not even a breath. It's a wound. Then, his breath hitches—shallow, broken—and blood bubbles at the corner of his mouth, dark and wet, catching the Door's light as it spills.

Something inside me shatters.

I don't have time to process. Rage spikes so violently I taste copper on my tongue—hot, metallic, primal. I launch myself at Dane again, this time faster, lower, using everything JP drilled into me. I feint low, cut high.

The blade whistles past his throat, and he tilts his head in a smooth, lazy motion. My knife still catches him.

Metal kisses skin. A strip of hair falls. The blade sinks deep enough into his collarbone to drag a sharp, involuntary hiss from his throat. Real pain, real surprise.

His eyes flare—not furious, not afraid, but thrilled. He reaches up with two fingers, plucks the knife free, and studies the smoking blood beading down the steel like he's admiring art.

"Well," he says, voice bright and pleased. "Progress."

He flicks the blade once between his fingers—effortless, taunting—before lowering his hand toward me. "Come now, Evelyn. You'll want this."

He opens his palm and lets the knife fall. Instinct overrides thought. I dive forward, snatching the hilt before it hits the asphalt. The metal is still hot—so hot it should blister—but my fingers don't let go. Not this time.

The moment the blade is back in my grip, Dane's smile sharpens, as if this was exactly the choice he wanted me to make.

Then, he raises his hand. Not fast. Not threatening. Just a simple, elegant lift of fingers.

Every demon left responds like a detonated bomb. They hit me in a single synchronized wave. Claws rake my shoulders. Teeth snap for my throat. Hands seize handfuls of my jacket, my hair, my arms, dragging me backward, sideways, down.

I twist hard, drive my heel into a knee—something snaps with a wet crunch. I wrench free from one grip, stab upward through a jaw. The demon dissolves into ash before it fully hits the ground.

Another lunges. I duck, slice across its throat. It bursts apart in a cloud of black dust. A third clamps its jaws around my forearm—teeth shatter and fall as my skin begins knitting mid-bite.

But they keep coming. There's no gap. No breath. No space. Just bodies. Just claws. Just weight and heat and pressure.

I'm fast. I'm vicious. I'm healing as I fight. But it's not enough.

A demon barrels into my side like a battering ram. Something in my ribs pops—sharp, white-hot pain streaking through my chest. My vision flickers. For the first time tonight, real fear digs its fingers into my spine.

"JP!" I choke out, not sure if it's a plea for help or an apology or a goodbye. He doesn't answer.

The demons tighten around me. Their breath is hot and wet on my skin. Their claws hook my clothes. Their weight crushes the air from my lungs. And through it—calmly, casually, like strolling through a garden—Dane walks.

His coat doesn't ripple. Dust doesn't cling to him. Nothing gets close enough to touch him. His eyes shine like he's watching a sunrise only he can see. He stops just outside my reach.

"Little Door," he murmurs, voice soft enough to be mistaken for affection. "Open."

Something inside me gives. Not bone. Not muscle. Not anything human.

It's the lock I've spent years bolting shut around the wild, wrong thing inside me. The piece that woke in fire once—and went back to sleep because a twelve-year-old girl needed to believe she could still be normal.

Grief tears it open. Anger holds it there. Love—stupid, fierce, aching love for the man bleeding behind me—pours gasoline on it. The world doesn't explode. It snaps. Like the air was stretched too tight and finally split open. And everything inside me comes flooding through.

Heat floods my veins—not surface heat, not burn-your-skin heat— but something deeper. Something incandescent. Like light forced inside bone, filling the hollow spaces and searing outward.

The air thickens. The sigil beneath us screams, silent but deafening. For a breath, I'm nowhere. No weight. No edges. No body. Just pressure—pure pressure—surging outward from the center of me in every direction, a shockwave tearing at the seams of the world.

The nearest demons don't burn. They unravel. Flesh cracks like dry paint. Their bodies split into seams of black dust. Ash bursts outward where they stood, then scatters on a wind that didn't exist a second ago.

The Door erupts, white, blinding, catastrophic light roaring up through the lines. The sigil thrums in time with my heart, reaching toward me, then recoiling violently, like it grabbed a live wire and couldn't hold on.

Dane staggers back a full step, the first real movement I've ever seen him make that he didn't choose. His coat snaps in a wind that doesn't touch anything else. His eyes go wide—then brighter, glowing with awe and hunger.

"Yes," he laughs over the rising roar. "There you are."

The power ripping through me doesn't feel like mine. It feels like standing next to a blaring storm siren—sound turned into vibration, rattling teeth, joints, marrow. My vision whites out at the edges. The necklace at my throat goes ice cold—a shock cutting through the heat.

Old concrete pillars crack without sound, fracturing from the inside out. They shear downward into dust with no flame, no explosion, just unmaking. Boarded storefronts blacken from the center, their wood curling inward before collapsing into soot that drifts like snow.

I fight to breathe. *Control*, JP's voice echoes—not from here, but from another night, a basement lined with mats, sweat and frustration in the air. *Breath, Evelyn. Footing.*

I drag air into a chest that feels too large for my lungs. My feet feel anchored and slipping at the same time, like sand is spilling out from under me. I reach for brakes—for something to grip, to slow, to stop—and find nothing.

Then, the surge shudders, like it spent what it came to spend. The light recedes a fraction, just enough for me to see again. The Door still glows, its pulse steady, alive. But not as blinding.

The remaining demons—two, maybe three—take one look at me, at the sigil, at what just tore through the world, and choose vapor over a second chance. They dissolve themselves, turning to ash in an instant.

Dane lifts one hand to shield his face from the fading glare, still laughing—delighted, reverent. The cut on his collarbone seals in seconds. "Enough for tonight," he says, voice soft and wrong in the suffocating quiet that follows. "You'll tear yourself apart if I let you keep going."

He kneels and lays his palm on the edge of the circle. The glow climbs his skin like a living thing licking along his fingers, tasting him, then settling. He stands and looks at me one more time. His eyes bright, greedy, triumphant.

"Soon, Evelyn."

A promise. A threat. A prophecy.

"Don't run from what waits inside you. The Veil won't." Then, he's gone.

No smoke. No blur. One blink, and he's not there anymore. The Door dims, its furious glow calming into a slow, heavy pulse.

My knees give. And I drop. The asphalt punches the air from my lungs. Pain hits late—then all at once—like a tidal wave roaring through every nerve. My muscles buzz with leftover power, flickering uncontrollably. Too much and not enough all at the same time.

"JP," I wheeze.

I crawl. The distance between us feels like *miles,* like crossing a world, but it's only a few feet of cracked, glowing concrete. I reach him.

He's sprawled on his back, face grey, lips tinged blue at the edges. His breath comes in shallow, ragged pulls that don't fill his chest.

Blood soaks his shirt, pooling thick and glossy under him, catching what's left of the Door's fading glow.

"Hey," I whisper, and my voice cracks clean down the middle. "Hey, I'm here. I'm right here."

His eyes—heavy, unfocused—still find me. Like they always do. Like they were built to. For a flicker of a second, they drift past my shoulder, drawn by something at the far edge of the lot. His breath stutters. His gaze sharpens. Fear? Hope? I can't tell.

I turn to look and, just for a heartbeat, almost as if the night is unsure whether to show her or hide her, she stands there:

Selene Pryce.

Blonde hair falling loose around her shoulders, a color too soft for a place like this. Eyes like storm light and dawn woven together. A face I've only seen in grainy photos shoved in old folders. A face I've pieced together from the quiet ache behind JP's eyes whenever her name came up in a breath he didn't finish.

My chest cinches tight. She's smaller than the legend I built out of JP's silence. More human, more breakable. But the air bends around her anyway—subtly, unmistakably—the same way it bent around Dane. Like the world is careful with her.

Her gaze shifts back to JP, and something cracks inside me at the look on her face—a soft, haunted sorrow I've never seen in the photos. She steps forward and kneels beside him, her pale fingers hovering an inch above the torn place under his ribs. Not touching. Just... near.

The bleeding slows, like someone pressed pause on his dying.

My vision blurs. Selene lifts her head and looks at me.

"Evelyn," she says quietly. And the way she says my name—like she's known it longer than I have—hits me like cold water. It feels

319

like remembering something I've been trying not to remember. Something impossible.

My throat seals shut. I can't speak. So I nod. Because any word I try to form might break me open.

A new voice cuts through the silence—clean, threaded with warmth, and horribly out of place.

"You need to call an ambulance," the man says. "Then, we have to get him out of the circle. This is a bad place to die."

I spin so fast the world smears. My knife is in my hand again—my body pulled it before my mind caught up.

A man stands a few yards away in the half-light, his long, dark coat brushing his boots. His iron-dark hair is threaded with silver at the temples, and his eyes look like he's seen every nightmare twice—and made reluctant peace with half of them. He smells faintly of smoke, metal, and cold night air.

He lifts both hands, palms empty, voice steady as stone. "Easy," he says. "I'm a friend. Volkov sent me."

"I'm done trusting strangers," I rasp.

"Good," he replies without missing a beat. A brief, wry smile tugs at his mouth. "Then don't." He taps his chest. "Malric Vale."

The name hits like a dropped weight. A ghost from JP's files. A rumor in the margins of old reports. The kind of man command teams whisper about and then pretend never existed.

My knife stays raised. "Prove it."

He doesn't flinch. Doesn't posture. Just exhales through his nose, tired and unimpressed. "You just lit up half the state, kid," he says. "Every hungry thing on both sides of the line felt that power. He'll be back."

His gaze drifts to the Door—its dying glow pulsing faintly—then, to JP bleeding out beside Selene. "And he won't be testing you next time," Malric finishes, voice dropping. "He'll be expecting results."

Cold settles in my stomach like swallowed ice. I swallow hard. "Help me get him to the truck," I say. "Now."

"Already on it." Malric steps forward, moving to JP's legs with the easy confidence of someone who's done battlefield extractions more times than he's eaten breakfast.

Selene watches him approach, her expression tightening—something brittling at the edges. Something old.

"You shouldn't be here," Malric murmurs to her without looking up, voice gentler than I expect.

"I'm not staying," she answers softly. The way she says it... It's not defensive, but resigned. Her eyes meet mine again and I see a hundred questions in that look. A hundred answers I'm not ready for. And no time for any of it.

Sirens wail in the distance, faint but growing, bouncing off cracked concrete and empty buildings: a reminder the world is coming back, whether we want it or not.

We move.

I wedge my arms under JP's shoulders. Malric hooks his hands beneath JP's knees. Together, we lift. JP groans—a raw, broken sound—and one hand twitches toward the wound like he's trying to hold himself together.

Selene walks beside us, her palm hovering inches above his chest, fingers trembling in the air. She never touches him... but the bleeding continues to slow. A gentle seep instead of a flood.

Every step we take away from the Door eases the pressure in my skull. The air stops vibrating. My bones stop humming. My

321

thoughts stop blurring at the edges. Just enough that I feel the crash barreling toward me.

When we reach the truck, the back door is already open. JP is heavy—too heavy. Not the weight of muscle, but the weight of a man slipping.

We ease him into the backseat. His head lolls. Blood slicks to the upholstery and my hands, warm and terrifyingly fast. I adjust him, whispering whatever lies I can make sound like truth.

"You're okay," I say, "You're okay. Stay with me. Please. Don't go anywhere."

His eyelids flutter. His fingers brush my wrist and leave a thin smear of red.

His lips move. I lean closer. "Good... kid," he rasps, voice shredded to ribbons. The words hit harder than any demon could.

"Yell at me later," I say, choking on something that isn't a laugh. "You hear me? You're not done yet."

He almost smiles. Almost. Then, his eyes roll back. His chest rises shallowly. Once. Again. Too shallow.

"Go," Selene says sharply, stepping back. "Now." There's no softness in her voice this time. Just urgency. I slam the door. Malric slides into the passenger seat like he's done it a thousand times, like he already knows where everything sits, where to brace, how to move in a crisis truck. I climb behind the wheel, fingers slick on the leather, heart beating somewhere between my throat and my spine.

The engine roars to life. In the rearview mirror, Selene stands alone in the loading lot. The faintly pulsing Door frames her in ghost-light. Her hair lifts in a wind I can't feel. Her outline seems too bright, too still—as if the world is holding a breath for her, the way it did for Dane.

She lifts a hand. Not a wave. Not goodbye. Something more like a promise. I blink, and she's gone.

Malric doesn't ask if I saw her. He doesn't tell me I imagined it. He just stares at the empty space where she'd been, jaw tight, something like regret flickering across his face.

I jam the truck into gear. Gravel spits. Headlights slash through the dark as we tear out of the lot. The sirens grow louder behind us—closer, faster—blue and red flickering against shattered storefronts as we hit the access road.

My hands shake on the wheel. Not fear—aftershock. My whole body hums like a bell struck too hard, still ringing, still vibrating with something I don't understand and can't put down.

"I won't let them take me," I say into the scraping silence. The words tremble out of me, cracked and raw, and I don't know who I'm promising. The night. The road. JP bleeding in the backseat. My mother's ghost. Myself.

Malric's profile is outlined by shadow, eyes fixed on the road ahead like it's an old enemy returning. "Good," he says. "Then don't."

The sirens sharpen behind us—closer now, bouncing off the abandoned storefronts, crawling along the broken asphalt like hounds on a trail. I push the truck harder. Gravel spits, tires scream. Malric's shoulders tense like he's bracing for the next blow.

I should feel relief. Distance. Safety buying us one fragile second to breathe. But something in the air changes instead. A pressure rolls through the night—quiet, deliberate—like the tide pulling back before deciding how hard it wants to come crashing in.

It's not loud. Not bright. No one outside this cab would feel it. But my bones do. My pulse does. The spark curled tight under my ribs lifts its head and *listens*.

Malric's eyes flick to the mirror, not in fear, but recognition. "Evelyn," he says quietly, "don't look back."

Which is exactly why I do. The mall sits in the rearview—broken skylights, dead signage, the loading lot yawning like a dark, open mouth. Nothing moves. No demons. No cultists. No Dane. No Selene. Just the ruins and the night.

But the circle—the circle isn't dark. It's not flaring or roaring to life. It's breathing.

A slow, inward draw—a quiet inhale—a pull I feel behind my sternum, like invisible fingers tugging gently on a string tied somewhere deep inside me.

Not opening. Not yet. But no longer closed.

A shiver crawls up my arms. The spark under my ribs answers with a faint, involuntary ache, a bruise pressed from the inside.

"Whatever you felt," Malric says, watching me instead of the road, "that was the first hinge moving."

I swallow, throat tight. "Can the others feel it?"

"Not the police," he says. "Not the town." His voice drops, low and certain. "But everyone who's been waiting for that Door—everyone who wants what's behind it—every power on either side of the line? They felt you ignite."

The sirens spill into the parking lot behind us, blue and red washing across the broken concrete. To them, the scene is destruction and debris. A fight. A tragedy. Something explainable.

Nothing supernatural. Nothing impossible. Not yet.

But the air in my lungs vibrates—subtle, ancient, patient—as if waiting for the next note. I face forward again, knuckles pale on the wheel. "So it's started."

Malric doesn't look away from the dark highway stretching ahead. "No," he says. And his tone is the coldest thing I've heard all night. "It's worse than that." A pause. "The Door has begun to notice you."

A cold pulse slides down my spine—sharp, exact—the same rhythm the circle breathed with. And far beyond the edges of this highway—beyond the empty fields and abandoned buildings and sleeping town—something notices back.

The spark in my chest flickers once—bright, startled—like it just received an answer.

I don't know what waits on the other side of this road. What I am. What I'll become. What it'll cost me. But I know one thing: This isn't over. This is the beginning.

And somewhere in the dark, the Door waits.